THE WAY OF TRANSGRESSORS

The Way of Transgressors

A NOVEL IN STORIES

EDWARD BROWN

TIDEWATER
PRESS

Copyright © 2025 Edward Brown
All rights reserved. No part of this publication may be reproduced, stored in a retrieval system or transmitted in any form or by any means—electronic, mechanical, audio recording, or otherwise—without the written permission of the publisher.

Published by Tidewater Press
New Westminster, BC, Canada
tidewaterpress.ca

978-1-990160-48-6 (print)
978-1-990160-49-3 (e-book)

Illustrations by Nick Burton (pg 5, 27, 43, 57, 78, 98, 108, 121, 139, 190, 211) and Shannon Leigh (pg 144, 160, 171, 244, 261, 274)

"Remember Me" first appeared in *Exile Quarterly*, Vol.42.3

LIBRARY AND ARCHIVES CANADA CATALOGUING IN PUBLICATION
Title: The way of transgressors : a novel in stories / Edward Brown.
Names: Brown, Edward, 1969- author
Identifiers: Canadiana (print) 20250176300 | Canadiana (ebook) 20250176343 | ISBN 9781990160486 (softcover) | ISBN 9781990160493 (EPUB)
Subjects: LCGFT: Novels.
Classification: LCC PS8603.R68318 W39 2025 | DDC C813/.6—dc23

Canadä

Tidewater Press gratefully acknowledges the support of the Government of Canada.

PRINTED IN CANADA

For Lidia
For Edward E. Brown (1939–2019)

*Good understanding giveth favour: but the way
of transgressors is hard.*
PROVERBS 13:15

TABLE OF CONTENTS

The Fifteen	1
Bones in the Hole (A Prologue)	3
Halfway to Queensville	5
The Handy Book	20
Brick (A Fairy Tale)	27
The Pulse of the Heart	38
Remember Me	43
Baby Farm	51
The Ballad of Robby Neill	57
Worm Syrup	72
The House on Defoe Street	78
Hobo Burglars	98
The Photography of Speech	104
Photo Album for Baby	108
A Bouquet of White Camellias	121
Settlement House	136
Honey for Andrej	139
Revival	142

The Lucky Coin	144
Badge	154
The Moore Park Murder	160
The Patsy	171
The Treatment	190
Poach	207
Bloodguilt	211
Malady of the Heart	237
Hard News	244
Heart's Content	253
I Sleep	261
A Policeman's Funeral	267
The Grave (An Epilogue)	269
Acknowledgments	273
About the Author	274

THE FIFTEEN

In September 2007, a backhoe uncovered a mass grave while excavating what had been the exercise yard of the old Toronto Don Jail. A total of fifteen bodies were discovered, the remains of inmates hanged on the prison's gallows between 1872 and 1930.

Mysteries to be solved, lives to be imagined, crimes to be dissected.

    John Traviss—hanged February 1872
    John Williams—hanged November 1877
    George Bennett aka George Dickson—hanged July 1880
    Robert Neill—hanged February 1888
    Thomas Kane—hanged February 1890
    Henry Williams—hanged April 1900
    Alexander Martin—hanged March 1905
    John Boyd—hanged January 1908
    Pavel Stefoff—hanged December 1909
    Pasquale Ventricini—hanged June 1910
    John Ziolko—hanged April 1915
    Hassan Neby—hanged January 1919
    Frank McCollough—hanged June 1919
    Frederick Davis—hanged May 1922
    Edward Stewart—hanged March 1930

    George Porter was inspired by a historical figure, a detective in the Toronto Police Service.

BONES IN THE HOLE (A Prologue)

Before the police or news reporters arrived, before detectives and the coroner started their brief investigations, and before the documentary film crew showed up and started shooting, Glen shoved the safety lock lever downward, undid his seatbelt, keyed off the Komatsu diesel engine, opened the door and stepped down from the cab of the yellow excavator to investigate something peculiar he spotted down in the trench.

It was early on a September day in 2007, and as the sun rose and morning peeked around the abandoned building where he was working, golden light reflected off a dull, whitish-yellow object below.

No one had arrived at the job site except for Glen and Luigi, the site foreman. Luigi always arrived before anyone else. He just sat in his van all day, smoked his little cigarillos, and drank cup after cup of black coffee poured from an orange thermos while slowly thumbing through *Corriere Canadese*.

Glen walked around the front of the building to where he'd parked his beat-up Honda, opened the rear door and removed a shovel from the messy backseat. A streetcar rattled by, filled with commuters on their way to office towers downtown.

When he came back around the building with the shovel propped on his shoulder, Luigi, seated in his van, looked up from the newspaper and waved. Before stepping into the trench, Glen waved back. Down in the trench, the scent of damp soil filled his nostrils.

The trench wasn't deep, under six feet.

The hospital next door had hired them to tear up the asphalt parking lot at the rear of the old building and haul away the debris. Later, they would grade the surrounding area. Instead of being demolished, the plan was for the structure to be converted into the administrative wing of the hospital.

Glen recognized the object unearthed by the basket. He poked it lightly with the shovel, then bent to pick it up. In the three years he'd been operating the excavator, the part of the job Glen liked best was unearthing interesting objects. It happened rarely and was never anything of value. He'd dug up dozens of antique bottles. An empty, rusted safe. An outboard motor. A rifle. Old coins. Cutlery. Knife blades. An anchor. Stuff like that. The coolest find to date was a bunch of hand-blown glass marbles.

This find was entirely different. He had dug up a human skull.

Glen hadn't noticed Luigi looking down at him until he heard the Italian exhale loudly and shout, "Hey."

Glen looked up into a plume of grey smoke to see Luigi crossing himself. "Hey. Hey. What do you do? You leave those bones in the hole. Get out here."

Instead, Glen examined the skull, about the size of a cantaloupe and the weight of a brass hammer. The bottom jaw was missing, and the top third sawed off. This was the first time he had ever seen a skeleton. Or part of a skeleton, anyway. More bones were scattered at his feet, along with what looked like shards of wood. He bent and picked up a crucifix clotted with soil.

"I'm calling the police," said Luigi.

The police showed up. The area was cordoned off. A tarpaulin canopy was set up over the open trench. Detectives and the coroner took photographs and asked a lot of questions. The detective who asked the most questions finished by telling him he had nothing to worry about because, according to the coroner, the remains he'd unearthed appeared to be over a century old. He explained that the old building was the former Don Jail, and the parking lot they were tearing up at one time was an enclosed exercise yard where convicted murderers were hanged and buried. There were likely more remains here. Glen stood at the edge of the scene.

What are their stories? Interesting things happened here once, and I'd like to discover what.

HALFWAY TO QUEENSVILLE

J. Traviss, 1872

JAMES QUINLEVEY, sworn
The prisoner came to me where I was chopping. He showed me a six-shooter and said he would let me see how he could shoot. He put two slugs into a hemlock tree. He said then he was going up to Old Johnston's.

Hard feelings between the farmer and his hired man erupted into the public sphere midweek after a meeting at the Methodist church in Queensville. The hired man, young John Traviss, a nineteen-year-old carpenter, stood four inches taller than six feet. Well built, he had a face that was not at all a bad one. East Gwillimbury was unanimous in that, until the rupture, Young John and Old John Johnston appeared well acquainted.

The laity met before dinnertime to confer on various topics, one of which concerned an accounting of the widows' fund. Throughout the meeting in the drafty basement, neither man displayed malice toward the other.

Narrow-shouldered with a long face, Old Johnston hobbled down the stone steps outside. The farmer brushed a powder of snow from the forelocks of his span of horses with his sleighing gloves. A serious man with a stern exterior, he concealed a gentleness of spirit easily overlooked by any unfamiliar with his old country upbringing. Arriving in Upper Canada from Kings County, Ireland, three decades earlier, Old Johnston had come into money, after which he allotted a half-acre of his holding to the Primitive Methodist Connexion. This place of worship owed its construction to Johnston's wealth.

Farmers stood outside the stone church in pairs and threes at twilight, discussing autumn wheat, a distressing calving, and MacGentry's wrecked harvest. Old Johnston gripped the halter, guiding his cutter from the carriage shed beside the churchyard. Lighting the candle lamps, he readied to leave.

John Traviss and his people were Primitive Methodists, as well.

No sectarian element factored into the slaying.

Hired by Old Johnston the previous spring, Traviss and his brothers spent the summer framing and constructing a new, larger farmhouse for the Johnstons. When the work was completed, the brothers' wages were paid in full.

No outstanding accounts contributed to the hostility.

Before Old Johnston departed church property, Traviss charged his sleigh, angry as a German wasp, shouting claims the farmer had traduced his name in the community.

"Why?" Traviss bellowed. "Why defame me after what you did?"

Johnston casually removed his bone-rimmed spectacles and exhaled on the lens, rubbing them on the checked woolen sleigh robe covering his lap.

Traviss seethed. "I could throttle you, man."

Johnston remained motionless. The other farmers drew closer. Mr. Porter, a well-knit wheelwright with a successful enterprise in the village, moved to stand between the angry young man and the sleigh, rubbing his pocked chin.

High-minded and just, Porter was acting county sheriff, appointed by the township reeve for a three-year tenure. The father of seven was in the constant company of his fourteen-year-old son, George, a thin boy with inquisitive eyes. Villagers addressed the youth as "Deputy." George relished the sobriquet.

The boy mimicked his father and rubbed his unblemished chin.

Barely able to control his rage, Traviss stepped back. He shoved his large hands in the pockets of his great black coat containing several walnuts, a McIntosh apple, a tin of clout nails, boiled lemon sweets wrapped in a stained cambric handkerchief marked E.N., and half a quid of tobacco.

He appealed to the farmers. "He whispers I am a tippler but have any seen me in the throes of whisky fever? What's more, he hints I run with the Tenth Line Blazers. Imagine me, cattle-lifting with those thorough-going rascals."

The farmers stared dispassionately. Traviss drew a handful of walnuts from his pocket, crushing several in his calloused palm. He hurled shell splinters and nutmeat at the frozen earth, lunging at the sleigh.

"That," he pointed at the ground, "is the mess of your brain after I beat your skull for tarnishing my reputation—and for what you did."

Johnston's team gave a start. He steadied the horses, his countenance showing no sign of intimidation.

Porter nudged Traviss on the shoulder. "Enough, son."

Traviss came at Johnston a second time. Several farmers struggled to hold him back before the teenager broke away.

George was knocked to the ground in the scrimmage. Traviss picked the boy up and righted him. "I'm sorry, Deputy. Are you fine?"

George, frightened by the suddenness of the incident, held in tears. "Fine. I'm fine. Just fine," the boy reassured him.

Deputy stood behind his father.

Traviss broke down. "Explain, Mr. Johnston, how, summer last, I was sober enough and honest enough to hire."

At the appearance of tears, some farmers glanced uncomfortably at their scuffed toecaps while others craned their necks, spying abrupt heavenly bodies behind clouds. White, hard, unblinking stars against a blue-black blanket of sky.

George glanced around his father, shocked at the sight of the big man crying.

"Mr. Porter, you know me," Traviss exclaimed. "You knew my father. He rests under the earth, right there." Traviss pointed at the collection of mute churchyard headstones. "Johnston challenges my repute, and I cannot stand it."

Old Johnston remained stoic.

Porter inquired, "Why would Mr. Johnston do such?"

"He has his reason, I suspect. It started when I began giving my addresses to a girl whose name I will suppress. Because of his innuendos, she no longer speaks to me nor will she see me. And her parents scorn me, too."

Porter asked Johnston, "Is there truth in what the boy asserts?"

The old man jeered. "Not on your tintype—"

"That's a horse's laugh," Traviss interrupted, turning a full circle in frustration.

"If neither agrees to bargain, then part, at least this evening." Porter inhaled. "More snow and cold coming."

Old Johnston twitched the reins and set off, his sleigh vanishing into the white concession road.

"This is far from done," Traviss muttered. He shook his fist, shouting into the fading light after Johnston, "I come from people that go to battle over slights or insinuations such as you spout, old man."

Farmers climbed into sleighs and departed. Porter and Deputy watched John Traviss walk purposefully across meadows toward James Quinlevey's place, the bachelor splitting stove wood beside his woodshed.

MARY ANN JOHNSTON, sworn
I am the daughter of the late John Johnston. John Traviss worked for my father off and on all last summer. Traviss took breakfast with the family. My father and the prisoner went to the sleigh. The prisoner was sitting on the left. I never saw my father alive after he drove away with the prisoner that morning.

Mrs. Johnston awoke before dawn, exchanged her nightdress for a green gown and, wrapping herself in a shawl, emptied the chamber pots of slop water. She lit the kitchen lamps, replenished the wood box, and stoked the fire. The night chill gripping the farmhouse began to recede. She commenced preparation of a large breakfast—porridge, salt pork, and tea—for her sleeping husband and three unwed adult children, still residing on the farm.

The house was quiet except for the snapping fire. Humming softly, she placed additional sticks of stove wood in the firebox and adjusted the damper. The predawn peace she relished came apart when an urgent thumping sounded at the back door. Startled, Mrs. Johnston saw the last person she expected at this hour, shivering on the enclosed rear verandah.

John Traviss.

The young man bid her good morning.

Mrs. Johnston held the lantern out for a better look at his expression. He appeared raddled. Rumours in circulation said he had taken to drink. Present when he had signed his temperance pledge, she had dismissed the innuendo as tavern gossip. His visit at this odd hour gave her pause, however.

"Get inside here, you big lunker. It's as cold as the grave." She pulled his sleeve. "What are you up to this early?"

Traviss entered, stomping snow from his calfskin boots, brushing the folds of his grey, cheviot-lined pants. Tugging off his mittens, he cupped his hands, blowing into the bowl of his fingers before rubbing his palms together vigorously.

In better light, she sized up his condition. She and his mother were well acquainted, currently serving on the Church Ladies' Aid Society. Mrs. Johnston knew John Traviss thoroughly.

Among the midwives at his birth, she had, on account of the livid-blue colouring of his eyes, given him the byname Lovely Boy, the endearment lasting into boyhood.

She caressed his smooth cheek, cold as marble, with the tips of her fingers. His bright eyes shone clear. The good-mannered young man she had known from infancy melted into view.

She inquired a second time. "Are matters all right? Why about so early?"

Traviss had always been fond of Mrs. Johnston. After the tragedy at the level crossing claimed his father's life, Mrs. Johnston visited more often than other farmwives. "Well, ma'am," he began, "forgive me. Upon returning from Quinlevey's last night, the road became impassable. I took the liberty of lodging in the old horse barn at the back of the lot."

Mrs. Johnston helped Traviss out of his great coat. "Upon my word and honour," she exclaimed at the coat's heft, "if I didn't know better, I'd suppose your pocket concealed a culverin."

John Traviss followed the lean woman into the stuffy kitchen, inhaling the scent of burning tallow, kerosene, and hickory. He continued, "I remembered the caboose stove inside the barn and lit a fire to save myself."

"Where did you sleep?"

"On the hearthstones. I saw your lamp just now in the kitchen. I came at once."

"Poor creature, you will catch your death. Let's get a warm breakfast for you. Sit. I'll bring tea."

In a few minutes, Mary Ann came downstairs in a flannelette morning wrapper to aid her mother. Traviss nodded to her, having lifelong acquaintance with all the Johnston brood. He had enlisted in the volunteer militia with her brothers. Greeting Traviss, Mary Ann put a white cotton smock over her dress. Traviss's presence at the oak table was unexpected but not extraordinary.

Water puddled at Traviss's feet. Mother and daughter wordlessly set about busying themselves in the spacious kitchen.

Near the end of the hour, John Johnston shuffled into the kitchen and hiked up his suspenders. Taken aback by Traviss's presence, he adjusted his spectacles.

Traviss checked his rage and grinned. "Good morning, Mr. Johnston."

Without pausing from their tasks, the women exchanged quizzical glances. The men sat silent until Mr. Johnston spat, "Is it official business that brings you at this hour?"

Traviss leaned forward, loutishly resting his elbows on the table. "No business. I explained to your missus already. Last night I—"

"No business? Leave." He pointed at the door.

"Now that it's mentioned, though, one account is outstanding."

Mrs. Johnston assumed the tension between her husband and Traviss concerned matters relating to the construction of the farmhouse. Her husband's business was his alone. She seldom pried.

Mrs. Johnston set a plate of hard biscuits topped with dollops of raspberry jelly on the table. She told her husband, "Get something in your stomach."

Traviss piped, "If it would please you, ma'am, I'll have a little."

Glaring at Johnston, Traviss broke a hard biscuit in half, plunging the morsel into his hot black tea. Johnston spooned heaps of porridge into his mouth. The men ate in silence. The kitchen filled with smoke. Mrs. Johnston scolded her daughter for not attending the flue, and opened a window a crack, creating a draft.

Mr. Johnston scraped his chair against the hardwood, pushing himself up from the table. "I have business at the Four Corners."

His wife inquired, "This early?"

"Yes, woman," he rejoined. "*This* early."

Traviss stood and wiped his face with the back of his hand. "Thank you, Mrs. Johnston. And you too, Mary Ann," and then to the old man said, "I'll join you in the sleigh. I have business on the road to Queensville."

Mr. Johnston was unprepared for the bold assertion. "Will you?"

In one stride, Traviss stood over the shorter man. He pinched Johnston's stubbled chin and held it. "I will."

The women watched, speechless. Johnston drew away. Without a word, he went to the horse stable to prepare the sleigh. Mrs. Johnston slinked upstairs to wake the boys. Traviss pulled on his heavy coat and wrapped himself in a scarf. He called out, thanking the women a second time.

"Goodbye, Mrs. Johnston. Goodbye, Mary Ann."

At the doorway, he stopped and turned. He peered into Mary Ann's close-set eyes. "Do you recall Confederation Day? The picnic at the big pond?"

Puzzled, Mary Ann said yes, she did.

"That day was nearest to my happiest." His eyes shone. Words came fast. "We rowed to the middle to watch the fireworks. You were there. Remember? I stood and sang "God Save the Queen" and upset the boat. We got a soaking. We all did laugh. Edwin and Thomas Porter were there. And Elizabeth Nichol, too." He removed an embroidered handkerchief from his pocket and studied it. "Even then, I was fond of her. She was fond of me, too. I always knew it."

Mary Ann hesitantly placed the dishrag she held beside a basin of water. Her voice cracked. "I don't understand. Why bring up events four years past?"

"Forgive me."

"For upsetting the boat? We were scarcely adults."

Traviss slid his other hand into his pocket and gripped the butt of the pistol concealed there. "No, not that. For future upset I cause." He closed the door and hurried to the stable.

Mrs. Johnston returned to the kitchen. Mother and daughter observed the sleigh gliding up the lane through frosted glass.

> GEO.WATSON, sworn
> I have known the prisoner from his boyhood. I never saw anything amiss about him. I was at a neighbour's that morning. I heard a shot. I did not take much notice of the report, as it is a time of year, we hear shooting. I saw John Traviss going very fast across the fields when I lost sight of him. He had on grey pants and a black coat with a scarf tied round him.

Sunlight crested above the horizon. John Traviss and John Johnston sat in hard silence, side by each in a sleigh on the road to Queensville.

The road lay pristine after the night of snow. Fallow fields slept beneath sugary drifts of white.

The span of horses was in good spirits. Jerking the halter, the sleigh approached the crossing where the Northern & North-Western bisected the concession road. Johnston removed a fob from inside his cloak and checked the timepiece. The morning mail train had steamed past twenty-three minutes earlier. Nonetheless, Johnston slowed the team to a walk.

Perched on a cedar post enclosing Joseph Blizzard's pasture, a grey shrike devoured a helpless waxwing. The horses' breast collars tinkled. The hungry bird chattered threateningly. Traviss shifted, the pistol pressing into his hip. He took off his mitten, reached into his pocket, and produced an apple. Splitting the fruit in two, he offered half to Johnston.

The old man looked annoyed.

"I insist," Traviss said, setting the sectioned fruit on the sleigh robe. Biting his portion of the apple, he chewed. "My father perished here." Pausing to swallow, he added, "Struck by the six-forty express." Traviss considered the wintery scene around him.

"I know the story," Johnston interjected. "I was among the men who collected the remains."

The two men studied the white guts of the apple against the checked sleigh robe.

"Story? It was my father's ending."

Johnston snapped the reins. The sleigh rattled over the tracks.

Traviss exhaled a plume of air. "I was in Niagara training with the Number Two Company but returned at once. After the inquest, we came to the crossing to gather Father's belongings scattered to the four winds. Pa was returning from the granary that day, and strange to say, the wagon was splinters, but the bags of grain remained intact. Never understood how the grain survived the catastrophe. For some reason though, that consoled me a little—"

The old man motioned to speak. Traviss curtailed him. "You have spoken enough. From here out, you're tasked with steadying the team and maintaining our course."

He put a plug of tobacco into his mouth and offered Johnston the same. The old man declined. He retrieved the white handkerchief from his pocket, "A sweet, then?"

"From you, nothing."

Traviss guffawed. "Right. You've already taken my sweet."

They rode in silence.

Traviss began, "Mr. Johnston, I am compelled to share a memory with you, and when the telling is complete, likely halfway to Queensville . . ." Traviss removed the pistol from his coat pocket, cocked the hammer, and laid the weapon across his lap, "I will send you to your long account."

Johnston became overwrought. "Are you mad? You want to kill me?"

Traviss interrupted. "You have too much jaw, man. Somebody ought to have darned a button on your mouth ages ago. Besides, if I am the liar you claim, you needn't worry."

Johnston's cheeks turned ashen.

Traviss commenced. "The spring I turned seven years, my father, brothers, and myself followed the three-day drove road to Toronto. Pa intended to sell a dozen white and red Angus and the Shorthorn bull for a reasonable price in the cattle market at St. Lawrence."

The old man glanced nervously at the pistol. Traviss instructed him to instead watch the road. "Some of the cattle had turned-in horns. Father was concerned they might not fetch top dollar."

The excursion to the city had been Traviss' first. He sat in the wagon, trudged on foot, and rode pillion with one brother or another on an old stager his father had purchased at auction. They lodged at inns and bivouacked in meadows.

Snow remained on the ground. One night a gentle east wind brought warm temperatures and an Old Testament plague similar to lice. In the morning, tiny black spidery creatures resembling coarse pepper covered the earth for miles. The infestation distressed young Traviss until his father explained snow fleas were harmless.

"When troubled, Pa could always settle me."

An American at the market purchased the livestock. The transaction went well. However, boarding the herd on the Lake Ontario steamer

Calamitas at Leak's Wharf, a cyclone commenced with winds keen and lethal. Fog bells rang. Their father hurried the boys to shelter in a nearby coalyard.

The city blew down. Families cowering in homes were crushed under falling houses, tree limbs, and stacks of chimneys. Young Traviss was petrified. His father soothed him.

"Lovely Boy, do not trouble."

The next day, the harbour master reported the storm had breached a portion of the peninsula enclosing the bay at the Don Marsh, washing away Quinn's Hotel. A broad and deep chasm formed a new island.

As his father had assured, they survived the worst of it and began retracing a path north. "Saturday night, we lodged at the limits of the city among the company of a travelling menagerie. With my father's permission, a man in a long coat and slouched hat allowed my brothers and me to throw corn cobs at chained monkeys. The next morning, unable to attend Sunday service, I still remember the scripture Father read, 'There is no fear in love. He that feareth is not made perfect in love.'"

The sleigh glided by pupils making their way on foot to the schoolhouse, including two of the Porter children, George and his younger sister, Beatrice. George raised his hand in greeting as his father often did, but the gesture went unacknowledged.

Traviss adjusted his frigid grip on the pistol and spoke rapidly. "I've become unsettled and without my father . . . "

He held the old man's gaze. "Until you, Elizabeth Nichol was fond of me." Before raising the pistol to shoot into Johnston's temple, he said, "I am not afraid."

Johnston's skull absorbed the lead shot like a soft apple. Traviss pulled the trigger a second time, getting his neck. Gripping the reins, he halted the team, calmly leaping to the ground, snow crunching underfoot. He thwacked the horses' rumps. Their master slain, the team remained stubbornly in place.

The walking children stopped at the report of the gun. They observed John Traviss moving very fast across fields toward his married sister's farmhouse.

George approached the sled cautiously. Beatrice followed a distance behind, the others lingering farther back still.

Mr. Johnston was slouched in the box, coin-size droplets of blood staining the snow.

George avoided stepping in Traviss's fresh boot prints as he circled the sled and studied the dead man's position thoroughly. Johnston's spectacles were askew. On the footboard lay the discarded six-shooter beside a piece of apple.

George surmised that a lone mitten half concealed in the folds of the sleigh robe likely belonged to the killer. He removed a jotter and a slate pencil from his shoulder bag.

Beatrice shouted, "Is Mr. Johnston ill?"

George was nervous and shouted back, "No, not ill."

The boy sketched the scene before him. Johnston's team of horses craned their necks, swatted their tails, whickered, curious of the boy's movements at their hindmost.

Beatrice inched closer. "What is it you're doing?"

George sketched the outline of the old man's slumped body. He pencilled in details of the kill. Two angry wounds. Skull. Neck. How odd, the boy puzzled: Mr. Johnston's left sleighing glove was half removed. Maybe, he contemplated, the old man was in the process of removing them the instant the initial bullet landed, but why?

He continued to sketch, too enthralled to hear his sister's shouts. "We should get Father. George, listen. We should get Father. We might get in trouble if we don't."

"We won't get in trouble. That's John Traviss's alone."

George admired his handiwork. He held the jotter out for his sister's observation.

"See? Father will approve, as well as Constable Cooke."

ISRAEL COOKE, sworn

I am a constable. Sheriff Porter instructed I arrest the prisoner. I told Traviss I arrested him on a warrant for shooting John Johnston. He did not deny the charge. He was handcuffed. The next day we came down to Toronto. Sheriff Porter's son, the one called George, accompanied. He attended as an aid. George had gone to the city previously on affairs similar. The prisoner was reading newspapers on the way down. We were not talking, then the prisoner said it was all on account of Miss Nichol that he shot John Johnston.

The bedlam Constable Cooke observed on the platform through the smoking-car window, the sheer numbers in attendance awaiting the arrival of the noon train from Newmarket, unnerved the peace officer from East Gwillimbury.

Never had Cooke witnessed a sight such as this. His face twitched as he, John Traviss, and the boy called Deputy disembarked at City Hall Station, greeted by the stationmaster. The crowd was close to unruly. Fearing the mob would pull down his train shed, the stationmaster dispatched Deputy to nearby No.1 police station with a plea for constables.

Hustling and shoving to get closer to the handsome suspect were women with grubby worsted wool sontags, who'd crammed into the ladies' waiting room for hours waiting for his arrival. Sooty longshoremen dusted brown from unloading lignite coal stole away from a nearby slip for a quick decko. A dark-skinned foreigner placed a purple felt fez at his feet and entertained on a flageolet for small coins until drowned out by the appearance of the De La Salle Institute Brass Band performing "The Battle of Waterloo."

Deputy returned short of breath in the company of policemen a few minutes later. Frenzied spectators grabbed Traviss's sleeves. Two drunks sharing a pint passed out on the station steps. Cutpurses made a killing. Constable Cooke lost his hat.

———

Placed in a prison van and whisked across the Don Bridge, timbers dangerously rotted in places, Traviss was afforded the privilege of Governor Allan's presence at the gaol door. After being led through the main hall to the search room, Traviss's name and description were entered into a book, and his possessions seized. Escorted to bathrooms downstairs, scrubbed with soft soap and a hard scrubber, he was dressed in grey, provided a tin dish, a rusty spoon, a straw mattress and two filthy blankets.

Until his trial in mid-January, he shared a three- by nine-foot unheated cell with three other inmates: a man with a venereal disease alleged to have stolen chickens, an inebriate who struck his wife with an iron, and Rick, an eleven-year-old sent down for stealing a mouth organ from a stall in the market. Rick crayoned dirty pictures and sold them for a small fee.

The din was unyielding, the stench worse. His first evening inside Toronto Jail was unusual because inmates and turnkeys alike permitted Traviss peace to indulge in a meal of black soup and a lump of bread. He passed the time in the exercise yard and the chapel and confided in Rick over games of draughts.

"Rick?"

"Yes?"

"She's going to forget me."

"She won't. Nobody will."

"What the old man did to her was unforgivable."

"I know."

Rick drew his chapfallen cellmate a dirty picture of a nude woman with lizard parts where arms should be.

Traviss gave it only a glance. Returning the crude erotica, he said, "You are like another boy I know, but you're not the same."

"How are we alike?"

"Same attentive spirit."

"How are we different?"

"You will always be in here. He will always be out there."

GEORGE PORTER, sworn
Heated words were exchanged between the carpenter, John Traviss, and another man, John Johnston, outside

the Methodist church in Queensville. I know it was a Wednesday and I was present in the company of my father. John Traviss pushed me down in error. My younger sister Beatrice Mildred Eunice Porter and I were the first to discover the deceased. Beatrice is a thirteen-year-old girl. I am a fourteen-year-old. Call me Deputy, if it pleases the court.

Hundreds packed into the Adelaide Street court gallery to observe the two-day trial, many spilling into halls and stairwells. Twenty-four witnesses answered to their names.

The court rebuked George Porter on the stand when he produced his jotter and displayed sketches of the deceased. His Lordship became repulsed, took the boy to task, and called the drawings an obscenity.

Twelve jurors deliberated an hour and forty minutes before returning a guilty verdict.

Sentenced to hang on the twenty-third day of February next, His Lordship asked solemnly, "Do you have anything to say?"

Traviss stood in the dock. "I have been found guilty and suppose I must suffer for it."

In a broken voice, he asked His Lordship to permit a final visit with his brothers and sisters and numerous friends who had made the trip to Toronto. Affected by the guilty man's plea, the judge complied, arranging for a last teary meeting in the grand jury room.

When George Porter stole into the room, Traviss told the boy, "You did a thorough job."

"But you will die because of it."

"I'll greet Our Creator with clear eyes. No part of you should apologize."

"No part of me will."

Returned to the jail, Traviss was placed in the heated death cell. Governor Allan saw that Traviss's meals were prepared by his staff, dinners consisting of roasted fowl and potatoes served on a fancy tray.

The end approaching, Traviss's cambric handkerchief, laundered and pressed, mysteriously reappeared on the stand beside his cot.

The day of his execution broke sunny and cold. One hundred and fifty inmates plus sixty shivering invitees gathered below the scaffold constructed in the exercise yard.

More spectators scaled the prison walls or found high perches on nearby rooftops. Contrary to custom, the hangman did not wear a mask. Before kneeling as if in prayer, a black cap over his face, Traviss shook hands with those on the scaffold and addressed the assemblage.

He apologized to his mother. "God has long arms. In this hour, My Father lifts me."

The hangman placed the noose around Traviss's neck, the knot beneath his left ear. The sun slipped behind a cloud. The trap was sprung. His corpse hung an hour, stiff and still like a dressed beef carcass. Cut down, Reverend Rice read a funeral sermon. Inmates lowered his coffin into an unmarked grave below the scaffold.

After the execution, citizens recognized the hangman boarding a train at the Don Station and beat him violently.

Before being released, Rick clandestinely etched *J.T.+E.N.* into the yellow brick above the place where the killer had rested.

THE HANDY BOOK

Two years before the Johnston murder, George awoke to the clatter of dishes coming from the kitchen downstairs. Outside, the dawn sky was a perfect delphinium blue. Beatrice woke a few minutes later in the bedroom she shared with her older sister, Lena. Lena, Edwin, Thomas, and Jean, who had completed their schooling but continued to reside in the family home, slept longer.

George and Beatrice washed and dressed. Their mother prepared sausage, berries, hominy, and beef tea for breakfast. They attended to morning chores and set to leave before seven, it being a good walk to Schoolhouse No.14.

"I'm thinking of a word, and it rhymes with pressed," Beatrice said.

The siblings, so close in age, kept one another good company. His sister was George's preferred companion; in winter, they skated on the big pond and, in summer, fished in Poplar Creek.

Beatrice stood at the bottom of the steps and looked up at her brother. "I'm thinking of a word, and it rhymes with pressed."

George adjusted the strap on his shoulder bag. "Is it a home for a bird?"

"What's that game you two are playing?"

Startled, the siblings turned to see Constable Cooke at the gate on his handsome black horse, Victor.

"Crambo. Surely you must have played it," Beatrice said, not shyly.

Israel Cooke was a modest, plain-spoken man with hazel eyes, a round, freckled face, and a horseshoe moustache hanging over his mouth. He wore his kepi at an unconventional angle. His grey uniform appeared slightly dishevelled this morning. Removing his hat, he ran his fingers through his thin, oily hair. In the job for the past seven years, the unmarried township constable prepared for the worst, but in a community populated mainly by pacifist Quakers, the worst seldom occurred.

"I'm here for the sheriff. There's a situation at the Peregrine farm."

"Father is confined to bed for days," Beatrice said.

Fair-haired and pretty with the hue of health in her cheeks, the youngster was enthralled by Victor and stroked the horse's silky breast.

"Confined to bed? Is it serious?"

"It's his neuralgia. Attacked his shoulders and arms this time," George said.

A few days ago, George's mother had sent him to get Doctor Fairwell to advise John Porter on a severe attack of neuralgia. The doctor prescribed heat, bed rest, and a complete water fast. In the interim, George and Beatrice's eldest sibling, Charley, would take over the operation of the wheelwright shop in the village.

"Is he awake? I must see him on the matter."

George shook his head. "This early? I can see."

"But, Pickle, we'll be late for school," Beatrice said.

Cooke dismounted and tied the steed to the hitching post. "Tell him, as acting county sheriff, his presence is required to execute a trespass warrant at the Peregrine farm on the Ninth Line. Kate Howard is up to it again. They keep sending her on her way, and she keeps coming back. They're demanding her eviction."

Kate Howard, known for being partially deprived of her wits, periodically entered homes and properties where she did not belong. Her people had abandoned her and moved to another part of the province some time ago.

Mainly innocuous, she vanished for periods only to return to the township and take up residence where she pleased. She was mainly tolerated unless she became an annoyance, most often through unclothing herself. When this occurred, strong drink was usually on her breath. In the winter, when she wasn't put up by locals, Constable Cooke lodged her in a room at the rear of the police office.

George quietly hurried into the house and upstairs. The blinds in his parents' bedroom were drawn. He tapped lightly on the partially open door before entering. His father was in bed on his back, and his mother was applying a hot, damp towel across his bare chest and shoulders.

In a subdued voice, George began, "Papa? Constable Cooke's outside. He has a warrant. He said you're required at the Peregrine Farm. Kate Howard objects to—"

George's mother turned toward her son with an annoyed expression. "Pickle, tell Izzy your father is in no condition—"

John Porter held the searing towel to his shoulder. "Your mother's correct," he grimaced. "Did he mention the class of warrant?"

"Trespass, he said."

"Hmm. You go in my place then."

"Me? In your place?"

"John, you must be feverish. He's twelve. You can't send a boy to perform a sheriff's duty."

"I'm not sending a boy. I'm sending my deputy."

"Deputy?" George's eyes widened.

"Don't be ridiculous," his mother countered.

"It's not a death warrant, Beth. According to law, it's permissible."

George's mother opposed the idea in the belief school attendance was more important.

"He'll be fine," his father muttered. "He can read. He knows his tables. He can sketch better than all of us, even." He beckoned George closer to the bedside and took his son's small hand. "When you address Kate Howard, speak gently, Pickle. She is brainsick but not contumacious. She will comply."

"Address her?"

"Constable Cooke will explain."

Outside, George relayed his father's intention to Constable Cooke.

"If that's Sheriff Porter's desire, so be it. Up you go, Deputy." Cooke lifted George into the saddle.

Craning her neck, Beatrice pleaded, "Pickle! What about school?"

High in the saddle, George said, "Tell Mr. Turner I'll return tomorrow. And don't call me Pickle anymore."

"What? What do I call you then?"

Constable Cooke answered for George. "Call him Deputy."

"What about our game, though?" she said. "It's your guess."

Cooke unhitched Victor, mounted the stallion and took the reins. He clucked his tongue, and the horse began a fast walk.

George looked down at his sister jogging to keep up beside them and said, "Is it worn under a frock coat?"

Beatrice stopped, dropped her school bag in the dust, and shouted after her brother, "No. It's not a vest."

They left Beatrice behind, riding double to the Ninth Line farm at a fast walk. The sun rose. George and the constable talked about different things. Cooke asked George to explain the game he and his sister played and reviewed all the words and clues provided. George asked Cooke what a constable did. Cooke inquired if George's father had tried the Holstein Milk Diet to combat his condition. "My brother swears by it."

"Mother applies heat. For the migraines, she administers Hawkes Hypnotic."

"What's that?"

"A laudanum."

Constable Cooke whistled through his teeth. "My brother says eight-ounce glasses of milk on the hour every hour, starting at seven in the morning and finishing at six at night, does it for him."

They rode silently, listening to birdsong until the Peregrine Farm came into sight at the top of a rise in the road. A rooster crowed.

George asked, "Why is the action against Kate Howard done so early?"

"At this hour, she should be docile. Hopefully."

Constable Cooke dismounted before removing George from the saddle. They came upon Kate Howard asleep under a buffalo robe on a pallet of straw in the cattle shed. Constable Cooke identified himself and the office he held.

Kate opened her expressive eyes, full of quiet fear. Gazing at George, she said, "Hello. A little boy. Who are you?"

Constable Cooke took an envelope from his pocket, opened it, and handed George a folded sheet of paper. "Read this."

George began to read to himself.

"Aloud."

"Catherine Elizabeth Caroline Howard," he stammered, "the people of the Province of Ontario, by the Grace of God, find you in violation of Section 57 of Her Majesty's Land Act and hereby, on the order of the Sheriff—"

"Deputy," Cooke interjected.

George read the entire trespass warrant. Kate Howard sat up, pulled her knees to her chest, and smiled. Cattle were lowing in their stalls. "I made my baby cry," she said.

"What?"

"I'm selfish."

"What?"

Constable Cooke put his hand on George's shoulder and nodded. "She's not—"

"I wouldn't have hurt her," she paused. "It was a game. The button game. What's your name?"

George cleared his throat, "George. George Porter."

"That's extraordinary."

"What is?"

"Your name. Extraordinary. It is extra ordinary." Kate sighed. "Will you be a mean one, Georgie Porter? Are you mean to me? Or will you be just?"

George's voice cracked. "No. Not mean. I'll be just."

Cooke interrupted, "Let's go, Kate. Breakfast at the police office. Come on."

Kate yawned. "Okay," she glanced under the buffalo robe pulled up to her neck. "George Porter?"

"Yes?"

"Can you find me clothing?"

George shrugged. "Yes. I think I can."

Kate was in the saddle, and George and the constable walked on the near side of Victor all the way back. Constable Cooke smoked his cutty pipe.

Constable Cooke lived in rooms above the police office and kept pigs in the front yard. He removed his belt slide holster, ground coffee beside the hot stove, and poured Kate a black mug with sliced bread and almonds. George sat at the table and swore an affidavit, as the law required. When Kate went outside and fed the swine, Constable Cooke removed a worn blue leatherbound book from a shelf and set it in front of George, who studied the cover before turning to the first page and said, "Jones' Constables' Manual?"

"It's the Handy Book," Cooke explained.

"What's that?"

"A must for constables across the Dominion. The criminal code neatly compiled for swift access. Details on fines, fee schedules, punishments, and crimes. Steps to avoid contaminating a crime scene. Proper chain of custody. It's an older edition, but yours if you want it."

"Really?"

"You'd make a good one."

"A good what?"

"Constable."

"Me?"

"Yes. And incidentally, Beatrice's word is arrest."

"What?"

"The game."

"Oh, yes. How do you know?"

"That's what I do." Cooke tapped the side of his nose. "Detection and deliberation. Followed by action."

"Detection and deliberation followed by action." George repeated. "I like that."

They saw Kate sitting on the earth in the piggery through the window, staring upward at the sky.

George asked what would happen to her now.

"Nothing. She looks happy, doesn't she?"

"She's fine." George watched her silently.

Then he asked, "Can I come back here?"

"As often as you please."

BRICK (A FAIRY TALE)

FRANCES

Mam praised education to the skies. Dada was perfectly illiterate. Compared with her twelve siblings, Frances resembled Mam strongest. They were both slightly built and possessed happy, pretty faces framed by mousey brown hair. Before the family's ruin, Mam and daughter passed for sisters.

Dada, a Liverpudlian with a dense Scouser accent, had a heavy head and brawny arms and walked with a stoop and slight limp. His appearance was plain, his temperament even and kind. Until abandoning the straight track, he touched liquor sparingly.

Frances adored her parents, enthralled by the story of their chance meeting on the creaking deck of a packet ship sailing for the Province of Canada. Holed up in steerage, each travelled alone, passage five shillings apiece. They possessed only the contents of his dressing case and her Saratoga trunk.

Mam's people were Irish. Shedding her fairy faith and fear, she fled the aftermath of the Great Hunger with some clothing, oddments, trinkets, and a periodical copy of Edgar Poe's "The Tell-Tale Heart," a story she could, in a short time, recite from memory: "Hearken! And observe how healthily—how calmly I can tell you the whole story . . ."

The ocean crossing was dull. Not a single incidence of cholera fever. The sea remained unusually placid, trade winds a steady fresh breeze. The pair commenced a twenty-three-day courtship beginning at the watery edge of Europe's continental slope with a meal of ship biscuits, potatoes, coffee, and butcher meat prepared in the crowded cook shop. Dada reclined against the mizzenmast for the duration, leisurely tying and untying a grief knot on the fag end of a rope.

Sails billowed. Mam perched on the gunwale and read Poe's treacherous tale aloud. Their first kiss occurred mid-Atlantic, two leagues above an abyssal plain. The night their vessel sailed calm waters over the Gully Trench, Mam slipped away from the ladies' cabin unnoticed to meet Dada topside. Together, they climbed the rigging to the foretop and lay side-by-side on their backs, gazing into the black, satiny sky.

Mam explained the star constellations, pointing. "That is Cassiopeia. That is Delphinus. Over there, Cygnus."

Dada asked, "What are the others titled?"

"Those? Those are ours to name."

Wrapped in a cutaway piece of flax sailcloth, tell-tails fluttering, the pair conceived Johnny, their firstborn, that night.

Mam recited Poe's story aloud for the twenty-third and final time, North America dead ahead: "Never, before that night had I felt the extent of my own powers—of my sagacity."

Nuptials were exchanged at the Port of Quebec. Mam was fourteen, Dada sixteen.

By the time they reached Weston, a suburb of Toronto, after stops in Cornwall, Ottawa, and Manitoulin Island, Johnny had four siblings, including Mary Ann, Frances, Eliza, and Adelaide.

Nearly to the end, Mam was with child.

Home was a rented labourer's cottage. Dada worked horny-handed in a local brickfield. Mam kept hens, sold eggs, made and peddled candles. She took in sewing. In the evening, she basted and read to the children by oil lamp. She taught them French.

Days were long. The brood eventually doubled. Emmie, Richard, Maggie, and the happiest baby in the Dominion, Sunny, arrived.

Mam taught each reading, writing, and arithmetic. She pledged them an education. Dada expressed no interest in learning.

On a Sunday morning, on the way to church, Mam suggested Dada create a venture and establish his own brickyard. With Mam's aid, he successfully sought bank financing and purchased a lot beside the river near the railyard.

By twenty-eight, Dada was self-made.

Mam attended to filing, form filling, and hiring. Outbuildings, a barn, and stables were constructed. Mam purchased additional moulds and a third iron pug mill. From digging flatland clay to grinding, screening, kneading, moulding, dying, and burning, the business of brickmaking was labourious. The operation expanded into the manufacture of pipe drains. With a reputation for quality, the business thrived.

After a succession of four more births, Carrie, Baa Baa, Harry, and Alma, the Williams relocated to larger living quarters. Now residing in a well-appointed red-brick house, they were as happy as Larry. A nursemaid was hired. Frances and Mary Ann matriculated in the Toronto Ladies School and boarded in the city. Johnny attended a business college at the corner of King and Toronto Streets. The younger children attended a local private school. When Mary Ann returned to Weston, she was hired by the grammar school and took a room nearby.

In the summer, Mam cared for the babies while Frances attended to the youngsters. Days passed playing knucklebones on a patch of dirt beside a vegetable garden in the fenced-in front yard or besting one another at games of cup-and-ball. Frances supervised dips in the Humber at a watering hole by the mill. When Ryan & Robinson's Mammoth Circus train encamped on a siding for a brief stay, Frances used the astonishing visit to provide lessons in zoology, explaining the pinstriped bands of zebras, the origin of hippopotami, and truths about trick horses. Placed in the howdah atop Old Romeo, the children went for a ride on the African war elephant's back.

Late in the evening, as he dropped into bed beside Mam, Dada drifted off, bemoaning the need for a man to supervise the third kiln. The following morning, Mam put Alma in a perambulator, wheeled her youngest to the post office, tacked a job notice to the public board, and returned home.

A blow-in named William Stones answered. Frances could simply have sent him away. The decision not to tortured her for the remainder of her years.

The sun was scorching. Frances went inside to fetch pink lemonade for the moppets and a bottle of Belfast Ginger Ale for herself from the icebox. When she returned to the yard, Stones, an open-mouthed ungainly man with large upper teeth, an untrimmed moustache, and very large ears, stood outside the gate. He unfolded a crumpled piece of paper from the pocket of his sack coat. Eyeing the property, he swigged gin from a noggin bottle tucked inside his shabby coat.

Frances squinted. The unexpected appearance of the unusual figure at the gate caught the teenage girl unaware.

"I'm here about the situation," Stones held up the paper. He stole another sip from the noggin bottle, belched, and dug a clod of wax from his ear with his baby finger. "Is Mr. Williams present?"

Carrie dropped the cup-and-ball handle in the dirt. Frances replied, "Our mam hires."

Stones placed his scabby hand on the gate latch. "Can I come in?"

Frances remained silent.

"I said, can I enter?"

Frances nodded reluctantly.

"It's not your mam I ask after." Stones opened the gate. He licked his pinkie finger, entering the yard, dragging yellow saliva across his lower, cracked lip. "I'm here for your father."

Frances stepped forward between the strange man and her charges. She replied reluctantly, "He is in the back, in the barn."

After Dada took Stones on, he transformed. He began laying off work, instead accompanying the scamp into the tavern in the Eagle Hotel. He wandered nights. He quarrelled. He was vulgar. The more grog Dada touched, the less human he became, tapping a previously unshown vein of violence. One evening he ravished Mam brutally before the children.

Pregnancy followed. April's birth was feeble. The sickly baby survived four months before she went to the ground at St. Philip's.

How quickly the brickmaking enterprise wound up. Insolvency, solicitors, the bank came and collected. Thirty labourers were thrown out, only a few hired back when the Baron Brick Co. of Chicago assumed the operation.

The Williams became destitute. They lived in squalor. The children of employable age worked. Frances abandoned her education and became a domestic in Toronto, boarding in the white brick mansion of her employer in the Queen's Park. She and her mam exchanged letters. Mam's inky scribble in one nearly illegible correspondence read, "Keep away. Your father is a changeling. He is going with the fairies."

The afternoon Frances received the telegram alerting her of the murder, the mistress of the house dismissed her explaining, "It is best for all."

RICHARD
Richard caught a silvery-green pickerel with an ash-wood pole, fishing below Wadsworth's dam, and brought it home. Mam was preparing a stirabout in the kitchen. The boy flopped the fresh, dead fish on the table. Mam expressed her pleasure. Richard remained silent, frightened by fresh bruising to her face as purple as a bullace plum.

Dada and Stones had been on whisky all day. Dada and Stones quarrelled and battered one another in the small, unkempt cottage. Children cried. Mam made an effort to break them apart. Dada knocked her in the throat. Stones laughed.

Dada threw his arm around Stones' shoulder and sang a song about the otherworld.

Mam went out back to milk the cow.

Dada sent Richard to Eagles to procure liquor. The boy slinked away to the railyard to hide, only to return very late.

BAA BAA

That night, a ruckus roused Baa Baa from sleep. Clutching a Frozen Charlotte china doll, she peeked into the darkened kitchen where Dada straddled Mam on the floor.

Frightened, Baa Baa hid in the Saratoga trunk.

Three months later, she went for adoption.

SUNNY

Mam's moans woke Sunny. In an insensible condition on the floor, Dada leaned against the wall, spat, slurred, and hissed. The boy kneeled by her side as she expired. He lost the contents of his bowels.

Fourteen years later, Sunny went to a barn, attached a rope to a beam, fastened it around his neck, threw himself from a fanning mill, and died.

MAM

Before giving up, she cried thrice, "Are you John Williams, my husband, in the name of God?"

CARRIE

Several minutes elapsed before Carrie roused Richard from sleep, instructing him to go at once for Mary Ann and Johnny. Carrie was adopted soon after by a family in a neighbouring community.

JOHNNY

The pug mill was outside the village, beside the river. Brickmaking begins sunup.

It has been fourteen months since I gathered my books and left home. When the weather suits, I sleep in the eaves of an outbuilding with other labourers like me who work in the brickfield. In winter, we huddle under the kiln. I have taught some to read. I continued to give Mam a portion of my wage to maintain her household. A smaller bit I set aside for education. I planned to resume business college in Toronto.

Then this.

Richard tracked the rutty path to the mill, teary-eyed and panting. I was kneading clay powder and water with a large wooden paddle when he entered, crying Mam was no more. Our poor Mam. Go straightaway, workmates instructed. I ran after Richard.

The labourer's cottage, where ten of my twelve siblings and my parents reside, was set back from the public road. A former icehouse and a disused byre beside the cottage provided additional sleeping quarters.

Policeman Brown and Policeman Porter stood around outside with their bare faces hanging out doing nothing to prevent curious villagers from traipsing in and out of the cottage. Policeman Porter, a cadet who looked scarcely twenty, said he took his orders from Detective Murray's command.

Quaking, I pushed my way inside. Policeman Porter followed.

Household furniture was upset. Broken crockeryware. A spattering of a meal. Torn books. Empty liquor jars. My parents' bedstead was broken.

Detective Murray was talking to Dada by the window. He wrote every word of their exchange in his occurrence book.

Policeman Porter received a dressing down from his superior after conveying my desire to disperse the crowd from the premises. I raised my voice and demanded the crowd withdraw. When they resisted, I went into the yard and retrieved an elm switch to drive them out.

"Get out," I shouted. "My Mam's house is not a theatre."

The cottage emptied. Mam was supine on the floor in the kitchen beside a wicker chair, her features unrecognizable and decimated. Brained repeatedly with a brick, wads of her hair had been torn from her scalp. Dark, clotted blood covered her chemise. Boot prints were all around. Horrorstruck, I covered her with a shawl.

Richard sobbed in a doorway. I asked him about our other siblings. Detective Murray paused a moment from questioning Dada and glared at me. Before he could say a word, Policeman Porter answered, "Safe. With a neighbour."

"Which neighbour?"

Policeman Porter opened his occurrence book. "The Holleys."

Then I snarled at Dada, "You have done it at last."

"Not me—"

Detective Murray interjected. "Then explain the blood on your pants."

"Blood? Not blood. Swamp dirt."

I shoved Dada. "Liar. It's Mam's blood. You know it."

He shoved me back. I went at him with fists. My physique was superior. Formerly thickset and imposing, once he could have easily throttled me. I forced him, weakened by drink, to his knees. Policeman Porter attempted to pull us apart.

Dada crumpled to the dirt floor, weeping. "Whisky did it."

"Whisky? This is all your hand." I turned to Detective Murray. "Apprehend William Stones. His hand is in this, too."

The detective sighed, resenting the interruption. He snapped an order at Policeman Porter, "Don't stand there. Go with the lad, then. Find this Stones fella. Shouldn't have to tell you twice."

"Yes, sir."

Policeman Porter and I hurried down to the flats. The cadet was chatty in a nervous sort of way, he told me had only just joined the force, but his kind and gentle voice did not lessen the shock. He instructed me to allow justice to take its course.

We discovered Stones concealed in his falling-down shack in a moist cedar bog beside the tracks, partially hidden in an abandoned industrial wash boiler. Stillness was interrupted by the low buzzy trill of a swamp sparrow in conflict with a rival male close by.

Policeman Porter tapped the wood-slatted door of Stones' shelter with his billy club and said to me, "Let me have words with him. You stand back."

I did not agree, instantly resolving that Stones, a filthy criminal with a starved body and black, perverted heart, would pay for his deed at my hand. My charge forward caught Policeman Porter unprepared. Fetching a washing paddle, I went at Stones, spindly and sunburnt, swinging widely, pummelling the pathetic, reprehensible creature. Stones did not counterattack as I split the scabby membrane of flesh pulled tight over his skull. I chopped at his head and the wounds bled liberally. Mouth pulped and teeth shattered, his unkempt moustache was soaked crimson red.

Policeman Porter ordered I desist. He pounced on my back and pulled me off, pleading with me, "The suspect is in my charge."

We rolled backward on the floor. "You know his type. You know what he did."

"The court will decide."

Back at the cottage, Detective Murray had Dada in bracelets. He evaluated Stones' condition. "What happened down there? Was the suspect recalcitrant?"

Policeman Porter explained I became extremely angry and flew into a rage. "Should there be a charge against him?" he asked the commanding officer.

Detective Murray appeared indifferent. He glanced at me and shrugged. "So he momentarily lost his composure? Who hasn't?"

The detective escorted Dada outside and I chased after, wailing at my father. "You turned wicked. I saw this coming. You'll get the rope." To my mother's corpse, I whispered, "You've been long in earning it."

In the next quiet moment came a sob from inside Mam's battered Saratoga trunk. I opened the lid where Baa Baa cowered inside, her stringy black hair plastered to her damp face. Clutching a doll, she sprang into my arms, trembling like a frightened bird. I hurried her outside.

MARY ANN

The wage at the grammar school was $600 annually. Some went to Mam. I resided in quarters at the Tyrrell House. When Richard arrived with the news, I sent him straightway to fetch Johnny, "Tell him to come without delay."

Class commenced in under an hour, but I started for Mam's regardless, frightened by the sight that awaited. Mam's strong words strengthened me: "You are a town lady. Be an example."

On Dada's sentencing, the school's administration replaced me with another teacher.

ELIZA
The tumult could not penetrate the thick, sedimentary stones quarried from the Humber River used in walling the icehouse. Eliza, Adelaide, and Emmie slept uninterrupted. In the morning, they shrieked as one at the sight of so much blood.

Eliza eventually went to a Hamilton family and vanished.

MAGGIE
The day following the slaying, the shy ten-year-old provided sworn testimony to the jury impanelled to consider how Ann Williams came to her death. Jurors strained to hear the little girl whisper, "I saw Dada stomping on Mam's head."

ADELAIDE
A church organist and her husband in Kingston took Adelaide.

EMMIE
Emmie eventually died from an ailment.

HARRY
Johnny took in his baby brother.

DADA
The convicted killer stated from the scaffold in a loud, firm tone, "I wish to make several remarks. I wish to thank Governor Green. I wish to thank my counsel. I am happy that I got a fair trial. I thank the public at large for what they have done for me. Also, my clergyman. Now dear children, you are alone in this world. That's all."

The noose followed.

Reverend Walsh commenced reading the Lord's Prayer, and when the words "deliver us from evil" were read, the platform fell.

Ribald laughter from boys perched on the wall filled the hushed jail yard. In the Don Valley, where all the leaves had changed and fallen, a steam train whistled a long, mournful lament.

BRICK (A FAIRY TALE)

ALMA
Alma learned of her adoption at sixty-eight and didn't tell a soul.

Fourteen years elapsed before she boarded a train bound for Toronto. The fact was she was too frail to travel alone. She had left Montreal, informing no one. By now, her children and grandchildren were frantic. She travelled with a single, light suitcase.

Upon arrival at Union Station, she hailed a yellow taxicab. She directed the cabbie in stilted English to take her to St. Philip's Anglican Church on St. Philips Road above the Humber River.

When they arrived, she instructed him to remain while she visited the grave of the mother she could not recollect.

The cabbie asked if he could assist her across the uneven churchyard lawn.

"*Non. Merci.*"

Fifteen minutes later, she hobbled back to the cab. She had been crying. The cabbie handed her a tissue, asking patiently, "Where now?"

Alma stared out the window. "*Un moment.*"

The cabbie removed a stubby pencil from behind his ear and did a few lines of a *Telegram* crossword puzzle.

Lost in thought, Alma muttered, "*Je me demande s'il y avait des soeurs?*"

"What?"

Alma absentmindedly repeated, "I wonder if there were sisters?"

She produced an address scribbled on wrinkled paper from her purse and passed it over the seat to the cabbie.

"549 Gerrard Street East?" Puzzled, the cabbie sought the old lady in the rearview mirror, "You mean the Don?"

"Oui. Yes. The Don. *Je veux voir l'endroit.*"

"Pardon me, please?"

"I want to see the place."

The yellow taxicab pulled to the curb in front of the imposing jail. The cabbie lit a cigarette, chuckling, "We breakin' someone out?"

"*Non.* No."

The old lady remained in the backseat staring at the façade of the jail.

The cabbie flicked the butt out the window, asking hesitantly, "Do you know someone in there?"

"No."

The cabbie lit another cigarette. Ten minutes passed. The cabbie flicked the butt out the window. "Meter's running."

Later, seated in a well-appointed hotel room across from Union Station, Alma called home.

THE PULSE OF THE HEART

The evening pleasantly began with George and other cadets attending a ten-round boxing match between Vint Harkness, the "Ithaca Giant," and "Washboard" Eddy Rochester. Harkness won a silver belt. Up to a point, in his ringside seat, George could say he was enjoying himself for the first time since his arrival in the city. However, the occasion proved to be a ruse by night's end.

After the match, cadets from the city hosted cadets from the country for a social affair in a private, second-floor convention room at the Clyde Hotel on King Street East. The desk agent's discretion was purchased, permitting alcohol from Kerby Henry's, a drinking saloon across the street, to be clandestinely conveyed onto the premises.

George was deceived into imbibing a significant quantity of spirits.

Police Cadet Wright, the brawny ringleader, initiated a hazing ritual after midnight. Several city recruits participated. Dickson, a courteous fellow from a village outside Hamilton, was forced to kill a chicken with his teeth. Another recruit with a cheerful smile was stripped, slathered in rendered bovine fat, and coated in eiderdown and ashes.

Recruits Hayward, McCowan, and Putnam restrained George while Seldon tied his hands. Mudd worked a blindfold over his eyes. George was shoved into a dark, cluttered storeroom containing a soiled mattress on a wickerwork cot. Inside, he was pushed against a whimpering hussy gagged with her silk hair ribbon allegedly paid to participate in a debasing episode. Gathering his wits, he sobered enough to persuade the young woman to unbind his hands, permitting both to escape out a fire exit to an alley.

She disappeared, but George was less fortunate. When his tormentors, led by Wright, caught up to him, they hauled him to Allen Gardens and dunked him repeatedly in the fountain until he was nearly drowned.

Coming out of that incident, he cemented a reputation among officers in the Toronto Police Force as a spoilsport. For the duration of training, recruits browbeat him unremittingly, just as Constable Cooke had feared might occur.

Even a patrol sergeant at the division where Cadet Porter trained joined others in the baiting. During third-watch training, hoaxers on the force arranged a prank with medical students from the university to obtain a naked corpse and dangle it on a meat hook over the sidewalk outside Langrill's butcher shop on Parliament Street. Porter, walking the beat at four in the morning, stumbled into the find and promptly cacked himself.

From then, rank-and-file taunted him as P.C. Privy Porter, or just Privy, a moniker that remained until he was made detective.

A winter harvesting ice on frigid Lake Simcoe added muscle to George's lean physique. Still, when he commenced physical training in Toronto that spring at the old lacrosse grounds, he remained unassuming and retiring.

George came to the city permanently before Easter arriving with few belongings in the company of Constable Cooke and Beatrice. His sister had made arrangements with a family from the township to reside in a residence they possessed on Rusholme Road. He rented a comfortably furnished parlour bedroom with an additional single room for $2.59 weekly.

When Beatrice visited, which she did often, she lodged in the spare room.

The Police Board received dozens of applications for constableship, accepting only sixteen. Constable Cooke had strongly recommended

George to the Toronto Police Force. Inquiries into his character and his family's position made him a successful candidate. Attaining top marks in reading, writing, and arithmetic, he easily met the academic requirements. His firearm-handling deficiency became plain when he was evaluated on his use of a revolver. However, after the Police Board noted George's brilliant deductive skills, they agreed to make an exception to the requirement that he hit a bull's eye at fifty yards if he pledged to practise and retest.

Beatrice fretted that George spent too much time alone in his room, reading and sketching. "At least sketch a self-portrait in your police dress, and I'll send it to mother and father."

To placate his sister, he gathered his sketching materials and posed in uniform before a cheval glass. After hours, armed with his .44 calibre revolver and extra ammunition, he went to the rifle range in High Park for practice.

In addition to a blue-coated uniform and blue and white helmet, he received a baton, handcuffs, whistle, fire alarm keys, and a small pocket lamp. He attended class daily for weeks, including parading and drill rudiments. Cadets also learned by-law regulations and the country's criminal laws.

Classroom instruction and physical training were a cinch. Walking a beat was a horse of a different colour, however. He was partnered with Gerald Brown, a constable with decades of experience. Brown, a morose, slothful alcoholic, was a poor instructor and left George to learn the ropes independently.

Assigned to a suburban division and placed on day duty, Police Cadet Porter rode the suburban train from Toronto to Weston, earning $1.35 daily. Weston had recently acquired a reputation for being lawless, and accidents were common.

On his first patrol, a six-year-old got his leg stuck in the spokes of a wagon wheel, and Police Cadet Porter escorted the boy to an infirmary. He also collected the body of a Jewish peddler whose cart became lodged on train tracks.

Intervention in domestic disputes was a daily occurrence.

Except for the Johnston murder, the police cadet witnessed more carnage, violence, and debauchery than he ever encountered back home in East Gwillimbury.

A man from the West Indies was kicked to death by inebriates at the Eagle Tavern. Patrons who watched refused to aid the investigation. A youth lost an eye in a knife fight. Porter stemmed the bleeding with a handkerchief he found discarded in the gutter. The youth lost the eye.

He investigated suicides, arson, and severe child neglect, struggling particularly with witnessing harm done to children.

The murder of Ann Williams proved nearly too much. He was the first to arrive on the terrible scene of what the newspaper labelled the "Weston Horror."

Returning from his shift downcast, he sat on the bench across the street from home, shocked that humans could hurt one another with such abandon.

The next day, he said to Beatrice, "I don't think I can do this."

"In fact, I'm sure you can."

"You don't understand what they inflict on one another. Even babies are not spared."

"It will get easier. Promise."

"That's my fear." George was close to tears. "Something of you vanishes every time you witness these brutalities. I'm afraid one day there'll be nothing of me I'll recognize."

Beatrice purchased tickets to a fancy roller-skating performance at the Princess Roller Skating Rink on Duchess Street to distract him from his thoughts that weekend. George reluctantly agreed. The doors opened at two, and the show ran until five.

The principal performer, the pretty Miss S. Martin, performed gracefully in a bright, gay costume with ribbons in her hair, giving a skilful roller-skating exhibition. George was secretly smitten, admiring how she could step in any fashion and turn her feet in potentially dangerous ways.

He continued target practise in High Park and saw a mild improvement in his accuracy. On a visit to East Gwillimbury, Constable Cooke mentored him on marksmanship.

Beatrice and George returned to the roller-skating show several times over the next few weeks to distract George from work.

To Beatrice's astonishment, George told his sister after a matinee, "Miss Martin is so merry and she is the pulse of my heart. I want to meet her."

After the show, introductions were made. Susan Martin was pleased to chat with the siblings about the modern form of entertainment and how she came to practise it.

Beatrice was amused when George requested Miss Martin's company on a future date.

"We could visit the park," George stammered, "and I'll show you my improved shot. Beatrice will tag along, too. Right, Beatrice?"

"If you agree to put on skates," Susan replied. "I'll agree to the park."

"I'm eager to see that!" Beatrice laughed.

Thus began a courtship that progressed famously. In the autumn, Susan accompanied George back home to East Gwillimbury to enjoy the seasonal colours and be introduced to his family.

They attended church and lectures in one another's company in the city.

Most of Susan's people resided in Calgary, but some were in Toronto. The Martins and the Porters merged two years later when George and Susan married in a ceremony officiated by the Chief Constable.

REMEMBER ME

G. Bennett, 1880

Ten minutes after the drop, George Bennett—alias George Dickson—was pronounced dead and his body cut down. Prone on the gravel in the exercise yard, Bennett's body, its ankles and wrists pinioned, was heaved onto a flimsy cart and wheeled inside the facility. A black flag was hoisted up the jail flagpole. The hangman removed the canvas mask required to conceal his identity, scratched his coarse cheeks.

Officials dispersed. Inmates dismantled the scaffold. A chatter of newspapermen departed. Outside the prison, the festive throng of spectators thinned. A small crowd lingered by the Don Bridge, shaded by a copse of black locust trees.

The hangman drew a small, hardback book from inside his jacket and made notations with a dull pencil. Gathering the half-inch soaped rope into a butterfly coil, he untied the noose and placed the rope into a sack. He stood a moment and gazed into the gauzy white face of the rising sun. At the base of the wall behind him, the inmate assigned to dig Bennett's grave went at the earth with pick and shovel, quietly humming "It Is Well with My Soul."

Before retiring to an unadorned apartment inside the jail where he had slept the previous night, the hangman collected his forty-dollar fee from Governor Green. Undressing, he leaned over a washbasin, splashed warm water on his face. He lathered shaving soap in a mug and shaved his cheeks smooth. Changing into a new black suit, he gulped from a flask. Sitting heavily on the stained mattress, the hangman unfolded a penny knife and cut lengths of rope from the cord that had recently launched Bennett into eternity. Placing personal effects into a carpetbag patterned with rosebuds, he lay back on the cot and catnapped.

An inquest was held pro forma in the small, black-and-white tiled prison hospital, austere as an anchorite's cell. Thirteen jurors were selected. Bennett's corpse was displayed on a table.

The black sack covering the condemned man's head was removed. The cord used to tie his wrists and ankles was cut and the corpse stripped of clothing.

Five feet, two inches, Bennett was below medium height and weighed one hundred twenty-six pounds. He wore a black Van Dyke beard. Between purplish lips, his tongue protruded, a black wedge of meat. His eyes were closed. His nose appeared to have been recently broken. Livid contusions marked his neck. His hands were a shade of blue similar to a morpho butterfly. The autopsy revealed congestion in the brain, lungs, and heart. The posterior ligaments of his upper vertebrae were separated. As a result of the drop, his spinal column had dislocated.

Medical examiner's conclusion: death was instantaneous. The jury's verdict, unanimous: the condemned had experienced no pain.

It was forenoon when the hangman approached the crowd lingering by the locust trees, rope sack, and carpetbag slung over his shoulder. In his free hand he held up samples of rope, repeating, "Souvenir? Souvenir. Justice is done. The righteous rejoice. The Honorable George Brown's killer, finished by this rope. An historic day. A souvenir?"

Horse blankets spread on the ground, a rank stench fouled the air as families fried carp livers, potatoes, and bay mussels on naphtha stoves, breakfasting in the fashion of a picnic.

The crowd surrounded the hangman. Boys climbed out of trees. Men in blue and white check vests and felt derbies ambled toward him, rubbing their bellies and inhaling deeply from hooked ceramic smoking pipes.

An emaciated teenage boy with a harelip and rags for clothing dangled from a tree limb kicking his spindly legs. In a voice like bone pressed to an emery wheel, he recited a Bible verse about the powers of darkness, shouting at the executioner, "What's it feel like killing for a living?"

The hangman's expression remained flat. Indecipherable. A weathered tombstone. "Tell me your name, boy," he shouted.

Perched above the crowd, the slender boy repeated, "What's it feel like killing for a living?"

"Well, if you must know, it feels like a full stomach and a clean suit of clothing. It feels like the taste of costly bourbon." His nostrils flared. "It feels like a close shave and like the scent of a perfumed lady." Locking eyes with the crowd, he concluded, "It feels like a downy pillow at close of day." He clasped his hands and mocked, "At least from my end of the rope, anyway."

The hushed crowd erupted in laughter. The rawboned boy appeared to shrink sizes. "Now," the hangman taunted, "tell me, what's the feel of hunger? How does it feel to have the face of a praying mantis? Tell me, what's it feel like to be insignificant?"

A woman seated with her back to a wagon wheel leaped to her feet, beckoned the hangman, and snatched a sample of rope. Strands of auburn hair came loose from her chignon. Her cheeks flushed as she clenched the fibrous twine, shoving it toward her husband. Face set in a moue, she sulked, "This is foul. I want it."

Her man paid with money from his purse.

After the hanging, Governor Green took breakfast. He instructed the chief turnkey to assign two inmates to prepare Bennett for burial, dressing the cadaver in clothing delivered the previous afternoon by Bennett's three siblings, Patience, William, and Julie, as well as a flaxen-haired gentleman in a waistcoat, striped trousers and Christy stiff hat also named William.

This second William went by Billy.

Patience, tall, comely, and darkly complected, had tugged the bell pull. William, a painter by trade, gripped a parcel of clothing wrapped in red butcher paper to his chest with whitewash-stained hands. Julie, the baby of the family, shaded herself under a parasol.

Carved into the alabaster keystone above the portico, the terrifying likeness of Cronos, the father of time, gazed into a blank future. Bald-faced hornets swarmed at the papery opening of a grey nest constructed in the architrave.

Following at least a dozen pulls, a turnkey with a tragic expression opened the heavy door.

"What?"

Patience murmured, "We're here to visit our brother."

Staring at them like they were zoo animals, he asked, "And?"

"And?" Patience cast a quick glance over her shoulder. "Allow us entry, please."

The turnkey studied Patience with agitation, suspicion. The intense midafternoon sunlight made everything appear increasingly queer.

"Who's your brother, then?"

"George Dickson," Patience said, before correcting herself. "Bennett, George Bennett."

"Bennett or Dickson? Which?"

"Bennett."

Their father was of West Indian origin but, unlike his brother and two sisters, Bennett took after their mother in appearance.

The turnkey was indignant. "Bennett? The white man?"

Patience unfolded the pass Sheriff Jarvis had provided that granted permission to visit their brother in the death cell. The turnkey scrutinized the paper as sounds of carpentry, hammering, and sawing came from the rear of the jail. Swatting at a wasp, Julie lost her balance, nearly toppling down the limestone steps. William reached for his younger sister's elbow. He dropped the parcel.

The contents spilled out.

The turnkey looked past Patience to Billy. "Can you vouch for the woman?"

Billy's Adam's apple rose and fell before he said, "The woman is my wife."

The door creaked closed. While they waited, a wasp stung Julie on the cheek. The white-hot sting brought tears. Helping their sister to sit on the steps, they comforted Julie.

Minutes lapsed before the turnkey reappeared. In a mordacious tone he snarled, "No."

"No? No, what?" Patience inquired.

"No visit," he smirked. "Not today."

"When? Tomorrow our brother—"

Julie pawed at her neckline. "My throat. I can't—"

William removed the gold pin engraved with her initials from the collar of her shirtwaist and dropped it on the step. Billy rubbed the back of her hand and attempted to settle her, repeating, "Sh, sh. It's okay. It's okay."

"I don't understand," Patience pleaded, holding up Sheriff Jarvis's pass. "We're permitted."

Julie panted, gasped, "Breathing. Difficult."

The turnkey uttered, "He wants visits from none of you. Bennett's words, not mine." The heavy door closed tight as a fist.

Jowls swollen, Julie clawed her throat, wheezing, "I can't breathe—"

Face pressed against the closed door, Patience pleaded, "Please. Please. At the very least, help my baby sister. She's only fourteen."

Julie's face and lips swelled terribly. A mud salve did not bring relief. Pleading to be rid of the pain, Julie moaned as they started for the emergency hospital. In their haste, Julie's collar pin was included in the parcel of clothing assembled into a neat pile and left on the steps.

Turnkey Wilson, a jittery man with a pronounced overbite, pulled aside two inmates, Deacon and Mann, before their work gang set out to complete landscaping work at Riverdale Park.

Wilson guided Deacon and Mann to the room containing Bennett's corpse. Deacon, a nasally woebegone grumbler as crooked as a corkscrew, was awaiting trial for housebreaking and petty larceny. Once set upon with a cricket bat, portions of his skull bone appeared to float under the scalp of his shaved head. Where his right eye had been knocked out during the assault, dense scar tissue formed a sphincter-like opening on his face.

Fourteen-year-old Mann, eyes as blue as deep water, had been arrested by Constable Porter and sent up for fifteen days for drunkenness. Two days remained on his sentence. Despite recent setbacks, Mann was, for the most part, a happy-go-lucky fellow.

In infancy, he had been left partially deaf after a bout of typhoid he had not been expected to survive. The gamins he ran with called their cheery friend Mann Lucky, Just Lucky, or Lucky. Upon release, Mann pledged to himself he would leave the jail, find a situation, and be done with the city. The black pox had taken his pop and his ma and his siblings. He had no one.

Resembling a grotesque bisque doll, George Bennett's sutured and stitched body lay unclothed on a table. A splendid black coffin ferried from Cobourg—the town of his birth—on the night steamer, *Mirth*, and delivered before dawn by a teamster from Small's Wharf, stood propped in the corner. The lid displayed St. Peter's inverted cross. Items of clothing sat neatly folded on a sturdy workbench.

Wilson turned up the gas, washing the room in sickly, yellow light. The prisoners paused at the sight of Bennett. Slowly, Mann removed his cap, crossed himself.

Deacon chortled, "What's this, then?"

Turnkey Wilson shoved the inmates forward. "Clothe and get it coffined."

"Wait now," Deacon whined. "This is women's work. Strumpets in the west wing could know better what to do with this bloke." Glancing at the coffin, Deacon added, "A Papist, too."

"Governor's orders," Wilson barked. "Get on with it before he's hardened."

REMEMBER ME

Deacon and Mann set to dress Bennett in fineries of the day, a double-breasted pine green frock coat with matching vest and trousers. Size five stacked-heeled cordovan leather shoes. A white collar. Loosely tying a barrel knot around his own neck before passing the tied cravat to Deacon, Mann gently cupped the back of Bennett's head, raised it slightly allowing Deacon to slip the black satin cravat over the scalp and around the dead man's neck. Wilson watched idly from the doorway.

Mann wiped a spot of grime from Bennett's ashen cheek with his frayed cuff, grooming the dead man's thick moustache with his fingertips.

Mann asked reverently, "Who is he?"

Straightening the cravat, Deacon shrugged.

Mann instructed, "Not too tight."

Wilson leaned in the doorway, chewing his thumbnail as the pair retrieved the coffin.

Mann grasped Bennett's shoulders, Deacon his ankles, and together they lowered the body into the box.

Mann knelt, smoothed Bennett's lapels, patted the dead man's firm chest. Lid set in place, the white metal thumbscrews remained unfastened.

In a pasture behind the jail, a dog barked.

Deacon and Mann turned to Wilson. Mann asked deferentially, "Sir? Now?"

Cast in yellow gaslight, the men appeared jaundiced. Wilson instructed each to turn out the pockets of their Garibaldi jackets. Without hesitation, Mann complied. Deacon stared at his boots, "I didn't nick nothin'."

Wilson jabbed his billy club into Deacon's throat, "Like I said, turn 'em."

Deacon removed an engraved silver pocket watch and a lady's gold collar pin from his pocket.

Wilson seized both.

"A fine timepiece," Deacon stammered nervously. "Too fine to bury."

The turnkey held up the timepiece, studied it. "Valuable," he murmured and, before slipping the watch into his pocket, glanced at the open doorway. "Valuable, indeed."

Deacon and Mann fastened the coffin lid in place. Wilson watched, hovering over their shoulders. Turning the collar pin over in his hand he asked, "Either of you know of this man?"

"Knew 'im? No, only that he ended another man."

Mann sighed. "Which man?"

Wilson winked. "The man. Brown." He tossed the collar pin at Mann, who reflectively snatched it out of the air. The turnkey said, "Son, in this life, there's profit in not knowing."

"Pardon?"

Wilson repeated himself, louder, "There's profit. In not knowing."

Mann sighed. "Oh. Profit. Of course."

Tightening the final screw on Bennett's coffin, Mann squeezed the collar pin in his palm.

The coffin was placed on a cart. Wilson ordered, "To yard."

Mann pushed from the rear. The exercise yard was ablaze with sunlight. Mann leaned down, placed his boyish face close to the seam where lid and coffin joined, and whispered, "Remember me."

These final words seeping into the dead man's box, Bennett joined the choir invisible in the ground. Reverend Father Egan recited a benediction. Puffs of incense from the polished brass censer drifted above the exercise yard, over the wall, over the river, over trees, over public roads, over Riverdale Park, to the top of the sky.

Upon his liberty, Mann was true to his word. He found a situation to convey him away from the city, replying to an ad in *The Globe* seeking agents to sell chromolithograph portraits of the late Hon. George Brown in townships throughout the province. He earned thirty-three cents on the dollar, plus a stipend for lodging.

With the take from a poker match, he purchased eel skin trousers, Chelsea boots, and a green vest. He sat in a haircutter's chair for his first fifteen-cent haircut.

The gold collar pin given to him by Turnkey Wilson pinned to his waistcoat, he walked the highway between Toronto and Cornwall hawking the likeness of George Brown.

"Souvenir? Souvenir. An historic day. A souvenir."

Passing through Cobourg, he saw a downcast, dark-complexioned woman in a satin polonaise, sitting on a covered porch, alone on a comfortable swing chair.

"Hello. I am thirsty."

She offered water.

The most exquisite lady he'd ever encountered eyed the collar pin fixed to his chest. For the first time in a long time, she smiled.

"The pin. Where did you come by it?"

"A long story."

"Sit. Please. Join me so I might hear."

BABY FARM

George cursed the rain, the wind, and the slippery sidewalk. He cursed the gawkers, always anticipating something never materializing. He cursed the night.

In the rush to leave the station, the constable had forgotten his Indian rubber rain cape in his locker. Now, standing sentry outside George Brown's handsome red-brick Beverley Street residence with P.C. Barrow, he found himself soaked through and miserable. Worse, word came that relief would not arrive until the end of second watch. He and Barrow would remain until at least the hour lamplighter Sullivan came around again at one in the morning.

Showers tapering to drizzle around midnight offered George slight relief. He complained to himself that the dank, night-chill springtime air would end him. Only later, at home, changed out of his soggy attire and into dry nightwear, would he acknowledge to himself, lying in the dark beside Susan sound asleep, that he had reacted brashly after flying into a rage and forcing the meddlesome swarm from the sidewalk.

His day had started well enough. Still newlyweds, he and Susan were trying for their first child but having a hard time with it. They enjoyed breakfast, chatting about plans for Sunday's Easter dinner in their home. Beatrice and her fiancé, Ted Gruber, principal harpist with the Philharmonic Orchestra, planned to join them.

P.C. Porter arrived at the station to begin first watch and had tea with other constables. Inspector Leith gathered a roster of policemen in the parade room announcing a deployment to search a rural property in Yorkville. Judge Nelson issued a warrant after a concerned neighbour reported discovering the operation of a suspected baby farm in the neighbourhood. Upon a visit to the residence, they spied around a half dozen mistreated little ones. They observed a baby in a bassinet beside a stove suffering a terribly intense fever. The complainant asserted the ill and neglected infant had been confined to the kitchen, hotter than a blacksmith's forge.

Inspector Leith explained records indicated the tenant, Gladys Hamilton, had previously been cited for the negligence of her own darlings and allegedly made a business of taking in newborns and infants of women attempting to conceal the fact they were mothers. Hamilton reportedly profited from child-selling.

Two rows of constables sat shoulder to shoulder facing one another on bench seats crammed into the rear of the grey, canvas-covered, horse-drawn police van. They made light conversation on the way to the abysmal rural property. Poor road conditions made for an unconformable ride.

P.C. Porter asked P.C. Patterson, a Scotsman with red curls, about the wellness of his family and what Easter Sunday service they would attend. Patterson responded that the wife was fine and their seven kids were bonny. They would attend a midday service at St. Paul's without him, though. The schedule said he worked.

Patterson ribbed Porter, "And Privy, how about you? Not in a family way yet, eh? And why?"

"We're trying," George replied. "Soon, I predict something will come of it," he chuckled bashfully.

Arriving at the dwelling, P.C. Porter became heartsick at the sight of Hamilton, half-undressed, and feeble children displaying reddish sores on their sallow faces, lying on the floor strewn with waste. Some reached out, grasping at the air as if blind, while others showed little spark. The police matron and a nurse attended to the pitiful creatures. At the same time, detectives questioned Hamilton and led constables on a thorough search.

Armed with spades slung over their shoulders, Porter and Patterson were assigned to the rear of the property. Porter held up the tool and asked a ranking detective, "What are the specifics of the search of the exterior?"

"In this circumstance," the detective explained soberingly, "more likely than not, some won't have survived these conditions."

Hamilton kept sheep and other livestock. Patterson entered a low-slung sheepfold, and the animals all ran to the farthest corner and cowered. Porter strode through the mud that reached nearly to his shins, the squidgy sound of soggy earth beneath his Wellingtons. A nanny goat and two curious kids trailed him into a rickety chicken coop. With nothing suspicious found there, he ventured toward the line where the property ended to examine a reeking mound of sheep manure.

The spade plunged into the rancid heap, revealing a tiny, flaccid arm.

"What in bloody hell—" George cried, jumping backward.

He threw the spade aside and went to his knees, digging furiously with his hands. He called for Patterson to come quickly. He had learned enough perched at the coroner's shoulder and asking questions to recognize that soil staining on the tongue and palate indicated the babe went into the pile alive, suffocated by clods of muck lodged in the pharynx.

On the ride back to the station later, the rear of the police van smelled of perspiration and damp wool. A detective had wrapped the pathetically tiny corpse in a patterned tea towel, laid it on George's lap, and instructed him to deposit it at the city morgue.

On the bumpy ride, George gazed in intense mute agony at the repeating pattern of pastel flowers. A seething voice hissed inside his brain, "Get it off me," but to the other constables, he appeared meticulously composed.

Patterson asked George if things were fine.

George nodded, "Yes. Fine."

"Lost in thought then, Privy?"

"I was just considering our duties," George swallowed, studying the lifeless bundle on his lap. "Funny. One day, I arrest a miscreant for theft of a milking cow or book a fourteen-year-old for public intoxication. Next, I'm in the backlot of a baby farming operation elbow-deep in sheep dung, delivering this defenceless little thing from a shallow grave with my bare hands."

The other constables in the small compartment stared at George in silence.

Patterson shrugged, "Sure, Priv. Funny. That's the word, is it? Funny?"

George sighed. "No. It's not." He was quiet then added, "But what is the word, fellows?" He looked at the others looking at him. "Describe it, in a word. What's expected of us?"

"Keep the heid, Priv. I don't wish you to crack. Not here," Patterson whispered.

As instructed, he deposited the remains at the morgue and walked alone to the station. His shift was nearly over. The constable filed the requisite paperwork and discussed the findings with Inspector Leith. His superior notified him an inquest into the infant's death was called for Saturday instead of tomorrow, seeing as it was Good Friday. His testimony was mandatory.

Leaving the station for home, frantic word arrived of an assassination attempt on the life of *Globe* owner and politician George Brown. Immediately, Chief Constable Draper issued an order to inspectors for all policemen to report to their division and those on duty to remain active until notified.

A young assailant had entered Brown's office at 4:31. Words were exchanged. A struggle ensued. Brown put up a good fight for a man his age until the perpetrator produced a pocket pistol from his coat and discharged a single shot, which entered and exited the victim's thigh. Office employees of Brown's instantly subdued the aggressor, a former *Globe* employee.

In minutes, crowds gathered outside *The Globe's* King Street East office. Later, a rumour circulated that Brown had been transported to his home and perished there.

Crowds formed outside his Beverley Street residence, where Porter and Barrow were on duty. The rain came heavily.

Porter ordered the throng, mainly ladies, older men, and children, to clear the sidewalk. They refused to comply. George ordered them a second and a third time and then aggressively herded them with his baton. Some lost their footing and fell, causing them to topple upon one another. They cursed the constable's hostility.

Fortunately, accounting for their sombre mood and P.C. Barrow's intervention, nothing escalated. "We are all saddened by events," Barrow projected. "We are anxious and praying for a positive outcome for Mr. Brown. This remains front of mind."

Barrow took Porter to one side, removed his rain cape, and gave it to his partner, suggesting the weary policeman put it on and stroll to the dark side of the road to recover his composure.

Between events at the Yorkville baby farm, working first and second watch consecutively, and then Saturday's inquest, George was in a low state Easter morning when the bells at St. Christopher's pealed. The chancel, font, and communion table were arrayed with vivid floral decorations. Congregates sang a rousing version of "Christ the Lord is Risen Today." Rev. Mockeridge sermonized on Jesus Christ's journey to Emmaus. The congregation relished the special musical selection by the choir. Susan did not expect George to decline partaking holy communion.

Later, for dinner, Susan prepared spring lamb and seasonal vegetables. Throughout the meal, Beatrice observed her brother's aloofness. Toward dessert, he barely expressed joy or any other emotion, for that matter. When Susan prepared the serve frosted cake and tea, Ted pushed out his chair, stood, took Beatrice's hand, and announced she was expecting.

"Are you glad for us, George?" Beatrice asked her brother. "Of course, we'll marry soon, and the order of things will appear natural. But still, George, are you?"

"Happy? Yes." George said flatly. "I am. Very. Happy."

In a few moments, he discreetly excused himself from the table and the cheery conversation and ventured to the basement. He sat at a gunmetal table cast in sallow lamplight in the company of the furnace, the pipes, and the ash pan. Above him, Ted played "Wiegenlied" on his lyre. The floorboards creaked with happy footfalls.

It felt like a cold, steel rail pierced George's heart. He cleaned his revolver and sketched, enveloped in the deep, woodsy smell of Hoppe's No. 9 gun oil.

THE BALLAD OF ROBBY NEILL

R. Neill, 1888

Despite being required to scrub the face off a man periodically, former bootblack Robby Neill, if given a choice, wouldn't harm a mite. As it was, no one who lived in Robby's Lombard Street slum was ever given anything, much less a choice.

Around here, if you wanted something, you snatched it. Lacking the courage to do so meant you never wanted it badly enough to begin with.

Robby barely cursed, avoided liquor, and shunned tobacco. He loved the street where he lived. He seldom visited the whores there. He was not a religious man.

Unbeknownst to a single soul except Detective Porter, Robby was a stool pigeon.

Solitary by nature, he had few wants except perhaps a heaping plate of Aunt Bridget's delicious sheep trotters with sugar beans or a visit to the zoo with his faithful beagle, Bugoff.

What he really wanted was to be left alone. This was never going to happen. Seeing how he possessed the strength of Theseus but the temperament of a Hibernian monk made the nineteen-year-old Lombard Street's reluctant bullyboy.

Great Lakes mariner Jeremiah Sheehan, retired from the *Defiance*—a well-equipped schooner among the fleet of stone-hookers docked at Queen's Wharf—snatched the title Mayor of Lombard Street from Danny "Paddy Rat" Dwan in plain view of other ward bosses, discrowning his rival during a red-hot match at the Baseball Grounds on Queen Street, east of the Don Bridge.

The Toronto Baseball Club and the Syracuse Stars game was called at three sharp. The weather was all that could be desired. A carbolic stench wafted over the field from the nearby soap works. Under the shaded grandstand, ladies and their escorts sipped refreshing soft drinks and lime cordial. In the general admission section, hecklers sat in the hot sun on green bleachers, gulping harder drink. Both sections indulged in tea and buns. Robby gave Detective Porter advance word that a significant event would play out at the afternoon match in the bleachers instead of the diamond. Detective Porter sipped his tea on the hard bench among baseball fanatics a distance away, eyeballing Sheehan and his boys.

Clenching an unlit cigar in his teeth, Sheehan watched the tournament intently, more than money riding on the outcome. In the same row, his shabbily dressed recruits horsed about despite instructions to carry on proper. Ropesy, Lusty, and Rose played games with knives. Dross and Moggy irritated spectators around them. Scian and Dave played bloody knuckles. Lord Nelson carved initials into the bleacher.

As for Robby, he sat beside Sheehan, Bugoff in his lap. Robby cared little for the game of baseball. Instead, his gaze drifted beyond the playing field toward smokestacks along both sides of the Don River, belching black fumes into the blue sky. He spied lofty church spires and tall, needle-thin masts of sailing ships moored in the bay.

Peek-A-Boo Veach, moundsman for the Torontos, dapper in a maroon cap, grey shirt, breeches, a gold belt, and white stockings, delivered a deceptive drop ball for strike three and the out. The crowd applauded. Sheehan elbowed Robby in the ribs. He stood, handed the soggy cigar to Robby, spat into his hands, and said, "Let's be havin' it, then."

Robby's pocket contained tools of his trade: brass knuckles, a garrote, and a throwing knife. He removed the skull crackers and handed them to Sheehan. Fitting them over his knuckles, Sheehan made a fist, glancing sideways at his homely band of ruffians. Scratching Bugoff under the chin and then making the sign of the cross, Sheehan said, "After this business today, Robby, we'll be outfitted proper."

The home team was up two. Several rows ahead, Paddy Rat, the fool, had made the lethal error of attending the game accompanied by only two lieutenants, Uncle Goat and Fingy, mushroom pickers with no fight in them.

The donnybrook erupted in the seventh, spilling onto the field near third base. Detective Porter sat up, opened his occurrence book, noted the time, and jotted down observations.

Players retreated to benches as Sheehan reorganized Paddy Rat's face. Fieldkeepers were ordered to separate the combatants. One look at Robby—Bugoff peeking from the haversack slung over his shoulder fashioned by Aunt Bridget from a discarded Five Roses flour sack—and they retreated.

Three thousand fans cheered Sheehan, planted on Paddy Rat's chest, battering his rival's face to a pulp. Umpire Cochrane approached, a meerschaum pipe in his mouth. An honest but timid fellow, the old man cleared his throat and said, "Sakes alive."

Cochrane removed his silver pince-nez, cleaned the lenses with a blue handkerchief, and placed them back on the bridge of his nose. He eyed Paddy Rat, prone on the turf, bleeding, and said to no one in particular, "From my vantage point, it appears that man is out. A goner." Cochrane sized up Robby and said, "And son, as for that dog," he pointed at Bugoff, "pooches aren't permitted on the playing field."

Robby said, "Is that a rule?"

The old man said, "Well, no. Not so much a rule, more a superstition."

Robby's sad eyes measured up the diminutive umpire and then gazed past him into the middle distance. Arms folded across his barrel chest, he asked Cochrane, "How much do they pay you?"

The umpire puffed on his pipe, confused. He straightened his polka dot bow tie. "Two dollars," he stammered.

Robby said, "An inning?"

Cochrane said, "No. A game."

Robby cocked his chin toward Paddy Rat, unconscious and bleeding profusely from his mouth and ears. "Two a game, eh? You ought to be paid more." He sighed. "My advice? Leave this alone. It's not worth it to you."

Umpire Cochrane took Robby's advice and slinked toward the Torontos' bench, shielding himself against a volley of fancy teacups and saucers launched onto the pitch.

In a desperate effort to restore order, game officials directed the band of the Royal Grenadiers to take to the field. The regiment presented their colours and struck up "Here's to the Maiden" to no effect.

Sheehan stood triumphantly and retrieved his unlit cigar from Robby. Winded, he removed the brass knuckles and wiped his bloodied hands on his waistcoat. He beckoned his boys over with two fingers. Surrounded in a huddle, he rubbed a Lucifer match on his pant leg, bit off the cigar's tip, and puffed.

Rubbing his palms together eagerly, he glanced behind him at Paddy Rat and then jabbed Moggy. Over the crowd's din, he instructed, "He'll be out of commission for a while, so send a packet 'round to his missus once in a month for the foreseeable." Next, he placed his hand on Robby's shoulder, "Arrange a meeting with the Yid."

Sheehan clapped and grinned wildly. Raising his arms victorious, he exclaimed, "Bedad, we're jack-a-dandies now, boys."

Before peelers from No.2 police station arrived to restore order, the newly self-appointed Mayor of Lombard Street, along with his louts, sauntered across the turf, slipping through a sliding door in the smooth left field fence used on rare occasions to retrieve balls hit beyond the boards onto Eastern Avenue.

Detective Porter headed for the turnstile.

True to his word, Sheehan accompanied his boys to R.H. Gray & Co, a Front Street haberdasher, outfitting each in matching short-brimmed plug hats, white collars, silk neckwear, Guyot suspenders and striped trousers, tight at the knee, lose at the ankle. Sheehan admired himself in the mirror, puffing out his chest. "We look deadly, boys." Pinning a sprig of red bittersweet berries to his lapel, he added, "Cock 'o the walk. From here out, we dress alike, live alike, fight alike, and die alike."

The part of the slogan about dressing alike didn't apply to Moggy, the syndicate's purser, or Robby, the protection. Moggy, a sportive fellow with a sloped chin prone to epileptic fits, wore instead a red-and-caramel County Tyrone tartan kilt and Ghillie shirts from the old country. Sheehan figured since no one fought like Robby, the demolisher could dress how he desired. Pleasing in appearance, Lombard Street's goliath went about without a hat, in patched-up clothing, his long hair cut straight across the forehead, hanging down his back in tresses.

Sheehan's new status meant the reorganization of rackets citywide. Of twelve ward bosses, only Morris "Icky" Goldstein—the Yid of St. John's Ward—rivalled Sheehan for power. Lesser bosses could be left alone to continue horse thieving, dog and cockfights, coal gleaning, and beak hunting. So long as these activities remained within their ward boundaries, they could continue petty humbugs and pickpocketing for all their born days. Sheehan and Icky would carve out spoils of larger criminal enterprises between them.

Robby met with Icky's number two, Lenny the Muskl, a surly bloke big as a tug with deep-set eyes, grimy hands, and protruding knuckles. The Muskl, in turn, arranged a midnight convention between his boss and Sheehan on neutral territory on the waterfront onboard the deck of a steam dredge docked at the Yonge Street slip. Nightwatchman Dobbs wisely stayed away.

Surrounded by his boys bathed in the sallow light of a hurricane lamp, Sheehan sat opposite Icky and pounded the table, "See Icky, Yids and Micks have a common foe. What say we hurt Orangie and take 'im for all 'e's worth?"

Icky agreed to have fingers in frauds, embezzlements, and counterfeiting on his side of Yonge Street. He would control docks west of the Custom House and skim the Northern Railway's busy freight shed at the foot of Brock Street. The western cattle market and the racecourse at the Industrial Exhibition Grounds were his. He would influence the teamsters' union.

Sheehan took Woodbine Race Course, the eastern cattle market, docks east of the Customs House, Grand Trunk and TG&B freight sheds. He controlled the streetcar and bricksetters' union and ran a protection racket. He snatched influence over Gooderham & Worts Distillery. Profits from bawdy houses, gambling dens, and whisky dives in their respective wards were excluded from the arrangement. Sheehan's domain included gypsy camps in the Don Valley. Newsboys and bootblacks belonged to Icky. Organizing prizefights would be a joint venture. Politicians were up for grabs, from aldermen to His Worship in the mayor's office.

The agreement was sealed with a spit oath.

Back on Lombard Street, Sheehan made things right. A third of a mile long, the overcrowded street consisted of drab lath and plaster row houses, hovels fronted by pigsties, privies, and waste lots. Few brick homes lined the impoverished street. There was a brewery, a sheeny man's storehouse, bawdy houses, a marble works, St. Nicholas's House, a corset factory, auction rooms, Ontario Lead & Barbwire Limited, a chophouse, and Madame Ristori's, a gypsy fortune teller.

One of the first things Sheehan set up was big feeds for Catholic orphans at St. Nicholas's. A magician, contortionist, and ventriloquist entertained. Wolf Weinstein, the sheeny man, henceforth paid tribute or else. Sheehan commenced collecting a cut from transactions at the auction rooms. When the Acoustic Telephone Company strung lines above Lombard to the rear of the post office fronting Adelaide one street south and then across to the courthouse and police station, Sheehan had the lines cut until the telephone company agreed to pay.

Patrol Sergeant Lally was paid off accordingly.

Now that he had a say in matters, Sheehan refused to live in the same vicinity as pigs or Protestants. Swine were barred from the gutters. Protestant residents were scrubbed from the block. Street preachers evangelizing against Pope Leo were pounded.

Robby oversaw Protestant evictions, inciting Young Britons to march. For consecutive evenings, The No Surrender Fife & Drum Band arrived at the top of Lombard Street ahead of the youth wing of the Orange Lodge. Young men uniformly dressed in white trousers and shirts, orange and blue sashes, and white straw hats carried torches and threatened the street. Cursing the pope, the mob stove in windows with stones and bricks.

Before unleashing his soldiers, Sheehan promised a bounty of twenty-five cents for every bloodied sash snatched from the intruders' waists. Hours-long mêlées ensued. For his part, Robby remained awake in bed, a candle burning and Bugoff at his side, until Sheehan sent for him. He pulled on overalls, slipped into a pair of gumboots, lumbered outside, broke several of the rabble-rousers, and frightened the rest away.

Sheehan installed himself and his family in a cleaned-up one-and-a-half-storey yellow brick home. Putting a match to their former shack, Sheehan told his wife, "We're rollin' in clover now, luvvie." He purchased matching upright pianos for each of his twin daughters. He set himself up with a proper bit of frock named Aoife, a curvaceous twenty-year-old who lived nearby in a house with her ma.

Robby and Bugoff, Ropesy, and Lord Nelson boarded next door to Sheehan. Ropesy, teeth rotted to a pulp, went about with a bullwhip fastened to his belt. Lord Nelson wore an eyepatch. Lusty and Dross encamped in a worker's cottage at Victoria Street; Moggy, Scian, Rose, and Dave at the opposite end at Jarvis.

Sheehan arranged for one of Lombard Street's oldest residents, the stooped spinster Bridget O'Loughlin, to lodge with Robby and company and keep house. Around Lombard Street, the old lady was known as Biddy O'Loughlin, but to Robby, she was always Aunt Bridget.

O'Loughlin's people settled on the street from County Tyrone ages ago when Lombard was still known as Stanley Street. During girlhood, her family of thirteen lived in a falling-down frame house. In twenty-four hours, a cholera outbreak consigned all but herself to the grave. In her dotage, she remained a good plain cook. She was fond of Robby, who regularly accompanied her to the market. She prepared his favourite meals. She was his comforter; he was her ministering angel.

Detective Porter and Robby periodically rendezvoused in the secrecy of the Don Valley in proximity to a gypsy camp. Both men got on well with the occupants. Sitting on a log under a canopy of leaves, they chitchatted.

"Is that a new hat?" Robby asked Porter.

Porter removed his grey hat, held it by the brim, and both men studied it. "Yes. From my sister. From Europe. She accompanied her husband on tour with the Philharmonic."

"What is the style called?"

"Fedora."

"Maybe I'll get one. What's your sister's name?"

"Beatrice. Likely they don't manufacture one in your size."

Robby informed the detective that Patrol Sergeant Lally was on the take and said others inside the No.1 were crooked, too.

The detective listened intently and didn't jot a single note in his occurrence book. That's not how this worked. Instead, he put everything to memory.

Bugoff sniffed around their boots, peed, and then leaped onto Robby's lap. The detective scratched behind Bugoff's ear.

"I don't like dogs, but I like this one," Porter said.

"I see that. He likes you. I can tell. Maybe one day you'll change your mind."

Before going separate ways, Robby declined Detective Porter's emolument, and as usual, the detective inquired why.

"I'm not a Judas. I don't do it for payment."

"Why then?"

Robby thought momentarily. "Like I said before, to keep the balance. Besides, I think we're friends."

Detective Porter said he didn't understand. "If we are friends, maybe you'll let me pay you back one day."

"Maybe."

"You know, Rob, things being what they are, I have a feeling if the tree had fallen the other way, you would have made a good copper."

"Thanks, George. The tree would never have fallen if I had a say in things."

"That's just like you, Rob. Always seeking the middle road, except when you're not."

Returning from ambles with Bugoff after visiting gypsy encampments on the banks of the Don, Robby would present Aunt Bridget with bouquets of daisies. When the others caroused in the evenings, he preferred to remain home and play card games like Spoil 5 and Maw with the old lady. She taught him how to weave a daisy crown. He explained the secret of breaking bones without leaving bruises.

On occasion, he borrowed a handbarrow from Costermonger Joe and, lining the cart with hay and a horse blanket, set her and Bugoff in the tray, pushing them to the zoological gardens.

Robby's bullyboy reputation spread citywide. Eyes were on him everywhere. Navigating crowded plank sidewalks and busy rutted streets, the odd-looking trio, wilted daisy crowns atop their heads, was given a wide berth. On the way, Robby paused at the GTR freight yard at the bottom of York Street on the Esplanade to filch yellow apples from an unlocked boxcar, a treat for lions Romeo and Juliet.

Romeo and Juliet became enlivened when Robby appeared outside the cage. Nudging their heads against rusted iron bars, Romeo chuffed as Robby stroked his snout and fed him apples.

Aunt Bridget smiled. In a voice as old as coal, she mused, "My mother used to say, out of the strong comes something sweet."

Robby said, "Would you like to pet him?"

Aunt Bridget said, "Yes, please. I'd like to very much."

One evening after the lamplighter had lit the gas, a stranger in kid gloves and expensive spats carrying a leather satchel appeared on Lombard Street. The visitor said he came to discuss a pressing matter with Sheehan.

Sheehan was leery.

The man said he represented His Worship, Mayor Howland. Sheehan was interested.

Citizens had elected Howland on his reformist "Toronto the Good" platform, a slogan the mayor himself coined. Among other initiatives, Howland limited the number of licensed taverns and he had a mandate to tidy slum neighbourhoods.

Before meeting in the rear of the dusty auction rooms smelling of camphor and naphthalene, Sheehan instructed Robby, "I want you there. Leave the dog but bring the bite."

Moonlight knifed the windowpanes near the ceiling of the cavernous warehouse filled with whisky barrels, tarped furniture, bronze sculptures, and machinery. Remaining in half shadows, Robby patted down the man for a weapon.

The man removed his derby hat and ran his fingers through his slick hair, whispering glumly, "His Worship has a problem."

Sheehan said, "Does the problem have a name?"

The man said, "George Morse."

Robby and Sheehan exchanged looks.

The man explained that Morse headed the largest cattle-shipping company in the Dominion: Morse, Nicolson & Marpole.

Sheehan interrupted, "Christ the night, you take us for muffs? We know who Morse is. So what? What of it?"

The man cleared his throat. "Morse intends to use influence to remove His Worship from office."

Sheehan said, "Yeah. I've heard."

The man said, "Due to carelessness on the mayor's part, His Worship is vulnerable."

Sheehan said, "Ain't we all?" and spat on the floor. "What's this have to do with Lombard Street?"

The stranger fixed his dark eyes on Sheehan and cleared his throat, "You're well aware, Mr. Sheehan, our shared interests benefit if Morse was to be silenced."

Sheehan said, "Silenced permanently?"

The man said, "Mr. Sheehan, just do what you do."

"I don't do a thing," Sheehan said, indicating Robby with his chin. "He does it."

The man removed a thick envelope from the satchel. "In appreciation," he said, handing it to Sheehan. He gave Robby several silver coins in a handkerchief. "A little extra for you." Before departing, the man said, "And Mr. Sheehan, if this endeavour is realized, your enterprise continues unimpeded."

Sheehan and Robby walked home together. The night air was breezy with the scent of flowering horse chestnut. Sheehan instructed Robby outside their Lombard Street residences, "Take care of Morse."

Robby said, "How I want?"

Sheehan said, "Yeah. Sure. As long as he's done with."

Robby said, "Can I just talk to him?"

Sheehan said, "Course." He grinned and put his hand on Robby's shoulder. "Talk long as you like, so long as the chat ends at the bottom of the bay. Yeah?"

Robby said, "I don't like doing it like that."

Sheehan said, "Yeah, I know. Too bad, eh?"

Not long after, Robby and Bugoff cornered Morse alone next to the dock behind the eastern cattle market. As prosperous as Morse was, the rough man appeared capable of handling himself at first. In the end, though, he proved all mouth and no trousers.

Robby said, "I want to talk to you."

Morse said, "Bug off. I know your type."

The beagle cocked her head.

Robby said, "Sure you don't want to talk?"

Morse said, "I said, bug off, so bug off." He swung at Robby with his walking stick. Robby sighed, "Suit yourself."

Robby told Bugoff, "Stay," and then ended Morse.

Several days later, grubby-faced newsboys hawking city newspapers hollered, "Body discovered in bay identified. Millionaire George D. Morse drowned."

Early Saturday, Aunt Bridget prepared Robby milk porridge. Children played hide-and-seek and red rover outside on Lombard Street. After breakfast, they had tea.

Robby said, "Want to go to the zoo?"

Aunt Bridget said, "No, son. Not today."

Robby prepared to leave. Clearing the dishes, she kissed Robby goodbye on the forehead and said, "Nothing in the world is as sweet as love, and next to love the sweetest thing is hate."

Robby and Bugoff left home.

A pong of coal tar stained the freight yard air. Lumbering between rows of rolling stock, Bugoff in the sack on his hip, Robby checked for an unlocked boxcar from which to steal a treat for Romeo and Juliet.

Quick bursts of a whistle sounded a warning to a flagman. The latch on a yellow boxcar unhooked. Robby placed Bugoff on the stony ground. He said "Stay," and hoisted himself up inside the boxcar.

Exiting a few minutes later, pockets stuffed with yellow apples, Robbie discovered a crooked constable known as Pug Nose and his partner Constable Reburn waiting. Pug Nose gritted his teeth and clenched Bugoff by the throat.

Robby said, "Put 'er down."

Pug Nose said, "Put 'em up."

Robby said, "Let 'er go."

Pug Nose said, "Go to hell."

Robby said, "Let's talk this out."

Pug Nose said, "We're through with you Catholic scum." He ordered Robby to his knees and instructed his partner Reburn to slap bracelets on him.

Robby resisted but before he could move on them, a third constable approached from behind, pressing the barrel of a revolver into his spine.

A voice instructed, "Don't even—"

Raising his hands, Robby said, "Please, don't hurt the dog."

Pug Nose said, "Then get to your knees, boy."

Robby hesitated. Pug Nose tightened his grip around Bugoff's throat. The dog yelped. Robby complied.

After Reburn had Robby in bracelets, Pug Nose said, "Crack 'em one. Split that popish bean of his in two."

Reburn raised his baton and struck Robby. Pug Nose threw the dog to the ground. Bugoff scampered under a gondola car.

Robby shouted, "Go home."

Bugoff cocked her head, panting.

"I said, go home."

The dog bolted.

Pug Nose kicked Robby backward with a boot to his chest, and then he, Reburn and the third constable thumped their captive senseless.

Appearing in police court the same afternoon, wirepullers from the Grand Orange Lodge made sure Judge Denison came down hard. Robby was transferred to Toronto Central Prison, sentenced to twenty-four months for stealing apples.

Warden Massie and Guard Rutledge, the sadistic chief turnkey of Cellblock 4, stood outside Robby's third-floor windowless cell accompanied by a trio of hard-headed political men from the Wardens' Association assigned to inspect provincial jails. Except for muffled footfalls on the polished ash wood floor, the Strachan Avenue prison was mournfully quiet, a policy of silence strictly enforced.

Earlier in the day, the gentlemen inspectors had assessed Central Prison's dormitories, cells, and domestic and industrial workshops, finding all shipshape. Quarterly inspections quelled public concern that brutalized inmates in the segregated industrial prison survived on a diet of putrid meat, rotted potatoes, and water.

Guards, Protestant to a man, allegedly meted out harsh punishment, particularly to Irish inmates in the Roman Catholic cellblock. Some were strapped to the triangle and lashed mercilessly, others branded with hot irons. Whispers of midnight burials circulated.

Warden Massie ordered Rutledge to open the door and light Robby's cell. Rutledge inserted a passkey on a ring attached to his utility belt into the padlock and pulled open the solid iron door. Assaulted by the stench inside, the inspectors reeled backward. Rutledge sniggered. The inspectors gawked at the motionless figure lying on the filthy floor, strips of flesh torn from his back.

Through pinched nostrils, a shrill-voiced inspector with a bushy walrus moustache said, "Why is the prisoner unclothed?"

Warden Massie said, "Unruly. Belligerent."

Since his confinement, Robby had kept to himself. Unmolested by other convicts, guards treated him with disdain. Rutledge in particular had it in for the big Irishman and did everything he could to provoke him, but Robby knew better than to respond.

Assigned to the shoemaking room, he laboured six days a week, meeting his quota beside unproductive, violent men. He cooperated, sang the good morning song with verve, and kept time when marching in formation.

Rutledge failed to get a rise out of Robby and fabricated an incident, identifying Robby in the complaint book as instigating a row. As punishment, Warden Massie ordered Robby receive twenty lashes on his bare back and confinement indefinitely to a dark cell. Robby, limited to bread and water, was tormented by Rutledge, who delighted in slipping an oilskin sack over his head, tightening the drawstring, then placing a pillow over his face and nearly suffocating the weakened Irishman.

The inspector made an entry on foolscap. He said, "Prisoner's name?"

Rutledge said, "Five-one-three-nine-one-two dash two-five."

The inspector said, "Don't be daft. His Christian name."

Rutledge said, "Oh. Neill. Robert."

The inspector tapped his pencil on the file folder and made an entry. He said, "Previous issues?"

Rutledge said, "Numerous. Documented in the complaint book, sir."

The inspector said, "We've seen enough. Clean this inmate up. Get me out of here."

A blue-eyed gypsy inmate was assigned to bathe Robby, swab his cell, and clothe him. Guard Rutledge propped a stool outside the open cell door, eyeing the inmates. He said, "No talking, neither."

Gently dabbing wounds on Robby's back with a sponge and warm water, the inmate whispered in Robby's ear, "The man in the grey fedora is a friend."

Robby gestured for the cake of soap and scraped s-h-i-v on the wooden floor.

Time passed. A little of Robby's strength returned.

One afternoon nearing the end of his shift, Rutledge removed his black worsted frock coat, hung it over the back of the guardroom chair, rolled up his sleeves, and entered Robby's cell. Robby lay on his back, eyes closed, arms at his side, motionless on the floor.

Rutledge kicked Robby in the ribs. No response. Second kick. Same. Kneeling, he tugged a sack over Robby's head, tightened the drawstring, and placed the pillow over Robby's face. Robby's arm lashed upward, snaking around Rutledge's back like a fly-eating vine, pinning them chest to chest. Rutledge flailed. Gasped. His breath grew thin. Robby squeezed Rutledge tighter in a killing embrace. With his free hand, he pulled a blade hidden at his side, spirited into the cell concealed in his slop bucket.

Rutledge's eyes flashed animal fear.

Robby slid the tip into Rutledge's back. Slow.

Robby said, "Shhh . . ."

The knife pricked Rutledge's heart. Robby pushed. Twisted. Slow. Mincing the vital organ. Rutledge became motionless, dead weight. Robby rolled him off his chest. Sat. Pulled off the sack. He tossed the blade into the slop bucket. Stood. Steadied himself. Wiped his hands on his yellow denim shirt.

He left the cell. The prison corridor was cool and clean. He walked toward an exit door in plain sight of the guardroom.

A shrill whistle sounded. Guards swarmed.

A guard shouted, "What the hell." He clubbed Robby. Another swung at Robby's knees. He said, "Where do you think you're going?"

Brushing them off like lint, Robby said, "Home."

Guards flooded the corridor. Robby was subdued.

WORM SYRUP

"Elements inside No.1 are rotten," Detective George Porter glanced at his occurrence book on his lap and read his notes to himself before informing his superior, "Mainly on third watch."

The Detective Sergeant rubbed his chin, leaned back in his red leather chair, looked out his large second-storey window at headquarters, and watched people going by below. "Yes, there's been whispers."

His deputy seated nearby nodded and repeated, "Whispers."

Since being promoted to detective, Porter had made it his mission to weed out crooked coppers. Nothing was more despicable than misconduct in uniform. He relished the challenge and would douse the entire force in worm syrup if left up to him.

"Who's your source?" the detective sergeant asked, leaning forward.

His deputy nodded, leaned forward, mimicking the actions of the ranking officer, and repeated, "Source?"

Porter closed the occurrence book, ignoring the query.

"Course you'd protect them," the detective sergeant murmured.

"Let's say I have it on good word that Patrol Sergeant Lally is on the take, meaning second and third watch are potentially compromised."

"Lally's easily dealt with. He's coming up to retirement."

"With all due respect, sir, his offences are more dire than drinking on duty or violence against the public. I've noted serious criminal offences. Corrupt acts. Hush money. A protection fund."

George was familiar with the roll at No.1 from his early days on the force. He didn't need to be told that P.C. Patrick "Pug Nose" Varley was among the ringleaders.

Varley had been the maggot in the apple crate all along. Porter looked into his background and discovered that, even in the old country, Varley had gotten up to no good. When constables at the No.1 initially enquired about the unsightly condition of his face, the former steam fitter for the City of Liverpool repeated the story about pressure built up behind a pinch valve and how a blown stopcock struck his ugly mug.

Porter drew a bead on Varley and knew the truth behind the sorry state of his face, which resulted from a pounding severe enough to convince him to flee for the provinces.

"You're a fine detective, Porter, and your diligence is worthy of a merit mark." The Detective Sergeant turned to his deputy and said, "Rope off what the detective has shared here from the press and keep them in the dark." Then he turned to Porter and said, "The administration appreciates your zeal. We'll see to the matter from here. Thank you."

"A message needs sending."

"Yes, Detective. Correct."

The Detective Sergeant's minion echoed, "Correct."

"Change is coming."

Porter pressed the issue. "For example?"

"The No.1 requires painting. We'll clean up and make some repairs. Add lockers. Enlarge the wagon house, as well. A message will be sent to rank and file."

"That's not the kind of message I had in mind."

"Detective, take some time off. You look weary."

Porter was diagnosed recently with Bright's Disease. The swelling, his run-down, scrofulous appearance, the back pain. Doctors prescribed an easy milk diet and temperate medicines such as bicarbonate of soda. Instead, he leaned into work to the detriment of his health, his marriage, and his mental equilibrium.

Preparing to leave, he considered telling his superior that jailers at the Central were also tainted. There was rot at City Hall, too. Lately, he had learned when to play a card, and when to hold and say no more. George stood to leave.

"One more thing," said the Detective Sergeant, "Where'd you get that hat?"

"That hat," the minion repeated.

"It looks like a woman's."

Detective Porter adjusted the brim of his fedora. "It isn't," he replied, closing the door behind him.

He often discussed work affairs with Beatrice, who was keen to hear every aspect of his profession. A few years earlier, Porter had considered quitting, but his promotion to the detective force reawakened his dedication.

Beatrice was fascinated with her older brother's work and, for ages, longed to pursue the same profession. The siblings ventured downstairs to his makeshift basement office if details were particularly offensive. On occasion, when she visited with Little Teddy, if her brother was not home and Susan was distracted with her nephew, Beatrice would sneak downstairs to poke through the contents of her brother's desk.

George maintained reams of notations from cases. Beatrice filched one of George's unused occurrence books, filling it with shorthand jottings, creating entwined hagiographies of offenders and victims and the policemen who disentangle them.

One evening in the basement, Beatrice shoved a crate beside the desk, littered with loose papers, files, and dozens of George's sketches. George sat on a stool. The lamplight was poor.

"You need to improve the light down here, or else your sight is done for." She casually opened a file and studied a booking photograph. "Who's this?"

"Thomas Cecil Bullard."

"Who?"

"Thom Bullard? Trombone Tommy?" Bullard derived his name from his skill as a musician.

"Oh. Him. He was in the papers."

"He was my collar."

"He was?" Beatrice exclaimed. "Why wasn't your name mentioned in articles?"

"Rather it wasn't."

George arrested Thomas C. Bullard, aka Trombone Tommy, a notorious American safecracker and skilled musician, while patrolling on third watch. Two of Bullard's criminal partners were also detained that night. The trio made a special trip up from Buffalo for the heist at a bank in the lower part of the city. P.C. Porter chased Bullard out of the building in the middle of the night and cornered him in a dark shed.

The photograph was a souvenir of sorts. The Police Board had relented to the Chief Constable's repeated requisition to acquire a camera; he predicted photography would play an essential part in combatting crime.

A constable trained on the device took the booking photo at headquarters when P.C. Porter returned with Bullard in handcuffs. The constable visited crime scenes and captured images, some of which were overly grisly. George befriended the constable for access and used the photos to facilitate his sketching.

The arrest of Bullard and his gang earned George merit marks and six months advance toward promotion.

"Are you being promoted?" Beatrice asked.

"They are recommending me for detective training."

"And?"

"And? I think I'm developing an ulcer," he paused before adding, "I'm resigning."

"What?"

"Quitting."

"Quitting?"

"It's settled."

"Does Susan know?"

"Of course not."

When Beatrice failed to dissuade him, she suggested he discuss the matter with Constable Cooke in East Gwillimbury.

"See a doctor, too," she pleaded, "It could be something else."

The population of East Gwillimbury had grown and the township had merged with the neighbouring municipality. Cooke remained a constable, but town officials had sold the old police office. Now, Cooke and the three other policemen on the force operated out of a leased office in a building between a small store and a hotel one town over, in Sharron.

Cooke rented a former caretaker's house, a handsome farm residence on a hillside beside the abandoned flour mill. Kate Howard followed him and lived there, too. There had been moves to institutionalize her, but Cooke refused to let that happen. Over the years, she'd mellowed and was less tormented than in the past. If she avoided drinking, Cooke reported that she remained balanced. She spent most of her time preparing the constable meat-and-nut sandwiches, whether he requested one or not.

The two lawmen sat on rocks by the brook near a broken-down windmill, passing Cooke's harmless .22 rifle back and forth, taking potshots at the remains of the windmill's creaking galvanized blades.

Porter missed every time.

"You're still a terrible shot," Cooke chided the younger man.

Porter pressed the rifle butt against his shoulder and squinted. "I retested." He squeezed the trigger. "And if you recall, I romped through it."

"As I recall, and Beatrice will back this, you passed adequately. You can't hit the side of a windmill."

The two friends laughed and then Porter sighed. "What should I do, Izzy? I'm thinking about leaving the force for good."

"Well, I know you'd make a decent detective."

"Did you discuss this with Beatrice?"

"She wrote." Cooke reloaded the .22, aimed at a slowly turning windmill blade, and squeezed the trigger. Plink. "If you made detective, what's the first thing you'd do?"

He handed George the rifle. He tucked the .22 in his shoulder and aimed. "I'd clean up the force for starters wherever I could. I'm aware of untrustworthy constables and higher-ups."

Plink.

"Good shot. That'll bring you popularity," Cooke said sarcastically.

"I don't want to be popular."

Kate brought sandwiches, a canteen, and grapes and sat with them. "Georgie?"

"Hi, Kate."

"Georgie, are you a mean one or will you be just?"

"You know George can't be mean, Kate," Constable Cooke bit into his sandwich and chewed. "Meanness has no hold on him."

George held a cluster of grapes and put a couple in his mouth. "I'll be just, Kate, I promise."

Kate smiled at him. "Can I have a try with the gun?"

THE HOUSE ON DEFOE STREET

Defoe St, 1890

From second floor offices at Central Police Station at 10 Court Street in Toronto, population 350,000, Detective George A. Porter, and eighteen other detective officers of the Detective Force investigated seven homicides in one year, including the remains of a male infant discovered concealed in an apple crate afloat in the bay. Two weeks later, a second infant, this time female, turned up in a shallow grave at the city limits. On August 31, police fished a third deceased newborn from waters off Queen Street wharf.

In other cases, Hugh McKay was charged with the death of his boss. Mary White went on trial for killing her brother, allegedly having dispensed a dose of Rough on Rats poison surreptitiously in his tea can. A resident of the Queen Street Provincial Lunatic Asylum slashed another inmate's throat.

Coroner Johnson concluded the infant killings, committed by parties unknown, were unconnected. Those responsible, likely debauched servant girls and parlourmaids, were never brought to justice. McKay was acquitted at trial, a jury found White not guilty, and the asylum inmate was deemed unfit to stand trial.

THE HOUSE ON DEFOE STREET

In November, Mary Kane was bludgeoned to death in her home, the city's seventh and final homicide of the year.

The semi-detached house stood at the northwest corner of Stanley Park, a wooded dale bisected by polluted Garrison Creek. Detective Porter watched neighbours traipse through the dead lady's house. Others remained outside, happy to peek into the front room through gaps in the shabby hessian curtains. Early Sunday morning, word had spread through the district and, before long, people as far as College Street and east to Bathurst were showing up.

Porter checked his timepiece. 8:47. Standing apart from the gathering crowd on the cobblestone roadway under a dismal morning sky, Detective Porter made a charcoal sketch of the façade of the roughcast house at 132 Defoe Street, as was his established habit, to aid his memory at trial. There were techniques he'd developed to bolster an investigation and achieve a conviction. Some he'd discarded, some cases he'd handle differently now, but those he kept to himself.

Detective Porter had served under two Chief Constables: Draper, and now Grasett, English blowhards to the last. In that time, Detective Porter learned a few things about murder and the carnage left in its wake. He also learned to resent busybodies poking about when he was trying to do his job. They had a way of getting his dander up. This morning, like flies around a horse in August, they swarmed outside the house when the initial call to police went out at dawn.

He noted the second-storey boarded-up window, the broken front door, the missing rainspout, and the sagging portico. The labourer's cottage was in falling-down condition. Judging by appearances, Porter knew whatever occurred in the house, dollars to dumplings, was fuelled by liquor. Every time he investigated a violent assault or murder where someone used his wife's head for a game of Aunt Sally, liquor triggered the event.

Well, almost every time.

Experience told Detective Porter that, when it came to murder, the more impoverished the circumstance, the more brutal the crime presented. The wealthier tended to display a certain reserve when killing their own. Take, for example, the Campbell killing. Last year around this time, Mrs. Campbell, a lady who moved in first circles, slew her husband, the scion of a dried bean interest, in their Glen Road mansion, thrusting a paperknife through his heart as he catnapped on a purple fainting chair in the great hall of their manor. A precise wound: neat, unexceptional.

Porter admired the unpolluted nature of a homicide displaying the absence of chaos. He recalled hovering above Campbell's lifeless body sketching the corpse. Except for modest discoloration of the flesh and a bloody worsted waistcoat, he was almost convinced the dead man was pretending sleep, that the unfortunate gentleman would be roused with a pronounced clap. Compare this to the Corktown nutter a few weeks later who bonked her old man on the head on Laetare Sunday with a cutlet bat, disembowelled him with a dull mincing knife, removed the Advent wreath from the front door, and plopped it atop the corpse's head like a crown, scrawling "The king is dead" in blood above the corpse.

A man with a vicious face stepped off the wooden sidewalk, intruding into Detective Porter's thoughts. "Hey."

"Hey, what?"

"You're the detective force?"

"How can you know?"

"I've seen you. I'm a cabman."

"And?"

"And nothing. I live on Stafford around the corner. Last night I drove two men from that house." He pointed at 132 Defoe. "Cross the whole city to Lombard Street. You remember a seventy-five-cent fare. Both were sullen. They didn't talk hardly."

Porter sighed. "Fine."

"Fine? Want to know or not who did this?"

"What makes you think I don't already?"

Porter closed the sketchpad and, crossing the street, wiped his hands on a cotton handkerchief. A pain in his back was killing him. He removed a pouch of chewing tobacco from inside his coat and shoved a pinch of black leaf into the corner of his mouth. He negotiated his way through an ill-clad throng of onlookers wearing jackets and shawls over morning dresses and nightshirts, grumbling. Shouldn't these gawks be preparing for church?

Porter noted the lot size, roughly twelve feet wide and thirty feet deep. Stepping over refuse, he edged his way to the rear of the house. A line of children ran excitedly from the backyard, cawing like a murder of crows. The rear door was nailed closed. Detective Porter heard people tramping about inside the house. Besides an abundance of pokeweed and a rusted piece of farm machinery, nothing in the backyard jumped out.

Returning to the front of the house, he observed a brownish-red streak smeared across the window's interior. Likely dried blood. An expression Central detectives bandied around, "poor slay poor, rich in gore," came to mind. Judging by the colouration of the smudge, with the mercury last night around 55°—warm for November—he knew without asking Coroner Johnson that eight to twelve hours had elapsed since the time of the murder.

Porter checked his timepiece. He entered a notation into his occurrence book, knowing in his bones to expect an appalling scene inside the house. People pressed their faces against the window, elbowing for a better view. "Look," one said, describing the macabre scene inside, "blood. Everywhere." A woman in a faded grey gown with a face like the bottom of a bucket marched out of the house carrying a baby on her hip, exclaiming to no one in particular, "Hag deserved it." A decrepit man in tattered clothing made the sign of the cross and looked skyward. "Poor lady. Sorry sight this is."

Church bells throughout the city began to toll a call to worship.

Police Constable Wright, sluggish with a heavy brow, stood idly by the doorway, tapping his baton against his thigh, passively observing the crowd. Porter approached, attired in plainclothes, and raised the lapel on his coat, revealing a silver badge embossed, "Toronto Police Detective Dept." Porter recognized P.C. Wright. With 264 constables walking the beat day and night throughout the city, Porter had a thing for faces. That, and they had a past. Wright had been on the force as long as Porter, never rising through the ranks. Regardless, protocol required the detective remain aloof. Abiding by rules provided Porter with an artifice of normalcy.

He acknowledged the veteran constable with a nod then introduced himself, "Detective Porter. Central."

"P.C. Wright. Number 3. I know you, Detective. Took you long enough, didn't it?"

Porter ignored the snide comment, "Who else is here?"

"P.C. McPherson."

"Who?"

"A cadet. Don't tell me you came alone?"

"No. Detective Cuddy's fetching the coroner and Dr. Powell." He looked over the restless crowd. "Send for more uniforms."

"Already did."

"And the wagon."

"Already did."

The crowd closed in. Porter spat a gob of brown saliva on the ground. "Been inside?"

Wright nodded. "Just for a peep." He grimaced. "A pretty bad affair."

"Look around," Porter sniped. "Hovels, sweatshops, and breweries. What do you expect on a street lined with deadbeats of the worst kind?"

Police Cadet McPherson, a beanpole still in his youth, appeared. Detective Porter flashed his badge, then opened his occurrence book. "What's your name, cadet?"

The cadet straightened his helmet. "Police Cadet Norman McPherson."

"Spell it."

McPherson shot P.C. Wright a nervous glance. "Spell what?"

Porter sighed. "Start with your surname."

"Aye." McPherson beamed. "McPherson. M-c capital P-h-e-r-s-o-n."

Detective Porter logged the time and noted the names of both uniforms in the occurrence book. He studied the young cadet. "New at this, eh?"

"Aye."

Porter resented the cadet's greenness. "The accent . . . English? From the north? Liverpool, maybe."

"Aye."

Wright interjected, defending McPherson. "He's satisfactory."

Porter sighed. He asked McPherson if this was his first homicide.

"Aye."

Wright smirked. "Easy, Detective. Remember the incident when you—"

"Enough," he interrupted. "I remember it well." Porter glared at the cadet. "A good story, lad. How about later, you and I meet at a coffee house and I'll tell you all about it over penny pies? What do you say, McPherson?"

"Aye?"

"Aye," Porter replied, parroting McPherson's accent. He knitted his brow and snapped at the eager cadet. "Not a chance."

Wright winked at Porter and chuckled. "We all get the shit sometime, McPherson. You'll have your chance, soon enough. Isn't that right, Detective?"

Porter ignored Wright and told McPherson, "Stay out of the way and learn."

Wright interrupted. "Easy, Detective. We'll see to our duty. You see to yours."

A breeze lifted. Dry leaves blew about in swirling eddies. Porter crouched and observed bloody shoe and boot prints on the threshold. He stood, flipped open his occurrence book, and checked his timepiece. After making a notation, he asked, "Any eyewitness evidence?"

Wright said, "Neighbours say they're drinkers. A cabman said he picked up a fare last night. I told him don't tell me, tell a detective when they get here."

"Then what?"

Wright shrugged. "Then waited."

McPherson echoed, "Waited?"

Porter inquired, "Waited for what?"

Wright exhaled, "You, Detective. Patrol Sergeant Pinker said to expect a detective from Central."

Porter studied the crowd and then asked McPherson. "What about you?"

"Me?"

"Yes. You. Any eyewitness evidence?"

Wright interrupted, "P.C. McPherson and me arrived together. See that lad over there?" Wright pointed at a stocky youth in a shabby peacoat sulking on the curbstone. "He was here milling about like a dimwit. Said he's the fellow that found the dead lady. His mum sent him to the call box. I told him to wait and tell a detective what he saw, and then I posted watch—"

McPherson cut in, "I talked to him. His mater, too. Boy's named Keith Sterling." McPherson grinned. "S-t-e-r-l-i-n-g. He's thirteen but big for his age, though."

Porter asked McPherson, "What did he tell you?"

The cadet opened a newly issued occurrence book and read aloud. "November 16. Sunday. Morning. At approximately five-thirty o'clock, Keith Sterling discovered the dead lady inside 132 Defoe Street residence." McPherson snapped closed the occurrence book, "His mater said the dead lady—"

Porter interrupted, "What's her name?"

McPherson cocked his head, "Whose? The mater or the dead lady?"

"The mum's name. What's the mum's name," Detective Porter said curtly.

"Aye. Elizabeth Sterling. Capital E-l-i-z-a-b-e-t-h, capital S-t-e-r-l-i-n-g."

"And the deceased?"

"The deceased what?"

Porter was shattered tired and lacked patience. "I'm asking, what's the deceased's name?"

"Aye. The dead lady. She's Mary Cain. Capital M-a-r-y, capital C-a-i-n."

"Did you ask?"

"Her? Course not. She's dead."

Porter rolled his eyes. "I know she's dead. Did you ask for the correct spelling of the deceased's name?"

"That's how Cain's spelled where I'm from."

Porter clenched his jaw and leaned aggressively into McPherson. "Is that so?"

Wright spoke up. "Lighten up, Detective."

Porter collected himself. He sighed. "What else did Sterling tell?"

"Lives next door with his parents and a sister. Through the night, Elizabeth Sterling, the mater, woke to screams from next door and wakes her husband and tells him look-see, but he just rolled over and told her to mind her business. She couldn't sleep a wink, and after a time it was deadly quiet next door, so she woke her boy Keith and sends him to see."

Wright snorted. "Terrible sight for a lad."

McPherson continued, "Cains 'ave lived here only a while."

Porter asked who else resided at the address.

McPherson replied, "Think only the dead lady and . . ." he flipped open his occurrence book, "Thomas Cain."

"Who's he?"

"Husband?"

"Did you ask?"

"No."

"Always ask. Anything more?"

"Aye. Mater said the boy returned out of sorts and said that Mr. Cain was drunk as David's sow out cold on the floor next to the dead lady whose brains were . . ." he paused and glanced at his notes, "Violently and fatally extravasated."

Porter arched his eyebrows, "He said extravasated?"

"Aye. I asked him to spell it even. E-x-t-r-a-v-a-s-a-t-e-d." McPherson shrugged, "Mater said the boy's a reader—"

Porter interrupted, "Where's the mum now?"

"Gone to Sunday School."

"Without the boy?"

"Aye. P.C. Wright instructed him to stay."

Wright nodded in agreement. "Good work, McPherson."

Porter rolled his eyes. "Where's Thomas Cain presently?"

McPherson pointed at the house, shrugged. "In there?"

"Did you look?"

"Nay. I'm not going in there."

Wright spoke up, "I told him not to go inside 'cause he didn't need to." Wright stared down Porter. "I went in. I looked. Cain's not in there."

Porter sighed. He took in the crowd. "I'll be inside." He asked Wright to borrow his baton. "Let's have that a sec." Standing by the doorway, truncheon raised, he shouted inside, "Everyone. Out."

People fled from the house in every direction. Porter returned the baton to the constable. "When Detective Cuddy and the coroner arrive, send them in." He added sarcastically, "And McPherson, good work."

McPherson beamed. "Really?"

"No."

The cadet rocked on his heels, "Looks dark in there, Detective," he said, handing Porter his pocket lamp. "Likely need this."

Porter checked his timepiece. He made a notation in his occurrence book. Entering the house alone, he forced the door closed, immediately struck by the ferrous stench of blood and perspiration, similar to the pong of a hog slaughterhouse.

Grey daylight seeped into the front room through gaps in the curtains. Butcher paper covered the window facing Stanley Park. In the moments it took his vision to adjust, Porter removed his coat and hat and hung them on a nail hook. Noting the home's condition, he thought, how do people live like this? Thanks to his Susan, his home was pin neat.

That morning, after the call messenger rang the doorbell at their St. Patrick Street house, Porter cursed at Susan's offer to prepare breakfast. No time, he told her.

She complained that he was too abrupt with her and that he hadn't always treated her this way.

Gawkers peered through the curtains. A woman wrapped on the pane with her knuckle and implored, "A cab last night—"

THE HOUSE ON DEFOE STREET

Detective Porter directed lantern light around the front room, pausing on an upturned cot. He poked around the semi-darkness, kicking an empty whisky jug and several Warner's Safe Cure bottles. Shining lamplight at his feet, he observed ash, sprinkled on the floor to soak up blood, swept into a mound in the corner. He browsed the room used to store wood. In the bedroom, the bedstead hadn't been slept in the previous night; coverlet spattered with blood. An open valise lay on the floor, contents strewn about. Bloody palm prints smeared the inside bedroom doorframe.

Back in the front room, he peeked inside a stack of paper boxes. Women's linen littered the floor. The detective dipped his finger into a basin of cold, murky water atop the rusty stove. He righted an upset stool beside the splintered ironing table. A flatiron, caked in blood, lay on the floor. Among trinkets cluttering a long, narrow tabletop, he examined an empty pay packet inscribed with the name Thomas Kane, jotting down the spelling of the surname. Beside the packet sat a hawk and trowel encrusted with dry plaster. He picked up a heart-shaped music box and wound the rusted key, brittle gears twanging like snapping bones before producing a short, tinny rendition of "My Love Is Like a Red, Red Rose."

The corpse of Mary Kane lay on the floor on her back, eyes open and fixed on the low, sagging ceiling, hands clutched in grotesque agony. One thumb was crushed off. Mouth an anguished maw, her teeth resembled broken crockery. Considering the battered condition of her face, Porter estimated her age between thirty-five and forty years. She was slight. Approximately five feet. Six-and-a-half to seven stone. Inferring from the blood pattern on the ceiling and wall, she received fatal blows here. Porter focused on a baking pan under the victim's head, placed there to collect fluid seeping from a posterior skull wound. The colour of the congealed blood in the pan informed him she was alive—but unconscious—several minutes after the skull fracture.

Crouching, he set the lamp on the floor and gripped her stiffened hand. No life here for hours. Her lower body was bruised from stomping. There were contusions around her ankles. Rolling her on her side, he parted her long black hair clotted with blood and probed the wound with his fingers. A solid object had crushed through the skull and laid bare the brain. He placed the corpse back as he found it and wiped his hands on his handkerchief.

A floorboard squeaked behind him. Standing abruptly, he shone lamplight toward the bedroom, demanding, "Show yourself."

A girl reluctantly entered the yellow circle of light. Porter cursed under his breath. He cast lamplight back on the corpse. "Is this your mum?"

"No."

"Come."

"No."

"Come here."

"No."

"Come here now."

"No."

Detective Porter relaxed his shoulders. He sighed. He softened his tone. "Come here. Please?"

She hesitantly stepped forward. In a small voice she said, "I came in to see the dead lady like everyone else was."

Porter seized upon the girl, snatching her by the forearm, hurling her at Mary Kane. Toppling onto the corpse, the child cried fiercely just as the front door swung open. Detective Cuddy, Coroner Johnson, and a man from *The Globe* entered.

Cuddy shouted, "In the name of the devil, what's going on?"

Bawling, the girl darted outside.

Detective Cuddy, a tall man with a sandy complexion, and not unduly bulky, opened the curtains. "George, you're in the dark." Stepping over the corpse, he went to the other window and tore away the butcher paper. "Get light in here."

The *Globe* man covered his mouth and nose with his hand, and taking in the room muttered, "An abomination."

Coroner Johnson set a black leather tote on the floor next to Mary Kane's battered head and knelt, casually adjusting his eyeglasses. He commented on cadaveric rigidity, rolling the corpse over with the ease of rolling a billet of wood. He examined the skull wound. "Looks as though the devil ground his heel into the back of her skull."

Cuddy picked up the flatiron, sniffed it. He glanced around the room and asked Porter, "Who is she?"

"Mary Kane."

Cuddy asked, "And the plain facts?"

Porter sighed. He noted the time on his timepiece. Standing by the door, he read aloud from his occurrence book. "Thomas Kane, plasterer, returned from work Saturday." Porter glanced at the corpse. "She was expecting his wages."

The *Globe* man took notes, "How do you know?"

"Know what?"

"His occupation."

"Tools. There." Porter pointed at the hawk and trowel. He continued reading from his notes. "Row started over finances. Thomas Kane's packet was empty. He'd been in the drink."

The *Globe* man interrupted, "How do you know?"

"Know what?"

"About the drink."

"Look around." Porter sighed. "Hold off on questions until I'm through, all right?"

Coroner Johnson nodded.

Cuddy said, "Continue."

"Saturday started normally. Thomas went to work. Mary did the laundry. She heated the basin on the stove. Baked bread, maybe." Porter sidled over to the stove. "Kane returns in the evening. Words are exchanged. Something sets him off. A spat broke out. Kane struck her." Porter crossed the room to the bedroom doorway. "She darts into the bedroom, shouting something like, 'This is enough. I'm leaving.' A struggle erupts. Thomas Kane socks her on the mouth hard enough to knock teeth loose." Porter felt around in his vest pocket, produced a tiny, greyish incisor, and held it out between his thumb and index finger for the others to observe. "Found this on the coverlet."

Porter directed lamplight toward the bedstead. "Mary Kane gets knocked to the floor. Thomas Kane drags her by the ankle, screaming. She grabs the doorframe for dear life. Kane's strapping. Judging from bruising on the body, a size thirteen boot. Six plus feet in height. She doesn't stand a chance against what's coming." Porter crossed to the front window. "She gets to her feet. Staggers to the door. He blocks her. She gets to the window. Waves for anyone's help."

Coroner Johnson pointed at the pane. "Explains that."

"Kane's temper is high. He finished her here." Porter pointed to the spot on the floor where the corpse lay. "Bludgeons her from behind with the flatiron. Continues bashing her brains after she collapses, then kicks and stomps her so hard he takes her thumb off."

Cuddy said, "Anything else?"

Porter nodded. "The pan under the skull."

"Yes?"

"Ever see that before?"

"No. Maybe. Why's it there? What are you figuring?"

"Staging like this indicates the nature of their relationship."

The *Globe* man asked, "How?"

"We're assuming they're man and wife. Placement of the pan could indicate otherwise."

The *Globe* man asked, "You can tell that from a pan?"

The question aggravated Porter. "I can tell that from experience. Often after a husband batters his wife to death, he'll conceal her face—mainly out of guilt—with anything available, an item of clothing, a blanket. Even roll her onto her stomach. Anything to avoid facing the act he's committed."

Coroner Johnson added, "Remember the Monroe slaying? Husband bound his dead wife's head in mutton cloth."

The *Globe* man asked, "So what's the case here?"

Porter said, "Perpetrator doesn't feel particularly guilty." He paused, searching for the proper word. "More like he feels responsible for the victim's care—"

Cuddy interrupted, "Begrudgingly, by appearances."

Porter continued, "When the Sterling boy next door discovered the body, he reported Thomas Kane passed out right there." Porter pointed to the floor next to the corpse. "Mary Kane was Thomas Kane's charge. The relationship was dutiful, not intimate."

Coroner Johnson agreed. "Explains the cot," he said, pointing at the upturned piece of furniture.

Cuddy questioned, "Siblings? Like the White murder in the spring."

The *Globe* man said, "But the jury found Mary White not guilty."

Porter said, "So? They were still sister and brother."

The *Globe* man replied, "But that doesn't—"

Coroner Johnson interjected, "Gentlemen, whatever the case may be, can we get on with it? Doctor Powell will arrive momentarily to perform the post-mortem." Johnson instructed them to clear the table and move it closer to the window. "Lift her on it. Can we get lamps in here?"

Cuddy, Coroner Johnson, and the *Globe* man rearranged the room. Porter said, "Leave her on the floor a sec," and went to the door and stood in the doorway looking up and down Defoe Street. The police van had arrived, along with additional constables. The bulk of the crowd had drifted a short distance, enticed by a street preacher named Simpson carrying an open Bible and haranguing onlookers against the evils of rumsellers, hollering, "Wine is a mocker. Strong drink is a brawler."

Porter stood in the entrance, waving to P.C. McPherson, "Come here."

McPherson followed Porter inside and began, "Somebody reported a cab—" but stopped abruptly at the sight of the deceased. His eyes widened. Removing his helmet, he knelt and pulled the hem of Mary Kane's underskirt over her knees.

"Leave it," Porter ordered, "Put your helmet on and lift the shoulders. I'll lift the legs. Get it on the table."

McPherson stood opposite Porter, reached under Mary Kane's shoulders, lifted. "She's light as a—"

"Shut your mouth."

A pocket of putrid gas found its way up her windpipe, escaping through the mouth, wafting up at McPherson. The cadet contorted his face. Porter smirked.

Wright put his head in the doorway and said urgently, "Detective, Kane's spotted by the creek."

Porter dropped Mary Kane's legs onto the table. McPherson lowered the upper section of the body, unhurried, and looking into the corpse's dead eyes, crossed himself and uttered, "You are protected in heaven, Mary Cain."

Detective Porter snatched his coat and hat from the nail hook. "Come with me," he ordered McPherson.

McPherson followed.

Outside, Porter said, "Incidentally, the surname? Spelling's incorrect. Know why?"

McPherson shook his head.

"She was never from where you're from."

McPherson shrugged.

"Always ask. Got it?"

Sparrows perched on bare branches chirped incessantly.

Thomas Kane, burly with cruel eyes, a small mouth, and dirty face, sat on a stone staring into the burbling creek. Working pants fastened with a length of leather plough line, his woven shirt was tattered and bloodstained. A misshapen felt bowler hat sat atop his large head.

Detective Porter stood on the path a short distance away. McPherson was behind him. "Hey. Kane," Porter shouted. "What's your game?"

Without turning, Kane lowered his head, replied, "I'm the man who done it."

"I know."

McPherson murmured, "He should know his rights—"

Porter abruptly raised his hand, fingers splayed. He shushed the cadet, muttering, "He speaks willingly. It's his choice."

The detective asked Kane plainly, "Why did you kill her? She your wife?"

"No. Not my wife. It's my sister-in-law. I was fond of her before, you know. But I'm glad she's dead. I should never have agreed—"

Detective Porter moved closer. "What did she do to deserve it?"

Kane flashed a revolver. "Stop."

McPherson slowly drew his sidearm and whispered over Porter's shoulder, "You're not armed, Detective?"

"No. Left the house early in a rush."

"Aye." McPherson's revolver trembled in the cadet's hand. "'ave this, then."

"No. Holster it. Won't be required."

"How do you know?"

"I know."

Kane waved his revolver. "Keep away, I said."

Detective Porter inched forward, repeated, "What did she do to deserve it?"

"I worked to keep that house. I did. Swear. I promised my brother. But Mary. She was too much."

"Your brother? Where's he?"

"Dead. Last year." Kane looked skyward. His hat fell off. "Edward. His name was Edward. His heart. He had a condition. Born with it."

Sparrows chirped maddeningly.

Kane laughed a sad laugh and continued, "We were at the zoo, once. At Exhibition Park. I remember Mary admiring the peafowl. A pair of them. A hen and cock. Mary said peafowl stay on with one another for life." He turned toward Porter. "She was wrong. Edward agreed with her, anyway. I told her that's not true." He exhaled. "Peahens can be vicious. Really vicious. And besides, does anything?"

Porter asked, "Does anything what?"

"Stay together. For life."

Detective Porter considered the question longer than intended. He looked at hosts of sparrows clustered on branches above, wishing they would shut up. He shrugged. "Wolves? They remain mates. I think. Read it somewhere. Maybe not." He glanced over his shoulder at McPherson and then back at Kane. "No, you're right. Nothing does. Not really."

Kane scoffed. "I didn't think so either and Edward knew she was wrong but he'd do everything and say anything to please her, you know, keeping her in clover."

McPherson piped in from behind, "But why would you do what you did to her, though? The violence of it. You wouldn't 'ave even put down a dog like that, would you?"

Porter told the cadet to shut up, but McPherson ignored the detective and continued, "Why not just leave 'er? Ever think going away before doing what you did would 'ave been better? That was an option, too. Just going away. Leavin' 'er alone." He paused. "Would 'ave been kinder to put a bullet in 'er face while asleep than to make 'er suffer like you did, too."

Kane shook his head. "Things got . . . carried away."

Porter ordered McPherson to stop talking, then asked Kane, "How did you get into this fix?"

Kane exhaled, slouched. "Edward asked me to see to her care if anything happened to him. Fuck. I should've said no, right?" Kane wept into his palm. "I should have said no. He was my brother, though."

Detective Porter was close enough to touch Kane's shoulder. "Need a way out?"

"What? Turn myself over to you, you mean?"

"No."

Kane looked puzzled.

"Is the shooter loaded?"

Kane nodded. "Course it is."

Detective Porter sighed. "Skin for skin, if I were looking at the rope, and I guarantee you're looking at the rope, I'd put the muzzle to my temple and finish it."

Kane wiped the back of his hand across his cheeks and runny nose. "What?"

"End it."

"End it?"

"Yeah. Finish it. That's what I'd do."

The creek burbled. The sparrows chirped. Church bells rang. Services were letting out.

Kane cocked the hammer. The cylinder clicked.

Detective Porter whispered, "That's it."

Kane angled the revolver under his Adam's apple. "I'm glad it's over—"

"Wait," McPherson shouted, "Everyone deserves at least a trial."

Porter sighed.

McPherson's voice trembled. "Put it down, Mr. Kane. There's another way."

Eyes wide, Kane slowly lowered the gun. McPherson pushed passed Porter. He snatched the firearm away and quickly secured Kane in bracelets.

Porter knelt, picked up the revolver as well as Kane's felt hat. "Don't forget this," he said, tossing the bowler at the murderer. It landed on the path at Kane's feet.

With Kane in bracelets, Porter instructed McPherson to pick it up. The cadet and the detective stared at one another until McPherson said, "Pick it up yourself," and led his prisoner away.

Constable Wright was waiting at the top of the path. McPherson was smiling when he arrived with Kane. Simpson the street preacher had departed. The crowd pressed around the cadet, the constable, and the killer.

Constable Wright asked, "The detective's not with you?"

"Nay. Collected the seven-shooter and went a-ways down the path. Wants to be alone to write in his occurrence book, I figure."

Kane went into the police van. Constables and detectives patted McPherson's shoulder. "Good work," they said. "Good work."

A few minutes after four o'clock, Coroner Johnson convened an inquest on the body of Mary Kane in the crowded lobby of White's Hotel on King Street West near Stafford. Twelve jurymen walked the short distance to the house at 132 Defoe Street to observe a body on a table covered by a sheet in the front room. Outside, a pregnant woman with glossy black hair tugged the sleeve of a juryman, asking, "They mention 'bout the cab?" before being shooed away.

Returning to the hotel, the inquest resumed at five. A crowd spilled outside. Constables were required to keep order. Coroner Johnson took the testimony of all persons concerned.

County Crown Attorney Badgerow was there for the Crown, James A. Macdonald for the defence. Robert Sterling testified he heard the row next door. "I didn't want to get mixed up in no family jar, though."

Elizabeth Sterling testified. "First I heard awful screams, then I heard, 'Tommy don't.' Then I heard nothin."

Keith Sterling affirmed. "There was a good deal of blood about the floor. Mr. Kane was out fast beside the body."

Detective Porter, sketchpad open on his lap, conveyed the content of his occurrence book. His testimony touched on the house's general appearance, the flatiron, boot prints, and the tooth.

When it was Detective Cuddy's turn, he backed every word of Detective Porter's.

Police Cadet McPherson detailed his first arrest but, following Constable Wright's advice, withheld details about Porter advising Kane to blow his brains out.

Dr. Powell told of bruising on the arms and legs and cuts to the head, concluding, "The viscera were normal and comparatively healthy. Several ribs were broken, and a thumb was crushed off. She hemorrhaged."

Additional witnesses were examined, including Kane's landlord and a neighbour, Esther Grey, who'd loaned Mary Kane a can of coal oil earlier Saturday.

The defence did all that was possible for Kane. "My client said he was down in the Ward the entire evening with two men and a woman named Liz."

Thomas Kane remained impassive throughout. Asked if he had anything to say, he muttered, "Can I have a glass of water, please?"

The jury considered the case for a few minutes, then brought in the verdict: Thomas Kane did forcefully and with malice afterthought slay Mary Kane.

At 7:15 o'clock, Coroner Johnson issued a true bill, committing

Thomas Kane to trial at the winter assizes. Kane was transported to a cell in the basement of No.3 station.

The crowd dispersed. Detectives, constables, the coroner, and Dr. Powell secreted into the barroom to celebrate McPherson's first arrest with whisky and cigars.

Detective Porter declined the invitation to join the others. Instead, he walked home, pausing outside the house on Defoe Street for one last look.

At a few minutes before nine, he arrived at his St. Patrick Street home. Pedestrians were not very numerous. The street was quiet. Inside, the lamps were turned down, Susan retired to bed.

Detective Porter remained outside on the sidewalk a long time, sketching his house's exterior under gaslight.

HOBO BURGLARS

? ? 1900

The sun was barely up. The November air was chilly. Detective Porter stood over the body splayed on the sidewalk. Congealed blood pooled underneath the dead man. Only a small crowd had gathered, but more would arrive with the coming light. Reporters from all the newspapers had already arrived.

Porter asked Policeman Willis, "You did this?"

"Mhm."

"You were the contact officer, correct?"

"Mhm."

Porter knelt. He could make out gunpowder on the deceased's palm. "Where's the firearm?"

"It was beneath him. He collapsed on it."

"Where is it now?"

"I don't know."

"You don't know?"

Porter studied the entry wound on the dead man's face, poking around the fleshy opening with his pencil. Noting flame burns and singed hair, he wrote "Rathole" in his notes, the word used to describe this kind of wound, one that appeared like a rodent chewed into the face.

"Close range?"

"Yeah. I was approximately here," Willis pointed at the pavement where he stood, "and he was about there."

"Got him on the button," Porter observed. "At a downward angle, too." Porter rolled the man's limp head to the side and felt around the scalp. "No exit wound. Hit the brain artery, I bet. The autopsy will tell us where the bullet ended up."

Porter stood. "What's his name?"

"Huh?"

"Name?"

"Oh. Right. McIntosh."

"M-c-I-n-t-o-s-h?"

"Mhm."

"And first?"

"Joseph."

"Joseph McIntosh. Age?"

"What?"

"Age. Come on, Willis. Work with me."

"Okay. Yes. Sorry. Looked to be in his twenties."

"Say, twenty-five?"

"Mhm."

Porter pointed to the compact chisel and a soap bar next to the body. "Hobo burglars. Not a Toronto man."

"He's not familiar to you, then?"

"Without a face, he's not familiar to anyone."

"I wasn't being—How do you know about him not being from here?"

"The soap," Porter said. "That brand. Le Bébé. It's only sold in Quebec."

"Oh."

"What else?"

The detective had already examined the primary crime scene on the second floor above the greengrocer, where multiple families dwelled. Witnesses stated that two burglars—McIntosh followed close on the heels of a second—burst into the room where they slept. There was a fight in the dark. An absolute mêlée. Furniture broken over heads. Gunshots followed. Shop owner John Varcoe received two bullets from a .38, one in the groin, the other under the heart, and died at the scene in a few minutes.

The burglars had gained entry through the back door and immediately went to the basement, assuming the safe was down there. The detective was shown dynamite, caps, fuses, and tempered drills left by the burglars. He attempted to question Varcoe's young daughters. Because he couldn't get more than sniffles and tears, he left it for the police matron to see what she could get out of them.

As the City Dairy milk wagon approached on Queen, Porter heard the rattling of empty milk cans. He instructed Willis, "Hang on," and crossed Queen Street to flag down the milkman, Sam.

Samuel Hazlett brought the wagon to a stop.

"Morning, Sam."

"'Morning, George. Sorry, Detective Porter."

"It's fine. Any chance of a spare bottle? Settles the ulcer. I skipped breakfast for this."

Hazlett reached behind his seat into a crate and handed Porter a bottle of milk. "What's happened here then?"

"Burglars. Murdered the shop's owner."

"No. Not John! He was a good man. Varcoe was getting married next week."

Porter took a long swig of milk and wiped his mouth on his sleeve. "Well, that's cancelled." He held up the bottle. "This helps. Charge the house account. Susan will see you're paid."

"No problem. You know, fellows were hanging around on an earlier run this morning."

"Here?"

"No. At the rear. Heard talking in the back of the alley. I drop Hayman's delivery early down that side lane."

"You say there were three?"

"No. Never said three. I said I just heard voices. Sounded like an argument, perhaps."

Porter took another swig. "Make anything out?"

"No. Just a disagreement. Nothing heated. Maybe a boy was there, too, or maybe the voice was a girl's."

"A female?"

"Yeah. Maybe. Probably not, though. Anyway, I got to get back."

Before Porter resumed talking with Policeman Willis, he offered the despondent constable a drink of milk. Willis ignored him and stared at the corpse.

"Hey," Porter shook the policeman's shoulder, "Come around, Willis. Gawkers are watching. Besides, it was you or him. Now give me details."

"Sorry." Willis gathered his thoughts. "He came out of that window. Up there. I was walking my beat. It was quiet. You know how it is. I was lost in thought when I saw this child in the doorway and said firmly, 'Boy, hey boy,' like that. It was after two, maybe closer to three. Then glass shatters, and this McIntosh falls out of the sky and lands with a thud. The next thing I see, he's coming up on a knee, struggling not to topple backward, and aiming a revolver. Frightened the living daylights out of me. I jumped behind this telegraph pole with enough time to draw, and then boom. Then the second mug, named Williams, comes tumbling out of the same window and slams the sidewalk hard, crying, 'Don't shoot me, Don't shoot me,' then hell breaks loose."

Porter took notes as Willis described what happened and nodded. "What did you do next?"

"The mob from the shop had them pinned. They weren't going anywhere. I chased after the boy to see if he was okay. I don't know why. I guess I was still startled because I fired a round at him." Willis paused. "I shouldn't have. It was heated, and my thinking wasn't clear."

"It's fine," Porter said. "Things were excited."

"But—"

He handed Willis the bottle of milk. "Hold this." He glanced at the shattered window and the broken frame fifteen feet above the sidewalk and jotted in his occurrence book. "Where's Williams now?"

"Who?"

"The fella who fell on the guy who practically fell on you."

"Oh. Henry Williams. In hospital. He was cut up and beaten pretty badly, but he'll make it. Getting back to the kid, I think he was sleeping in the doorway, and the commotion woke him up."

"Yeah. Probably."

"You get a look at him?"

"I think so."

Porter wrote down every word Willis spoke but stopped when the policeman said, "I feel bad, Detective."

"Bad? Why?"

"For him."

"For this refuse?" Porter nudged the corpse with his shoe. "Are you kidding me? The shop didn't even contain a safe. All this was for nothing."

Willis shrugged. "But I killed—"

"If you feel bad for anyone, feel bad for them." He pointed at Varcoe's daughters inside the shop, "That one's Meta Varcoe. She's six. The younger one is Olive. She's four. Their mother's dead. Died earlier this year. They went to bed with a father and woke up orphans."

Detective Porter left Policeman Willis and walked across Queen, heading east toward an alley.

Policeman Willis followed a few steps before stopping. "Where you leaving to?"

"To see what I can find of the boy."

"The boy?"

"The one asleep in the doorway."

"He's long gone."

"I'll look around a few corners, anyway. See what I can see. When I come back, we'll work on a sketch. Meantime, get McIntosh under a sheet until the coroner arrives."

The overcrowded hospital ward smacked of phenol. Detective Porter showed his badge to the constable assigned to guard the prisoner seated at the foot of the cot. Williams, eyes closed, lay on his back, stripped to his waist. His face was gashed and gouged.

A doctor with a venerable beard informed the detective that the patient had been administered doses of scopolamine and morphine and wouldn't be too responsive. "He's not alert."

"I'll try anyway."

"Suit yourself. He's received a sound thumping. I've diagnosed broken bones from the fall and am checking for a brain hemorrhage."

"Will he recover?"

"Likely. Unless things take a turn."

Detective Porter shook Williams on the shoulder and patted his cheek. "Wake up."

Williams grimaced and opened his eyes. "Huh?"

"You're in a hospital. I'm Detective Porter. McIntosh is dead."

"Poor Joe," he slurred.

Porter held a sketch close to Williams's face. "Who's this?"

Williams mumbled, "Don't know."

"Who is he? Your spotter. A name."

"He?" Williams swallowed and rolled his head side to side. "He was never a he."

"What?"

The doctor stood behind Porter and said, "He's not alert. Like I said."

"Let him talk."

Williams closed his eyes, turned his head, and slurred, "Leave me alone, copper."

Porter sighed. He slapped Williams's face hard. "Hey. Hey, buster. Come to. I want a name."

"Leave me alone—"

"Cuff him to the bedpost, constable"

The doctor interjected, "But his wrists. The carpal bones are fractured."

The constable hesitated.

"So what. Do it," Porter ordered.

Williams's yelping filled the ward.

Williams's appearance improved. He was arraigned at police court and then transferred to a jail cell. The detective questioned him about the third man every chance he got.

Taking the stand in his own defence at his trial, Williams blamed McIntosh for the slaying. When questioned about the accomplice who remained at large, he told the court, "I don't know anything about that."

Porter badgered Williams to the end. Williams remained obstinate, playing checkers all day and evening with guards. Throughout the night, he wrote letters to his parents and acquaintances.

A few days before his sentence was carried out, Porter visited the convicted killer's death cell one more time.

Williams paced miles in his cell. Porter relaxed against the wall.

"I don't need you to find him."

"Him, eh? Why are you here, then? Find 'im yourself."

"I intend to."

"You got nothing and never will."

"We'll see—"

Williams stared down Porter. "You don't even know what you're looking for." Then shouted, "Guard, get him out of here. I don't want to see that face no more."

Henry Williams hanged the day after Good Friday. The jail surgeon, preparing his remains for the coroner, discovered a folded envelope inside the trouser pocket of the deceased addressed to Detective Porter containing a blank sheet of paper.

THE PHOTOGRAPHY OF SPEECH

Beatrice answered an ad in the classifieds. *Become a stenographer! Private lessons in shorthand. Reasonable.* Teddy was now fourteen and well able to care for himself, and Ted was often away on tour with the orchestra.

THE PHOTOGRAPHY OF SPEECH

After her first week of stenography lessons, she enthusiastically discussed the course with George and Susan during the Gruber family's weekly Saturday visit to the house on St. Patrick Street. The May weather was pleasantly warm, and the group sat convivially on the front porch. Susan knitted, Ted perused the newspaper, and Teddy excused himself and retreated to the conservatory.

"The instructor's a pleasant fellow. A bachelor. In fact, he's rather effeminate," Beatrice said. "I suspect he's a homosexual. He told me something charming after class yesterday. He said, 'Stenography is the photography of speech.' What a lovely turn of phrase."

Ted announced from behind the raised newspaper, "A dispatch to the *Evening Mail* says Oscar Wilde has been found guilty of gross indecency. He's been sentenced to two years hard labour."

"Is it true?" Beatrice exclaimed. "I do admire his writings. George, remember I dragged you to his lecture at the Horticultural Gardens?"

George uncrossed his legs, adjusted his hat. "Yes. Ages ago. Wasn't Teddy still a baby?" He lit a cigar.

"Yes. Ted had a performance, so Susan watched Teddy so we could attend."

Susan looked up from knitting, ignoring her sister-in-law and scolding George, "Take that to the back porch, please."

George took a puff. Beatrice took the cigar from him and followed suit.

"Honestly, Beatrice?"

Beatrice and George walked around the house to the small wooden porch off the kitchen at the rear.

"Have you ever encountered homosexuals?"

George exhaled a cloud of smoke. "Yes. And Sapphic women." He passed the cigar back to Beatrice. "You resemble Mother."

"I don't. Tell me about the lesbians."

"We recently broke up a dancing party."

"Where?"

"A hotel. On Ontario Street."

"Ted said their orchestra's first bassoon is a molly."

"How does he know?"

"He said he's quite fastidious. They say that's how you can tell them from others. Have you heard that, George? About them being fussy?"

"I've heard everything except why we don't leave them alone."

"Where do they meet?"

"Why the sudden interest?"

"For something I'm writing."

They passed the cigar back and forth.

"Writing?" When Beatrice didn't elaborate, he continued, "They meet at the usual places. Parks. Hotels. Restaurants. Like us."

"How do they behave?"

"Like us. Come downstairs. I want to show you some photographs I obtained of a dreadful murder–suicide."

"It's so pleasant here. Let's finish this," she put the cigar to her lips, "then take a peek." Exhaling, she explained how she was one of only two women in her class, and when an exercise required a partner, the two were always partnered up.

"It seems you hardly ever work with a partner at your work, George."

"That's not true. I do, on occasion. Truthfully, I don't believe others want to work with me. Besides, I bounce possibilities off you."

"Likely against rules and regulations, I'd imagine."

"I know it is, but to paraphrase our friend Machiavelli, the ends justify the means. My clearance rate is high. Don't tell, and I won't."

"You mean, our clearance rate is high," Susan corrected with a smile.

"Do you know, George, that there is an opening for a stenographer at Osgoode Hall trial court? I intend to apply." Beatrice planned to join the Canadian Shorthand Association when she completed her course. She confided in George that her goal was to be independent and contribute to the household income by making a living as a writer. "*The Standard*'s published one of my stories already."

"Really? I didn't see it."

"It appeared under a pseudonym."

"Which was?"

"Bash Melmoth."

"What was the story about?" George asked.

"Siblings. A brother and sister discover a well-known figure in their community has been murdered."

"Set in winter?"

"Yes."

"Is the victim discovered slumped his sleigh?"

"Yes."

"And by what means did the victim perish? No. Wait. Let me guess. Shot?"

"Through the head and the neck."

"I've heard this story before, or it sounds vaguely familiar."

"Does it?"

"Yes. It does. The older of the two, the brother, does he go off and become a peace officer? And eventually a detective?"

"No. Breaking convention, the younger sister does."

George grinned, "What did you title it, Beatrice?"

"Road to Kingsville."

"Interesting. It could be part of a serial story. Perhaps *McClure's Magazine* would be interested?"

Susan opened the door from the kitchen. "Would you two like some tea?"

George winked at his sister and stubbed out the remains of the cigar, calling after Susan, "We'll come to the front, Sue, and join you and Ted."

George took his hat back. Beatrice said, "One day, I'll let you read something of mine. Ted likes it but claims it's a mite too graphic coming from the pen of a lady."

"A lady?" George laughed. "I thought you authored it?"

Teddy joined them on the porch. He kissed his mother's cheek and said, "You smell like Uncle George's cigars."

PHOTO ALBUM FOR BABY

Notes for potential article in Canadian Magazine *(Vol. 25 no.7, 1905) by Beatrice Gruber under the byline Bash Melmoth. Including a selection of photographs and a single Tarot card.*

Baby, this is not the city you think you know. This is the city where displaced Englishmen snap papists' teeth clean off without second thought. It is a city of churches where hoity-toity Tommy Toronto drives Hebrews from burrows of their own making into a labyrinth of rutted streets & laneways. Chased through St. John's Ward, captured, taken by the whiskers, stoned, tarred & crucified by steel-pipe dreams of monarchy.

Street Arabs filch queendom dreams of WASP supremacy. First-ranked ladies promenading Yonge Street & King Street, the Crystal Palace, the Opera Hall, Saint Lawrence Hall are splashed with urine-topped syringes. The culprits tuck away into cigar stores, billiard rooms & other dens of this nature.

The Canary & Caged Bird Society meeting is interrupted by stone-throwers. Last night, 435 hungry men lined up outside the Yonge

PHOTO ALBUM FOR BABY

Street Mission. Wycliffe College students gave them supper. The sika deer at the Riverdale Zoo was fed a shard of glass. Rats ate 24 wild duckling eggs.

The Allan Gardens domed floral dream, refuge of Toronto's lovesick, is a lie. Children wintering here freeze to death in the frigid park, little bodies rigid as wintered-over redbud, solid as mahogany. Let's be straight, Baby, the city stinks of effluvium marsh gases. Night soil settling beds. Pork packing. Coal fire. City stables. Sandpit crematoria. Slaughterhouses. Tannery Hollow.

Girls contort themselves into frontier prostitutes, misshapen & grotesque. They hawk their wares to iron-hearted soldiers slinking across bleak parade grounds renamed Stanley Barracks. Mothers slay newborns in abundance, concealing corpses in the likeliest places. Fleshy water coffins jettisoned from the end of Queen's Wharf into Lake Ontario.

Baby, consider fathers. Why do they fail?

———•··———

Warning: This one's hard to look at.

Tarocchi was a two-year-old Italian pointer. Speckled coat the colour of sandpaper. A fine bird dog. Energetic & obedient, her keen abilities, her soft mouth made Albert Damer's bitch the envy of sportsmen at Maple Leaf Hunting Club.

In autumn, Albert took down his Browning double-barreled breechloader, put it to his shoulder & walked Tarocchi four miles to where the Don River forks. They hunted bevies of quail in grassy tableland above the valley. Albert, wearing red flannel, was all smiles back at home, picking cockleburs from his sleeves & removing quail after quail from hunting coat pockets.

Tarocchi enjoyed the outings as much as her master.

Outside birding season, Albert keeps Tarocchi sharp with fetch games played in reedy Coatsworth Cut beside the low edge of a sheetpiled breastwork south of the channel near home on Coxwell Avenue. Early morning on a sweltering day in August, Albert leads Tarocchi to the marshy shoreline. Dragonflies dart & dive about Albert's yellow cap. Tarocchi becomes alert to game Albert fails to observe. Without a command, Tarocchi lowers her head, gazing through the reeds at lapping lake water. Forepaw raised, her sinewy body becomes needle straight. Steady. Steady. The dog breaks point suddenly & turns & looks at Albert. Albert commands, Halloo.

Tarocchi leaps beyond the shallows, into chilly Lake Ontario.

Tarocchi returns through rushes. She obediently releases a corpse, rubbery & bloated, clothed in a white dress, the size & weight of a ringneck pheasant, at her master's feet.

Baby, it's you.

Albert's skin pebbles. He gasps & falls down. Tarocchi whines, turns a circle, licks Albert's face. Soaked, Albert mutters, Good God. After some moments, he stands, rubs Tarocchi's crown & rewards her. Good Tarocchi. Good dog.

Bullfrogs harrumph. A raft of black coots paddle through the clogged & reedy marsh. Man & dog hoof it to a Queen Street East callbox. Albert, out of breath & perspiring, is nearly run down by a messenger boy on a bicycle. Albert pats Tarocchi's crown & tells her Detective Porter has been dispatched. They wait beside a sheepcote, Tarocchi alert to sheep penned inside, shoulders & rumps marked with green paint.

Albert envisions fellows at the Club green with envy when he boasts Tarocchi's incisors didn't even puncture the thing's pellucid, bullet-grey flesh. They will pat Albert on the back, squeeze his shoulder & praise him because no dog has a mouth as soft as Tarocchi's.

Detective Porter arrived in the company of a uniformed officer carrying a camera. He eyed Albert & Tarocchi & said, Nice dog. Tarocchi wagged her tail. In a flat, hollow, disinterested tone, Detective Porter asked, Where is it, then? Albert replied, This way.

They walked & walked. No one spoke until Albert said, I didn't realize Tarocchi & I had gone so far. Detective Porter asked, Who's Tarocchi? Albert pointed at his brindled dog.

Tarocchi wagged her tail. Detective Porter asked, That's a dog's name?

The detective stood over you, Baby, face down in the marsh. He removed his hat, wiped his brow, looked at the sun & muttered, Bloody hot as hell. He flipped you face up with his boot, This is it, eh? A boy. That a birthmark or a bruise? he asked, referring to a bottle-green fish-hook-shaped blot on your right temple. Albert shrugged. The detective removed an occurrence book & a pencil from an inside pocket.

Baby, the look in the detective's eyes changes. A mechanism in his mind switches on. He fires up his scenario-generating machine, allowing him to envision infinite possibilities to explain how you arrived at your ending. He noted the time, knelt, & made a notation regarding what appeared to be a blue paint smudge on your left parietal bone. He mumbled, Interesting. Albert asked, What is? Detective Porter said, Does that look like blue paint to you? Albert said, I guess. Detective Porter said, Yeah, but what shade of blue? Albert said, I don't know. Are there many? Detective Porter said, About two-hundred & forty. Albert said, Oh. I only know one. Blue.

The detective snapped an order to the officer with the camera, Get a shot of that, pointing down at you and then asked Albert the proper spelling of his name, first, middle & last. He made a hasty sketch of the scene. Albert inquired, Is there a reward for finding it? The detective looked into the endless sky, rubbed his pocked chin & sighed, No. As an afterthought he added, Probably tossed by a chippie.

Additional detectives arrived. They consulted one another. Tarocchi barked. Albert snapped his fingers, Shush. Detective Porter said, My feet are wet.

———•••———

Let's back up a little, Baby. Here's a photo from the day of your parents' marriage. They eloped on Christmas Eve. Alex Martin pinned a red carnation to his lapel. Ethel Bye tied a grey crepe ribbon in her hair. He was twenty-one. She was seventeen & eight months pregnant.

With nothing to do after city hall, the newlyweds followed tides of passers-by browsing hand-painted winter scenes displayed in scarlet & green in King Street storefronts. They shared gin from a flask. Stores remained open until ten.

Outside Dunlop's, Alex elbowed his way from the curb to the

window where white doves soared heavenward on silken ladders. He pressed his nose against the glass & remembered boyhood. Alex pleaded with his new wife, Let's go inside. Ethel refused, Don't be simple. Alex edged his way to the entrance, customers cursing as he stepped on toes. The doorkeeper barred him.

Ethel convinced Alex to steal a little cart drawn by a brown pony. The couple made their way up Yonge Street to the Lennox Hotel near Tannery Hollow in the north end. The hotel porter greeted them heartily, Merry Christmas. He asked about valises. Alex said, Stolen. Concerned, the porter replied, Did you report the theft to the police? Ethel answered in the curt tone of a first-ranked lady, No need. The pony was stabled in the hotel's livery.

They interrupted the hotel clerk seated in a panelled booth arranging red & white checker pieces on a board & registered for the night under a false name. The clerk assigned them an upstairs room in the back. Beside one another on a sagging mattress, Ethel unbuttoned her blouse, We should do it. Alex stood, peeled his suspenders off his shoulders, pulled his trousers to his knees. He reached to turn down the gas lamp but Ethel said, Don't. She hiked up her petticoat & gripped the bedpost, Put it in from behind. Alex said, It'll hurt the baby. Ethel was aroused, Just do it. He did. She yowled with pleasure.

In a few minutes, the clerk wrapped on the door, inquiring, Mr. Wentworth, is anything the matter? Ethel squealed, Leave us alone. The illuminated gas lamp bubbled & glowed like a sore.

Later, they went up to the roof & smoked little cigars nicked from Captain Andrew's Cigar Store on Yonge Street. The streets below were empty. Trolley service ended hours earlier. It wasn't as cold as you'd expect & the sky was clear. Ethel leaned over the brick parapet & spit. Alex glanced at the red carnation still fixed to his lapel. He said, It's Christmas. Ethel ignored him, lit a cigar, pursed her lips & exhaled a loose string of grey smoke, asking, How much could we get for the pony? Alex said, Not much. He put his hand across Ethel's shoulder & observed, You forgot your ribbon in the room. Ethel said she didn't care. Alex squeezed her shoulder.

Ethel twisted & pulled away. Don't touch me.

Back in their room, they considered burgling the suite next door or robbing a guest. Ethel mused about lighting the mattress on fire & burning the whole place down. Instead, they skulked down the fire stairs to the alley & walked to a Bloor Street cabstand near the crematorium. An albino deer up from the Rosedale Ravine bounded across the street.

It was still dark by the time they arrived at their one-room apartment in a burned-out, abandoned building. Alex knelt by the hearth & lit a fire. Ethel removed a sterling silver thimble from her pocket & gave it to Alex. Alex said, What's this for? Ethel said, Christmas. Alex gave Ethel his comb. Ethel gave it back. She rubbed her stomach, I don't want nothing. They lay together in their clothing on a rusty iron bedstead under a heap of coats & blankets. Ethel complained, I'm cold. Alex mused, We need to get a job. Ethel yawned. Then get one.

Baby, I know Detective Porter well. He is my brother. He avoided the camera whenever he could. There is a photograph of him on file, however, taken outside a police station. Drab fedora. Hooded eyes. Pained expression.

That day in the marsh with man & dog, Detective Porter appeared dispassionate. However, don't be deceived, he will be your champion.

Coroner Fleming was summoned. Authorities at the Health Office were contacted. Detective Porter sealed you in a water-repellant canvas pouch, fastened it, placed you on the bench seat beside him in the police van & removed you to Brown's undertaking parlour.

The caretaker awaited your arrival at the rear entrance.

Detective Porter transferred you deferentially, carrying you as though handling a jewelled egg or stemware from Waterford.

With the sooty eyes of a sawtooth eel & sideburns that hung on either side of his face like two squirrel pelts, Dr. Hutchinson performed a post-mortem examination, promising a thorough study.

The doctor's deft handling of dissecting forceps & cartilage knife was impressive. Detective Porter observed, sketched & created a record. He peppered the doctor with questions.

THE WAY OF TRANSGRESSORS • Edward Brown

The doctor retrieved a loupe to see better & using tweezers, removed wood splinters submerged in the papillary dermis of your scalp. Porter remained until you were sewn up like a raggedy doll.

Doctor Hutchinson submitted his findings to Coroner Fleming at the inquest opened later in the evening: Death occurred within days. Your skull was fractured & there was an absence of water in the lungs. By simple way of explanation, Baby, the evidence revealed you were done for & then lobbed into the bay.

The witness, Albert Damer of Coxwell Avenue, recounted how he & his champion bitch discovered the remains.

Detective Cuddy presented a theory that the mother likely also met her death in the company of the infant, either by her hand or another's, & to expect her remains to wash ashore forthwith. Detective Porter created a rankle in the department when he took the stand & publicly challenged Detective Cuddy's postulation.

The inquest was adjured at nine o'clock, your death ruled homicide.

On a hunch, Detective Porter grabbed a late bite at a York Street eating house, then went to City Hall & convinced a clerk overworking to assist him in compiling a list of boathouse operators licensed to rent pleasure boats to the public. Experience informed Porter the slaying was impulsive & performed in seclusion. Judging by the blue paint smudge on your flesh, the splinter evidence, & his knowledge of lake currents, he supposed that you likely were pummelled with an oar & then tossed over the gunwale of a rowing boat east of Coatsworth Cut.

He arrived home after midnight. His wife was asleep.

―•―

Baby, come hot on the heels of their December nuptials, you were born the following January. You were very tiny. The doctor who delivered you went unpaid. Alex found work in a tailor shop. Ethel complained it was too hard to carry you everywhere. She found a lady to take care of you while she waited tables at the Jubilee Restaurant. The manager gave her free food & she stole food. Alex fashioned a wine cask into a cradle. Ethel laughed & said it reminded her of a casket.

The city burned in April. Ample photos are available. An inferno of flames, ash & fear. A futile effort to save wholesale houses, shops, manufacturing & the like was underway. Column after column of orange blazed into the night sky.

Ethel carried you as she followed Alex up a rickety staircase onto the flat roof of the three-storey building where you lived. It was cold, blustery. Streets below echoed with shouts, galloping horses, the clang & gong of fire brigades. Wooden buildings veneered with brick bent & fell. The firestorm excited Ethel's wickedness. A burning wind rushed over her. As the world came down around them, she said, I wish I'd started it.

Ethel lobbed you at Alex. You hung in the air like an apostrophe before landing in Alex's arms. He shouted, Hey. Careful. Unsure what to do with you, he laid you on the tarpaper roof away from the edge. Ethel asked, What are we drinking? Alex gave her a flask of Old Irish. You curled into a comma to keep warm. Waves of ash, hot embers, descended like singed feathers.

The fur-lined cloak Ethel had stolen from a customer at the restaurant where she worked caught fire. As Alex patted the flame with his hand, he asked, Is smoke bad for the baby? Ethel ignored him, replying angrily, Why'd you do that? Alex shook his head, confused. She sneered, If I catch fire again, I want to burn.

Ethel picked you up. You were pale, almost albino, with hunger. A gust momentarily lifted clouds of smoke, revealing the bay. Ethel said, Let's rent a boat. Alex added, We could row to the Island. Visit the fair at Hanlan's Point & see the Daredevil Dash, or we could just take the ferry.

Back in the apartment, Ethel dropped you in your cask, speculating, I bet a lot of people died tonight. Alex answered, Suppose you're right. Ethel was aroused. They fucked. She made noises & spoke in voices like an animal. Alex wanted to stop. Ethel said, No. The building was abandoned. No one complained about noises she made.

No one perished in the fires that night or the next day or the day after that.

Baby, this one is frayed around the edges: a partially submerged rowboat at the mouth of Don River. At the beginning of August, the manager of Hick's Boathouse confirmed to Detective Porter he recalled renting Alex & Ethel a rowboat. Twenty-five cents for an hour in the bay. A receipt revealed their names.

The morning after the inquest, on four hours of rest, Detective Porter arose early, dressed, shaved, & skipped breakfast, intending to get away while Mrs. Porter slept.

They would remain childless their entire marriage. They tried for a child and came close on occasion, but Providence chose otherwise.

Before the noon hour, Detective Porter visited five boathouses east of the Cut—Britannia Boathouse Club, Hick's Boathouse, Dean's Boathouse, Fawley Court Boathouse & Hendrie's—each licensed to rent rowing boats to the public.

Sound leads came out of an interview with the manager of Hick's. He remembered you well, Baby. Remembered the couple argued about who would hold you. Remembered, as the boat started out on the lake, the lady with a fish-eating grin played "This Little Piggy" on your toes.

They return to the city late at night aboard a ferry without you.

The detective took possession of a cerulean blue oar, put it on his shoulder, & set off for Central Police Station. On his return, he was accosted by a glad-handing man with a neglected appearance executing a please-lend-me-a-nickel act & threatened him with a charge of vagrancy. A little further along, the detective pushed aside an Italian fortune-teller working a sidewalk operation. He studied Porter a moment & then prognosticated a return to his watery path. The soothsayer promised Porter that, for a small fee, he would tell Porter the secrets of his life, including the hour & manner of his death.

Billy Assen, a newspaperman with the *Evening Standard*, looking to scoop other crime beat hacks, confronted Detective Porter outside the Court Street station, asking for developments in what his daily labelled "The Coatsworth Mystery." Assen asked eagerly, Where's the oar from? Porter replied, Hick's Boathouse. Assen inquired, Is it the object used as a weapon to extinguish the babe's life?

Baby, one thing you can say about Porter is, he was experienced enough to know when using newspapermen to further an investigation could be advantageous & responded, Yes, it could be or one just like it.

In the afternoon, Frank Stauffer, a well-known resident of Cleveland who was visiting a relative in the city, came forward to give his statement to Porter. Stauffer & another witness said they were out in the boats when they saw a couple with a baby row from Munroe Park toward the Island.

Detective Porter secured an excellent description of the couple & their clothing.

Another witness reported that she spied a couple in a boat on a picnic trip to the beach with her two children. The man held a youngster. The lady rowed. They were close enough to shore to hear the lady curse.

The dinner hour approached. Porter sent a boy to his home with a message for his wife that he would work late & not wait up.

A booking photograph reveals Ethel was arrested outside the Jubilee. Detective Porter kneed her in the groin. Next, he apprehended Alex hiding in a horse stable at Stanley Barracks, where he'd enlisted a few days earlier. Iron-hearted soldiers drilling saw him cuffed & escorted across the parade ground. The detective thumped him in the kidney with his billy club & ordered, Stop resisting. Alex winced, I'm not.

Charged with child murder, Ethel & Alex were held separately in the Toronto Jail, Alex in the east wing, alone in the death cell. Ethel was placed in the west wing with ninety-eight other females.

Ethel shared a cell in the basement with women in their late teens. Other inmates were in their early twenties. Still others were pitifully old. Most had disagreeable diseases. Some were insane. Everybody hurt everybody. A simple-minded, bright-cheeked thirteen-year-old in for over a year ate bread soaked in phosphorous poison to deal with the rat problem & died.

Vanzant, governor of the jail, was no goody-goody man. Governor Vanzant called female inmates hens. He took liberties with them in his apartment office. Except for the oldest, the infirm & ones married to men of inferior races, he pleasured himself by making them do things they didn't want to do.

Ethel had a hard go. She was despised, beaten & choked with undergarments. She broke an inmate's collarbone in a fight. At night she lay awake on her iron cot, considering the jam she was in. A lawyer was appointed to her case. A trial was scheduled. Ethel thought hard on how to avoid the noose. One afternoon she met an inmate named Rebecca Revis, arrested for telling fortunes. Revis had a pegleg. Pegleg Revis agreed to read Ethel's cards for a dime. Ethel had no money. Instead, she offered to allow the fortune teller to watch her touch herself. They went to the woodyard. Ethel leaned on a cord of wood, pulled up her skirts, reached between her legs & frigged herself with a piece of bark.

Later, in a cell, Ethel turned over the five of wands, the nine of swords, death, the eight of wands, the ten of cups &, from the bottom of the shuffled deck of Tarot cards, the hanged man.

Before she began the reading, Pegleg Revis asked, What do you seek? Ethel replied, A long life. Pegleg Revis sighed & became agitated. As she gathered the cards back into the deck, she said, You don't need these to know what to do. Get pregnant. A jury will never convict you in a state like that.

Ethel went to Vanzant eagerly. By the opening of the trial in November, she was showing.

Baby, the trial was swift with hardly time for a photo. The accused sat closely together in the dock. Ethel took the stand. Her lawyer cautioned jurors, This woman is on trial for her life, & the law doesn't make any distinction in the sexes, so I ask you, gentlemen, to weigh the evidence carefully.

Ethel blamed Alex & vice versa.

The verdict came back. The foreman stood & pronounced, We find Alexander John Martin guilty of murder. We find the prisoner, Mrs. Martin, not guilty. Ethel dabbed her eyes with a white handkerchief, pretending to cry bitter tears. She stretched her belly, leaned over, whispered mockingly in her husband's ear, By my lights, this city's no place to raise a child. Don't feel bad, either, he could've been anyone's.

 She kissed Alex on the mouth & left the docket free. Alex was sentenced to be hanged by the neck until he was dead.

This one is a hard one to look at, too. Hangman Radcliffe reported to Sheriff Mowat, who gave instruction. Radcliffe saw Vanzant at the jail. The scaffold was erected in the yard. The condemned was visited by his father & two brothers. A farewell visit. Alex handed his father a sterling silver thimble & said, Give it back to her. His father examined the trinket bewildered, Who? Ethel? She's left the city. Alex sighed, Already? One of his brothers asked, What do we tell Mother? Alex thought a moment, Tell her I wasn't the only one who failed.

 Eight the following morning, on the first warm day in March, Alex stomped up the stairs to the scaffold, followed by Reverend Vipond. He was pinioned & positioned over the trap. A black cap was placed over his head. The noose was adjusted. Sheriff Mowat asked firmly, Have you anything to say? From beneath the course sack, Alex said, Simply this, you are hanging an innocent man. Sheriff Mowat exhaled. Anything else? Alex asked Reverend Vipond to pray him across. The reverend turned away, It's out of my hands.

 Radcliffe shot the bolt. Twenty-five people watched Alex drop into the pit below & die in nine minutes.

Months later, a rumour rippled through the city that your half-brother, Michael James O'Leary, was born. Billy Assen, the dogged reporter, chased down Ethel, clenching the new baby. The photograph made the first page of his newspaper. In the image, you can see a large, oar-shaped birthmark on the infant's right temple. Baby, don't envy Michael.

The final photo, the one I've saved for last, is the only one in existence proving you were more than an afterthought, more than an ampersand between a brute & a coward.

Baby, you were precious. You had a name. Put this photo to memory. I will put this story in fire & it will burn & nobody will ever read it again.

I've looked & looked & my brother claims to not know where your bones are interred in the gay white city on the lake.

A BOUQUET OF WHITE CAMELLIAS

J. Boyd, 1908

"Shine, boy."

John Boyd, a courteous, gentle, wholesome man with penetrating pearl-grey eyes was the bootblack and restroom attendant at the Grand Union Hotel. Unlike any restroom in the city, its high coffered ceiling, embossed copper inlays, polished marble columns, plaster scrollwork, mahogany panelling, and brass faucets were reminiscent of the magnificent cathedral church on King Street.

At the beginning of each shift, John placed fresh flowers in a crystal vase on the quartz countertop. John considered this room the most beautiful in the city. He whistled, "You're the Flower of My Heart" and the restroom walls whistled back.

The only thing John loved more than this beautiful room was Naomi Evans. Alone in the restroom, he studied his upturned palms darkened by polish oil. He remembered riding the steam-powered carousel at Scarboro Beach Amusement Park, her hand in his. When no one was looking, he kissed the dimple on her—

"I said I need a shine, boy." A conventioneer staying at the Grand, a stout man in a plug hat, snapped his fingers, pulling John from his reverie. John stood, put his hand to the brim of his silver braided cap in acknowledgement. "Have a seat." The conventioneer stepped up, sat in the raised, heavy leather armchair, and placed his feet on the footrests.

John knelt beside the brass spittoon and polished the man's shoes to gleaming.

After John completed the shine, the conventioneer dropped pennies on the embossed silver tip tray. He helped himself to a complimentary white handkerchief before leaving, not once making eye contact with the bootblack.

John washed his hands. He looked at his reflection in the mirror and straightened the stem of the camellia he had placed in his lapel buttonhole, then tidied his workstation and swept the restroom floor.

The Grand was opposite the train depot. When their schedules coincided, after work John walked ten minutes from the Front Street hotel to the corner of York and Queen, a short distance from the New York Chinese Restaurant, and waited for Naomi to complete her shift waiting tables.

Constables from the Agnes Street police station a few streets over frequently dined at the New York Chinese. The proprietor, Edward Wandle, was on good terms with constables at No.2 station. At Wandle's insistence, the constabulary received complimentary meals at the eating house, even though it went against police policy.

Before Wandle permanently exiled him from the premises, John waited inside if the restaurant wasn't busy or if the weather was inclement. He would wait by the entrance or sometimes take a seat at a nearby table in the corner by the window. The restaurant's pale yellow paintwork and shabby decor gave the New York Chinese a homey feel. It was nothing fancy but an improvement from other dives on York Street. Sometimes Henry Woo, the bar attendant, served him something from the tea menu.

The bootblack always insisted on paying.

Late in the afternoon, before dinner service, Naomi was finishing her shift and the restaurant was empty of customers except for Constable Cross and his partner Ogilvy, who routinely flaunted the chief's policy, dining gratis at the New York Chinese. Downing the last of their beef tongue sandwiches and fruit salad jelly, Wandle, his coal-black face scarred from bouts of acne in his youth, entered the dining room from the kitchen and briefly joined the policemen at their table. Naomi served them coffee. She spied John sitting alone in the corner by the window and smiled furtively.

Wandle unexpectedly shoved his chair backward, crossed the room, and slammed his thick hand on the table where John sat, startling the timid bootblack, upsetting the teacup, saucer, and cutlery. Wandle pointed to the door. "Get out of my restaurant."

John knew better than to react. He sat motionless.

Constable Cross called across the dining room, "Need assistance over there?"

Through gritted teeth, Wandle said harshly, "Unnecessary."

Naomi slinked unnoticed into the kitchen while John abided and went outside.

A few weeks later John stood out of the rain in the restaurant's alcove beside a nickel-in-the-slot gum machine waiting for Naomi. Wandle came out and barked, "Get off my property."

John abided and moved to the curbstone.

On another occasion, Wandle glared at John through the restaurant's picture window. After a minute, he stood framed in the entranceway, shouting, "Get off my sidewalk. You make me nervous." Wandle raised his cane as if he would strike the bootblack. John crossed to the opposite side of York to a spot under a buttonwood tree in the public-school yard and waited for his beloved beside an Italian peanut vendor.

A few weeks later, Wandle was nearly struck down by a one-horse shay when he charged across bustling York Street waving his cane above his head demanding, "Get off my street."

Henceforth, John waited for Naomi by the cast-iron baffle gates at the front of Osgoode Hall among swarming murders of black-caped barristers and the cries of newsboys hawking dailies.

One afternoon while walking their beat, Cross and Ogilvy encountered Boyd loitering there and instructed him to move along.

John complied.

John walked Naomi to her home, a flat she shared with Angela, another waitress at the New York Chinese. The couple planned to marry eventually. She wore John's resized signet ring on her pinkie. For the time being, they kept their engagement a secret. If John had his way, Naomi would find work someplace else. A different restaurant. Any place would be better than working for Edward Wandle.

John didn't place demands on his fiancée but cautioned, "Wandle is not a good man."

"I know. But did you know he's a churchgoer?"

John repeated, "Love, he is not a good man."

Naomi was white. Orphaned at a young age, she was from a town in Alberta. John was from a village in Indiana. Naomi was fragile; she had a past. John was not naïve. When she was ready, he knew she would tell him.

In the evening the couple attended an outdoor concert by the Woodmen Band at the Allan Gardens pavilion. The late spring air was fragrant. After the concert, they walked arm-in-arm to the streetcar stop. John wore his burgundy uniform, a white camellia in the lapel buttonhole. Naomi had changed out of her work clothing into a striped dress. Passersby stared at them with open curiosity.

Naomi teased, "It's because you're young and handsome and look like an officer in that uniform." Naomi was a decade older than John. Sometimes John had the urge to tell her that, where he came from, men like him swung from branches by the neck for this simple, pleasant act, but he suspected she already knew.

On the sidewalk outside her home, she whispered suggestively, "Tomorrow is your birthday."

John nodded.

Naomi bit her bottom lip. "Come up. Angela's out." She tugged John by the arm. "I have an early present for you."

Neither noticed Constables Cross and Ogilvy approaching from behind. Ogilvy stood by the curbside. Cross pushed the tip of his baton to the bootblack's chest and eased him backward, glaring at Naomi. Cross asked the waitress, "Is he the cause of a nuisance, madam?"

John began to answer, but Cross cut him off. "I'm not addressing you. I'm talking to the lady."

"Everything is fine, Constable. Thank you."

The constables left them in peace.

Again, Naomi asked John to come up.

John was resolute. "Not until we're married, love."

Tomorrow, he turned thirty-three. He walked home to a room he rented in a house at Bay and Adelaide. That night, near midnight, he took down a bottle of Scotch, poured a glass, drank it, and put the bottle away until next year.

Forty-six-year-old Edward Wandle was bad tempered. He walked with a cane. The cane was an accoutrement, hollowed out and filled with lead. He'd been born in Georgia; twenty-six years ago, he fled his home state and eventually the US. Wandle resided in Windsor for a spell, married, moved to Toronto, opened the eating house, and gradually became a pillar in the community. Wandle had friends at city hall. His wife's name was Jemima. Intimates referred to her as Jenny. They had two daughters, both enrolled in finishing school, where they boarded.

Wandle was a prominent member of the Beverley Street Baptist Church. When he passed them on the boulevard, gentlemen tipped their hats and greeted him, "How do you do, Mr. Wandle?"

The Wandles lived in a handsome house on Palmerston. Once or twice a week, Wandle brought home a handbag full of money, stuffing it in a cupboard under the kitchen sink or a compartment under the floorboard beside his bed.

Jenny was sleeping when Wandle came home after one. As he stole into the bedroom, Jenny sat up. "Eddie?"

"Expecting someone else?"

She switched on the electric bedside lamp and struggled to sit. Rubbing her eyes, she asked, "How much?"

"Twelve hundred and change."

She laid back down. "Don't forget to tithe."

Lowering the floorboard in place, Wandle counted $110 and, opening the wardrobe, tucked the folded bills into his grey flannel church-suit pocket.

"Take yourself a rest," he told her. "I have something late to do." Wandle closed the bedroom door. Halfway down the creaking staircase, Jenny called, "Don't cheat God, Eddie."

Only Jenny was permitted to call him Eddie, and only in the privacy of their home, never with their daughters present.

A lodger at the hotel, a husky man wearing a black coat and a stiff hat, entered the restroom. John stood attentively while the man admired his reflection in the mirror. He removed his felt hat and gave it to John to brush.

The man combed his hair and washed his hands. John turned off the faucet. He held a towel out to the man. Drying his hands, the man glanced under the stalls furtively, and leaned toward John. "Any games tonight?"

John feigned ignorance. "I'm sorry, sir. Games?"

"You know, games?" The man winked.

"I understand the Orioles play the Maple Leafs but that's tomorrow afternoon at Diamond Park—"

"I'm talking about some action tonight." The man cleared his throat. "Know what I mean, right?"

Edward Wandle provided incentives to housekeepers, clerks, porters, bellhops, attendants, and the like at various hotels, including the Grand, to direct lodgers seeking vices to an operation Wandle ran out of the back of his restaurant.

John didn't play along. "Oh. I understand. Tonight." John winked. "College Street Baptist hosts a Bible study at—"

The man scowled. "Are you mocking me, boy?"

"No, sir."

The man regarded the bootblack. "Have you worked here long?" John straightened. "Yes, sir."

"They said you'd—"

"See Mr. MacDonald," the bootblack interrupted. "The house porter. He can direct you better."

The man put his hat on, pulled a nickel and a penny from his vest, dropped them on the tip tray, and left the restroom.

John organized his workstation, collected the man's tip, polished the faucets, and placed the gold-handled hat brush on the tray beside a dry sponge and a brown reagent bottle of peroxide of hydrogen used for spot cleaning. He studied his reflection, straightening the camellia in his buttonhole. Assuming he was alone in the restroom, he began to whistle a full-throated version of "You're the Flower of My Heart." To his astonishment, a baritone voice from inside a stall accompanied him, singing the opening line, "In the evening when I sit alone a-dreaming . . ."

John fell silent.

The cubicle door slowly swung open. "Of days gone by, love, to me so dear...Why'd you stop?"

A man with a grey fedora emerged, raised his arm, and made a sweeping motion around the ornate restroom. He adjusted his hat. "Fancy operation, Mr. Boyd," he said, craning his neck to take in the restroom's sophisticated décor. He asked the astonished restroom attendant, "Who taught you how to whistle, by the way, Old Man Wind himself?"

John draped a fresh white monogrammed towel over his forearm in preparation to serve the patron.

"That won't be required."

John was confused.

The man walked to the exit as though to leave, his heavy soles clicking on the polished marble floor. Rather than exit the restroom, John heard the bolt click, locking them inside.

John was nervous, quickly looking for an item to defend himself with if necessary, eyeing the crystal vase. Roughs had robbed him in the past, desperate young louts who managed to evade the hotel doormen. John sensed this individual was of a different ilk.

"Quite the palace," the man said. "I lack the means required to lodge in such opulence." He reached into his coat. "Not on a—"

John moved toward the vase.

"—detective's salary," he finished, producing a shiny silver badge and holding it out for John to view. "Detective Porter. Toronto Police." He allowed John a moment to process, then said, "Mr. Boyd, I have a proposal to discuss with you."

John turned on the faucets, stepped backward, and prepared to hand the detective the towel after he had washed his hands.

Porter turned the faucets off. "Unnecessary. I slipped in unnoticed during the exchange with the previous patron. Haven't used your facilities but thank you nonetheless."

John nodded.

"Like I said, a proposal."

"Concerning?"

"First thing first. May I?"

"Certainly."

Porter helped himself to a small whitish-green mint from a silver dish on the countertop and placed it on his tongue. Working the candy around his mouth he said, "I admired the manner in which you dismissed the previous patron. The lodger 'looking for some action,' as he put it." Porter nodded in approval. "It refreshes me to know men of integrity—"

Before he could complete the sentence, someone rattled the door from outside the restroom, attempting to enter. Porter crossed to the door and shouted, "Out of service."

The muffled voice opposite whined, "Come on. I got to go."

"Find someplace else."

They heard a muffled curse as the frustrated patron departed.

"I have to perform my duty, detective," John said politely but firmly. "Please broach the subject to be discussed."

Detective Porter climbed into the leather armchair seat, indicating that John should sit on his stool. "The New York Chinese."

"What about it?" said John, sitting.

"Your friend, Miss Evans, is employed there."

John was startled. "Is Naomi well? Has something occurred?"

"She's fine."

Another patron attempted to enter the restroom. "Closed," Porter's stern voice echoed. The handle was yanked a few more times. "Place is busier than Union Station—"

"It's Wandle, isn't it?" John said.

"Yes." Porter tapped his chin. "What do you know of him?"

"He's the proprietor."

"Henry Woo informs me you've had words. Tommaso Esposito said Wandle practically assaulted you with his cane."

"Who?"

"Peanut vendor. Across the street?"

"Oh. I don't know him."

"Well, he remembers Wandle charging at you with a full head of—"

"True."

"I've had eyes all over the Chinese New York for months."

"For what purpose?"

"Place is a front."

"I know."

"I know you know. That's why I'm here. There's an old warrant for Wandle's arrest in Macon, Georgia, but I'll put him in cuffs before they ever do."

The detective explained in more detail that the gingham tablecloths, panelled mirrors, and chicken, beans, fish, and banana cream pie menu concealed the restaurant's true purpose. The premises were used to fence stolen property and sell illegal cigarettes out the rear door. A backroom contained an opium den. Wandle ran a gambling operation—dominoes, colourful fan-tan tables—and prostitutes in the city.

"What about those two constables—"

"Cross and Ogilvy. A disgrace. I'll see to them."

"So, what do you want from me? If I'm denied entry—"

"But not Miss Evans."

"I don't want her mixed up in all this."

"Nothing risky. Maybe she looks around his office. Inside a drawer or two. Sees what she can see. Tells you. You tell me. Easy."

"Not a good idea. Wandle's unpredictable."

"I can only ask." Detective Porter exhaled. "But if you agree, I'll assist you somehow when the future comes."

"Let me think on it," John said.

"I don't have to tell you how one hand washes the other." Detective Porter stood. "Thanks for the mint," he said before unlocking the restroom door to leave. "One more thing. Don't trust the hotel detective. He's on Wandle's payroll, but you probably already know that, too."

The popular light-opera singer Grace Von Studdiford was in Toronto to perform three shows at Shea's Theatre and was staying at the Grand. Like John, Von Studdiford was from Indiana. Their families had lived in the same town. When he knew her, she was still Grace Quivey. John's father worked for Mr. Quivey in his gasworks.

The black-and-white checkerboard floor in the foyer of the Grand gleamed. A sweeping dark-wood staircase with brass balustrades showcased the lobby. Tropical flowering plants and miniature palm trees grew from iron urns around the perimeter. Magnificent oil paintings in ornate gilt frames hung from wainscoted walls. Guests lounged in velvet armchairs and overstuffed chaise lounges by a fountain. A splendid eight-foot carved oak grandfather clock kept time as bellhops flitted about like moths. A portrait of Edward VII hung in a place of prominence above the front desk.

The voluptuous singer wore a sensational theatre hat topped with a mass of ostrich plumes. She stood by the register holding a cascading bouquet of flowers surrounded by her retinue, newspapermen, and admirers. Von Studdiford spotted John crossing the lobby and called to him. John stopped and turned. Everyone looked aghast when Von Studdiford acknowledged the restroom attendant by name.

"I'd recognize those eyes anywhere," Von Studdiford said pushing her way through the crowded lobby. "What are you doing here? This is my first time performing in Toronto." She studied his burgundy uniform, surprised. "You're a porter?"

He corrected her. "Restroom attendant."

Forgetting the swarm of people that pushed in around them, she asked, "When did you get here? Are you alone? Do you have someone? John, you were always so clever—"

Feeling put on the spot, John blurted, "I'm to be married."

"Lucky girl. What's her name?"

John looked at the white faces staring back. He stammered, "I'm— I'd—"

Von Studdiford interrupted, "You must attend my performance. I'll have two tickets sent."

A newspaperman piped, "To his office in the loo?" Everybody laughed. When his shift ended John discovered two tickets for that evening's performance on the tip tray.

John and Naomi meant to attend the Von Studdiford performance, but on the way to Shea's, they rescued a small grey owlet stranded in the middle of the car tracks at Adelaide and Yonge.

Rushed for time, John was still in his attendant's uniform. Naomi wore work clothing. The owlet was not much bigger than a sparrow. John went over and picked up the tiny bird. A boy selling chestnuts from a pushcart offered him a paper bag and after cutting air holes into it, he put the bird inside.

Instead of attending the theatre, they took the owlet to the Riverdale Zoo, arriving after the Winchester Street gate had been closed. On the walk there, John told Naomi about his conversation with Detective Porter. The zoo's superintendent, a man named Goode, resided with his family in a brick house on Winchester next to the gate. Goode's wife, Eleanor, answered the door. John and Naomi explained how they'd rescued the owlet from the busy street and placed it in the paper bag.

Eleanor said, "That was kind," and invited them to stay for supper. After the meal, the four Goode daughters, all under the age of ten, insisted on giving John and Naomi a private tour of the zoo. The girls took turns carrying the paper bag with the owlet inside. Before placing the chick in the aviary with other birds, they made a game of naming it.

John and Naomi stayed late and were invited back. It was the greatest night of their lives. Their rescue of the owlet, the accolades heaped upon them by the Goodes, and the invitation to return made John and Naomi feel closer to one another than ever before. It was their last supper together.

The next day, Wandle raped Naomi in his private office above the restaurant after catching her rifling through a filing cabinet.

After work, John waited for Naomi as usual by the gates at Osgoode Hall. She never arrived. Same thing the next day and the day after. Concerned, he visited her flat. Angela unlatched the door. In three years of courting, he had never been inside the apartment.

Angela pointed at a closed door. "In there." Before she went to put the kettle on, she added, "She should have gone to the Emergency Hospital."

John removed his cap and knelt at the foot of the bed. From under the covers, Naomi told him what happened.

He wept. "I'll murder him."

"No. Don't do anything."

"Then we'll go to the police."

"The police won't do anything."

"They'll horsewhip him."

"No, they won't."

Naomi sobbed into a pillow. Behind them, in the doorway, Angela blew on a cup of hot tea. "When they find out she's with you, they'll say she deserved it."

Before leaving, he removed the wilted camellia from his lapel and placed it on the nightstand.

In desperation, the bootblack considered approaching Constables Cross and Ogilvy but thought better of it. Instead, he went to Detective Headquarters to search for Porter.

Porter was in the first-floor foyer about to leave the building when John approached him. Requesting a moment of the detective's time, Porter directed him into an alcove for privacy. Certain no one was in earshot, John explained in a muted tone, "Wandle's done something despicable."

The detective remained expressionless. He took out his occurrence book, checked the time, and prepared to make an entry when John told him to put it away.

Porter folded his arms across his chest. "What's happened?"

John explained Naomi's recent experience in Wandle's private office above the restaurant. "She went up there for me as a favour for you and—"

A constable interrupted, tapping Detective Porter on the shoulder, seeking a signature on an official document.

John would not be deterred. "Detective, are you listening to me?"

"Yes. Of course. And there is indisputable evidence this occurred? Not only her word? It would be better if she could secure a witness."

"A witness?" John was growing indignant. "Why would she create such a claim if it weren't true?"

Porter retorted, "I know. It's just that according to the law—"

"At the least, do something. Anything. A word with Mr. Wandle, even."

"No. Things are at a sensitive juncture."

"Unbelievable. What about what you said about one hand washing the other? Then take her complaint to the Police Magistrate and let them decide," John pleaded.

"No. Absolutely not. Wandle gets the heads-up, and my entire investigation falls apart."

Incensed, John raged, "And you don't care about anything else?"

Porter glanced around the foyer, instructing John to lower his voice. "I'll take care of the matter. Now, don't do anything rash. Understand me?"

"Take care of the matter? Do you understand me? He raped her."

"I said I'll take care of it, and I will."

In six years, John had never missed a day of work, but instead of the restroom, John stayed home. He took down the bottle of Scotch and finished it, then walked from his room to the New York Chinese. Out of his uniform in blue denim overalls, a flannel shirt, and a dark jacket, he went unnoticed by waitstaff serving the lunch crowd. He scanned the dining room. Henry Woo approached.

"Where's Wandle?" John demanded.

"In the back. In the kitchen."

John glanced at the kitchen entrance covered by a damask curtain.

"You can't go in there."

John stepped around Woo, his expression determined, and started toward the kitchen.

Woo went after him. "What are you going to do?"

"Talk."

Woo pleaded, "Mr. Wandle doesn't talk. You should leave." But John didn't.

Moments later, diners looked up from their dishes at the sound of raised voices in the kitchen. Patrons gasped when John suddenly pinwheeled backward into the dining room, pulling down the rod and curtain from the top rail above the frame. Wandle struck John repeatedly with his cane. A gash opened under his eye. Outside on the pavement, John fell to his knees, protecting his head with his arms as Wandle hit him mercilessly.

When John returned two hours later, the lunch crowd was gone. His face was bloodied and bruised and one eye terribly swollen. A stairway led to Wandle's second-floor office at the end of a poorly lit hall. The office was off limits to everyone, including Jenny. John entered without knocking.

The windowless room was cluttered, the air fusty. An unmade cot in the corner was heaped with soiled bedding. Wandle looked up from behind the desk. "Well, I declare." He stood, hands on his hips, flabbergasted, then reached for his cane. "If I didn't know better, I'd suppose you were stronger than an acre of garlic." He dismissed John with a limp wave of his hand in the direction of the partially opened door. "Boy, get along."

John turned toward the entrance. Wandle snickered. Instead of departing, John closed the door. "I cannot abide you."

Wandle grinned. "Are you serious, boy?"

John removed a pistol from inside his coat and shot Wandle. The restaurateur recoiled. John pulled the trigger again, the second bullet striking the centre of Wandle's chest. Wandle collapsed, kicking over a chair. He writhed in a spill of blood. His spine arched. John went around the desk and a third bullet passed through Wandle's throat, embedding itself in the hardwood floor. Wandle's body tensed, spasmed, became slack, then dead still.

The office was smoky. John released the magazine. Unused bullets clinked to the floor. He slipped the pistol into his pocket and walked toward excited voices at the bottom of the staircase.

"I'm coming down. The gun is not loaded."

John Boyd exited the New York Chinese unmolested. He sat on the curbstone, set the unloaded gun on the pavement beside him, closed his eyes, and put his face in his hands.

Policemen arrived. John was placed under arrest. He made no resistance. People gawked at the bootblack, handcuffed at his back. Constable Cross stood over John. Constable Ogilvy stood beside him.

In a few minutes, Detective Porter shoved his way through the crowd and approached John. Constable Cross blocked his way. Porter jammed his finger into the constable's chest. "Back off!"

Porter held up his badge before Cross could go for his baton. "Dare you," Porter snarled.

Cross backed down. Porter leaned in, whispering in the constable's ear, "You and Ogilvy are through."

The detective knelt and sat beside John. "I said, don't do anything rash and what did you do?"

John glared at Porter. "Shot him in the arm. Shot him in the chest. Shot him in the throat," the bootblack hissed. "And I'd do it again."

"Why? Why would you do such a thing?"

"Because of what he did to my Naomi." He paused and looked around. "I am unapologetic."

"You appoint yourself judge, jury, and executioner? This was my case. I follow a process."

"I'm sure you do."

John was transported to Agnes Street Station No.2, booked, fingerprinted, and photographed.

The trial of John Boyd lasted two days. Thomas Robinette K.C. failed to convince a jury John acted in self-defence. The judge ignored their strong plea for mercy and sentenced him to death. As the day of execution approached, workers moved the gallows from the exercise yard and permanently installed them in a former second-floor restroom.

On a cold January morning, they came for John and escorted him a few steps to the converted restroom. He wore patent leather shoes and a grey suit.

Detective Porter stood in the corridor.

A noose was dropped over John's head and with a few quick jerks tightened around his neck. John closed his eyes and imagined a white camellia in his lapel buttonhole, marble columns, brass faucets, and the scent of polish oil. From next door came the sound of the D'Alessandro's Orchestra performing "You're the Flower of My Heart."

John whistled and the walls whistled back.

George Porter couldn't bear it. He covered his ears.

SETTLEMENT HOUSE

Susan arranged the table in the drawing room of her home in preparation for another small afternoon tea, filling a Burmese vase on a centre of white silk with a mass of deep red Richmond roses. Her guests, Mrs. Edna Simpson of Sherbourne Street and Mrs. Mary Miles of King Street East, were not expected for another hour. Like the Porters, the Simpsons and the Miles were congregants of St. Christopher's

Presbyterian, and like Susan, Edna, and Mary volunteered at the settlement house operated by the church to provide services for several classes of foreigners. Mary volunteered as a creche worker. Edna provided lessons in the household sciences. Susan taught Women's English on Tuesday evenings for one hour, commencing at seven o'clock.

Beatrice, Ted, and Teddy attended St. Christopher's sporadically. Many years ago, George wanted to cease attending Sunday services entirely, but Susan insisted, so he went to placate his wife.

———

It was the second last day of the Exhibition and George, who had an infrequent day off, had agreed to put aside his preference to shun crowds on condition that they visit the Innovations building to view the "The Camera as a Detective" exhibit presented by Scotland Yard. He wanted to learn more about the incredible potential of coloured photography to aid in crime detection and pictures dealing with forged bank notes. The exhibit contained objects of interest, including the latest apparatus required for lifting fingerprints, burglary tools displayed in a glass case, and the infamous two-bladed, white-handled pocketknife connected to the unsolved Whitehall Mystery from years ago.

Porter also hoped to make the acquaintance of Detective Drew of the Yard, who was overseeing the agency's exhibit. Susan hoped to meet up with Teddy, who she saw infrequently now that he travelled so much as a piano tuner for the Morris Piano Co. Teddy was attending the exhibition on behalf of his employers, who were exhibiting in the Manufacturing Hall. His hammer, forks, and felts at the ready, he spent his days in the beautifully appointed recital room.

The Porters were due to set off when word arrived of a slaying in the city. George was furious that the chief inspector wanted him to be the lead detective on the case. A Macedonian had allegedly axed a countryman to death in a boarding house crammed with numerous other non-English speakers.

"There aren't enough interpreters as it is. And now a houseful of foreigners must be interrogated? God damn it—" George ranted to Susan as she tied his silk cravat around his neck.

"George! Don't be so impertinent."

"Sorry. It's frustrating. I know for a fact the force has only a single Macedonian interpreter on contract, and if say he's not available, then what?"

"I understand, George. But there's always a solution—"

"Like what?" George snapped.

Ignoring his abruptness, she helped him with his coat and, handing him his hat, said, "Here's a suggestion. Contact Professor Petre Ivanov at the University of Toronto."

"How are you familiar with him?" George inquired.

"From St. Christopher Settlement House."

George's expression remained blank.

"Where I volunteer?"

"Oh. Of course."

"Professor Ivanov teaches Men's English in the classroom across the hall from mine. He's fluent in several languages. If able, he will assist. I'm sure of it."

At day's end, Susan couldn't wait to share with George what she and Teddy got up to at the Exhibition. She'd ridden a rollercoaster and tasted a red-hot for the first time. The goldfish Teddy had won for her at the shooting gallery swam lazily in a bowl on the kitchen table. She wasn't surprised when George arrived home late. As he breezed silently past her in the parlour, she asked, "Did the professor work out?"

"Yes. He was a great aid in getting the witness's statement filed. He was a fourteen-year-old boy, with almost no English. If I had one complaint, it's that the apostrophe key sticks on my typewriter."

"What?"

"Nothing. I'm going to speak to the inspector about retaining the professor's services."

Susan was about to tell him about the goldfish and Teddy's accuracy with a gun but George was already tramping downstairs, files in hand.

"Goodnight," he called back.

HONEY FOR ANDREJ

My English not good. Professor Ivanov tells me begin with name and how old and where live. The detective will use typewriter to put my words on paper. His name Detective Porter. I am MARKO NIKOLOVA. I am 14 years. I live at 16 Eastern Avenue. I come here from Macedonia. It is small house. There is kitchen. There is 2 rooms. One is for sleep. Bunks there are for me and 9 men from same village. They are Vani Simoff, Kale Miceff, Pavel Stefoff, Vanas Tipeff, Flipp Miceff, Jodor Trocanoff, Andrej Imeri, Done Stefoff, Thiesto Miceff. My English better than those men but Vani English best. Everything I see happen in morning from hide in coop behind house. There I smoke cigarettes with pigeons. Vani say cigarette bad for me but I don t care. I hate work at Dominion Brewery. All men in house arrested because Pavel kill Vani. We no kill Vani. Pavel kill Vani. I say I work at brewery, yes? Detective Porter say tell him what I see will be for the court. This easy. I see this. I see Pavel kill Vani. First, he choke him. Then kill with axe. So much blood. This Detective Porter say to tell more. So I tell everything what happen. First, today I no go to work in morning. I see Pavel and Vani talk. They get loud. Then talk more. Vani was good. He says we are brothers. But too many in house. House too small. We no fight because Vani. When I finish cigarette, through hole in wall I see Pavel hit Vani on head with axe. First, he chokes. I cover mouth so make no noise. Oh no I say, oh no. Pigeons fly around coop. Oh no I say but I am quiet all the time. I know I do nothing. I should do something, right? This bad for Vani. There is blood. Before this happen, Vani stop at store for honey. Beekist Pure Honey the most perfect of all food. I read labels for make English better. 15 cents for jar. Vani said we need learn English better. Others no learn English. I learn English. We all arrested. You know, 15 cents is lot of money. Detective Porter say me to start from beginning so I do. For 1 week Vani work night clean ash pits at roundhouse. Before come home in morning, he say to Pavel he go to greengrocer for honey. This word greengrocer is funny to my ear. From greengrocer Vani buy honey for Andrej. Andrej Imeri. He live here. Already I tell this? Andrej cannot drink mountain tea he need to stop pain in stomach without honey. I like Andrej. He play mandolin. Sad music he play make me think home. I miss. Andrej teach me how play Tablanet game from Macedonia like men in village play. Andrej should go to doctor. Doctor so much money. Too much money. Andrej go still to work with pain in stomach. Other workers hide him. He need go back to village. We save the money for this. Every time we save more money for this to send Andrej back to village. Pavel he no save the money. He work not too much. Vani smart and English good so he keep money for Andrej to go back. 140 dollars saved for Andrej. So much money. Vani hide on belt. He say he guard with life. It is morning when I hear Vani come home, it is 7 o clock. I hear door key in morning. I know 7 o clock whistle make at Sunlight Soap across river. I be at work but not go. I go be with pigeons to smoke. We keep pigeon for egg to eat. Everyone work today. Vani and Pavel only here. Pavel beside stove in middle of kitchen wait for Vani. I take newspaper from in hole to stop cold from go inside house. I see Vani in kitchen put lunch pail on table. His face is with ash from corner of eyes. He say Pavel why no work? You talk Dimitrij at Sunlight Soap? I tell you

HONEY FOR ANDREJ

about Dimitrij? He from village near us too. They need worker. Pavel walk around kitchen say he want to go home to village. He miss village. Vani say English speak English Pavel you no learn if you no speak. It is dark in kitchen but light come in window. Kitchen is so dirty. I see Pavel lean over on back of chair by table then Vani open lunch pail say sorry brother I want you for try English to learn. He get jar of honey out of lunch pail he look happy, say look Pavel for Andrej. Honey for Andrej. He hold jar. Pavel see. Vani open honey. He say Andrej like. It is good. They look long time at each other. Pavel look sad. He try English not good he say Vani I no like here. Vani say it get better. We move. You see. Vani puts hand on here, on this part, chest, yes? I see belt money under shirt. Pavel see too. Pavel say loud he no like here. He say other things loud I no understand. Vani smiles say you no like city, okay no like city. Vani say about honey, we take little? With tea? He say Pavel put on the kettle. We take honey in tea. A little. Andrej no mind we take little honey in tea, yes? He call Pavel brother. Vani get two cup on shelf. Pavel say he miss home. Vani say he miss home too but live here now. Pavel face change. Get mad. Pigeons fly around. Vani no see Pavel behind him. He choke Vani. Vani fall on back on floor arms like this out. Pavel with axe under stove hit Vani. Ax go in Vani s head. His face. His head. His head. His face. His face. Pavel do again. Again. Again. He so mad. Oh no, I say. Oh no. Honey fall on floor. I see Pavel beside Vani no move. Pavel open Vani shirt. Open pants. Go in pocket. Blood and honey everywhere. I think help Vani but I no do. I no do. I see through hole Pavel take money for Andrej to go home. He put in pocket. He wash in sink to get blood off with coal oil. I smell. I put newspaper in hole. Pavel hear me I think. He go to front door. I think, he come to coop? It all over in 2 minutes. I run to Mr. Baily across street. Tell him what see. Police come. We go to station. Pavel lie. He say he come home from work and Vani dead. I tell the detective this story I see. Pavel lie. Detective Porter say him to explain blood on pants. He can t. Vani has wife. He has child 2 years. Here Pavel hang for kill Vani, yes?

REVIVAL

"I think your goldfish is sick," Beatrice said, peering into the bowl. Its tail fin appeared shredded, and its dorsal fin collapsed. "Look," she pointed, "There's mottled green spots on its scales." She flicked the water's surface, momentarily startling the pathetic goldfish to life.

"We mustn't mention this to Teddy." Observing the bowl over her sister-in-law's shoulder, Susan added, "He won it for me at the shooting gallery at the CNE."

"He's twenty-nine, Sue. He's able to handle it."

"Yes. Of course. I know. It's just that he was thrilled by the win and insisted I select his prize."

Susan fetched the yellow- and black-striped tin of Justrite fish food from the cupboard, crushed a wafer between her fingers, and sprinkled flakes into the water. "Maybe all he needs is nourishment."

The women stared into the fishbowl, watching for movement, but saw none.

"My afternoon with Teddy made me realize the pointlessness of all of what I do."

"Nonsense," said Beatrice. "You have volunteer work. George. He loves you. Teddy adores you. You maintain a lovely home. Look around. Most employ a hired girl. Not you. This fine home, this accomplishment, is all yours alone. George appreciates how you take care of him, give him a good home, so he can do his job well. He even boasted to me the other day how you helped him to obtain a witness statement."

Putting a teapot on the table, she sighed. "My life's sole purpose sometimes feels like keeping the Mazawattee Tea Company in the black," Susan confessed. "I used to be so much more." She poured the tea into two pretty cups. "If I compare my life to yours . . . I've never worn trousers or ridden a bicycle or been to Europe, and you, you've done everything!"

"Absurd," Beatrice said, taking a macaroon from a dish on the counter.

"Is it? You're one of those 'New Women.' Work. Raise a child. Marriage. Your stories appear in *Saturday Night*—"
"Only a few stories," Beatrice corrected.
"Only?"

Before retiring for the night, Susan checked on the goldfish, who appeared to have experienced a revival.

George, arriving late as usual, placed his hat on the hat rack and asked, "How was your visit with Beatrice?"

"The usual. She is quite the *raconteuse*."

"That she is."

"You know, George, none of my acquaintances ever ask about my life and me."

George checked all the doors and windows to be sure they were locked.

He changed into sleep clothes. She put on a nightgown. They turned down the bed and lay side by side. "George?"

"Yes?" George yawned.

"I've decided. I'd like to take an evening class. I'd like to discover other things that interest me." She paused for a moment. "George?"

George was asleep.

Before dimming the gas lamp, Susan sat up, got out of bed, put on slippers and a robe, and went downstairs into the drawing room to check on the goldfish again, swimming in slow circles.

A soft blade of yellow light emitted from a St. Patrick's Street gas lamp sliced through a small opening in the window curtains, reflecting off the fish globe and flickering a magical pattern on the ceiling.

"You're fine," she said out loud to the dark. "And why wouldn't you be?"

THE LUCKY COIN

P. Ventricini, 1910

He learned the only English he would ever speak in the dank confines of the lower deck of the overcrowded SS *Royal George*, destination Montreal, Quebec. Port of calls included Rome, Marseille, Valencia, Lisbon. The passage was stormy. The Mediterranean Sea ran dangerously high. The steamship coaled in Liverpool before commencing the ocean crossing. Heavy weather was encountered on the Atlantic.

Fourth-class passenger Pasquale Ventricini, a distinguished man with a handlebar moustache, suffered terrible seasickness. He remained uncomfortably in the corner of his bunk during much of the voyage, a discarded tobacco tin permanently held below his chin. Between retching, he befriended Ringo, a resourceful, mussy-haired fourteen-year-old from a village outside of Naples. Ventricini, travelling alone, shared the ill-smelling berth with Ringo, Ringo's family—momma, papa, four sisters, three brothers—and some caged fowl, a goat, and a dozen suspicious individuals Ringo referred to as cousins. Ringo was the eldest among his siblings. Foul weather for much of the crossing forced them to remain below deck. Momma knitted and tended to her brood. Papa napped in a hammock. He'd periodically grunt himself awake, fart, sip from a flask, and resume sleeping.

A week into the sea voyage, Ventricini threw up on the goat. Since boyhood, he has suffered periodic seizures. Roiling seas, frequent vomiting, and fatigue now triggered the condition. When a fit passed, and he came around, he was confused, unaware of his surroundings.

Ventricini apologized, "*Scusami.*" He wiped stringy bile from his chin.

"What is wrong with you, old man?" Ringo asked in Italian from his bunk. "Kicking. Flapping like a fish. Foam in your mouth. You scared my little brothers and my little sisters. My cousins say you are cursed. You are like Jonah, they say. I stopped them from throwing you overboard."

Ventricini apologized again. "Excuse me. I have never been on the ocean."

Ringo sat up and swung his feet over the edge of the bunk. "Look around. None of us have. Fifteen hundred passengers. Only you vomit on our goat."

Papa opened one eye, muttered something, and handed Ringo a flask to offer Ventricini.

Ventricini waved it away. "Spirits make it worse. They make me violent."

Momma rooted through a crate, prepared something, and handed Ringo a sticky glob resembling brown rice and honey on a long, wooden spoon. He offered it to Ventricini. "Here. Eat. Momma says it settles the stomach."

Ventricini hesitated, reaching for the utensil. "What is it?"

Ringo shrugged. "Who cares? Just take it."

Nothing remedied his nausea. In the artificial light of the berth, Ventricini's pallor resembled dull copper. The ship's surgeon was sent for but failed to appear. With no portholes in steerage, the stench was unbearable.

When Ventricini threw up on Ringo's little brother, Ringo said, "Enough."

Weakened, Ventricini gathered himself and prepared to leave the berth. "I'll go to the companionway. Stay there."

Ringo nodded, "In this weather? Okay. But you will die."

Ringo thought a moment, tapping his index finger against his smooth chin. "Wait. You need a distraction." Glancing at Momma nesting in her lower bunk, children clustered around her like fledglings, he asked Ventricini, "Do you knit?"

Ventricini sighed. "No."

Ringo went on tapping his chin. "Hmm . . ."

Ventricini brightened, "I draw."

"Do you have charcoal and a sketch pad?"

"No sketch. But I have book." He produced a blue, hardback book resembling a Bible from inside the haversack.

Ringo's eyes widened. "A story of adventure? Read to my little brothers and sisters. It will take their minds off the sickness. Hold it up. Read the title." Ringo's siblings watched in earnest. The cousins were uninterested. "Ignore my cousins," he muttered. "They're stupid, from another village."

Ventricini smiled a little for the first time since boarding in Rome. Positioned close to the electric light, the coal-dark eyes of Ringo's siblings watched him excitedly. Ventricini cleared his throat before reading the title aloud, "Italian Code of Criminal Procedure—"

Ringo leaped at Ventricini, snatched the book from his hand, and studied the cover. "*This* is the book you want to read to my brothers and sisters? We will all vomit. From boredom." He tossed the heavy book, striking a cousin in the head. "Why did you bring this book?"

Ventricini stammered, "It's my work."

"You are a lawyer?"

Ventricini felt woozy. "No. Carabinieri."

"You? A policeman? No."

Ventricini nodded. "Yes. I will be in Canada, too."

"In Canada? In Canada you are nothing. How will you be police?"

THE LUCKY COIN

"I will show them my book. I will be carabinieri."

"You even speak English?"

The ship rolled over a swell. Papa farted. Ventricini leaned forward and threw up in the tobacco tin. "Heh," Ringo exclaimed. "I know. *I will teach you English.*"

Ventricini gazed over the rim of the tobacco tin. "Yes?"

"For one lira, I will teach you the most important English."

Ventricini grinned. "Yes. You speak English?"

"Yes. I will teach you the one sentence to make the Canadians happy."

"What is the sentence?"

"What is your name?" Ringo said in English.

"That is the sentence?"

"No. We call you Jonah, but what is your real name?"

Ventricini leaned back in his bunk. "Oh. My name?"

"Yes."

Ventricini placed the tobacco tin on his lap, "Pasquale Ventricini."

Ringo nodded, then said in English, "Hello, my name is Pasquale Ventricini."

Lessons commenced. Over the next few days, Ventricini's nausea passed. Momma fed him. His strength returned. The fits ceased. Pasquale Ventricini mastered the only English he would ever speak with the North American coastline in sight. Before disembarking, as promised, Ventricini offered Ringo a one-lira coin.

"What is this?"

"One lira. I promised. You helped me."

Ringo stared at the tarnished coin on his open palm for a long time. "You know, Momma said you are not cursed. You just have bad luck." He returned the coins to Ventricini. "In Canada, these are worthless. You keep them."

Ventricini smiled. "Thank you. I will keep them. And remember you. A memento."

"No. Keep it for good luck. Momma says you need it."

SS *Royal George* dropped anchor in Montreal harbour. The ship's iron door opened. The gangway was lowered. The port bustled. Dockside, haversack slung over his shoulder, Ventricini fell to his knees and kissed the hard ground, declaring in perfect English, "Hello, my name is Pasquale Ventricini."

———•••———

As Ringo had guessed, Ventricini did not become a policeman. He lodged in an Italian boarding house on Manning Avenue and found work as a brick mason—an occupation he loathed—after taking a crowded westbound passenger train to Toronto. Life was hard, and Ventricini was unhappy without his family.

He had a smithy punch a hole through his lucky coin, strung it on a leather cord, and wore it on his neck.

At times, particularly in the evenings or during the unbroken stillness of the night, he grappled with a deep sense of loneliness. He would lie on his cot in the crowded lodgings he shared with others like himself, herded together in sleep, staring into the soiled darkness of the room, the air thickened by the scent of moist washrags, boiled garlic, and cabbage.

Without disturbing his housemates, he'd remove the blue, hard-backed copy of the *Italian Code of Criminal Procedure* stowed in a footlocker under his cot, strike a match to light the stubby remains of a candlestick and, as pale shadows flickered across the sagging lath and plaster ceiling, thumb the pages to where he tucked away a frayed, black-and-white photographic portrait of his beloved Carolina. As a tide of emptiness washed over him, he closed the heavy tome and blew out the candle, thinking maybe it had been a big mistake to come here.

Some nights he skulked the empty streets around his boarding house. The black blanket of sky awash in brilliant stars was the single feature he learned to cherish in his adopted country.

Once, he trailed behind a lone constable, young and handsome, on his beat through the quiet neighbourhood. Ventricini concealed himself in doorways, behind a mailbox, crouching by an iron bench, and hiding behind a hedge. It felt dangerous, but he did it anyway.

Walking on the inside of the pavement near the storefronts,

similar to the training Ventricini once received, the lynx-eyed policeman remained unaware of his pursuer.

Stealthily observing the patrolling sentry casually twirl his baton and rattle locks to confirm they were secure, Ventricini was reminded of his former life and, growing overwrought, began mimicking the policeman's gait to improve his spirit. The constable turned unexpectedly and glimpsed Ventricini ducking behind a horse fountain and dropping to the ground.

The fearless constable investigated what Ventricini was up to. When the foreigner muttered several times in pathetic English, "My name is Pasquale Ventricini," the copper assumed he was tipsy and asked, "Did you fall down?" He reached toward Ventricini. "Let me help you up."

"*Grazie.*"

Three years passed without Ventricini seeing his boy and his girl and he worried they wouldn't know him. He had saved enough money for Carolina and their two children to journey to Canada, and stopped at St. Peter's Church every chance he could, begging St. Christopher for their safe passage. Worry evaporated, along with his loneliness, the instant they were reunited on Platform No. 5 at Union Depot. Taking Carolina up in his arms, he kissed her and exclaimed, "Hello, my name is Pasquale Ventricini."

Carolina was impressed. She looked at her husband and exclaimed in Italian to their travel-weary children, "Papa speaks English!"

Ventricini caught both up in his arms and spun in a circle, repeating, "Hello, my name is Pasquale Ventricini."

Carolina asked, "Signor Ventricini, do you know more English?"

Ventricini twisted the tip of his well-groomed moustache, smirked, and said, "No." It was funny. Everyone laughed. Ventricini took them home to their new lodgings, a larger room on Clinton Street.

For the first time in ages, surrounded by his family, Ventricini felt like himself again. The children enrolled in school and quickly picked up English. He formed friendships with his Italian coworkers, and as his skills improved, he grew to like his job. Carolina worked at a shirt factory. The family attended mass at St. Peter's and watched baseball clubs compete at Bickford Park.

A special outing for the Ventricinis included boarding the *Luella* at the foot of Bay Street on a run across the bay to Island Park or Hanlan's Point Amusement Grounds, admission five cents.

When the sun came out strong, they passed entire Sundays on the island, picnicking and walking the pebbly Lake Ontario shoreline. A favourite spectacle in the Amusement Grounds was Professor Herbert's Dog Circus, where a small, clever canine ran up a vertical ladder forty feet high and dived into a blanket. The children loved the Japanese acrobats and the Hurgle Gurgle slide.

In the early evening, as the stars were turning on, the family, exhausted from a full day, leaned on the rail on the top deck of *Luella*, watching the city come into view. Ventricini's daughter tugged the collar of her blouse, attempting to lick clean a stain left there from the frozen custard she had earlier, absentmindedly asking her father, "Can we get a dog?"

"*Italiano!*"

"*Possiamo prendere un cane?*"

"*No.*"

Ventricini's son interrupted, pointing over the rail and asking in Italian, "What is that unusual star?"

Everyone in the city had been discussing the appearance of a peculiar celestial object in the night sky lately. Ventricini studied the whitish-yellow anomaly and shrugged. "Just a star."

"But it has a tail."

"*Italiano!*"

"*Ma ha una coda.*"

Carolina clicked her tongue, shook her head. "It's a bad omen."

Ventricini dismissed her with a wave of his hand. "*Uffa.*"

The streetcar ride home wasn't long, but the pitch and sway of the trolley lulled Ventricini's daughter to sleep. At their stop, he carried her the remainder of the way, head resting on his shoulder. Before the family rounded the corner onto their street, they saw a patch of sky glowing with angry orange intensity. They encountered a commotion outside a clothing store, ablaze. The intense heat pushed the large crowd of spectators back off the sidewalk and onto the road. The sizeable shop windowpane shattered. Flames licked out of the opening, choking black smoke issuing from upper windows.

Ventricini hurriedly passed their daughter to Carolina and, followed by his son, pushed his way through the throng. A half-suffocated woman in tattered clothing stumbled outside toward a police constable ordering the crowd to move further back. Between coughing fits, she pounded her chest and gasped, "My children. They're inside."

The policeman's eyes widened. "How many?"

"Nine."

Ventricini asked his son, "What did the lady say?"

"She said her kids are *inside*, and the policeman asked *how many*, and she said *nine*."

Ventricini put his hands on his head. "*Nove? Mamma mia.*" In the next second he was charging inside the burning building, the constable in pursuit.

Caroline shoved forward with her daughter in her arms until she reached her son. "Where is your father?"

"In there. He ran inside. And then the policeman ran after him."

Carolina slapped her forehead. "Madonna!"

Fire reels arrived. The flames were doused.

A total of twelve—nine children and three adult boarders—had narrow escapes from death that evening thanks to the heroism of Pasquale Ventricini and the constable.

Ventricini sat panting on the curbstone, his children crowded around him, gathering his breath. Wiping his blackened soot-covered face and singed moustache with Caroline's scarf, he kissed the lucky coin around his neck, tussled his son's hair, and smiled at his wife. "*Vedi, buona fortuna.*"

Life improved even more for Ventricini when his friend Raffaele Di Fabbio arrived in Toronto from their village in Italy. Ventricini and Di

Fabbio had been close, almost like brothers growing up. Ventricini got him a job with his employer. Di Fabbio sent money home, anticipating the day his family arrived. Ventricini helped his friend when he could, remembering his loneliness upon arriving. Di Fabbio visited his friend's home often and the Ventricini children called him Zio Raffa.

The city contracted Ventricini's employer to enlarge the monkey house at Riverdale Zoo. The zoo received some chimpanzees, a yellow baboon, and a black ape named King William, requiring additional space. The larger enclosure opposite the alligator tank would also house colourful macaws and parrots, and include a big tree.

Bored chimpanzees in the crowded enclosure sat on their haunches, grooming one another, indifferent to the brick masons in faded monkey jackets over bulky coveralls installing the block foundation of their future home a short distance away. King William watched the workmen with suspicion, a mass of hair around his face and a mouthful of awful teeth.

The unusual object in the night sky continued to create a stir in the city. Digging a trench, Ventricini asked Di Fabbio, "What is that star with a tail I see at night? Carolina said it is a bad omen."

Di Fabbio stopped and leaned on his shovel. "I do not know. I heard the English foreman call it a shooting star, I think."

"What is the name they call it?"

"Halley."

While they spoke, the crowd of patrons gawking at primates turned to gawk at the Italian workmen speaking in their southern dialect. Ventricini waved to them, shouted happily in a singsong voice, "Hello, my name is Pasquale Ventricini."

The two friends laughed. A macaw squawked. The crowd dispersed. King William threw shit everywhere. The brick masons resumed shovelling.

After work, both Ventricini and Di Fabbio joined several workmates at a College Street taphouse. Ventricini intended to remain only a short time, but he staggered toward home with the others hours later. They stopped to search the starry sky for the celestial body talked of so much lately. Ventricini was behind Tony, a man with a scarred face. Clustered beneath a streetlamp, Ventricini slurred, "Too much light. We go there." He pointed down a dark alleyway. Drunk and almost senseless, he lost his footing and stumbled into Tony, who attempted to right his drinking companion.

"Don't touch me." Ventricini flung an arm over Tony's shoulder. He pointed upward. "I know what the English call it."

Tony pushed Ventricini's arm away. "Call what?"

"What do you think? Your sister's—"

Tony slapped Ventricini playfully on the arm. "Don't talk about my sister."

Ventricini slurred through gritted teeth, "I talk about whoever."

Tony pushed Ventricini, sending him pinwheeling backward. Tony was angered but maintained his temper. He shouted, "We are drunk. I won't cut out your tongue. But don't speak of my sister."

Ventricini got to his feet and charged Tony. Tony punched Ventricini in the chest. The former policeman cuffed Tony in the side of his head before falling to the ground. A brawl ensued. A knife dropped to the pavement. Men shoved and hollered profanities at one another. Bottles broke.

A kick in the mouth. Ventricini stiffened. His jaw clenched. Comet-speed fury electrified his hot brain. Confusion. He entered a quiet, violent dream and f l o a t e d.

Corpo. The word ricocheted inside his head. Nothing. Makes sense. Stringy currents. Underwater terror. Black. Out.

Di Fabbio recognized Ventricini's distress and pulled men off his friend. He knelt, shouted, "Give him space."

A blade. A flash. Thrust. Pin sharp pain through Di Fabbio's heart.

When Ventricini came around, he was under a bed. The room smelled of shit. Ventricini had soiled his trousers. His mouth tasted of blood, and his shirt was torn. Detective Cuddy hauled him by the shoulders out from under the bed. The only light came from the hallway where Detective Porter stood, jotting notes and sketching. Constables linking arms held back a hysterical crowd attempting to push their way into the messy bedroom. Terrified children in nightclothes huddled on springy beds. A sobbing old woman in a colourful shawl gripping a rosary crossed herself and rocked back and forth on a hard chair.

Porter placed him in bracelets. Ventricini felt woozy. He tried to focus, looking deep into the detective's eyes as he mumbled, "My name is Pasquale Ventricini."

Detective Porter replied, "Pasquale Ventricini, I am arresting you."

Ventricini vomited.

Commotion in the stairwell. Carolina pushed her way in through the crowd. Someone shouted in broken English, "She is the wife of him."

Detective Porter ordered, "Let her pass."

Ventricini stared vacantly at Carolina, a face he recognized. He squeezed Ringo's coin strung around his neck and, gazing around the bedroom, asked his wife, "Where is this?"

Carolina fell against her husband's bloody chest. She wept. "Fabbio was stabbed dead."

"Dead? How? By who?"

She covered her mouth, "You."

BADGE

"You know, Signore Bruno, observing how deft you are at your *business* back here, I ask myself, is he an exterminator who serves as a court-appointed interpreter or a court interpreter who exterminates dogs and cats," said Detective Porter, standing in the doorway.

Bruno whistled, casually preparing to dispatch another dog in the lethal chamber.

"Isn't that the same thing?" he said, bunching the sleeves of his soiled white laboratory coat up to his elbows.

"I don't believe so."

"And please, Detective, call me Mike," the tall, slim, congenial man said over his shoulder as he hauled a yelping cocker spaniel by the scruff of the neck from the dog catcher's wicker basket, placing the canine in the device's wire cage. "We've known each other long enough, eh?"

In addition to operating the lethal chamber installed off the alleyway in a repurposed brick bicycle shed at the rear of No.2 police station, Bruno provided interpretation services for non-English speaking Italians who appeared before Magistrate Denison in Police Court.

The Detective Force depended on Signore Bruno's services during interrogations, as did the Crown in court proceedings.

Before he settled in the city decades ago, Michele Bruno belonged to a troupe that travelled Europe with a maul of performing bears. Quitting that, he came to North America to work for Barnum's Circus as an animal trainer until one of the big cats nearly bit him in two.

While mending from the incident, he came to Toronto, eventually finding work as a court-appointed interpreter.

As the former method of dispatching worthless, aged, ownerless, or vicious dogs and cats fell out of favour with the public, the Humane Society petitioned for the installation of a lethal chamber at the Agnes Street station. Bruno, versed in the temperament of animals, was a natural fit for the role, and truthfully, nobody else wanted the task.

Bruno latched the lid securely and pulled a mechanism that lowered the cage into an airtight compartment. In the sudden darkness, the panicked canine scratched violently on the chamber's smooth, seamless interior in a pointless attempt at escape.

The exterminator slipped on thick, elbow-length rubber gloves. Before he pulled down a cumbersome respirator over his face, he directed Detective Porter, "Move back. More. Go outside, but don't close the sliding doors. The chamber leaks a little. And watch for caca, too. There's shit everywhere back there."

The detective followed Bruno's recommendation and surveilled the process from outside through the open panel doors. The afternoon air was still, the milky blue sky interrupted here and there by gauzy ribbons of clouds. A dishevelled rag-and-bones man passed in the alley, his rig pulled by a ramshackle old nag. Porter, moved to recreate the scene with a charcoal pencil, produced a small square sketching pad from an inside pocket. He heard a hissing sound as Bruno released a chloroform spray into the chamber, entering the polished steel enclosure through a red hose to render the mongrel unconscious.

The yelping, scampering, pawing frenzy gradually ceased.

Next, Bruno turned a toggle, generating the gas mixture in a steel retort from a pasty chalk and water mixture that combined with sulphuric acid to produce fatal fumes.

As Porter sketched, he noticed a slatted wooden crate containing cats and a lid held down with a brick on a bench beside the door. Paws jutted through the openings, swatting madly; distressed meows filled the air.

Porter removed the brick, lifted the lid slightly, and peeked inside. Behind him, a mangy, black-and-white fox terrier with lesions on its snout tied to a post lay in the dirt and whined, unambitiously chewing the discarded leather sole of a shoe. Beside it, a critter concealed inside a cinched canvas sack struggled hopelessly to find a way out.

In a few minutes, Bruno removed the scratchy respirator and the rubber gloves. Trailed by a wafting chemical scent, he joined the detective outside. Before he lit an Old Chum cigarette, he offered one to Porter.

"No. Thanks."

"You okay? You look off."

"Just my back." Detective Porter studied the canvas sack flopping around in the dirt. "What's in that?"

"I don't know. A puppy. Or a kitten. A raccoon, even. What the catcher shows up with makes no difference to me. I make the same sixty-five cents for whatever I dispatch."

"How much do you get paid for your interpreting services?"

"A dollar a case."

"That answers it, then."

"Answers what?"

"You're the latter."

Bruno, confused, spit a shred of tobacco leaf off his tongue and said, "So, Detective, what can I help you with? Not to rush you, but at least half a dozen cats are in that crate and must be finished individually. They're a chore. They get wild."

"I notice something. When you're at that," Porter nudged his chin toward inside the bicycle shed, "you whistle a certain song. I've heard you whistle it before back here. What's it called?"

Bruno whistled a few notes, "That one? It bothers you?"

"No. Not at all. Just curious. What's it titled?"

"Tarantella Napoletana. From my village. It's a folk song. In English, you say maybe, Dance of the Spider."

"Why that one?"

"Why any song? But truthfully, whistling calms me. And you know, it calms them, too."

"How so?"

"You ask lots of questions. I guess that's your job, right?" Bruno grinned momentarily, blowing a steady stream of smoke between his pursed lips. "That song is cheerful but . . . " he stammered, "a little sad, too. A poisonous spider bite causes uncontrollable dancing. Then you die. See?"

"No. Not really."

"All I know is I want the pitiful creatures to know they're not alone at the end. Someone's nearby. They hear me." Bruno looked up into the sky and his voice cracked. "I'm not a monster, you know, I'm just helping them die."

"I know you're not. You're just another civil servant like me doing a job."

"Remember the old way? Remember? Hanging. The hammer. *Mio Dio*. That was inhumane even with the—"

Before he could finish, the crate holding the cats tipped over off the bench, and cats darted in every direction.

"Jesus, Joseph, and Mary," Bruno cried.

Porter smirked, "Looks like your cats flew the coop."

"How did that happen?" Bruno eyed the detective. "You did something."

Porter shrugged.

"You did, I know you did."

"Forget about the cats for a minute. I want to ask you about something."

Bruno crouched beside the upset crate on the ground, discarding his cigarette butt in the dirt. Remaining crouched, he said, "What do you want from me, Detective? You hardly come back here and nobody else comes back here either, 'cept mean kids sometimes. Even the constables avoid coming back here unless they have to."

"Keep this dry, all right? I want to sound you out on a subject. Talk *in camera* if you get my meaning."

Bruno stood and lit another cigarette. "*Inteso*. Understood. I get it. Wait. This hasn't to do with the former *carabinieri* charged with murder the other day, does it? The 'Hello, my name is Pasquale blah, blah, blah fellow?'" Bruno jabbed the air with his finger. "Because if it is, we can't discuss the case. Not outside the courthouse."

"We're not talking about the case, we're talking about the blah, blah, blah."

Bruno exhaled. "You see how he looked around police court during his arraignment, so confused. Like he just woke up. And repeating his name over and over got His Worship's dander up. He's sketching all the time, too. Kind of like you. Is that something they teach you? You know he saved an entire family a while ago from burning to death in a house fire? Ran in. Pulled them out one by one. Anyways, what do you care? 'cause he was a copper back home? Don't get soft, Detective."

"No. That's not it." Porter knelt and picked up the wriggling canvas sack, going at the tight knot that prevented whatever was inside from escaping. "Well, it might be. I'm not sure. It could be a professional courtesy. I placed him in cuffs. He was a mess. It was a scene. His wife was hysterical. Later, when I found out he was a constable back home, I thought, I don't know, I've put a lot of fellows in cuffs, and this one didn't seem the type, but it appears he's just as guilty as all the others, so—"

"So what?"

"Did he say anything about what led up to things?"

BADGE

Bruno became serious and lowered his voice. "You know I can't tell you what he discussed in the presence of his lawyer. I will tell you this, however, he has a medical condition that influenced his homicidal action."

"That so?" Porter loosened the knot and pulled on the drawstring. A black-and-tan pup emerged, panting and licking Porter's hand. Impulsively, the detective said, "This one's coming with me."

"What? No. I've lost my afternoon already, and I suspect it's because of something you got up to."

Porter tucked the squirming puppy under his arm and removed his billfold. "Here's a dollar. Keep it all."

"And the cats? How about them?"

Porter scratched the puppy's chin. "I'm not reimbursing you for them. Besides, they'll be recaptured eventually." Porter turned and walked toward the alleyway. "Thanks for the chat, signore."

Stepping over the sickly terrier, Porter looked down at the ugly mongrel and said softly, "Sorry, fella, can't save you all."

A youngster playing with a hoop on the sidewalk in front of the police station on Agnes Street paced beside Porter and asked, "Are you a policeman?"

"Yes," Porter replied.

"Can I see your gun?"

"No."

"Can I see your badge, then?"

"No."

"Jeepers, mister. What's the pup's name, at least?"

Porter stopped, looked down at the boy, and then at the retriever. "Badge. His name's Badge."

"Can I pet 'im?" the boy asked excitedly.

"No."

The boy remained on the sidewalk, watching Porter cross the street before heading toward detective headquarters.

THE MOORE PARK MURDER

J. Ziolko, 1915

"Hey, kid. Get me your dad's hammer. The one with the claw." John Ziolko's dark eyes flashed with fury. He intimidated everyone in the cramped tenement where he resided.

The boy, who lived across the hall, wished he hadn't answered the door. "My dad's not home. He'd say no." The boy started to push the door closed. "I'm not allowed to lend his tools."

Ziolko stomped his foot in the doorway. "I borrowed it before," he lied. "Get it."

Frightened, the boy stared at Ziolko's boot, snow melting like tears on the splintered wood floor. "Okay, okay," he said, backing away and returning quickly with the tool. "But bring it back, all right?"

Halfway down the hall, his back to the boy, Ziolko replied, "Don't worry, you'll get it."

Ziolko met Tom Cekoski later that day in the lobby of a burlesque theatre on Bay, attempting to steal into the show.

"I don't have no money," he admitted to Ziolko.

"Neither do I. I know how we can get some, though."

They lingered in the lobby, talking until the younger man reluctantly agreed to help Ziolko carry out his plan.

City Hall contracted Godson Paving Company to construct a trunk sewer beneath the streets of Moore Park, a new subdivision near the city limits. The company hired dozens of foreigners—Italians, Irish, Albanians, Greeks, Bulgarians, Macedonians, Russians, and Poles—to perform the backbreaking underground work.

John Ziolko and Tom Cekoski were tunnellers. Their acquaintance, Bagago Trendo, was a bricklayer. The trio periodically ate together when the lunch hour whistle blew and, on payday, joined their coworkers for drinks in the taproom at the Rosedale Hotel.

The first portion of the Moore Park trunk sewer, thirty feet below Summerhill Avenue, was completed in the autumn of 1914. Godson then dismissed the workers with the promise of rehiring in January.

This meant weeks without work. By the middle of December, Ziolko and Cekoski were desperately low on funds and behind on their board. They visited the Salvation Army soup kitchen and schemed to survive.

Trendo's situation was less dire. Through his diligence, he got a dinky job doing piecework as a coremaker at a non-union factory, working any shift available. A saver who socked away his money in an astonishingly bulky wallet, he boasted to friends he had enough to get him through to January when work on the trunk sewer resumed, but he pursued factory work to be safe.

The day before Christmas was sunny, clear, and chilly. Ziolko and Cekoski initiated Ziolko's scheme and crossed paths with Trendo on a downtown street, seemingly by chance.

Sidewalks were crowded with cheerful, last-minute shoppers.

The three men huddled in the recessed doorway of a barber shop. As Ziolko had instructed, Cekoski lied and told Trendo that Godson had begun rehiring workers for phase two. "He'll believe you more 'cause of your baby face," Ziolko had predicted.

"Really, Tom?" Ziolko forged surprise. "Then we should get up there before others get all the jobs, right?"

Tom's reply caught in his throat. "That's right. Before the jobs are all gone."

"Should we go right now?" John suggested.

Cekoski nodded enthusiastically.

They stared at Trendo, anticipating his reply.

"Right now? To the hiring shed? In North Toronto?" Trendo said. "But it's Christmas Eve. Will anyone even be there?"

"Come on, Bagago," Ziolko blew into his cupped hands. "What do you say?"

Trendo considered, then shook his head. "No. I promised my landlady I'd attend her church's Christmas Eve service. She's nice to me and the other boarders. It's at St. Basil's. After, there's a free meal for congregants in the basement—"

"Can we come?" Cekoski eagerly blurted before Ziolko gave him a shattering glance. "I mean, forget it."

"Maybe the day after Christmas, then?" Ziolko suggested, "We'll meet right here at three."

"That's Saturday, though," Trento countered. "Boxing Day. Are things open?"

Tom then suggested Sunday.

"No," Trento said, "Sunday's church."

Ziolko was growing impatient. "Monday, but no later."

Trendo agreed to Monday and departed, leaving Ziolko and Cekoski shivering in the doorway.

Come Monday, Trendo failed to appear. Ziolko and Cekoski caught up with him the next day.

"We waited too long, and most positions are probably taken, Bagago. If we're going to do this, we should go now."

The sun was nearly behind the office buildings when Ziolko, Cekoski, and Trendo set out. It was bitterly cold and snowy. They smoked cigarettes, stomping their feet to stay warm until the streetcar arrived, boarded, and travelled east to Yonge Street. Next, they transferred to a northbound car. Ziolko complained loudly that the streetcar was too chilly. He confronted the conductor and, pointing back at the heating stove near the streetcar's centre, demanded that additional coke be added.

"Talk to the motorman. I'm busy."

Boisterous, red-nosed recruits headed for battlefields in Europe boarded at Bloor, greatcoats and kit bags layered in snow, cheerfully singing bawdy songs and excitedly discussing pending adventures. Buildings lining the streetcar route eventually gave way to empty lots. Approaching city limits, the recruits exited at a level crossing. They traipsed off into history through blowing snow toward a low-slung, modest train depot near Price Street.

Ziolko, Cekoski, and Trendo exited the streetcar at the next stop, outside the Rosedale Hotel. The streets were empty except for a few people around.

"Let's get whiskies. Let's get beers," Ziolko suggested before they continued to the work site.

Trendo resisted. "It's getting late. Let's get them on our way back."

"They're on me, though. I'm paying," Ziolko said.

"Really?" Cekoski chirped, knowing Ziolko was penniless. Getting into the act, he turned to Trendo and said, "Come on. Let's go inside at least to warm up. See how Old Boy's doing. It's been a while."

The stuffy taproom inside the hotel was shabby and rundown. Old Boy, the bartender, glanced up when the trio entered and appeared to ignore them.

They took a table.

Ziolko went to the bar.

Old Boy said, "Hey, Ziolko."

"Where's everyone?" Ziolko asked.

"Everyone? It's Christmas, where do you think?"

"Three whiskies. Three beers." He turned, pointed at Trendo, and lowered his voice. "Bagago's got this round."

They remained drinking for nearly two hours, and when they left, they were last seen staggering east along Shaftsbury Avenue, vanishing into the ravine in a gray-white wall of driving snow.

The discovery of a body with a battered skull in the Moore Park ravine near the end of December upended Detective Porter's expectation of having New Year's free after working Christmas Day. Because the homicide occurred at city limits, Detective Sergeant Cuddy assigned him to assist Provincial Detective John Miller of the Criminal Investigative Branch.

Porter stood, file in hand, in the doorway of Cuddy's office. "Assist? Miller? Really?"

The Detective Sergeant rocked backward in his chair. "I know. There's history. Get on with it, though."

"What about Levitt?"

"He's four days into a case on the attempt on Reverend Scott's life."

"Come on, Al, I can't—"

"George, it's you. End of discussion."

"Miller's incompetent."

"A wall of citations and an armful of Meritorious Service Decorations from the AG's office says otherwise. Not to mention newspapermen adore him."

"We both know he was slotted for something political ages ago—"

"That comes with having a Queen's Park office *slotted* between the Attorney General's and the Premier's."

Porter scowled. "He's half our age—"

Cuddy grinned. "George, that's not nearly true."

"You know what *is* true? What he *actually* has a knack for, Al? Collaring pickpockets. Not a difficult feat considering, in this city, dips are as common as shit in a cowbarn." Porter sighed. "And don't get me started on the newspaper poppycock about his 'extraordinary gift' of a photographic memory—"

"George, I get it. You don't get along—"

"That's putting it mildly. Besides, I promised Susan New Year's off. At least designate me co-lead."

"You know the AG's policy about co-leads."

"And New Year's? Susan?"

Cuddy glanced at his desk calendar. "Make an arrest in two days—"
"And bolster Miller's clearance rate."

Snow had stopped falling, and the temperature had climbed. Detective Miller arrived with uniformed constables in the ravine before Porter.

Upon Porter's arrival, it was evident that Miller hadn't preserved the crime scene, compromising its integrity.

A frozen corpse lay face down beside a wide path, partially submerged in a snowdrift. Opening his occurrence book, Porter asked a constable, "Coroner hasn't arrived?"

A breeze rustled through tall, bare trees. Branches creaked. Chickadees trilled, flitting limb to limb.

"No, Detective."

Porter made a notation.

Detective Miller was chatting with a constable about his splendid Christmas dinner with the Solicitor General a few days earlier when he overheard Porter ask, "Does Jack Frost have a name, yet?"

Miller hurried over and said, "I was getting to that. What are you writing in your book, Porter?"

Porter ignored the question. "What have you been doing?"

"Securing the scene."

"This scene? Secure? The snow has been thoroughly trampled, and your perimeter is far too narrow—"

"Listen, Porter. This is how *I* do things. I'm lead, remember."

Constables in earshot pretended not to listen. Porter beckoned one over. "Hey. Come here."

"Yes, Detective?"

"When was it you arrived with Detective Miller?"

"About an hour ago. Did he mention the mitten?"

"Mitten?"

"A man's mitten. I found one. Half a mile that way." He pointed down the path. "Tough slog through the snow. There's a name inside it, too."

"Good find. I'll get a look at it momentarily," Porter said, asking the constable for the correct spelling of his full name before asking Miller, "You've been standing around in the freezing for an hour and haven't even attempted to garner the victim's name?"

"I'm working on it. I searched the area and found the mitten, didn't I? About to check for a wallet when you showed up."

"A wallet? There is no wallet."

"How do you know?"

Porter knelt. "We're looking at robbery. Fellow was lured here. It's obvious. No one was out walking last night in that blizzard by choice. Likely tracks were left, too, but they've been trampled over. Deceased's been in this condition for at least ten hours. Look at the colouring of the pooled blood." Porter removed his glove and examined the head wound with his fingers. "Fractured skull. Three blows—"

Constables shuffled nearer to hear Porter's assessment when Miller interrupted. "*Bam.* First blow from behind. *Bam.* Drops to his knees. *Bam.* Face first into the snow. Last one finished—"

"That's what happened? And what do you suppose the weapon was?"

"Huh. Umm. A blunt object."

"Good guess." Porter felt the wound again. "Perforations are jagged. Bone fragments protruding outward. I suspect the perpetrator likely used a claw hammer. Judging by the wound, I'd guess a twenty-eight ouncer."

"I was going to say that—"

"Sure."

Before sarcastically requesting permission from Miller to turn over the corpse, Porter beckoned over the constable assigned to take photographs, advising him to capture images of the deceased from various angles.

After that, Porter crouched and unbuttoned the victim's leather coat, discovering a name sewn into a patch in the fur lining. "*Bagago Trendo.* Sounds Macedonian."

He tugged the victim's mittens off and studied his hands. "It's hard to distinguish from frostbite, but it looks like he may have been a mason." Constables leaned in. Porter continued, "See there? Alkaline in the mortar causes skin irritation like that."

Porter stood and made notations in his occurrence book.

"What are you writing?" Miller asked.

"It's not your concern." Porter glanced around. "I notice you never take notes. Oh, wait, don't tell us, photographic memory."

Constables barely concealed their laughter.

"Yeah, and your doodles, those stupid sketches, they're so important?"

"It's *procedure*—observe, report. Honestly, I don't know how you get away with what you—"

Miller snapped, "Here's what'll happen next, Porter. After the coroner gets here, he'll transport the body to the morgue. We'll know more after the autopsy."

Porter wiped his hand on a kerchief and put his gloves back on. "You're going to wait on autopsy results before your next move? Mr. Trendo won't thaw for three days. New Year's Day. I'll have made an arrest by then."

"We'll see."

The mitten proved significant. Its discovery led Porter on a three-hour trudge following the route he suspected the perpetrator had taken, ending at the Riverdale Zoo. He requested the headkeeper show him the night watchman's logbook. An entry made just after midnight noted two suspicious individuals lurking outside the elk enclosure. The watchman pursued them as far as Gerrard, where the pair boarded a westbound streetcar.

Porter visited the home of the individual who originally stumbled upon the remains.

A streetcar conductor told Porter a trio disembarked at the Rosedale Hotel stop the night in question. He remembered one complaining loudly. Old Boy provided Porter with three names.

One name, John Ziolko, matched the name inside the mitten. Porter laid into contacts to ascertain an address.

Meanwhile, Miller spent two days on the ravine's edge overseeing the futile search by a cadre of constables for a blunt object buried in snow.

On New Year's Day morning, Porter accompanied constables to search John Ziolko's apartment and discovered Trendo's wallet.

Ziolko claimed the robbery was Cekoski's idea and that the younger man delivered the fatal blows.

Porter was leading Ziolko in cuffs down the hall when a door opened behind them. A boy stepped out and shouted, "Hey, where's my dad's hammer?"

Tom Cekoski was arrested within the hour.

While Porter processed both men at the station, Miller visited Government House, where the Premier hosted his annual New Year's Day levée, glad-handing the chief justice, the AG, politicos, and dignitaries.

Later, newspapermen snapped photographs of Miller posing with a bloodied hammer triumphantly held up over his head, and another of him escorting Ziolko and Cekoski into the rear of a police van.

―•―

Their first-degree murder trial commenced four weeks later. The Crown presented solid evidence backed by witness testimony. The hearing lasted two days. After two hours of deliberation, the jury returned guilty verdicts for both defendants, resulting in mandatory death sentences.

Ziolko broke down, shouting, "No, no, no! It wasn't my idea. I have a wife, a daughter back home. Please."

Before he brought the gavel down, the justice commended Provincial Investigator John Miller on his thorough investigation.

―•―

Bored inmates confined three to a cell clanged enamel-coated steel mugs against cell bars and shouted obscenities.

Porter stood in the middle of the death cell, studying Ziolko slouching on a chair while Cekoski slumped on the sagging cot. Father Hinzmann leaned against the wall, clutching a Bible.

"In the end," Porter asked, "what was the take? Eighty and change?"

Ziolko folded his arms. "Who cares—"

Porter continued, "I'm curious, though, who schemed up the idea originally?"

During pretrial questioning and testimony on the stand, Porter concluded that Ziolko likely masterminded the plot and influenced the younger Cekoski to participate.

Ziolko said, "Can't make a difference now."

"Not for you, in any case," the detective glanced at Cekoski, "but could for him."

Cekoski looked up. "Me?"

"Yeah," Porter replied. "I'm certain it wasn't your idea."

"I thought we were just taking money, 'til he pulls out the hammer—"

Ziolko leaned forward and interrupted. "What difference does it make now?"

"A big difference. If you confess the scheme was your idea, and you committed the homicide, there's a slim chance Tom here gets a reprieve—"

"But not me, though?"

"His sentence will be life at Kingston Penitentiary, but he will get out in twelve for good behaviour. Then he promises to return to whatever the village is you're from to take care of your wife and daughter and see they don't forget you."

Father Hinzmann stepped forward. "That would be the Godly thing to—"

"I'll think about—"

"What do you mean, 'I'll think about it,'" Cekoski interjected. "It's my fuckin' life—"

Porter turned to leave. "Well, for your pal's sake, think fast. Less than forty-eight hours to—"

"I said I'll think about it," Ziolko sulked.

That night, Ziolko requested Father Hinzmann's presence, admitting he planned the robbery and that Cekoski had no hand in the killing.

Without delay, Father Hinzmann eagerly informed the Crown of Ziolko's confession, who petitioned the Department of Justice to commute Cekoski's sentence to twenty years imprisonment.

Hours before hanging, a telegram from Ottawa spared Cekoski's life.

The morning of John Ziolko's execution, a shackled Tom Cekoski boarded a train headed to Kingston Penitentiary, escorted by Detective Porter.

The train hissed out of the station. Cekoski did not utter a word. Porter stared out the window, asking himself why he did what he did.

THE PATSY

Hassan Neby, 1919

When Detective Porter arrived at the crime scene, Provincial Detectives John Miller and William Greer of the Criminal Investigative Branch were huddled outside the boarding car with Coroner Hunter, a bespeckled Irishman with a toothy grin. A short-line freight train roared past. A crowd of locals watched from a safe distance.

The previous night, a homicide had occurred in a Canadian Pacific Railway Co. boarding car on a siding at the nine-mile marker approaching the Humber River Bridge. George Tucker, nineteen, a member of an eight-man section crew assigned to track repair, was dead.

The three men observed Porter approach. He opened his occurrence book, cleared his throat, and began to make an entry when Detective Inspector Miller asked, "What do you want being here?"

Glancing at Miller, he replied, "I could ask the same thing."

Miller rolled his eyes and moved toward Porter. "The homicide occurred on federally regulated land—"

Porter stepped toward Miller. "—in the City of Toronto."

"Yeah, Porter, in the City of Toronto. You think you know

everything? The Railroad Act of 1903 requires a *provincial* investigation body lead the investigation—"

"So why'd Detective Sergeant Cuddy order me here?"

"I don't know. And I don't care. To observe? To learn something, maybe? And that lunker of a partner of yours. Where's he?" Miller chortled, "Heard the big ape has a name down at the department. Something like Noisy?"

"Shut it, Miller. Don't bring him into this—"

"Hey," Greer stepped between the quarrelling detectives. "Cool it. Both of you. It's just jurisdictional. We'll investigate this jointly, as equals," he added, forcing Miller back a step.

"No, we won't," Miller countered, glaring at Porter over Greer's shoulder. "I'm the lead. Porter's here to observe."

Porter composed himself, adjusting his fedora. "Okay. I'll observe." He paused. "So, the body. Where is it? In there?" he asked Coroner Hunter, pointing at the boarding car.

"Nope," Miller answered before Hunter could reply. "Undertaker took it."

"The body's been removed already?" Porter asked Coroner Hunter pointedly.

Coroner Hunter nodded nervously, stammering, "Detective Miller gave the directive, and I—"

Porter hurried inside the boarding car. The interior walls were dark tongue-and-groove wood panelling, and the blinds were partially drawn. The cramped living quarters contained a pair of metal-framed bunk beds, a wood-burning stove for heating and cooking, a wood box containing firewood, a dining table, furniture for stowing belongings, a washbasin and stand, and additional accoutrements.

Miller, Greer, and Hunter trailed Porter inside.

Porter took a minute to adjust to the change in light, looked around, and said, "Tucker was killed in here? The place is pin neat."

"A little too neat," Hunter mumbled under his breath.

"What's really going on, Miller?" Porter asked.

"Coworkers returned to the rail car last night and found him dead on his bunk. There's been a lot of labour strife lately between Maintenance of Way workers and foreigners gunning for their jobs. The previous crew, all foreigners, were recently canned for demanding a wage increase. Tucker was a new hire. Guess a disgruntled ex-employee visited to make a point."

"Murder? And no struggle? Nothing upset? Not a drop of blood even?"

"Killed in his sleep. It's a robbery gone bad."

"And you know this how?"

"I questioned his coworkers. They reported some valuables missing."

"You questioned all seven of them? Thoroughly?"

"Yeah. Thoroughly. I'm efficient, Porter, unlike you and that apish partner—"

"So, which is it? Robbery or labour strife?" Porter sighed. "Probably lined up a suspect already, too."

Miller jabbed himself in the chest. "It's whatever I conclude it is. Get it? And as a matter of fact, got some sound leads already."

"A foreigner?"

"Yeah. A foreigner. How'd you guess? Secured an eye witness, too."

"Really."

"A night watchman named Blair working his shift at the foundry down the way said he went outside for a piss when a big fellow shuffled past, and when he slowed to say hi, he noticed blood on his shirt."

"Slowed to say hi? After committing a homicide? And the eyewitness sees bloodstains on his shirt? In the dark? Ridiculous."

"It was a full moon last night, asshole. I checked. Did you?"

"No. Got me there."

Back outside, Miller and Greer talked to a reporter as Hunter guided Porter around to the opposite side of the boarding car, out of earshot of the provincial detectives.

Hunter lowered his voice. "Something hinky's going on, Detective. Tucker was a giant fellow. He could have taken care of himself, all things being equal."

"What do you suspect?"

"That his slaying was carried out someplace else and the body placed here for convenience."

"Let's keep this between you and me for now, agreed?"

"Agreed."

Acting Detective Frank "Noisy" Williams was almost too large to fit in the booth. Flipping through the menu, he started with a slice of fruit pie, fries, and a cream soda. Sitting opposite, Detective Porter ordered tea and a ham sandwich. Nasmith's Lunch Counter on King Street was the detectives' usual haunt.

Porter chewed the last of his sandwich and said, "We've been reassigned to the Tucker case."

Williams sipped cream soda through a straw. "Who's Tucker?" He grinned, looking over the menu. "I feel like something else. Do you?"

"No. Do you ever read my briefing notes?"

"You write those? How's the broiled chicken?"

"Do you ever stop eating, Noisy?"

"'Course. When I sleep. I'm kidding. The Tucker case—the Weston murder. I know it."

Porter gulped the last of his lukewarm tea and rubbed his sternum.

Williams observed and said, "Ulcer?"

"Yeah."

"Oww. Ice cream relieves that."

The younger detective had been recently promoted and partnered with Detective Porter for his smarts and intuitive abilities. Easygoing and bright, the broad-shouldered, six-foot-four giant with huge sloping shoulders and simian arms could hit like a pile driver when provoked. Porter wouldn't admit to it, but there was something about Noisy he liked, which was unusual for him.

Porter said, "You got ketchup on your face."

"Me? Where?" He dabbed his face with a serviette.

"Who else? Right there. No. Lower. The chin—there."

Williams wiped his chin, then crumpled the serviette.

THE PATSY

"Detective Sergeant Cuddy directed us to suspend the theft-ring investigation temporarily to focus on the Tucker murder."

"Really? Who's the lead?"

"Detective Inspector John Miller. Investigative Branch. Know him?"

"Heard the name. He's provincial police. Also heard you and him have history."

"Yeah. It's nothing. Cuddy said Miller needs guardrails. I said we'd rather not, but he said we don't have a say."

"So, we're guardrails?"

"Appears so. I've known Cuddy for a long time. I can tell it wasn't his decision."

"Feels political."

"It is. Something's up. Some poor sonofabitch is about to be railroaded, and I suppose assigning the two of us to the case makes the final outcome appear legit."

"Think someone's hoping you and Miller *intentionally* bang heads?"

"Hadn't thought of that. For what purpose?"

"Cover their tracks? Shift blame if things go topsy-turvy? Go after your job? Who knows."

"Get me fired?"

"Suspended, at least. We playin' ball?"

"Yes. And no."

"I'm going to order waffles. We got time, right?"

"Nope."

Williams grinned, ignored his partner, and waved the waiter over. "Joe, a stack of waffles for me and a dish of vanilla bean for the sourpuss."

A few days later, Detective Miller announced to reporters that authorities were closing in on a suspect. Behind the scenes, a sting operation was set up.

Through information provided by CPR police, it was learned that twelve recently fired workers—all Albanians—were owed a final cheque. Coordinating with the payroll department, detectives arranged for the terminated workers to visit their former employer's downtown office tower in the morning to receive their last payout. William Blair, the night watchman who claimed to have seen the killer up close, stated he could identify the individual.

The CPR company was headquartered in an opulent, fifteen-storey skyscraper. Arriving early after completing an overnight shift, Blair was positioned in the two-storey marble ticket lobby with an unobstructed view of the street-level entrance. Detectives Miller, Greer, Porter, and Williams concealed themselves behind soaring columns and waited. Plainclothesmen inconspicuously ringed the building outside, watching should anything go haywire.

The cavernous hall hummed with activity. One by one and in pairs, grubby men in greasy overalls and soiled denim work clothing arrived, crossing the gleaming lobby to the elevator and up to the payroll department.

Ten of the twelve suspects appeared in a few hours, collected their pay cheques, and departed. Blair had been instructed to indicate the killer's presence by pointing at him, but seemed exhausted and could barely keep his eyes from closing. Under no circumstances was he to interact with the individual.

Detective Miller grew frustrated watching Blair slouch in a wing chair, sometimes appearing to drift off. The undertaking seemed all for naught until Blair sat upright and pointed toward the entranceway at a man smoking a cigarette.

The individual he indicated stood around five-six and weighed roughly one hundred twenty-five pounds. He had dark eyes, olive skin, a pronounced dimple, a reddish moustache, and a high forehead. He wore a faded brown coat, loose trousers, and a tatty felt bowler hat pitched backward.

The detectives remained in place until the suspect crushed his cigarette under his heel, made for the elevator, and disappeared.

The detectives clustered around Blair. Miller asked, "That's him? You're sure?"

Blair nodded.

Williams gave Porter a queer look before Porter interjected, "Impossible. He's half Tucker's size and twice his age."

Miller thanked Blair for his service. "We're satisfied. It's an accurate identification."

A few minutes later the suspect returned to the lobby and exited. Police observed him board a westbound streetcar.

The twelfth dismissed worker—Sam Ali—never came to collect his severance.

Near the end of the month, Detective Miller instructed Porter and Williams to rendezvous at the suspect's residence at a King Street address around four in the afternoon. When Porter and Williams arrived, the three-storey residence housing twelve Albanians was already cordoned off. Three tenants present were rounded up and put in a front room. The rest returned home in dribs.

Meanwhile, Detectives Miller and Greer searched the premises and assigned duties to uniformed police. Miller instructed Porter to see what he could get from the three Albanians.

"They don't speak a lick of English," Porter protested.

"Then keep an eye on them."

"Listen, appoint a uniform for that. I'll assist in the search."

Miller responded, "No. You listen. It's an order."

Porter observed the trio of Albanians staring in mute distress at the detectives, lowered his voice, and said, "It's just, well, the word is you've bollixed things already, and I want—"

Miller interrupted. "Get over it. Okay? Follow my order. Understood?"

Porter and Williams exchanged looks before the detective conceded. "Understood."

Minutes later, Miller thumped down the narrow staircase, stopped before reaching the bottom, held up a suitcase, and triumphantly announced, "Lookie, lookie. I found Tucker's ID card inside, too. Now it's just a process of finding out who the suitcase belongs to."

Porter said snidely, "Convenient."

"Isn't it, though?"

"And the smoking gun? That's inside there, too, I suppose?"

"Matter of fact, there's a little .38—"

"I assume you've read the coroner's report—"

"Get over it, Porter. Be a team player. You'll go further."

Porter, frustrated, shook his head. "Not if it means going with you."

By six o'clock, eight Albanians had returned home and all were detained. The suspected murderer, Hassen Neby, was separated from the others.

"Place them in the police vans and get them to Central," Miller instructed.

Porter asked Miller about the absent man.

Miller sneered. "What about him?"

Porter said, "We should wait him out."

"Wait? And if he never shows?"

"There could be more to it, or it could be nothing. If he doesn't show up, we should look into him."

"Get over it, Porter. We got our man."

"We do?"

"Yes. We do. Have a problem with that?"

"At the least, we should confirm the absent man's name. Compare to see if he's the same one who didn't show up for his last cheque."

"I said, get over it. Let's get them in for questioning."

"Look at them. They're terrified. They will tell us whatever they think we want to hear."

"I know. I've done this before, Porter. A lot."

Before they departed, Porter took one Albanian aside and, along with the translator, asked him the name of the housemate who had failed to return home. The man was reluctant to answer.

Porter said, "Tell him it'll be worse if he doesn't."

The exchange between the Albanian and the translator went on for longer than Porter expected. "Tell him to give me the name. That's all. The name."

The translator replied, "He said he doesn't want to be involved."
"He already is. Tell him."
"He said he's afraid. He doesn't want to say the name."
Porter tore a blank page from his occurrence book and produced a pencil stub. "Tell him to write it down, then."
"He doesn't know the English, though."
"In his language."
The translator spoke, and then the man hesitantly wrote something in looping Albanian script.
Porter snatched the paper from his hand. "What's it say?"
"It says Sam Ali," the translator replied, adding, "He says this Sam Ali is *huadhënës*."
"Which means what?"
"Lender. He's a moneylender. Do you know this name, Sam Ali?"
"Yeah. Heard it before."
Outside on King Street, Porter rubbed his back and told Williams, "Learned something interesting."
"What?"
"A name."
"Whose?"
"The name of the fellow who didn't pick up his cheque? Same name as the fellow who was a no-show today. Guess what else?"
'What?'
Porter twisted and made a face like he was in pain. "Guy's a loanshark."
"That *is* interesting. Your back hurts?"
"Yeah."
"Go home. Rest. I'll cover for you."

THE KING V HASSEN NEBY, PART 1

A Freedom of Information request from the Canadian Justice Project is pending for records of confidential police informants of the time.
An understanding of historical events occurring at the time

of the murder investigation into the slaying of George Tucker is critical.

During the First World War, Toronto was English Canada's largest urban centre and the headquarters for military operations in the province. As the war dragged on, citizens' intolerance of ethnic minorities increased exponentially. The established populace routinely questioned the loyalties of Balkan immigrants to King and country.

By 1918, when the events being examined unfolded, hostilities routinely played out in the streets, with violent acts openly carried out against minority groups. Perpetrators rarely faced consequences. Behind closed doors, authorities expressed growing concern about the potential for rioting precipitated by predominately Anglo-Canadian members of the community.

It was in this environment that Hassen Neby, an ethnic Albanian, appeared at a preliminary hearing before Magistrate Brunton at County Police Court. He was not represented by counsel. Several of his housemates spoke against him.

Newspaper reporters learned a little more about the thirty-six-year-old, illiterate Albanian immigrant: a Muslim who did not speak English, he had arrived alone in the city three years earlier, leaving his wife, children, mother, and sisters, in Krujë, a town an hour north of the capital, Tirana. Neby had worked as a labourer, first at Dominion Glass Co. and then at the John Inglis Co. plant. For a brief time, he was a member of the CPR section crew that worked the section of track where Tucker was murdered.

The victim was described as passive, a loner, and quiet. His aunt, when interviewed, was surprised to learn he was killed in his sleep; she knew he liked to go walking at night alone and figured that's what he was up to the night of his death.

THE PATSY

People who lived in proximity of the rail siding informed the detective that on the night of the killing, they observed Tucker alone inside the boarding car around 8:00 that evening. Others swore in the previous two or so weeks to have witnessed foreigners showing up at all hours and sabotaging railroad property. CPR police were informed but appeared to take no action.

One witness, who lived in a home with an unobstructed view of the rail siding, reported venturing to the rear of her property around midnight to check on her chicken coop and seeing a truck arrive with its headlamps off. Three figures exited the vehicle carrying something bulky before disappearing behind the boarding car.

Through a translator, the Albanian described himself to the court this way: "I work with pick and shovel. I do not learn to read or write."

Neby was formally charged with first-degree murder and committed to stand trial at the fall assizes.

On King George V Day, a statutory holiday honouring His Majesty's birthday, Porter accompanied Susan and thousands of others to the park behind the Legislature to attend royal salutes fired at noon. Streets adorned with bunting and flags were crowded with office workers and schoolchildren enjoying their liberty. Shops displayed photographs of His Majesty in their windows.

In the afternoon, Porter and Susan visited Beatrice and Ted in the East End for a late lunch. The family intended to walk to the amusement park beside the lake.

There were many guests at Beatrice and Ted's lunch in their back garden. After the meal, Porter informed Susan he had to leave.

Susan asked, "Are you not fine? Is it your back? You look tired."

He explained that a work-related issue had arisen and told Susan to express his regrets.

"At least inform Beatrice you're leaving."

"No. You know her. She'll ask too many questions and hold me up."

"Will you be late?"

"Don't wait up."

On a hunch, Porter visited impresario Paul Pattillo in his spacious office that doubled as a gym on the upper floor of a building on the north side of Wellington Street, behind the Soldiers' Club. Years ago, Porter had arrested Pattillo, once a sensational light welterweight furious with his left, on larceny charges. Nowadays, Pattillo operated a charity for Hebrew newsboys. Clever for a former boxer, he appeared to avoid mischief and keep out of trouble, but Porter knew otherwise. The detective kept Pattillo close on account of the sort of people Pattillo fraternized with.

A warm breeze rippled in through openings in the floor-to-ceiling plate glass windows. Red leather heavy bags attached to rafters by chains swayed in the draught like elephant rumps.

Porter found Pattillo catnapping, leaning backward in an office chair with his hands behind his head, displaying his bare feet on the desk. He startled the former pugilist awake, swiping his feet off the desktop. "Show respect for His Majesty on His birthday."

Pattillo, groggy, ran his fingers through his hair. Collecting himself, he stood and stepped into his shoes. "Did you bring a cake?"

"No sass, Pattillo."

Pattillo smoothed the front of his rough suit, which anyone would know cost a lot of money, sat back down, and poured himself a drink from a bottle stowed in the desk drawer.

He wasn't happy to see Porter, but that wasn't unusual. Nonetheless, he offered the detective a drink. Porter declined.

"What do you want, then?"

Porter dropped into the chair opposite Pattillo. "That's a nice suit you got, Pattillo. Expensive. Where'd you get it?"

"You want one?"

"No."

"Then don't ask."

Porter showed Pattillo a sketch of Hassen Neby. "Recognize him?"

"No. Maybe. Should I?"

Porter sighed. "Not a difficult question. Either you don't, or you do. Judging by your response, I suspect you do."

"I recognize him from the newspaper, maybe."

"Whichever it is, I'm looking for someone who might know someone who might know an Albanian shark named Sam Ali."

The men talked a while longer. The direction of Porter's questions made Pattillo fidgety. To get rid of the detective, he scribbled a name on a scrap of paper and pushed it across the desk. "You didn't get this from me."

Porter read the name aloud. "Whoa. This isn't nobody."

"In these circles, he's known as Money Spider, and listen when I tell you, he presents a web of trouble."

Porter read the name aloud a second time and whistled through his teeth. "You're positive? Because this is substantial."

"As substantial as sin." Pattillo exhaled. "Some advice, Porter. Tangle with him, and someone gets hurt, or worse."

Porter and Williams went behind Cuddy's back in the ensuing weeks to juggle cases.

Williams focused primarily on their investigation to dismantle a dangerous criminal organization selling high-value items, including artwork, furs, Packards, and Buicks. Porter split his attention between the theft ring and the Tucker case. They regularly met at Nasmith's during work hours and after work at Porter's home to catch up.

Porter pursued the Sam Ali lead alone. He drew a bead on the Money Spider fellow, whom Pattillo identified as a "fashionable usurer." Among other ventures, Money Spider advanced money to society men with expectations but no cash available. Porter's sleuthing revealed that Money Spider also advanced loans for enterprising criminals, mainly foreigners with few options.

Money Spider owned interests in breweries, a racehorse stable, an extensive real estate portfolio, a construction company, and a chain of theatres. His influence reached corporate and public boards, including the Canadian Pacific Railway.

Privilege insulated Money Spider from the prying detective's dogged inquiries with waitstaff at exclusive restaurants, Grand Opera House ushers, Royal Canadian Yacht Club deckhands, and Rosedale gardeners tasked with maintaining tall, impenetrable hedges surrounding estates.

Money Spider evaded Porter until the frustrated detective made an impromptu early morning visit to the Syracuse Club, an exclusive venue for top-tier citizens. Jimmy, the door attendant who also ran the lift, attempted to deny Porter entry even after the detective flashed his badge. Porter pushed past the white-haired man and walked purposefully across the club's empty, ornate main hall, plush crimson carpet underfoot, into the oak-panelled dining room with twenty-five-foot ceilings inlaid with crystal where members consumed the most expensive viands and sipped aged wines.

Porter recognized the distinguished, clean-shaven man wearing a black-trimmed smoking jacket seated alone in a private corner of the cavernous hall, partially concealed behind a painted screen. He was sipping black coffee and perusing stock market indexes in the pages of the *Financial Post*.

Porter sat.

Money Spider spoke from behind the newspaper without a hint of irritation. "Detective Porter. My, my. You're as welcome in here as water in my shoe."

"Not very welcoming when you phrase it like that."

"You don't belong in here."

"You don't belong out there," Porter replied, hiking his thumb over his shoulder toward the entrance. "You belong in prison."

"Do you know who I am, Detective?"

"Do you know what I want?"

"Not in the slightest."

"Sam Ali."

Money Spider exhaled. He folded the newspaper. With a relaxed smile, he asked, "Are you one for superstitions, Detective?"

"No."

"You don't strike me as the sort. Likely then, you don't know the one about the money spider?"

"No."

He laid the folded newspaper on the table and leaned forward.

"You know what a money spider is, I assume?"

"Yes."

"The diminutive Linyphiidae. It's said that if the little red arachnid appears in your garden, expect good luck and money. However . . ." he paused, sipped his coffee. ". . . the superstition goes, if the same little fellow has a black stripe on his back, anticipate the opposite."

"Quaint. Tell me about the Albanian, Sam Ali."

Money Spider forged a confounded expression.

Porter produced the Hassen Neby sketch. "How about this sucker. Know him?"

"I do not."

"How about the Tucker case? The Weston murder? Any bells ringing?" Porter slammed the tabletop.

"What are you driving at, Detective?"

"I believe you know, but I'll tell you anyway. I think this Sam Ali fellow owed you, or somebody connected to him that you know owed you a favour. I don't think it was him, but someone visited the rail siding on your order, maybe your strong arms. You sent goons to frighten someone because labour strife isn't good business, and you and your boys wanted to send a message, but something got fuddled. Someone showed up unexpectedly or something like that. Whatever, things got carried away. They went too far and, well, this Tucker kid ends up jagged, and before you could—"

Money Spider sat upright, annoyed. "Stop talking," he hissed. "We can't have this conversation. Not here." He snapped his fingers. Jimmy appeared, followed by two imposing waitstaff.

"Jimmy, see Detective Porter out."

Porter was already standing. "No need." He turned to walk away.

Money Spider folded his arms, leaned back, and called out, "Ask yourself, Detective, when the money spider appears in your garden, will it have a black stripe?" After a pause, he concluded, "I suspect so."

Porter continued toward the exit. "I'm not one to spend time in the garden. I'll have to take your word for it."

"For shame. They tell me it's quite relaxing. Gardening, I mean. And Susan? Is the wife much of a gardener? Or Beatrice, that sister? How about that fledgling partner of yours? The one they call Noisy. Don't be surprised if he has a streak of bad luck."

A few days later, Detective Sergeant Cuddy summoned Porter upstairs. In preparation, Porter drafted his suspicions in a report.

Cuddy was indifferent. "Miller's got it sewed up."

Porter dropped the file on Cuddy's desk. "I disagree."

"Disagree at home, then. You're suspended."

"What? Suspended? Come on, Al, we've known each other for ages."

"I know, George. It's not you. It's politics. It's coming from up top."

"I'll talk with the Chief, then."

"Higher."

"Oh," Porter's eyes widened. "From outside."

Cuddy nodded. "The conversation is over. Go home."

"How long?"

"Until informed otherwise."

Arriving at his house unexpectedly in the afternoon, Susan asked if he felt ill and wanted tea. Instead, he took Badge for a long walk. Later, Detective Williams visited Porter's home.

The two men sat in the parlour. Porter instructed Williams to keep poking around. He warned his young partner to keep an eye out, though.

"For?"

"Anything. Everything."

Noisy grinned. "That doesn't help me."

Susan, who had been fond of Williams from the moment she met him, interrupted their discussion, asking, "Frank, stay for dinner?"

Before Noisy could reply, George said, "Stay for dinner? On my salary, we can't afford to feed him."

Williams grinned sheepishly. "I'd be pleased to, Mrs. Porter."

"Mrs. Porter? I'm not your schoolteacher. Call me Susan."

"All right, Mrs. Porter," he grinned endearingly. "I mean, Susan."

THE KING V HASSEN NEBY, PART II
To date, no response to the FOI request.

The first-degree murder trial of Hassen Neby before Chief Justice Sir Glenholme Falconbridge and a twelve-men jury commenced in the Criminal Assize in November. Barrister Thomas Agar appeared for the Crown. The accused was without counsel, and the court requested barrister William Henderson represent the prisoner. Hassen Neby was arraigned and pleaded not guilty through the aid of a translator. After the court established Neby's inability to understand English, his lawyer informed his Lordship the prisoner waived his right to the Court-appointed translator without explanation. Justice Falconbridge accepted the motion.

The Crown presented its case. George Tucker's missing money; identifying witnesses testified; Detective Inspector Miller provided his evidence. Mr. Henderson's efficient cross-examinations brought to light inconsistencies, admissions of uncertainty, and contradictory testimony.

The courtroom was pin-drop silent when Hassen Neby swore an Islamic oath and took the stand in his defence. Through a translator, the Albanian admitted Exhibit No.9—the black suitcase—belonged to him but did not know how it came to contain the incriminating items. He answered questions about his work history, residence, and activities on the evening of the murder. Henderson asked directly, "Did you murder the man Tucker or have anything to do with him or know anything about him?" Through the translator, he replied, "No, I do not know anything about that. I cannot do such a thing."

The trial lasted two days. Possession of George Tucker's

identification card was damning. The jury deliberated for seventy minutes and returned a guilty verdict. Falconbridge sentenced Hassen Neby to hang on January 3, 1919. The judge brought down his gavel.

Confined in the death cell, Hassen Neby initially maintained a stoic silence. Guards thwarted his attempt to pick the lock on his cell door with a spoon stolen from a meal tray.

For the two following months, a guard taught Neby some English and gave him cigarettes. In exchange, Neby performed Albanian folk dances and sang.

Citizens wrote letters on Neby's behalf supporting his innocence or pleading mercy for the convict. The Minister of Justice denied requests for a reprieve. Citizens wrote more letters on Neby's behalf. Justice Falconbridge refused the application to commute the sentence to life imprisonment. Neby's request for a *sajjāda*, a prayer rug, was rejected.

Neby declined a meal of his choosing, which he was entitled to on Christmas Day.

To the end, Neby denied any wrongdoing.

At 7:28 a.m. the cell door rattled open. The jail physician entered and gave Neby a grain of morphine.

They came for him at 7:58 a.m.

Neby collapsed on the scaffold. The hangman struggled to put the noose around his neck. The trap was sprung. Neby dropped seven feet, six inches. The jail physician checked for a pulse. He checked again. Hassen Neby survived another seventeen minutes—the longest for a man to live after the lever was sprung.

Neby was cut down at 8:21 a.m. A newspaper reporter asked the jail physician to explain why he survived as long as he did. The physician responded, "He must have had a big heart."

THE PATSY

After the execution, Porter encountered Miller, smoking a cigarette, on the steps outside the City Hall courthouse.

"You're okay with this?" Porter said.

"Yeah. You're not?"

THE TREATMENT

F. McCullough, 1919

FILM TITLE: *No Tears to the Gallows*

Logline: After the cold-blooded murder of a rookie police detective, a mysterious woman, and teenage girl coerce a prison guard into facilitating a jailbreak that sees the killer almost escape the gallows while a detective pursues an alternative path to justice.

OPENING TITLE CARD: Most of what follows is true.

TITLE CARD: "It is no exaggeration to say that no case heretofore has aroused as much public interest as the events in the case of Frank McCullough." *Mail & Empire,* June 14, 1919

TITLE CARD: Palmerston Avenue
Leroy Swart, alias FRANK MCCULLOUGH, 26, reclines uncomfortably on a small canopy bed in a frilly room with his back to the wall, reading

a dime store novel, Jesse James on the cover. Frank is a charismatic fellow with a slight overbite and ears that stick out. At 5'9, he walks around like he is 6'4. His sultry blue eyes attract the ladies. American by birth, he deserted the US army in 1917 and fled north. He did time at a remote Ontario prison farm for shop-breaking. Upon release, he came to Toronto, attempting to keep his past a secret.

Beside Frank sits a picked-over plate of chicken bones on an open sketchpad displaying a drawing of the exterior of his Palmerston Avenue rooming house. Curtains flutter. A car horn and children's laughter are heard outside.

Someone knocks on the bedroom door. Frank sighs before quickly covering the plate of chicken bones with the Jesse James book. Door opens to reveal DORIS MYTTON, 16, gangly, perceptive. She informs Frank her mom said his rent is late.

He says, *Tomorrow.*

Doris answers, *You said tomorrow last week.* She suggests he get a job.

He counters she should go to school.

She replies, *It's Saturday.* Backing out of the room and closing the door, she comments he looks ridiculous on that bed, adding with a knowing smirk, *and Mom said no eating in your room.*

Shouts and cursing replace joyful noises outside. Curious, Frank parts the curtains and observes POLICE and uniformed VETERANS clashing in the park across the road. Police strike veterans with their batons. Veterans fall to the ground, injured. Recently returned soldiers, convinced foreigners have taken their jobs, resent police, who appear to side with newcomers. Veterans also resent the fact many police officers received deferments and avoided going to the Front.

Frank is shocked by the level of violence that he witnesses outside his window.

TITLE CARD: St. Patrick Street home of Detective George Porter
DETECTIVE GEORGE PORTER, stoic, sits on the edge of chesterfield opposite rookie detective FRANK "NOISY" WILLIAMS, 24, hulking, earnest. Porter pets his dog, a black and tan retriever, Badge. The pair,

engaged in intense conversation, are interrupted by George's wife, SUSAN PORTER, kind looking. She invites Williams to stay for dinner. Noisy thanks Susan and accepts.

Later, Williams pushes himself away from the table and prepares to depart. The detectives stand in the doorway and shake hands.

TITLE CARD: November 18, 1918, near King Street and Bathurst
A chilly autumn afternoon. Frank McCullough and another man, ALBERT JOHNSON, 30, crooked-nosed, brutal eyes, stand in shadows in lane beside a horse and buggy. Frank holds reins. Sign overhead reads, Cross's Livery, Horse & Buggy Rental. The lane is accessible from busy King Street. At the top of the lane, a mooned-face NEWSBOY paces sidewalk exclaiming, *Police use batons freely in dealing with crowd. Battles in downtown streets.*

Albert gestures his disapproval, whistles, removes wad of cash from coat pocket. We see the butt of a pistol glint in his waistband. As he is counting bills into Frank's palm, Detective Noisy Williams slinks round the corner unexpectedly. Both recognize the detective even in plainclothes.

Albert fidgets. *Shit. Noisy. There's a price on him.*

Frank tells him, *I know. And look at the size of 'im. But he's a cop. Stay cool.*

Both steal sideways glances at fur coats, store tags attached, stowed in box of buggy.

Noisy approaches cautiously, spots stolen goods, eyeballs crooks, and asks, *What do we have here, boys?*

Frank chirps, *None of your business, Noisy.*

The detective flashes his shield. *I beg to differ. Where'd the coats come from?*

Frank coolly explains. Noisy isn't buying it. Albert's nervousness doesn't help. Noisy snatches reins from Frank and ties them to a hitching post. He informs both he is placing them under arrest, instructing them to accompany him inside the livery office, where he will telephone for the patrol wagon. The pair do not resist.

THE TREATMENT

The men enter a dark corridor. Suddenly, Albert draws the concealed pistol from his waistband, turns, points the barrel at Noisy's gut, and squeezes the trigger just as Frank knocks the weapon out of his partner's grip. The shot goes wide, splintering the doorframe. Pistol lands with a thump. Blue smoke snakes from the muzzle. A tremendous battle ensues. Instead of his service revolver, Noisy draws a small baton from inside his topcoat and swings wildly. Albert squirms free of mêlée, breaks for it, and vanishes through the doorway.

Frank and Noisy commence a pitched battle for the pistol. Frank wins. A second shot is heard. Bullet shatters Noisy's ankle. Going hell for leather, Noisy batters Frank's head with baton; still Frank refuses to release his grip on pistol. A third shot goes into the ceiling. Frank appears down for the count until a fourth shot is heard. Noisy's arm tenses mid-strike.

Combatants lock eyes. Expanding red stain darkens fabric of Noisy's topcoat. He crumples to floor, dead.

Frank bolts, battered and bloodied, indiscriminately knocking into pedestrians horrified by his appearance. He flails wildly down sidewalk.

Newsboy, unaware. Frank pinwheels toward him.

Newsboy exclaims, *Police batter protesters with batons. Protesters respond with brickbats, bottles.*

Frank collides with newsboy, falls unconscious into gutter.

TITLE CARD: St. Patrick Street

We see a MESSENGER BOY knocking on the front door of George Porter's home. Porter opens the door. Susan, behind him, peeks over his shoulder. Messenger boy looks up into Porter's stern face and hands him a slip of paper. Porter reaches into his vest pocket and casually drops a coin into the messenger boy's palm. Without turning, Porter reads the message. His expression changes noticeably.

Now facing Susan, he mutters something inaudible. She falls into his arms in tears. They embrace.

She sobs into his ear, *Find out who did this, George, and see they don't do it again.*

We see Porter's bearing change from stern defeat to one of resolve.

THE WAY OF TRANSGRESSORS • Edward Brown

TITLE CARD: January 23, 1919, City Hall, Courtroom No.4
ATTRACTIVE WOMEN, veterans, and NEWSPAPER REPORTERS crowd the unruly public gallery. Doris Mytton is seated in the row behind Frank. JUDGE, stern, aloof, pounds gavel. Frank's face has healed, but there is a noticeable scar where his left eyebrow was stitched up. Beside him sits his LAWYER in a bespoke suit. Frank glances over his shoulder at spectators and appears to be sketching the scene behind him. Among the agitated crowd sits MYSTERIOUS WOMAN, composed, dressed to the nines in a mink stole, expensive bag and gloves, and a pearl bib. Her hat's net veil conceals her identity.
    Detective Porter sits in the back row, taking in the scene, sketching.
    Judge lectures twelve crusty old JURYMEN on their duty to fairly judge evidence heard in a two-day trial before reaching a unanimous verdict. Judge restates Frank's claim he acted in self-defence, fearing for his life as Detective Williams battered him senselessly. According to law, however, the judge explains that if an unruly suspect resists arrest, a peace officer is entitled to use as much force as necessary to subdue them.
    Boo birds sound off in public gallery. Judge pounds gavel. Jurymen warned to ignore courtroom outbursts. Suddenly, a BUSTY WOMAN in a cloche hat disrupts the procedure, proclaiming her undying love for Frank. Porter shakes his head in disbelief. Judge pounds gavel. BAILIFFS haul busty woman from the courtroom, inciting veterans to hoot and wave canes in support. Judge pounds gavel. Exasperated, he threatens to clear the courtroom.
    Jurymen shuffle out of the jury box. Unlike Frank, who appears buoyed by the public's support, his lawyer appears concerned.

TITLE CARD: Ninety minutes later
Jurymen file into jury box and sit. Judge instructs Frank to stand. He does so with hands behind his back. Public gallery is on edge.
    JURY FOREMAN rises, reads verdict: Guilty.
    Courtroom erupts. Teary-eyed Doris flees the courtroom. Porter follows. Frank's mouth is agape. He gazes at the coffered ceiling. When he

brings his hands around to the front, he discovers a scrap of paper in his grasp. He glances around the chaotic courtroom, mystified.

Outside Courtroom No.4, we see the back of Mysterious Woman. Her heels click as she vanishes down an ornate marble staircase.

Back in the courtroom, Frank quizzically studies the handwritten note, and his lips move as he reads, *We shall be dangerous.*

Bailiff handcuffs Frank. Frank studies his partially drawn sketch of Mysterious Woman, asks Bailiff if he can take it. Bailiff considers a moment, then furtively stuffs paper into Frank's shirt pocket.

TITLE CARD: Paul Pattillo's Gym
Boxing impresario PAUL PATTILLO, forty-one, and Detective Porter have a history and this evening the last person Pattillo wants to see darken the doorway of his empty gym is Detective Porter.

The detective forgoes pleasantries, grabs Pattillo's collar, and shoves him against the wall, demanding, *Where's he hiding?*

Pattillo's eyes are wide with fear. Frightened of the consequences of not answering, he mutters, *I don't know what you're talking about.*

Porter isn't having any of Pattillo's posturing. *McCullough's going to hang. Now give me his partner. The gutter scum who killed Noisy.*

After an animated conversation that includes Pattillo pleading for his life, Porter departs with the information he sought.

TITLE CARD: Death Cell
A spear of predawn light enters small barred window, lands on Frank asleep in corner on tiny cot in sparsely furnished cell, bare except for cot, potbelly stove, two chairs, a table, and bucket behind screen. Newspaper folded into a cone serves as a shade to defuse the continuously burning lightbulb on wire overhead.

Overnight guard ERNEST CURRELL, 33 and aged beyond his years, sits at table wearing bifocals. Sips steaming coffee, reads early edition of daily newspaper.

Footfalls outside cell. Currell checks pocket watch as his replacement, MUZZY, Fatty Arbuckle in appearance, enters cell. Currell makes notations on clipboard. The guards exchange nods. Currell empties coffee cup, puts on cap, exits. Frank continues to sleep.

Later. Muffled shouts echo through jail. Muzzy, seated at table, works on a crossword puzzle. Frank is behind screen doing his business.

Muzzy chews the end of his pencil, glances over newspaper at screen, Hey Frankie. Beyond harmful. Six letters.

Frank appears around screen carrying bucket and approaches Muzzy. Both glance at contents in disgust.

Frank hands bucket to Muzzy and says, *S-H-I-T-T-Y?*

Frank, bored, sits on his cot leaning against the wall. Feeling caged, he stands, positions the chair below the window, steps up, grips iron bars, and stares outside. Drifting into a daydream, chirping birds replace the voices of shouting inmates. Frank gazes beyond the wall enclosing the jail and across the valley. He sees Riverdale Zoo patrons strolling the grounds on one of the first days of spring. Far up the valley, a sooty black steam train appears and whistles.

Suddenly, he glimpses Mysterious Woman in raccoon coat just beyond the wall as she dashes behind a tree. This is not Frank's first time spying Mysterious Woman outside the wall. He has seen her on nights when he can't sleep, when he's pulled the chair over to the window to look outside. Presently, he squints, thinking he is delirious, until Mysterious Woman waves.

Frank's attention is pulled away by a knock on the cell door.

Muzzy announces, *Visitor*.

Frank sees the heavy door hesitantly creak open but resumes scanning for Mysterious Woman, who has vanished. Agitated and with a scowl on his face, Frank hops down from his chair, expecting to see a lawyer or jail staff, not Doris Mytton, framed in the doorway, bag slung over her shoulder, smiling coyly.

Frank is surprised. So is Muzzy.

Doris glances at Muzzy's crossword before asking guard for privacy. Muzzy complies.

Frank is awed, *How did you do that?*

Doris replies, *I asked nicely.* She removes a bundle of Jesse James dime-store novels, a small plate of chicken, a sketchpad, and pencils from bag and places items on table beside incomplete crossword puzzle. She explains these gifts are from members of her church.

Frank drops to cot, speechless.

Doris elaborates. Overnight guard Ernest Currell attends her church, The Church for the Stranger.

She explains, *Currell served with my dad in France*. She describes how Currell informed the congregation about Frank, saying he's a nice guy, just misguided. The congregation agreed to help get Frank's sentence commuted to life imprisonment through letter-writing campaigns and protests. Currell informed Doris the surest way to arrange a visit and get items inside the death cell.

Frank becomes emotional and stammers, *I was scared. I'd do anything to change what happened. People judge without knowing what really happened.*

Doris says, *Counting other people's sins doesn't make you a saint.*

Frank sniffles, *Is that in the Bible?*

Doris shakes her head, *No. Jesse James said that.*

Frank's mood changes, and his eyes become wide. *Really?*

Doris shrugs. *Maybe. He could have.* She asks Frank about his spiritual advisor.

Frank replies he doesn't have one.

Doris recommends Reverend Nelles from her church. She studies her wristwatch. She must go. Before she leaves, Frank asks if she knows the Mysterious Woman outside.

Doris turns back and replies, *Nope.* Doris exits.

Muzzy returns to the cell, sits, and resumes working on his crossword. Frank lies on the cot in awe, flipping through one of the books Doris brought. As he does, Doris unexpectedly pokes her head around the partially open cell door. She humours Frank. *I told you to get a job.*

He partially sits up and smiles, remembering. *I told you to go to school.*

Doris adds, *But seriously, I forgot to ask, my mom told me to find out what we should do with all your stuff at the house.*

Frank tells her to put it out for trash.

Doris winks. *If you say so, but you might need it.*

Without taking his eyes off the crossword, Muzzy mumbles, *Not where he's going.*

Doris ignores this comment and says, *By the way, Frank, you look ridiculous on that little cot,* and then, before leaving for good, turns and says to Muzzy, *Twenty-three down? Six letters? Beyond harmful? Think about it. L-E-T-H-A-L.*

CUT TO Detective Porter
Alert, stealthy, following a path in a wooded area strewn with garbage on the city's outskirts. It is early in the season, and trees are budding. The woods appear damp. A crow caws. Up ahead, off the path through the trees, Porter spots a ramshackle cabin. He approaches with caution.

CUT TO cabin interior
Porter inside the cluttered cabin, a small filthy window the sole source of light. Porter is seated in a worn wicker chair, concealed in shadows. He wears a pair of black leather second-storey gloves. The detective appears tired, having been sitting for some time, but becomes alert to a sound outside the cabin. A twig snaps. We hear the sound of squishy, wet leaves underfoot.

The cabin door creaks open, framing Albert Johnson in the doorway, the butt of a pistol visible in the waistband of his trousers. When he spots Porter, Albert's expression runs the gamut as he considers his next move. Before he can draw his weapon, Porter reveals his revolver, which has been trained on the cop killer the entire time. Nudging the barrel, he instructs Albert to get inside and close the door behind him. Albert hesitates. We hear a click as Porter cocks the hammer of his revolver.

Porter says coolly, *I know you know who I am. I know you know why I'm here.*

Albert appears flustered, *I should have cut out when I still had the chance.*

THE TREATMENT

Porter responds, *You never had a chance.* He repeats his instruction to come inside and close the door.

Albert does as told. *Guess you're going to run me in, now. Guess I'm done for.*

Porter smirks. *Not exactly. This plays out differently than expected.*

Albert's ebbing courage is returning. He guffaws. *What are you going to do? Shoot me? You're a cop.*

Porter counters. *Not exactly. Not presently. I'm suspended and possibly dismissed. So, it's a grey area, at best.* Porter rises from the wicker chair and, holding up his revolver, moves toward Albert. Porter removes the pistol from Albert's waistband and, in an impressive display of dexterity, confirms the weapon is loaded while keeping his revolver on Albert. Porter holsters his revolver while keeping Albert's pistol pointed at the lawbreaker.

Porter says calmly, *I hazard to guess I'm better at my occupation than you are at yours.*

Albert is confused and backs away. *My occupation?*

Porter counters. *Yes. Your trade. You're a crook. I'm a detective. Being a crook was your profession before that terrible career move when you killed my partner.* Porter pauses a beat to gather his thoughts before continuing. *You never considered it like that, did you? That's why you've never been good at what you do.*

Albert backs into the wall.

Porter shoves the barrel under his chin. He continued, *I'm good at what I do. I've been doing this a long time. I've investigated dozens of homicides and more suicides than I care to recall and learned to spot the difference in a trice.*

Fear and confusion appear in Albert's eyes.

Porter guides Albert to the wicker chair. He instructs him to sit.

Albert complies as though in a trance.

CUT TO cabin exterior
From outside, we hear Porter. *Good. Now, lean your head back like this. Good. Sideways a wee bit. Good. Open your mouth. Wider. Wider. Perfect.*

Now place your hand here, like this. Good. Remain perfectly still and imagine you're having your photograph taken. That's good, Albert. You're finally good at something. Hold it. Hold it. Now, say "prunes."

A gunshot echoes through the woods followed by the clunk of Albert's pistol dropping to the floor.

We see Porter following the path away from the cabin.

TITLE CARD: Riverdale Zoo

A cluster of boisterous CHILDREN gather in front of a cage containing Toby, a mangy little black bear. Children squeal when KEEPER enters the rear of the bear enclosure and tosses Toby a loaf of stale bread. They shriek when the keeper engages Toby in a playful boxing match.

Doris observes from the bench. Toronto Jail is visible in the distance.

ZOO PATRONS include uniformed veterans. Detective Porter moves clandestinely among the crowd. Mysterious Woman appears and sits beside Doris. As usual, she is fashionably attired. A real beauty, up close her amber eyes are flecked with sadness.

She makes small talk with Doris until Doris says abruptly, *You were at the trial. Frank's seen you outside the jail.*

Mysterious Woman's eyes widen. *You've spoken with him?*

They study one another before Mysterious Woman introduces herself as Vera Lavelle.

Doris asks contemptuously, *Do you love Frank?*

Vera removes a creased photograph of a handsome soldier from her purse. The resemblance between Frank and the man in the photograph is uncanny. Vera dabs her eyes with handkerchief. She explains Frank's hanging would be like losing something precious a second time.

BALLOON SELLER in a funny hat, big shoes, ambles passed hounded by youngsters. Doris's kid sister, EDITH, 6, interrupts the conversation, pestering her sister to buy her a balloon. Doris tells Vera she is the eldest of four sisters and explains her family took Frank in as a boarder when their papa left for France. Doris sniffles. After their papa was killed, Frank's presence was comforting. Doris recognizes Frank is guilty as sin but doesn't want anyone else to die.

THE TREATMENT

Edith continues to plead for a balloon. Vera reveals she financed Frank's defence and asks how Doris finagled her way inside the jail. Doris informs Vera about Ernest Currell.

Vera beckons the balloon seller and buys a balloon for Edith and all the other children as well.

Doris explains her church's strategy to squelch execution and their belief that citizens' aversion to recent police action helps their cause.

Vera says, *Let's work together on something more significant.*
Doris is curious. *What do you have in mind?*
Vera grins mischievously. *A jailbreak.*

CUT TO a busy diner, a few days later
Vera Lavelle, Doris Mytton, and Ernest Currell are seated around a table visible from the street. Across the street from the diner, sitting behind the wheel of a parked car, we see Detective Porter watching the confab.

TITLE CARD: Outside Toronto Jail
A smattering of protesters, including Doris Mytton, wave placards and sing hymns. REVEREND NELLES, 45, high-wattage smile, exits taxicab clenching Bible. Scales jail steps two at a time. Enters, signs register, trails guard through the clamorous facility, and arrives at Frank's second-floor death cell.

EXTERIOR SCENE REPEATS. Each time, the number of protesters increases. Detective Porter conceals himself in the throng. The crowd swells to the point where police are required to maintain order. Doris, Edith, their two youngest sisters, and their mom wave placards.

CUT TO Frank's cell
Mailbags accumulate in the corner of the death cell. Reverend Nelles admires sketches taped to the wall, pointing to an incomplete drawing of Mysterious Woman.

Nelles says, *She's lovely. When will you complete it?*
Frank smiles knowingly. *One day, soon.*

Later in death cell, Frank and Ernest play chess and talk into the night. In the wee small hours, Ernest tells Frank about his battlefield terrors. He describes his feelings of hopelessness, carnage, and loss.

Late at night, protesters continue to gather outside the jail. Frank, perched at the window, is overwhelmed by the sight of torch-bearing supporters and confesses he is at a loss to understand why citizens have taken up his fight.

Ernest explains, *It's simple. You represent everything they've lost, and in a twisted sort of way, if they can prevent your death, a fraction of their hope might be restored.*

TITLE CARD: April 15, 1919
Ernest enters the cell carrying a fancy box of chocolates concealed under his coat. Frank is on his back, reading on his cot. Muzzy, the day guard, prepares to leave and makes notations on the clipboard. He inquires about the chocolates. Ernest opens the box, explaining they are a gift for Frank from his church congregation, and nervously offers one to Muzzy. Ernest says, *Help yourself. Frank won't mind, will you, Frank?*

Muzzy's hand hovers over the selection of chocolates. As he is about to make his selection, Ernest discourages him. *Not that one. You won't like it. Cherry filling.*

Muzzy replies, *But I like cherry.*

Ernest counters quickly. *But you won't like that cherry. It's cherry from Madagascar.*

Muzzy is puzzled. *Where?*

Ernest says, *Exactly.*

Muzzy shrugs before settling on a chocolate. He pops the sweet into his mouth, chews, nods approvingly. *Mmm. Good.* He pops a second one in his mouth. Before leaving, Muzzy says, *So long, Frankie. See you tomorrow.*

Frank mumbles, *Not if I can help it.*

Very late. Frank and Ernest exchange clothing. Ernest, seated, stirs coffee. On the table sits an open packet labelled Veronal. Ernest is drowsy and inadvertently dribbles coffee on his shirt. Frank loosens lightbulb. The cell goes dark. Ernest struggles to remain awake. His head lulls to one side before passing out. Frank removes tray of chocolates from the box and discovers a note, tied to a hacksaw, that begins, *My bold companion* . . . Before Frank positions the chair below the window, he takes down the incomplete sketch of Mysterious Woman from the wall, folds it, and puts it in his pocket. He stands on the chair, rubs the hacksaw blade with a bar of soap disguised as a chocolate, and begins sawing through bars on the window.

Early next morning. Bells ring. Frantic footfalls echo throughout the jail. Ernest, startled awake, rubs his eyes, looks down at his clothing, and then looks up at the sawn iron bars on the window. A swarm of panic-stricken GUARDS burst into the cell. The packet of Veronal has been replaced with a note from Frank testifying to Ernest's innocence.

TITLE CARD: Hideout near King Street and Bathurst
The sparsely furnished room with shades drawn contains a hideaway bed, kitchenette, icebox, hotplate, desk, and chair. Frank, in a change of clothing, peeks nervously outside.

Footsteps are heard in the hallway. Distinct tapping is heard on the door. Frank hesitantly opens the door, finds Vera Lavelle, dressed down. She enters. They speak in hushed tones. Frank asks why she assisted his escape.

Vera replies, *I financed it. The rest is the girl.*

Frank is anxious to flee the city immediately. Vera convinces him to stay put longer. They talk late in the night. Before Vera leaves, she promises to come back and provides him with cash to use if necessary.

She departs and we see Vera furtively making her way up the darkened street near the hideout. Detective Porter watches her from a distance, concealed in a doorway.

CUT TO the next day
Frank sleeps during the day and wanders the neighbourhood in a partial disguise after dark. He visits the corner store and purchases newspapers

and Eskimo Pie. He revisits Cross's Livery. Observes bullet hole in the ceiling, splintered doorframe, bloodstained floor. The memory of murderous actions overwhelms him as he considers the current outpouring of support.

Vera visits again, and we hear her familiar tap on the door. She tells Frank arrangements are in place for him to depart. She says they won't see one another again, and as she caresses his forearm, she recites: *Defeat, my Defeat, dearer to me than a thousand triumphs, my bold companion, we shall be dangerous.*

Frank completes the sketch of Vera seated on a bed illuminated by a sliver of moonlight.

Before departing, Vera tenderly kisses Frank's cheek and whispers, *Get as far away as possible.*

Frank asked her to consider going away with him on the lam. She declines.

He pleads with her to change her mind, reminding her they will likely never see one another again.

She says her happiness will be just knowing he's alive.

Vera slinks out of the hideout as before, vanishes into an alley, weaves down another, and is finally whisked away in a chauffeur-driven luxury car. Detective Porter, silhouetted in darkness, tracks her every move.

CUT TO the next night

Frank packs items into a small travel bag.

Spread out on the cot beside the bag are forged identity papers, tickets for various bus carriers, colourful maps of different regions of Canada and the US, bundles of Canadian and American currencies, a sketchpad, charcoal, and a Kahlil Gibran book of poetry.

We hear Vera's familiar knock. Frank's expression changes from anxiety to relief. He hurries to the door. Instead of his patroness, it is Detective Porter, pointing a revolver. Frank knows a copper when he sees one.

Porter says, *Evidently, you were expecting someone else.*

The men sit opposite one another. Frank slouches.

THE TREATMENT

Porter looks around and says, *Cozy.* He notes the sketchpad and charcoal and admires Frank's completed drawing of Vera. Porter asks, *You sketched this? It's admirable. I sketch, as well.*

Frank perks up a little. *Sketching relaxes me.* Porter nods in agreement. Frank perks up further. *We're more alike than you'd imagined.*

Porter scoffs. *Hardly.* Porter removes a folded newspaper from his coat and places the late edition on the tabletop before Frank. The hoodlum's eyes widen when he reads the headlines: "Socialite Held for Questioning in McCullough Jailbreak. Charges Pending." Bold letters below a photograph of Vera in handcuffs inside Toronto Jail reads, "Judge Orders Lavelle Held Until McCullough's Recapture."

Porter explains the Crown considers Vera an accessory to murder in Detective Williams's death. Frank has a choice: Give himself up tonight, and before he goes to the gallows, he can explain Vera had no hand in the detective's death, and she'll walk free. Or make a run for it, and who knows what happens to her? Porter glances at the revolver turned on Frank. *Either way, you're not going to make it far. Your pal Albert faced a similar dilemma, he chose felo de se.*

Frank asks, *What's that mean?*

Porter replies, *He killed himself.* Porter stands and moves toward the door.

Frank is surprised and asks, *Where are you going?*

Porter responds, *Home.*

Frank is flabbergasted. *Without taking me in?*

Porter replies, *I'm suspended.*

Frank is aggravated and demands, *So why did you come here?*

Porter shrugs. *To look into the eyes of the poltroon who killed my partner and to see what's there.*

Frank demands to know, *And?*

Porter thinks a long time before replying. *Nothing.* Before he leaves, he tells Frank, *Give up. Make a run for it. No skin off my nose. Either way, you're as good as dead.*

We see Porter exit the building and disappear down the darkened street. Frank hurriedly follows a few minutes later, travel bag slung over his shoulder. Expecting the cavalry to arrive any second, he looks up and down the deserted street. When nothing happens, he walks with purpose in the opposite direction to Porter.

Rounding a corner, he spots a POLICEMAN, fresh-faced, walking his beat. The policeman is young, a rookie. Frank stares at the cop for a long time, considering his options.

Unbeknownst to Frank, Porter has been stalking him since he left his hideout. Porter, lurking in the shadows, draws his revolver. He has a clean shot.

Frank unexpectantly whistles, waves his arms, and shouts, *Hey, you, flatfoot. I'm who you're looking for.*

Porter lowers the weapon.

The policeman initially doesn't recognize Frank. Frank grows frustrated and hollers, *What's a guy got to do to get arrested around here? Shoot somebody?*

The rookie cop approaches Frank, recognizes him, and makes arrest without incident.

Detective Porter reappears, identifies himself to the cop, kneels beside Frank, who is sitting on the curb with his hands cuffed behind his back, and says close to the thug's ear, *I couldn't decide. Except that I knew I wouldn't let you die back there comfortable in that cozy love nest. Would I get more pleasure shooting you in the back in the street, knowing you died alone, bleeding out in the gutter, or instead see you strung up by the neck?* Porter chuckles, *Neck or back? What would you have preferred, Frank? Me? I'll get pleasure out of the neck.*

TITLE CARD: Toronto Jail, June 2, 1919

Doris Mytton and family among thousands surrounding facility singing hymns. Mob violently rocks police van transporting HANGMAN, impassive, into jail.

Jail is pin-drop silent. In cell, the window through which Frank previously escaped has been removed and the opening bricked in. Reverend Nelles prays with Frank. JAIL PHYSICIAN appears, offers Frank sedative. Frank declines. WARDEN, other officials, appear accompanied by a REPORTER. Frank's wrists are pinioned. Procession walks solemnly forty paces to the death chamber where Hangman waits. Reporter asks, Last words, Frank? Hangman slips black hood over Frank's head.

    Frank's voice, muffled, confident. *Tell them there were no tears at the gallows.*

FADE TO AUDIO: Shuffling. Murmurs of The Lord's Prayer. Long silence. A heavy clank. Gasp. Thrashing. Rope creak.

TITLE CARD: Vera Lavelle served two months at a work farm for her role in Frank McCullough's escape.

TITLE CARD: Ernest Currell was convicted of assisting Frank McCullough escape custody but his conviction was overturned on appeal.

TITLE CARD: Doris Mytton escaped prosecution.

CLOSING TITLE CARD: The End

FADE TO black.

POACH

Early Sunday, Porter walked Badge to the park. Sidewalks were mostly bare. The detective was aware he was being followed for several blocks: a young fellow, early twenties, on the short side with a reddish complexion and receding hair on his temples. Judging by his comportment, Porter surmised the stalker was unarmed.

    Ducking into the deep, narrow doorway of a closed carriage shop, the detective commanded Badge, "Sit. Quiet." The obedient dog complied. Porter looped the leash around the brass doorknob. When his pursuer skulked past moments later, the detective took him by the collar, yanked him into the doorway, and pinned him against the wall at the throat.

"Why are you following me?"

The pursuer's eyes bulged. He stammered, "Please. I'm a private investigator. Don't—"

"You? A P.I.?"

With the lightweight pinned against the brick, Porter turned the man's pockets inside out until he found a red leather wallet containing identification. "Bryan Hogan. Private Investigator. Hogan Detective Agency." Porter released him. "Your tradecraft could stand improvement."

Porter unwound Badge's leash, guiding the dog onto the sidewalk.

Panting, Hogan straightened his collar, adjusted his tie, and put his wallet away. He handed Porter a square card. "That's Bryan with a Y—"

"I can read. Why are you on my tail?"

"I want to hire you."

Porter sighed. "The Ambrose Small case?"

Hogan's eyebrows arched. "Yes!"

"The answer is no."

Detective agencies periodically tried to poach Porter, usually when an intriguing case surfaced in the news, but Porter never took the offers seriously. High-class firms like Pinkerton could match his salary, and the job was undoubtedly cushier, but he doubted he could endure the tedium of searching for runaway children of the wealthy, divorce cases, or civil litigation.

However, after Noisy's slaying, his clash with Miller, and his months-long suspension, now over, he had half convinced himself PI work mightn't be so terrible. Maybe cushy was precisely what he needed. And the disappearance of multimillionaire Ambrose Small was intriguing.

Hogan was chatty. He asked Porter if he could tag along with him and Badge.

"It's a free country."

As they walked toward the park, Hogan asked, "Do you know much about Small's disappearance?"

Porter lied. "No."

"In the newspaper, Chief Grasett posted a $500 reward. And Small's wife is offering much, much more. $50,000 more."

"Every man on the street with a hunch will chase a reward that size. Has Mrs. Small hired the Hogan Detective Agency?"

"No. Not exactly."

"What's your game, then?"

"You and I locate Small and divide the reward equally."

"Is that so?"

"Then publicity will generate more cases."

"More cases?"

"Yes. We'll be partners in an enterprise."

"Interesting."

"I can't tell if you're being sarcastic."

"I thought I was being obvious."

Porter hadn't been assigned to the Small case but, through contacts, he heard whispers that Small's enormous gambling debts had come due. Thus far, newspapers had chosen to suppress that information.

Porter judged the young fellow to be harmless. It wasn't in him to tell Hogan that, from what he was hearing, Small was already done for, his remains reduced and concealed either in a Rosedale garbage dump or inside a barrel buried in the Rouge River. No reward would likely ever be collected. "I'm declining your offer, Mr. Hogan."

PI Hogan's face flashed with disappointment. "Oh." They walked silently for a few paces before Hogan asked, "Out of curiosity, what case are you currently working on?"

"Nothing in particular." Another lie. A cold case concerning a midget wrestler's disappearance recently crossed his desk. More significantly, the investigation potentially linked a person of interest in the case to another from years ago that was not entirely sewn up to his liking.

"Keep my card if you have second thoughts."

"I'll keep that top of mind." Third lie.

"Can I ask another question, Detective Porter?"

Porter nodded.

"Back there in the doorway, you didn't draw your revolver. How did you know I wasn't concealing a weapon?"

"How do you suppose?"

"You're actually unarmed, yourself," he countered eagerly.

Porter opened his jacket slightly to reveal his holstered Colt.

"So how?"

"Your gait. The way you carry your hands. And that ill-fitting tweed suit. It's two sizes too small to conceal even a baby pistol."

"And if I draw a blade?"

"A manageable situation. Didn't you study all this in private detective school?"

Hogan smiled. "Private detective school? Such an institution exists?"

BLOODGUILT

If a man is burdened with the blood of another, let him be a fugitive until death; let no one help him. PROVERBS 28:17

There is a dream she dreams where the city is as quiet as a mausoleum. Violetta Limoncello stands, naked as Eve, on a crowded street corner, making no effort to conceal her flesh. She does not recognize the part of the city she is in, but she knows she is in Toronto. It is at once a long time ago and today. The city becomes a museum. Citizens observe her as though she were behind glass or on a stage. A policeman in an olden-day uniform strolls in her direction. He holds a large camera in one hand, and in the other, a gun. She doesn't recognize the camera but knows it belongs to her. The policeman seeks the audience's opinion. "Shoot? Take a photograph?" Before they reply, he levels the gun, taking direct aim at the centre of Violetta's chest. He throws the camera to the ground; it turns to sand. Violetta becomes conscious of her naked state and transforms into Violet Lemon, the middle-aged woman she is today. The policeman's eyes become wax and melt like broken egg yolks down his cheeks. The audience is dead silent. An elephant trumpets. Everything is bathed in stark light. The policeman flails. Where are you? Violet pleads silently. I am afraid. The policeman can see without eyes. Before squeezing the trigger, he asks directly, "What is this that you have done?" The hammer strikes the primer. A bullet is expelled. Violet observes sunburst-orange muzzle flash. A puff of soot-grey smoke. Oddly, there is no report. The unusual silence is unnerving. The bullet's trajectory is menacingly slow. Violet finds this at once amusing and horrifying. Twin girls in pyjamas appear, effortlessly pulling the limp body of a man across a stage and vanishing through a doorway. An elephant trumpets. An angel with wings of ice crashes into the sidewalk like a sack of wet oatmeal. A disembodied voice whispers, Run. Violet is in the hold of a ship. She is a child, paralyzed by fear. A small object as sharp as a spear and at the same time as dull as a potato presses against her heart. The hull splits open. A rush of air. She is falling.

Violet awoke, clenching her throat. Hew to the line and let the chips fall where they may, the time had come for Violet to confront Meta.

The first time Violet mustered the courage to board the No.415 trolley to North Toronto was the Saturday after St. Patrick's Day. An unpleasant sky threatened rain. She wasn't sure, but she suspected she was being followed by a black sedan with a dented hood and fender. Near her destination, it began to shower and, lacking an umbrella, she cowered at Stop 13 and turned tail for home.

Rather than return to an empty apartment, she sat unnoticed on a bench sheltered by a chestnut tree across the street in Allan Gardens. Hands buried in the pockets of her tweed knickerbockers, she wore a man's mackinaw jacket over a loose-fitting checked shirt. She concealed her cropped, raisin-black hair slicked with ointment smelling of burnt leather under an eight-panel tweed cap. At four feet tall, with her boyish figure, Violet passed for male.

Sitting in a fine drizzle, she watched a raft of knockabouts play chess in a gazebo and share a bottle of cheap red concealed in a soiled paper bag. By the time she slogged across Carlton, through the lobby of the Sheldrake Apartments, onto the elevator, and up to her flat, her white canvas tennis shoes were soaked through.

The following day at work, Willy offered Violet a banana Life Saver. Violet and Willy worked side by side in the sorting department at the postal depot inside Union Station. The workmates took breaks and lunched together every day, sitting on a low parapet overlooking the labyrinth of conveyor belts moving parcels, canvas mail sacks, bags of securities, money packages, and registered materials into and out of bandit-proof grey container cars.

Violet and Willy–short for Willomena–were the only female sorters at Postal Station A. Willy, big-boned and muscular, held the candy roll up to Violet. "Tell you a secret?"

More than once a day, Willy posed this to Violet, and because Willy was dull as a result of being kicked in the head by a barn animal as a child, Violet never knew what she would come out with.

This morning Violet was distracted. "Huh?"

Willy smoothed the pussy bow knotted at her throat and straightened her collar, repeated, "Tell you a secret?"

Violet squinted. She looked into her pal's mud-coloured eyes. "Okay."

"I don't like Life Savers anymore."

"That's the secret?"

Willy shrugged. She looked offended. "You're not yourself."

Violet said, "Huh?"

Willy had a five-year-old at home she called Little Pretty. The little boy had the prettiest hazel eyes. Little Pretty's father, Kneehigh Jackson, was a pint-size wrestler, the offspring of an Italian merchant and a Mississippi sharecropper who'd trained with Mickey Boom-Boom at the Arena Gardens. Along with five thousand other fanatics, Willy and Violet faithfully attended Saturday bouts at the Mutual Street Arena. Post office salaries afforded them dollar-fifty ringside seats.

Willy had no use for men but desperately wanted a baby. It appeared hopeless until opportunity fell into her lap or, more accurately, Violet's. Willy and Kneehigh met in the third round of a bout after an undercard from Toledo, Ronny the Steamer, tossed Kneehigh off the mat and over the top rope, where he landed on Violet.

Willy shouted, "Can I have him?"

Violet shoved the little man onto Willy's lap. "He's all yours."

Willy and Kneehigh became attached at the hip. In the ring, Kneehigh was bombastic, but outside the Arena, the straw-weight was anything but. Reserved and diffident, he went around in secondhand corduroy suits, checked shirts and a misshapen velveteen hat.

It wasn't long before Willy whispered to Violet, "Tell you a secret?"

"Okay."

"Kneehigh taught me the wrestling move that puts a baby in you."

Kneehigh vanished while Willy was expecting. If people asked, Willy said he went for a walk. Pressed by Violet, she claimed he walked as far as Medicine Hat, where he'd died of something with a long name. Violet asked Willy about a funeral. Willy shook her head no.

"Can't be one. Doctors said even dead he's still contagious."

"Really?"

"Yep."

Violet shrugged.

"Tell you a secret?"

"Okay."

"I don't know where Medicine Hat is. Do you?"

"Alberta."

"Have you been there?"

"Uh-huh."

"Is Alberta far?"

"Uh-huh."

"Too far for Kneehigh's little short legs to walk?"

"Uh-huh."

"You believe me though, right?"

"Uh-huh."

Willy considered Violet a dear. Likewise, Violet regarded Willy as the big little sister she never had. After Little Pretty was born, Willy gathered items stowed in Kneehigh's Indestructo wardrobe trunk he'd kept at her house—mainly costumes, barbells, Roman sandals and clothing—dug a pit on her property, placed all of it in the hole, and, except for the shirts and some caps she gave to Violet, burned everything.

Now, when Violet wore clothing that had belonged to Kneehigh, Little Pretty called her daddy.

A whistle sounded. Break ended. Violet and Willy returned to the sorting tables. Willy spat a Life Saver on the floor and repeated, "You're not yourself."

"Have I ever been?"

"Have you ever been what?"

"Nothing."

The second time Violet boarded the trolley to North Toronto was two months later, on Empire Day. Instead of getting off at Stop 14 at Eglinton, she sissied out and rode the streetcar all the way to the Glen Echo Road terminal.

The steel car clanked into the city limits' terminus. The motorman sounded the air whistle, applied the handbrake. The conductor in a shiny black suit jacket walked the length of the car on spindly scissor legs, stooping to collect balled-up Kleenex and discarded cellophane candy wrappers. At the centre doors, he snapped his fingers and pointed at Violet staring out the window. "Hey. Boy. Cash fare back into the city. Five cents. Pay or get."

When Violet turned, he realized his mistake and mumbled an apology. "A nickel just the same, lady."

Violet hurried off the trolley, telling herself she was hungry. Inside Conery's, the commissary next to the terminal shed and car barn, motormen and conductors sat in seafoam-green leather booths, smoking, sipping coffee, and chewing the fat. The township food market across the street had closed early for the holiday. The taxi stand was empty. A pair of mustachioed transit workers in soiled blue overalls sat opposite one another, leaning away from the table, hands of cards fanned close to their chest, playing Irish Switch.

Violet ordered the blue-plate special: egg salad sandwich with yum-yum pickles, a side of potato chips and a glass of pop. The waitress removed a pencil from the chest pocket of the yellow bungalow apron she wore over a uniform as white as Monday's clothesline.

"What kinda pop?"

Violet asked if she could instead have a glass of milk. The waitress clicked her tongue, her narrow, disapproving face hovering above Violet. "Why not? It's your half dollar."

Perched on a chrome stool, elbows resting on the countertop, the waitress brought her order.

A man in an overcoat breezed into the diner and, without removing his fedora, sat in a corner booth and eyed Violet when he assumed she wasn't looking in his direction.

Violet requested a straw, then pushed aside the plate and nibbled on a potato chip. She removed an envelope from her pocket addressed "Meta Robinson, 2497 Yonge Street, Toronto, 9." Pressing the envelope on the counter, she read the address again. The stern image of King George peeked through the black cancellation mark over the four-cent, sun-gold stamp in the corner. In nineteen years at the post office, this was the only item Violet had ever filched.

The waitress broke into Violet's thoughts, placing the bill on the counter. "Somethin' wrong?"

Violet crumpled the envelope in her hand. "No."

"It's hardly touched."

"I wasn't hungry."

The waitress clicked her tongue. "Suit yourself."

Violet returned to Allan Gardens in the evening and stayed until the Toronto Police Silver Band arrived for a performance in the pavilion. Rather than stick around, Violet escaped through the wrought iron gate undetected. Inside her little third-floor flat, she closed the windows, pulled down the blinds and put an Enrico Caruso recording on the phonograph player. Lying on her back on her bed fully clothed, she stared at the air above her, Caruso's voice a fortress against the failing daylight.

At the depot the next day, Willy told Violet that Little Pretty had learned the reverse headlock move.

Violet said listlessly, "Nice."

"You don't like Little Pretty anymore?"

"You know I do. I love Little Pretty like I love the morning."

Violet recently gifted Little Pretty a mechanical rag doll as big as the boy himself that, when shaken violently, said "Daddy." Punched in the stomach, the doll said "Momma."

They sat in silence on the parapet until Willy said, "Tell you a secret?"

"Okay."

"Don't get mad?"

Violet squeezed Willy's large hand. "Never."

"Promise?"

"Promise."

"If I go away, you get Little Pretty."

"You're not going away."

"Not even if police take me?"

"The police? Take you? Why?"

The third time Violet boarded the northbound trolley was on Father's Day weekend in June. The black sedan with a dented hood and fender tailed her. At Stop 13, her courage wavered.

She disembarked south of Mount Pleasant Cemetery and sat on a bench coaxing herself to continue on foot. She pretended not to notice the black sedan round a corner and disappear. Under the old Belt Line bridge, a messy-haired teenager wearing a North Toronto Collegiate letter sweater and driving an old bucket rolled up beside Violet.

"Hey, pal. Need a lift?"

Violet glanced at her dusty tennis shoes.

"Get in."

Violet glared at the teen.

"Beg pardon, ma'am. Thought I knew you from school. How far you headed, anyway?"

"Eglinton."

"I'll drive you." When Violet hesitated, he added, "It's what we do in this part of the city."

She stepped on to the running board, riding like those Chicago machine-gunners she read about in the dailies. "Easy on the bumps."

They passed a market garden, an apple orchard, and a jersey cow. The driver made a mooing sound. Rolling through the intersection at Yonge and Davisville, he waved enthusiastically at a trio of blind Great War veterans, side-by-side on a bench outside the general store, staring mutely at the sky.

Shouting above the rattle of the engine, he told Violet, "They're from the convalescent hospital."

When Violet didn't respond, he added, "Blind. Chlorine. Fuckin' Krauts. Pardon my French."

Plumes of grey smoke drifted above the smokestacks at the Millwood brickyard. A subdivision was being constructed in a field south of Eglinton. Near the town hall at Roehampton, Violet shouted, "Here's fine."

The car slowed and Violet stepped from the running board. "Thanks. I'll walk the rest."

She milled about in the shadow of the Capitol Theatre marquee. Across the road, Violet spied a woman about Meta's age behind the display window of Robinson's Radio Parlour and felt as though she was being kicked in the heart. A mother in a seersucker dress and straw hat pushing a perambulator looked at Violet, doubled over, panting. "Are you okay, son?"

Panicked, Violet ducked into the Capitol. The girl in the ticket booth looked up from the folded paperback she was reading.

Violet asked, "What's on the screen?"

"It says on the marquee."

Violet glanced outside in time to spy the black sedan with a dented hood and fender glide past. "Just tell me."

"It's called, *Love, Lick and a Promise*."

"About what?"

The girl sighed, rhyming off a prepared description of the film printed on a cue card. "A happy-go-lucky bandit in Arizona plays cat-and-mouse with the sheriff pursuing him while romancing a local beauty." She glanced at her wristwatch. "Starts in three and a half minutes."

"I'll take one."

Violet sat in the back row of the darkened theatre, munching popcorn, watching the man in the overcoat and drab fedora from the diner who slinked in after the newsreels started. Seated off to her right, a section away, he watched her pretend to watch the film.

Violet left long before the credits rolled.

Back at her apartment, Violet put on Turandot. She watered the red geraniums on the sill.

Sitting on the end of her bed, she absentmindedly observed youngsters playing in the fountain across the street in Allan Gardens. Older children played prisoner's base. She wondered if Meta's life had turned out fine, after all.

———

Tuesday following Dominion Day, Violet left work early. The sun was hot and strong.

She walked to the Simcoe Street Loop beside the Daly House Hotel, knowing better than to look back over her shoulder. Boarding the trolley northward for the fourth time, she reached her destination without caving.

Willy had said something during break Violet couldn't shake. Sitting beside one another on the parapet, Willy had said, "Tell you a secret?"

"Okay."

"Police came again."

"Police? Came again?"

"Yes."

"What do they want?"

"It's a secret."

"Did they say their names?"

"Yes. I called them policemen. They said, we're detectives. I said that's the same thing, though. They said, no."

"What did they want?"

"One was Detective Porter and the other one that didn't talk as much said he was Detective Beany, I think. I don't remember. The ones dressed like normal policemen brought shovels."

"Shovels?"

"They dug the yard and searched the cellar, dug the garden and rummaged the attic and looked under the sink and through closets."

"For what?"

"It's a secret."

"Can you tell me?"

"Not yet."

"When did this happen?"

"A week ago. Or two weeks ago. Or three weeks ago. I can't remember. But they came before, too."

"Why didn't you tell me?"

"I did."

Violet steadied herself on the sidewalk outside Robinson's Radio Parlour, feeling scared inside her chest. Banners, bunting, Union Jacks, and Red Ensigns attached to storefront awnings drooped in the still air. The street was tame. Children and mothers strolled this sleepy stretch of Yonge. It occurred to Violet she knew nothing about this part of the city because nothing ever happened here.

Inside the shop, Meta stood behind glass, quizzically studying Violet. In her late twenties with the chubby face of a cherub, Meta's armour-grey eyes resembled the underside of rain clouds. She jerked open the door. "Telegram?"

"What?" Violet swallowed.

"I'm sorry. I mistook you for—You've been looking inside a few minutes. I thought you were a messenger boy."

Violet suppressed an instinct to bolt. "I need a radio."

"Come in." Meta opened the door wider. "Look around."

The showroom was expensively carpeted. A row of handsome radios, some as large as curio cabinets, lined an entire wall. Violet slinked around the shop's periphery, tennis shoes swishing over carpet. Her plum-sized heart fluttered against her ribcage like a moth's wing.

Meta tucked a loose strand of long, black hair behind her ear. "Here's an appealing model." She crossed the showroom floor. "Mercury Super One. Retails at ninety-five dollars, excluding tubes and batteries. There's also the license at two dollars annually." Meta tapped the top of the radio with her fingernail. "All in all, not a bad little unit. Pulls in London. In the evenings, of course."

Violet studied Meta. "I don't—"

Meta asked, "If you're interested in our payment plan, we can—"

"Are you Meta Varcoe?"

Meta appeared uncomfortable. "Yes. Varcoe was my maiden name. Why?"

Violet felt weak. She went to the door and locked it. Meta looked confused as Violet returned to one of two chairs placed beside the display of radios. "Can we sit?"

Meta eased herself into the other wingback.

Neither spoke as two men in black flannel suits, serious faces partially concealed by fedoras, materialized on the sidewalk in the doorway of the shop.

Meta laughed nervously. "What's going on? They look like detectives."

"They are detectives."

Meta stood and moved toward the door.

Violet said, "Don't. Tell them you're closed."

"What? Why?"

"Tell them to go away," Violet said. "There's something I have to tell you."

Meta turned to Violet. "Are you going to hurt me?"

"No. I want to tell you something. Then I'll leave. Just tell them to go."

"What do you want to tell me?"

"First, get rid of them. Trust me."

"I don't even know you."

"Yes. You do."

Meta's eyes darted between the two grave figures outside and Violet seated in the wingback. After a long pause, she raised her voice to be heard through the glass, waved her hands, and said, "No. Closed. Sorry."

One of the men casually tugged his sleeve to check the time on his wristwatch. He slowly shook his head. The other man glared past Meta, his eyes locked on Violet. He mouthed something before the duo vanished as quickly as they had appeared.

Meta asked, "Do you know him? What did he say?"

"He said he'll be back." Violet held out her hand. "This is yours."

She handed Meta a locket. "Sit down. I have something to tell you."

"What?"

"It's a long story. I will read it to you."

Meta said, "I don't understand."

"You will."

Violet unfolded pages of paper on her lap and cleared her throat. Before she began to read, she looked Meta square in the eye and said, "First thing I need to tell you is, I murdered your father."

———•••———

This is my confession: I am Violetta Limoncello. I am a fugitive. I was born on an active volcano in the Mediterranean. I resided there until Mama and Papa died one afternoon while out shooting rabbits on a scorched plateau. Because I was a girl who resembled a boy, church fathers had no use for me. Villagers cast me out. They put me on the German ship SMS *Veil Glück* bound for North America. The day I sailed, the mayor tied a lanyard around my neck that included my name, birth year, and a message: This orphan is not a boy. It belongs now to Uncle Veto in Brooklin. I still remember the mayor's parting advice. Be quiet. Wear quiet shoes.

I was seven.

The crossing to the Strait of Gibraltar was atrocious. Some crew mistook me for a *Klabautermann*, a malevolent sprite and harbinger of doom. The rest assumed I was the ship's boy and mistreated me accordingly. I was terrified. If not for a kind-hearted English boatswain named Van Wart who sheltered me in the forehold, I might have perished. Van Wart secreted me rations of oily stew and pretzels and gave me his waterproof edition of the King James Bible. He taught me English. My voyage lasted one hundred seventy-eight days with several ports of call. Van Wart told me I was bright. I made it through the first chapters of the Book of Genesis.

The captain, unsure of my precise destination, unloaded me on the Chimneys, a guano-encrusted rocky outcrop off Morgan Point, midway between Brookline, Massachusetts, and Brooklyn, New York, in Long Island Sound. I was rescued by a tug and deposited on a wharf in New Haven. After being processed, I set out afoot on Union Avenue to the turnpike, following the New England coastline north, sleeping under trees and begging for food. In Providence, I lodged in a doss house, shined shoes, and stole to survive. By the time I walked to Boston, I had read to the Book of Esther. I worked as a chimney sweep and dabbled in daytime burglaries.

I was nine.

Northward from Boston, I read Jeremiah's sad dirges and slinked into Bangor, Maine.

One morning, while picking pockets at the rail depot on Exchange Street, a green-eyed Queen of Thieves, Phoebe Gilbert, tapped my shoulder with her shillelagh and said, I observed you back there. You move quietly. I could use you, lad. What are you called?

I said, Violetta.

She said, Violetta? That's a gal's name. Violetta what?

I said, Limoncello.

She said, You're Vincent Lemon now.

I said, But I'm a girl.

She said, Violet Lemon then.

I said, Okay.

Gilbert draped her arm over my shoulder and said she intended to make a righteous burglar out of me. I liked her. She was kind. She taught me how to move in darkness. She taught me you don't look, you see; you don't hear, you listen. My job was to reconnoiter, climbing veranda posts to unfasten windows, entering premises through the slightest cranny. I scouted for alarms and booby traps. If I encountered a clerk burning the midnight oil, a dozing watchman, or even a watchdog, I would slink back outside and call off the robbery.

Profits were high. The risk was low. I continued reading the Bible—Jonah, Micah, and Nahum.

Because of my cautiousness, no one met harm.

I was twelve.

In the next four years, I graduated into a first-class sneak thief, trekking across the Dominion, east to west and back again. It had taken a decade, but eventually I read the Bible in its entirety before arriving in Toronto.

I was sixteen.

At the tag end of summer, I hopped a westbound freight on a siding near Cornwall, Ontario. Inside a livestock car, I met Joe and Hank, raddled hobo burglars as poor as Job's turkey, and Princess Rita, a two-thousand-pound baby elephant. Secured with chains, the seven-month-old male calf, about my height, was destined for the Toronto Zoo.

The train accelerated. Joe possessed the submissive temperament of a coward. He was pleasant. Hank was brooding. I got a bad sense from him.

Joe said, I'm Joe. This is Hank.

Hank nodded. He had a habit of chewing his droopy moustache.

Joe pointed at the Indian elephant swaying with the train's momentum and said, That's Princess Rita.

I said, I'm Vincent.

Joe said, Pull up a crate.

The honeyed smell of elephant dung permeated the stock car. Damp, ankle-deep straw covered the slatted floor. Joe offered me cold tomato soup in a cracked Kilner jar, a piece of stale bread, and salmon from a can. In return, I offered my new travel companions oranges, chipped beef, and a can of peaches stowed in my gunny sack.

Hank paused from chewing his moustache to ask, What are you?

The question confused me. I said, What?

He said, What are you, angel?

I sipped from the Kilner jar before passing it to Joe who said, We burgle. Hank's asking what a sweet-looking lad like you does to get by in the big world—

Hank interrupted. Ain't what I'm asking.

I dragged my sleeve over my mouth and told them, I sneak.

The train rocked comfortingly, panel door wide open. The blue St. Lawrence breezed past before giving way to a blur of green-gold countryside.

Hank and Joe told dirty stories, played mumblety-peg, and dozed. I collected orange rinds and fed Rita, scratching the elephant's chin. I picked the lock and removed the chains, allowing the poor creature to lie down. Rita responded by flapping his ears, wagging his tail, and trumpeting.

The freight approached the Toronto yard in a few hours and slowed. I left Princess Rita unchained in the stock car and Joe and Hank south of the quarter-mile bridge in the Don Flats.

Rita proved a popular family attraction. Parents paid five cents for their children to ride on his back and gouge his sides with their heels down in the valley, over the Winchester Street Bridge.

Lodging in a room across from Riverdale Park, I often stole onto the premises and into the elephant house at night with treats. Rita purred when I petted his leathery flanks. The next day Rita would trumpet when he spied me among the crowd pinching valuables from the throng outside his enclosure.

One afternoon I found a folding pocket camera on a bench near Rita's pen. I intended to keep it until a boy in a sailor suit said, Hey, fella. That belongs to my ma. She'll photograph me when my turn comes on the elephant.

I looked around and said, Where is she?

The boy said, Princess Rita?
I said, No. Your ma.
He shrugged. I don't know. She told me stay here.
I returned the camera to the boy.
A policeman approached.
The boy smiled, Hello, Officer Henry.
Before I could slink away, Officer Henry clutched me by the arm. He asked the boy, Everything fine, son?
The boy stammered nervously, Yes. Why wouldn't it be?
Officer Henry eyed me doubtfully, making sure. The officer gave me a shake and asked the boy, What did he say? What does he want you to do?
He gave me back my camera, the boy said. He told me to tell my ma next time be careful.
That so? Officer Henry tightened his grip. What are you doing here, boy?
I'm here for a ride on Princess Rita, like him, I said.
Officer Henry stared at me hard.
The boy took a deep breath. Scared of getting in trouble he pleaded, You know my ma, Officer Henry, right? And you know my dad, too, right?
Officer Henry attempted to settle the boy, telling him, It's okay, son. You didn't do anything wrong. It's him I need to keep my eye on.
He released me. I scarpered.
It was over for Princess Rita a short time later when a carpet tack embedded in the elephant's gum resulted in the calf refusing food. It abscessed. He died. Julian Leather Goods Co. was hired to remove the carcass to their King Street tannery. They peeled his hide and tanned and stitched it into expensive purses and wallets. My stomach turned when crowds gathered to view Rita's embalmed head, trunk, and tail displayed in the storefront window. I broke into the leather goods shop, removed the remains, and gave him a proper burial.
On the second of November, I attended an All-Souls' Day service at St. Simon's.

Entering the vestibule, I snatched a leather pocketbook. During Canon Dann's homily on the thieves crucified with Christ, I rubbed the stolen wallet concealed in my pocket with my thumb and thought of Rita. Names of deceased congregants were read aloud. The choir sang "I Need Thee Every Hour." The boy soprano's solo made me cry. When the collection plate came around, I contributed the bills and coins from the stolen pocketbook. After the service, I crossed the Glen Road Bridge and chucked the empty pocketbook into the valley, my pocket-picking days over.

On a shortcut home through St. James' Cemetery, Bible under my arm, I happened upon Joe and Hank breaking into mausoleums, smoking Old Abe cigars, and kicking a bleached skull around like a ball.

Joe, wearing a sooty top hat, shouted, Vincent.

I weaved my way through tombstones, across the spongy, leaf-strewn lawn toward them. Hey, Joe. Hank.

Hank kicked the skull toward me, Hello, Bible boy.

The skull rolled to a stop at my feet. Joe chuckled and asked, Where are you coming from?

Church.

Joe was tipsy. Hank sniggered. He was drunk. He chewed his moustache, pointed at the skull. Kick it here, angel.

I picked the skull up, placed it on a marker, and said, It's a person, not a game.

Crows circled overhead.

Joe exhaled a ring of smoke. We could use your help.

I asked, For what?

Hank said, Lookout.

I said, Where?

Joe said, Greengrocer on Queen. Gunna blow his safe.

Hank stumbled into me, nearly bowling me over. He grabbed my arm and twisted. You in? Out?

A week later, I reluctantly met them in the alley behind Varcoe's Groceries in quiet shoes and dark, close-fitting clothing. A full moon hovered over us like the silvery eye of God. I was nervous. Until then, I was never nervous. We greeted one another in hushed voices. Joe knelt, unrolled a burglar kit that contained dynamite, and told me the plan. He had a .32 in his waistband. Hank had a .38.

I pointed at the moon and said, It's too bright. I say postpone.

Hank scowled. Who asked you? Besides, place's empty.

I sighed. You sure?

He said, Yeah. It's tonight.

I said, No. I mean, are you sure no one's inside?

He said, Yeah.

I pointed at Joe's waist. What are those for then?

Hank slapped my hand. Just in case. He glanced up and down the alley. You know, angel, you got girl's hands. Just go around front and whistle when you see something.

Joe said, Keep it down, both of you.

I pleaded, Gimme a sec inside.

Hank said, What for?

I said, It's what I do. Five minutes. I'll locate the vault and open the door.

Hank pushed me backward. You know what? We don't need you. He turned and palmed the door and said to Joe, Let's bash it in.

Joe said, No. Too noisy, then looked at me, pointed at the cellar window, and said, Five minutes. Go.

The window-catch unfastened with ease. I slid open the narrow pane and slipped inside. The unlit cellar was crowded with merchandise. The dirt floor silenced my footfalls. Climbing the stairway on padded feet, I explored the shop, noting the absence of a vault. I spirited by half a dozen rooms in the apartment upstairs, counting numerous snoring figures outlined under bedclothes.

Pussyfooting into a bedroom where two little girls shared a cot, I nicked an almond-sized locket off the bedside table and slipped it into my chest pocket. Slinking from the room, feet barely touching the floor, a voice so quiet I almost thought it was my own said, Momma.

I froze.

A girl sat up in bed. Momma? It's Meta.

A second voice, higher, more excited. Momma?
I held my breath, whispered, Go back to sleep.
They obeyed. It was quiet a moment, then, Momma? It's Meta.
I whispered back, Yes, Meta?
Meta whispered, I miss you.
Back in the alley, I pleaded with Joe and Hank. There are families in there.
Hank said, So, and padded his waist. We got these.
I said, And children.
Hank sneered, Go round front. Whistle for trouble.
I didn't move. He shoved the .38 under my chin, snapping my head backward. The hammer clicked. He snarled, Don't think I won't. Done it before. Do what I say and don't run out on us either 'cause your ass is in the jackpot, too.

Queen Street was as quiet as a mausoleum. Crouching in the doorway of the carriage works next door, I rubbed my hands together against the chill of the bright November night. The spire atop Cooke's Presbyterian Church pointed heavenward, a rigid, cautionary finger.

A policeman approached on the sidewalk. Instead of whistling a warning, I crouched lower, the stolen locket pressed against my chest.

Too late. The policeman made me out in the moonlight. Hey. Boy. What you up to there?

A sunburst flashed above, followed by the report of a gunshot. Glass shattered. More gunshots. Girls screamed. The policeman drew his gun and ducked behind a telegraph pole. Glass and splinters rained down. I heard grunts of men in battle. Joe, cut to ribbons, landed like a sack of wet oatmeal on the sidewalk. Hank followed with a thud. Blood bubbled from Joe's lips. He writhed in pain, making a feeble attempt to stand.

He saw me and whimpered, Run.

The policeman pulled the trigger, putting a lead ball through Joe's face.

Hank cried, Don't shoot.

Men in night clothing spilled out from the shop, pummelled and kicked him unconscious. In the confusion, I ran, policeman in pursuit.

Stop, he commanded.

A bullet traced past me. I escaped down an alley.

It was over for Joe. For days and weeks, police cast a dragnet over the city in search of the third accomplice. As for Hank, a jury sentenced him to hang for the murder of shopkeeper John Varcoe.

The Saturday before Easter, I sat on a bench at a cab stand outside Toronto Jail disguised in a walking skirt and lady's buttoned boots, opened Bible on my lap. Over the wall in the exercise yard, you could hear a mouse sigh. At half-past eight, a black flag was run up the flagstaff. The jail bell pealed. It was over for Hank.

Too tired to continue to run, I threw my Bible in the lake and remained in Toronto, masquerading for a time in ladies' clothing. I found work at Fielder Box Co., and then the post office.

I am thirty-seven. I am alone. I wish it were over for me.

Violet finished her accounting. For a long time, Meta sat in shocked silence.

Violet knew Meta and her husband were childless. Meta's younger sister, Olive, lived in Vancouver. Except for the odd dream about her deceased mother, who had died from TB earlier in the year of her father's murder, Meta didn't recall a thing from the night her father was gunned down.

Before Violet left the radio shop in North Toronto, Meta asked, "And Uncle Veto?"

"Who?"

"Uncle Veto? Brookline? Did you locate him?"

"No."

Meta walked Violet to the door. "What do I tell the detectives if they come back?"

"They will."

"What do I say?"

"Whatever you want."

"Violet, or whoever you are, don't ever come back here, okay?"

"Okay."

"I don't want to see you again."

"Okay."

"Ever."

"Okay."

Instead of her apartment, Violet visited Allan Gardens, hid inside the Palm House, and wept. The sky darkened. Through the domed glass ceiling, she observed one star after another burn into existence. It was sweltering. She passed out.

Months later, on an overcast autumn afternoon, Violet had nearly reached her apartment building when the black sedan with a dented hood and fender cruised to the curb beside her. The driver leaned over and rolled down the passenger-side window. He held up a metal badge. "Detective Porter. It's unlocked. Get in."

It began spitting.

Violet ignored the detective's request and continued on the sidewalk. The black sedan with a dented hood and fender jolted forward, balloon tires bumping over the curb and onto the sidewalk, partially blocking her way.

Porter shouted over the juddering engine, "Just want to talk."

Violet sighed.

Facing Violet, one hand gripping the wooden steering wheel, the other clasping the top of the bench seat, the detective leaned forward and shouted, "Suit yourself. Bet your girlfriend—or whatever she is—will be more talkative." He held Violet's gaze. "Either way, won't leave you alone 'til you answer some questions."

Violet looked up and down the sidewalk.

Porter's manner changed. "Come on. It's about to pour. You'll get soaked. Those tennis shoes of yours are already wet."

"I'm nearly home."

The spit became a drizzle. In the distance, thunder.

"No. You're not."

The door creaked open. She stepped up onto the running board and climbed into the car. The seat springs were shot, and the upholstery was stained. Violet could barely see over the wood-panelled dash. A steady downpour pelted the windshield. She rolled up the window. The interior stunk like a bag of soiled laundry, perspiration. Fingernail clippings dusted the muddy floormat.

They cruised the rainy city for a long time in silence, wipers swooshing hypnotically, struggling to repel the deluge. The windshield fogged. They drove around the waterfront. Porter rolled his window down a crack and instructed Violet to do the same. They drove downtown. They drove through the part of the city where well-heeled people lived. They drove around factories beside the river.

Violet spoke first. "Is there a point to this?"

Detective Porter harrumphed. "I'm trying to unnerve you. Get you to say something incriminating. It's a way of getting you to talk. I'm wasting my time, though. You're good at this. I can tell you've done it before."

"Now what?" she shrugged. "What's your plan? Your idea didn't work."

"You're right. Okay. It didn't work. But I want to take you somewhere and show you something."

"Is it close? Because I got things to do."

"Yes. Close. After, I'll drop you off straight away outside your apartment. Promise."

Rain fell harder.

"Miss Lemon, or Violet, may I call you Violet? That's the name you go with?" Porter's eyes never left the road. "Odd how I couldn't find a thing on you. Nothing. Not at the post office. Stumped the super in your building when I went poking around there. Nobody seems to know about you. Odd. Even the rum-hounds across the road from your apartment, you know, the boozers who play chess all day in the park. Don't know a thing about you."

"Why would they?"

"That's me being thorough. What is your real name, again?"

"You know my name."

"Okay, then, Violet. You're from where originally?"

"Come on. Is that what this is about? Where I'm from?"

The black sedan left the busy boulevard for a quiet residential street lined with naked trees and shabby brick homes.

Porter talked faster. "They assigned me a detective from the provincial police to help with the Kneehigh disappearance. They do that sometimes when it comes to cold cases. Anyway, I prefer working alone. His name's Detective Greeny. Truth be told, I'm not fond of him. I don't like him. Something about him. I don't know. Certainly don't require his assistance. And he's got all the bad habits. Clips his fingernails wherever. Pushes people's buttons. You know the type. Do you know the type?"

"Uh-huh."

Porter stopped the sedan by the curb on Queen Street. "See that place across there? Used to be a greengrocer. Look familiar?"

"Nope."

"I need to be honest with myself, Violet. It could be I resent him. Could be that, right? I have to accept it. I'm not saying it is, or I'm not saying it's not. Where you from again?" He paused, anticipating an answer. Violet stared straight ahead. Porter continued, "The obnoxious sonofabitch—pardon my French—was forced on me, you know, by the higher-ups."

Porter pursed his lips to whistle. Violet stared straight ahead.

Porter continued, "I don't like him. But I got to work with him, so I work with him. You ever work with someone you didn't like?"

Violet stared straight ahead.

Porter said, "Hey, look. Look at me for a sec. Light's terrible in here so I'm going to try to sketch you later from memory."

Violet stared at Porter.

Porter whistled through his teeth. "Boy, do you ever look like a boy."

She reached for the door latch. "It's a twenty-minute walk home. I'm leaving."

Porter ignored her. He continued talking. "Wait. I got a feeling you'll want to hear the end of my story."

Violet rolled her eyes.

Porter said, "Going around like he's a big deal 'cause he's a member of the Department of Criminal Investigation's bandit squad. How old are you?"

Violet sighed.

Porter plowed on. "Know what it is? I'll tell you what it is, Violet. I'll tell you this. Greeny's clearance rate doesn't touch mine, not by a far piece. You know what I mean by clearance rate, Vi?"

"Nope."

"I think you do, Vi. But for emphasis, I'll explain nonetheless. Clearance rate is the number of arrests I make stick. My department at the division has a seventy-eight percent clearance rate. Anything above eighty percent is unheard of. Mine? Mid-nineties."

She stared straight ahead.

"These are class one offences I'm talking here. Robbery. Theft. Rape. Forgery." He turned to Violet. "Look at me."

She turned her face toward his.

"Homicide."

They stared at one another in silence until Porter said, "What that means is, well, I always get my man." Sizing up Violet, he added, "Or, you know, whatever."

Violet cleared her throat. "You sure talk a lot."

This struck Porter as humourous. He laughed. "That's a first." Then turning serious, ordered her, "Open the glove box."

She resisted.

"Come on. Open it. Nothing in there 'cept a piece of paper."

She turned the latch. The small door dropped open.

"Take it out. The light in here's not so great but look at it."

It was a sketch. A boy.

Violet studied the yellowed paper.

"Familiar? No? From a case. Just over twenty years ago. Not my best work, I'll admit. A greengrocer shot to pieces in his bed above his shop. Right over there, in fact. It just happens a constable's hoofing this stretch of Queen when it occurred. I got the file. It was my investigation. Must have interviewed that cop, the first one on the scene who put a bullet through the guy's face, a hundred times. He told me there was this kid, a boy, and he practically tripped over him. A small fellow. Described him pretty well. Well enough for me to do that sketch. About the size of you, in fact. Could have been sleeping in a doorway. Likely startled by gunshots. The commotion. The cop told me he took off like the devil." Detective Porter exhaled.

"The point?"

"I didn't possess the knowledge I have now. Didn't process like I do today. Anyway, it's all for nothing. The case is closed. One perp expired on the sidewalk, right there." Porter pointed across the road. "The other got the noose."

Porter was quiet, events from the past playing out in his memory.

"Years later. Literally. It occurred to me, perhaps," he paused, "the boy was the lookout."

"Uh-huh."

"What do you think, Violet, a lookout?"

"Sure. Uh-huh. Guess you'll never know. It's a good story, though."

"Guess you're right. You know, the longer I do this job, the better I get."

"That so?"

The rain stopped. The sun was nearly gone.

Violet leaned against the door, pushed it open, and got out.

"Thanks for the drive," she said, slamming the door hard enough to rattle the glass.

Porter leaned over and cranked the window down. "I'll drive you back."

She walked away.

"Suit yourself."

Violet stared straight ahead.

"Hey. Hey. Violet," Porter shouted, "Something I didn't mention."

Violet knew better than to stop and look back.

"I never told you his name. The greengrocer."

The Friday before Christmas, an evergreen decorated in coloured electric lights adorned the sidewalk outside Postal Station A. The post office was busy with the holiday rush. It was past the supper hour when Violet and Willy punched out. As part of their Friday routine, they picked up fish and chips from a Bay Street lunch counter then drove to Willy's home in Todmorden, where she rented a farmhouse on the edge of the valley where the macadam roads ended.

The sidewalk bustled with shoppers. Outside the lunch counter, Willy pulled off her mittens and said, "Little Pretty asked Santa for snow. It's all he wants but five days 'til Christmas and not a flake."

Violet pulled up the collar of her coat, glanced at the empty sky, and said, "What's he really getting?"

"A sleigh. An air gun. A shooting game. A muskrat. A Bowie knife. Gifts like that."

A black sedan with a dented hood and fender slid to a halt at the curb without warning. Men in duffle coats and salt-stained utility boots with two-ply soles sprang from the automobile. They parted the crowd with, "Back up. Get. Everyone. Back."

Willy gripped Violet's hand. "Don't worry, sis."

Detective Porter showed Violet his metal badge. "Hello again, Miss Lemon. This is Detective Greeny."

Detective Greeny presented his metal badge. He stared at Violet and adjusted the brim of his drab fedora. "I'm from the bandit squad."

Willy snapped, "Thanks, Detective Beany, but we know who you are."

Detective Greeny said, "Willomena Duncan?"

Willy snickered. She glanced sidelong at Violet. "These are the dicks I told you about. They're here about Kneehigh."

Detective Greeny opened the car's rear door, ordering Willy to get in. People stared. Willy grinned, wide as a piano. "Am I being arrested?"

Detective Greeny said, "No. Get in."

"Get in yourself. I got a lawyer. He said no body, no crime. And not to talk to you no more. Let's go, Vi."

At Todmorden, Willy lit the stove and warmed dinner. Little Pretty and Violet set the table. Willy made a celery salad. Violet poured three glasses of milk.

Later, Willy said, "Let's cut a tree down."

Outside, Willy lit two acetone-soaked torches and gave one to Violet. Violet put on a toque that had belonged to Kneehigh and followed Willy to the shed to retrieve an axe. They trekked to the edge of the property. Little Pretty carried the axe on his shoulder. A whitish haze in the distance hung in the sky above the city.

Little Pretty found the perfect tree, a nine-foot balsam fir. Willy handed the torch to her son in exchange for the axe. "Hold this."

Practised with the sharp tool, she swung the axe again and again without ceasing. Woodchips flew in all directions. The tree was down in no time. Back at the house after she washed up, Willy said to Violet, "Tell you a secret?"

"Okay."

"I'm not as dull as they tell me I am."

Little Pretty ran to the window, pointed, "Mom. Daddy. Look. Snow."

MALADY OF THE HEART

There were moments early in the mornings during his shaving ritual when, gazing back at himself in the mirror, George realized that, with sixty-five in sight, the time to throw up the sponge approached.

George poured hot water into his shaving mug, dabbed the brush in the scalding water, rubbed the cake of soap, and lathered his face and neck in a circular motion. Swiping the straight razor on the strop a few times, he leaned toward the mirror, reached over his head to the opposite temple, and tugged the flesh below his sideburns up, scraping the blade downward as he considered his life's work. Over forty years and, except for one suspension, no official reprimands, black marks or fines. A respectable clearance rate. George was aware of officers with nearly an equal number of years in uniform who remained constables for the duration of their time on the force. In '19, he was made detective sergeant.

Tilting his head back to expose his jaw, he recognized he was not obligated to drop out. Deputy Chief Stewart would be seventy-two on his next birthday. However, rank-and-file members expressed considerable resentment when older officers at the top refused to die or retire.

When done shaving, he rinsed his face with cold water and patted it dry with a clean towel. As he splashed aftershave on his face, the icy antiseptic stinging his cheeks, Porter looked at his reflection and reassured himself he had at least another five to seven years and would know when to step out.

Then 1921 happened.

Three people close to the detective went into the ground in seven months that year. Teddy in the spring. A grief-stricken Susan a few months later. Izzy Cooke that autumn.

Except for his work and Badge, he lost his purpose.

Teddy was forty-one when he went skating on the big pond by Poplar Creek. The father of three, including Teddy the Third, he'd married late to a lovely Japanese girl, Hatsu Kondo. They met at a recital, when she had accompanied the Berkshire Small Chamber Orchestra on the piano. Hatsu was an exceptional pianist. One look into her magnetic eyes, and Teddy was smitten. After years of travel, Teddy quit the Morris Piano Co. for a teaching job at the Toronto Junction College of Music.

The weekend visit to East Gwillimbury in early spring was routine. Teddy, Hatsu, and their children, along with Beatrice and Ted, loaded into the McLaughlin Model D for the rough ride north of the city, only a portion of the drive on paved motor roads. The enlarged Porter residence of Beatrice and George's childhood on Bolton Street remained in the family.

Instead of church on Sunday morning, a skating party was planned but Beatrice and Ted demurred, citing the chilling temperature. The children then complained it was too cold and begged to remain with their grandparents. At the last minute, Hatsu decided to stay with the kids.

Teddy went skating alone.

It had been a long, cold winter. Sunlight glared off the frozen blue-black surface of the pond. The pristine fractal-patterned ice sheet resembled the frozen fingers of a lightning bolt. Teddy carried an ice chisel with him and, before lacing up, checked the ice thickness. Investigators later discovered the small opening he smashed in the ice near the bank frozen over.

Speculation was that the ice thickness above deeper water in the middle was thinner, and he broke through on his first stride. After a long struggle, he climbed on top of the ice again and crawled to the bank, exhausted by injuries received on the jagged ice. The big pond was about half a mile from town. Everyone was in church. The temperature hovered around thirty-four degrees. In the throes of hypothermia, he did not get far. Later, someone reported hearing cries but had attributed them to a howling dog.

Hours passed. When Teddy failed to return, Hatsu went to find out why. She discovered him in a badly frozen condition, partially concealed in a drainage pipe in a gully. Some of his clothing had been removed.

Hatsu was inconsolable, as were Beatrice and Susan. They wondered if there was more to Teddy's death than it appeared. What explained his attempt to hide himself in the drainage pipe, and why would a person freezing to death partially disrobe?

Informed of the circumstances behind his nephew's demise by the coroner, George kept to himself past observations that, in hypothermic deaths, victims sometimes display a sort of burrowing behaviour, perhaps in an instinctive misdirected effort to save themselves or conceal themselves. Contradictory disrobing was a common practice, likely a result of the victim entering a delusional state. Upon an inquest, the coroner reported the cause of death to be hypothermia, and the jury classified the mishap a death by misadventure.

Susan had considered Teddy the son she didn't have. She took his passing profoundly. When she wasn't sleeping late, Susan abandoned social interests to tackle household chores in a state of automation, beside herself with grief. She scrubbed every surface, beat the carpets, and waxed the tiled floors. Two men from Wilson's Cleaners took down curtains and sent them out for laundering.

One afternoon, George came home unexpectedly and found Susan outside in a downpour, going at the back wooden steps with a brush and pail, knuckles chafed and bleeding. Badge watched George gently touch her shoulder from the window. "Susan, please. Come inside."

After helping her stand, George slowly guided his wife up the steps and through the backdoor into the antiseptic-smelling kitchen. He sat her at the kitchen table and made tea for both of them. Badge turned a few circles under the table, dropped, and curled at her feet, panting.

Seated opposite, George held Susan's hand, palm raw and chapped, and felt the faint pulse of her wrist. He knew he needed her close, but she was far away and almost gone.

"We could hire a charwoman," George suggested, observing the dimmed light in her eyes.

Susan sipped her tea. Through the faintest smile, she answered, "No."

A few mornings later, George awoke to find she had died in her sleep beside him, taken by an unsuspected malady of the heart.

Badge came as far as the open bedroom door, flopped to the hardwood floor, and remained there, George's sentry.

George recognized the routine stillness of death, but this was the coldest, strangest feeling. He opened the window covering only enough to permit a single finger of the dawn to enter, and he rendered a sketch of his wife for the only time in his life. He washed and shaved and dressed and lay a moment beside her on the coverlet before sending for an ambulance to commence the organized confusion of death.

Israel Cooke's coffin was draped with the Union Jack. Constable Cooke's confreres, including George, wore black armbands. Beatrice was among the mourners who filled the small Sixth Line chapel. The obsequies included prayers and a scripture reading, and, as Izzy had requested, George recited Whitman's "O Me! O Life."

The cemetery was along a country road where golden orioles flashed in the trees. A brief graveside service followed. The grave was on a hill overlooking the town. Stores closed out of respect, and Main Street was silent in the warm autumn sunlight.

MALADY OF THE HEART

Leaving the cemetery, Beatrice linked arms with George to steady him. She asked if he recognized any of the constable's family among the mourners.

"No. None of his people came up from Kitchener."

"So sad he never married."

"That was never for him."

Beatrice stopped and looked inquisitively into her brother's face.

"Why not?"

"I thought you knew. Izzy was a homosexual."

"How would I know? How did you know?"

"He told me. Ages ago. He said liars make people uncomfortable. He didn't want me feeling that way." Over Beatrice's shoulder, George saw Kate Howard. "There's Kate. Give me a moment. I want to talk to her."

It was Kate who discovered Izzy Cooke in the horse barn. He had gone to check on Victoria, his big, white mare. At eighty, Izzy could not ride the horse, so he walked her to the pasture daily for runs. Recently, Victoria had stepped on a sliver of hardwood in her front foot, three inches above the hoof. The constable pulled it out with pliers and cleaned the wound thoroughly. The sore was healing nicely.

The afternoon his heart gave out, Izzy went to check on the injury and, while brushing the mare's silky breast, clenched his chest, lowered himself down to the clay floor, and died in Victoria's stall. The affectionate horse nudged Izzy, and when she didn't get a response from him, she whinnied and blew forceful expulsions of air through her nostrils to get someone's attention.

"Hello, Kate. It's me. George. The Deputy. Remember?"

"I'm Kate. That's right," she said, leaning against the iron picket fence enclosing the graveyard. She was dressed plainly, a black leather strap-purse slung over her shoulder. Her brittle grey hair was combed back off her face.

"I didn't see you in the chapel?"

"I couldn't come in. I have a baby, Georgie. A little, little baby."

"Do you? You're more than seventy, Kate. A baby?"

Beatrice came and stood beside George. "Hi, Kate." She smiled a warm, resigned smile. "Do you remember me?"

"I remember. You are Beatrice. Izzy said, 'Teddy is dead, Kate. He went on the big pond, and he is dead, and when you are dead, you do not come back. Izzy always, always, always, always, always, always said," she dropped her voice an octave, "'do not ever go on the ice, Kate. Do not ever go on the ice. Your Teddy should have listened to Izzy, too, right, Beatrice?"

Beatrice's eyes rimmed with tears. "That's right, Kate. He should've."

"Izzy told me everything, you know. All the time. He talked to me, and I listened to him, and then I talked to him, and he listened to me. He was my friend." She looked at George and said, "Friends tell friends things. He told me what you did in the cabin with that man. He was bad. A bad man. You fixed him, Georgie, you fixed him good. Izzy was right about you. You are not a mean one. You never were."

Beatrice, uncomfortable, dabbed her eyes with a hankie and paused to ask George what Kate was referring to.

"I don't know," George said, looking to see who was in earshot. "Whatever Izzy told you, though, Kate, he wouldn't want you to tell anyone else. Right, Kate?"

"Right, Georgie. Right." She looked at Beatrice, beckoning her closer and whispering in Beatrice's ear, "Izzy told me how much you loved Teddy and how much Teddy loved you."

Beatrice pursed her lips and nodded.

"Want to see my baby?" Kate asked cheerily. She opened the black purse slung over her shoulder. "Look—"

Inside was a grey kit and a scattering of sliced carrots. The baby rabbit looked up and twitched its nose, sniffing.

"Sweet," Beatrice said. "Where'd you get it?"

"Under a tree with other ones." Distracted momentarily by passing buggies and cars lifting dust into the air, she asked, "Where do I live now?"

Driving back to the city, George pulled the car to the shoulder of the two-lane asphalt highway. There were no other vehicles in sight. A farmer on the far side of a field seated atop a red tractor planted a cover crop for winter. They sat in silence until George said, "This is the place. Where it happened. Just right up there." George pointed out the windshield. "Near that culvert, there."

"Where what happened?"

"Where the Traviss boy murdered Mr. Johnston. Remember?"

Beatrice surveyed the autumnal landscape. "It looks different now."

"It was a long time ago." They sat quietly, remembering the event before George said, "Do you know why he really did it?"

"Who did what?"

"Traviss. Why he was compelled to murder the old man."

"No. Do you?"

"Traviss told me and the constable on the train to the city that day. He said the old man raped the Nichols girl, and when she said she was going to tell Traviss, the old man spread rumours to defame the boy's name or at least muddy the water some. Izzy and I talked about that case a lot for a long time. It never made sense to us."

"That didn't come out at the trial? About the rape?"

"No. Traviss wouldn't tarnish the Nichol girl's reputation. There's something else I want to tell you. That thing Kate mentioned back there about the man and the cabin."

"What did she mean?"

"I killed a man, you know. Shot him. Made it appear like suicide. And it did."

"Why are you telling me this now. Or ever?"

"Liars make people uncomfortable."

"Was he a mean one, George?"

George nodded.

"Then okay."

HARD NEWS

With J. Davis, 1922

Knowles took notes. Porter chewed an antacid. Wickett smoked a Craven "A". Boyo adjusted the camera. Davis had an erection. An unseen armed guard in the grey gun tower above the facility's entrance observed each man's movements below. Outside the high stone wall enclosing Auburn Prison, State Street was slick with drizzle. No one was out this early except for a passing bread truck.

Unfavourable weather didn't bother Porter. Or the chill in the autumn air, lack of sleep, or hunger. Instead, he focused on the task of removing the handcuff connecting him to Davis. Unfastened, he rubbed his wrist and then straightened his fedora. Adjusting his tie, he picked up his valise and faced the photographer. Prison gate at their back, Porter ordered Davis, "Stand straight. Look into the camera. Don't move." Next, he instructed Boyo, "Take it."

Boyo wasn't ready and continued to fidget with the camera, the size of an electric toaster. "Wait a sec."

Porter glanced up at the gun tower. "We don't have a sec."

HARD NEWS

Wickett looked at the time on his expensive wristwatch. "Train pulls in soon."

Boyo suggested Wickett pose for the photograph, too, adjusting the Speed Graphic's settings. "Stand on the other side," he told Wickett, "with the degenerate in the middle."

Wickett said, "Uh-uh. Davis wasn't my collar—"

Porter interrupted, "Take the damn photograph."

Porter suffered terrible heartburn and a backache. Wickett had a stake in a racehorse named DeathOnTheOtherHand. Knowles jotted in a steno pad with a yellow pencil. Boyo had witnessed the horrors of the Great War up close. Davis was small and diseased.

Porter snapped his fingers impatiently. A wood pigeon began to coo nearby. Boyo adjusted the camera's aperture. "What do you expect?" Boyo complained. "It's raining and dark, and freezing as hell."

Davis twitched and fidgeted and glanced nervously up and down the street. Porter noticed and said to him, "Don't get any ideas." He instructed Wickett, "If he makes a move, gun him down."

Wickett nodded.

Boyo said, "Almost ready."

Porter said, "Then take it."

"Almost there."

Porter gritted his teeth. "You're a pain in the back. That's the third time you've said that."

"Yeah," Davis whined in a staccato voice. "This chill is the death of me and you handsome fellows are to blame."

Porter said, "Who asked you?"

Davis trembled. His eyes rolled abnormally. A frightened expression appeared on his face. He bared his teeth, grinned, and confessed to no one in particular, "I killed him with a knife I made from a hacksaw."

Boyo looked up from the camera, mouth set in a tight line. "What did you say?"

Porter interjected, "Doesn't matter. Not important. Take the photograph."

Davis's declaration stunned Knowles, who jotted the statement word for word into his steno, asking Porter disingenuously, "Shouldn't you advise him against—"

"He's been cautioned."

Davis twitched, grimaced, and scratched his palm aggressively.

Wickett ground the Craven "A" into the pavement under his heel and said with a wry smile, "Shoulda been in the booby hatch a long time ago."

Boyo sighed. "Okay. Ready."

Porter and Davis posed, stock still. Boyo raised the camera, centered their figures in the rangefinder, counted three, and pressed the shutter release. The magnesium flashbulb detonated a white burst of light.

There was shuffling in the gun tower. Porter asked, "Good?"

Boyo slowly lowered the camera. "No."

"No? Why no?"

"He smiled."

"What?"

"The freak. He smiled."

"He smiled?" Porter dropped the valise in frustration. Rage building, he repeated, "He smiled." Porter loomed over Davis, a man half his stature and, yellow with anger, railed, "Did I tell you to smile? In Warden Jennings' office, you promised to cooperate. I said do what I say, follow my instruction, we're back in Toronto in no time. You said okay." Porter made a fist as though to strike Davis. Davis recoiled, cap falling to the pavement, setting his wig askew.

Knowles said, "Hey. Not so rough."

Porter said, "I didn't lay a finger on him. Yet." He stepped toward the prisoner and Davis winced a second time. Porter said, "Pick up the cap. Fix the rug. Look into the camera. If I see so much as a smirk, believe you me—"

Knowles said, "Is that necessary?"

Porter said, "It's a ploy."

Knowles countered. "He's sick."

"Well, the sonofabitch is giving me heartburn." Porter popped another antacid into his mouth and chewed, adding, "His health isn't my concern."

Porter repeated his demand that Davis retrieve his cap, stand beside him and look into the camera. Instead, Davis yowled like a rabid animal, dropped to his knees and bit through his tongue. He spit blood on the pavement, pleading, "Help me, help me, help me."

The snap of a high voltage switch reverberated from the gun tower, illuminating the men in a searchlight's bright column of light. A disembodied voice from the tower demanded, "What's that racket down there?"

Porter cautiously raised his hands and stared unblinkingly up into the light. In a deferential tone, as though God manned the tower, he spoke, "I'm Detective Sergeant George Porter. Toronto Detective Department. I'm the detective-in-charge. We didn't mean to cause a disturbance. I apologize. I'm here with Detective Wickett." Porter glanced over his shoulder. "Show them who you are, John." Then, addressing the voice in the tower, continued, "I'm responsible for this prisoner transfer. The extradition papers are signed by the governor." He indicated to Davis, curled at his feet. "A little misunderstanding. Everything's in order down here."

"Did he spit on my sidewalk?"

"Who? Him?" Porter nudged Davis with his shoe. "No, no one spit. The prisoner is just under the weather. He's a little overwhelmed."

"What about that butt?"

Wickett quickly stooped and pinched the remains of his crushed cigarette between his thumb and finger and concealed it in his pocket.

The voice said, "Okay. Get."

Porter stooped and took Davis at the shoulder and coaxed, "Come on, Fred. This wasn't my idea. Upsy-daisy." Davis slowly rose to his feet. "It's the chief, my boss, and the newspapers, they want the picture." Porter cajoled, "Get it over with. What do you say? Look at the camera. Boyo, retake it."

The searchlight remained on.

Wickett retrieved Davis' cap and placed it on the prisoner's head. Boyo replaced the flash, raised the camera to his face, and took the photo.

Porter squinted. "Got it?"

"Yep."

Across the road, a Canadian Pacific New York–Toronto express passenger train hissed to a quick stop at the depot. Porter cuffed Davis to his wrist. "Let's go."

The searchlight clicked off. Auburn, New York, returned to darkness.

The locomotive left the depot.

Porter was relieved. Boyo glared out the window. Wickett was handsome but sloppy. Davis was forty-six years old. Knowles was a softy.

Toronto authorities had telegraphed a desperate appeal to Lehigh Valley Railway to make an exception for an unscheduled early morning stop at Auburn depot after Porter encountered unexpected delays. At the last minute, Warden Jennings had required that he obtain the signature of Governor Miller, sending him to the capitol building in Albany. The railroad agreed under conditions: the prisoner remain cuffed to his escort and confined to the compartment car for the four-hour passage.

Sunrise gouged the horizon.

With an empty, deadly stare, Davis sat between Porter and Knowles recounting violent details of his crime, beginning when he first laid eyes on the boy at the victim's shabby McCaul Street residence where booze was sold in teacups, to concealing the body in a field of pigweed in the shadow of Sacred Heart Orphanage. He described eighteen months on the lam and his eventual arrest and conviction in Rochester for theft.

Wickett sat opposite and rested his eyes. Porter remained alert. Boyo contained his rage. When Davis finished describing his crime, he said he was hungry. Knowles lay the steno notebook on his lap, wedged his pencil behind his ear, and watched a purple-orange ladder of veiny dawn sunlight climb the sky.

Fields and valleys rolled past. The train screamed through another town. Another white church and steeple.

A dining-car attendant wrapped on the door with a carafe of black coffee.

Porter ordered a tapioca pudding to soothe his heartburn. When the attendant returned with the dish, he couldn't eat it without removing the handcuff so left it untouched. He cursed under his breath and chewed another antacid. Wickett killed a Craven "A" in the ashtray. Davis had untreated syphilis contracted from a prostitute when he was twenty. Boyo, looking sucker-punched, filed his fingernails with a five-inch ebony nail file he'd taken from a dead German soldier at Herve, near Liège. Knowles felt sorry for the prisoner.

Silence fell. The train rocked. Davis cast his jaundiced eyes around the compartment car. A strange and terrible expression appeared on his face. He said to Porter in that grating staccato voice of his, "I'm really, really hungry. Are you going to eat that pudding or what?" He indicated toward the dish. "It gets a skin on the top, you know?"

Boyo sat across from Davis studying dried specks of blood on the prisoner's white shirt. When Porter didn't reply, Davis resumed talking rapid-fire about his crime. "He said hey mister give me ten cents I want to go to a show he said he liked the pictures so I took him after we had vanilla bean ice cream."

Boyo recognized a perverse version of the thousand-yard gaze in Davis' eyes. Davis tilted his head back and stared up at the compartment car ceiling, his words coming faster. "He cried and cried and cried and cried but I said don't cry don't cry don't cry then I put the blade in." Davis made a squawking sound. His voice changed, becoming deeper. "He was a fucking Jew so what I killed a Jew so what there's more of them coming everywhere."

Wickett said, "That's evil."

Knowles said, "Give him a break. It's an illness."

Porter cleared his throat. "Moral turpitude."

Davis chuckled. "Guess where I put my thing after that?"

Boyo could take no more. He lunged across the aisle at Davis, pressing the nail file to Davis' throat. Knowles pushed himself against the compartment car window, distancing himself from the confrontation. Wickett spilled coffee reaching for his holster.

Porter commanded his partner, "Don't."

They froze.

Boyo said, "I wish you'd shut up."

Davis laughed. "Don't get so hot. The kid was a Jew."

Porter said, "Boyo. Listen."

"He was a fucking—"

"Boyo, listen to—"

Boyo panted. "You slit a boy's throat."

"Boyo, listen to me."

Davis laughed.

Boyo pressed the file into Davis' flesh. Blood appeared.

Porter demanded, "For Christ's sake. Cut it out. Sit down," shoving Boyo hard back into his seat.

Boyo composed himself.

Davis grinned a smug, shit-eating grin.

Porter leaned in and whispered into the child killer's ear, "It would be no skin off my back you dying right here, so cut out the yapping."

Davis's eyes widened. A wet patch appeared on his lap.

Wickett snickered, "Look. The nutter pissed himself. What'd you say to him, George?"

"Told him to behave himself."

Knowles said, "He's to be pitied, not laughed at. He's insane. That's an illness."

Boyo said, "Shut up, Kenneth."

Davis began to rock. His knee trembled. "I'm sorry. I'm not a bad fellow at heart." He wiped his nose on the back of his hand and then looked up and asked Porter with dead eyes, "So are you eating that pudding or what?"

At the Buffalo terminal, the train took on water. Porter showed a border officer his identification and the required paperwork for the prisoner transfer. Knowles stretched his legs on the platform. Wickett wore cheap cologne. Boyo apologized to Porter for losing it back there. Davis had the mental capacity of a seven-year-old.

The lead attendant came to the compartment car before they got going again to inform Porter that his party was required to change trains.

Porter said, "May I inquire as to why?"

The attendant said, "It's not you, constable. It's the trash you're escorting back to the city. It's no longer welcome on this train."

"Who decided?"

"Everyone."

"Everyone?"

"The crew. The entire train."

Porter stood. He instructed the others to gather their belongings, then told the attendant, "By the way, I'm not a constable. I'm a detective sergeant. Learn the difference."

They collected their baggage, located the proper platform, and boarded the Buffalo–Toronto Flyer No.8, a third-class train running on a short, fast freight line.

The change resulted in a two-hour wait plus an additional charge of three dollars and ten cents.

Before the No.8 left the terminal, Porter cuffed Davis to Wickett. Wickett wasn't keen on the idea, but what could he do? Boyo stared out the window, considering his next assignment, the Santa Claus Parade: Saturday, starting at two-thirty. Knowles was a quarter of the way into a novel he had been secretly writing and would never complete. Davis closed his eyes and fantasized about an incident in a prison stairwell a few weeks ago involving a vulnerable inmate. Porter opened a sketchpad.

Just when they had got going again the train came to a sudden stop after Merritton on the Canadian side of the border. Porter asked Boyo to go and discover the cause of the delay. Ten minutes later, he informed Porter a stray cow was on the tracks.

Davis was giddy. He said, "Did we hit it all over the place?"

Boyo sat and said, "Shut up."

The train lurched forward. They were moving again. Porter sketched Davis. The compartment remained quiet until Porter looked up and said unexpectedly, "When I think about it, my career began on a train. Newmarket to Toronto."

Davis said, "Nobody cares."

Porter looked Davis in the eyes and said, "I know. Why would anybody?"

In that instance, Porter decided he had enough and to call it quits.

Knowles said, "I care."

Boyo said, "That's your problem. You care for everything."

Porter thanked Knowles. Knowles told him to continue talking about his law enforcement career. Instead, the detective tore the completed sketch of Davis from the pad, crumpled it, threw it on the floor, and stared out the window.

The train moved rapidly, countryside flying passed at fifty-one miles an hour.

Approaching Toronto, Wickett said, "Things being what they are, George, I don't want photographs with this piece of shit clamped to my wrist."

The detectives exchanged seats and Porter cuffed himself to Davis.

Davis said, "No one likes me."

Boyo scowled at the child killer and said, "Boo fucking hoo. What's wrong with you? What happened to make you like this?"

"I don't know. The doctor said probably my mother."

In the throng at Union Station, Porter and the prisoner attached to his wrist went unnoticed. Porter and Wickett took Davis to No.1 police station by automobile.

Porter processed Davis. Wickett visited the men's room to wash his armpits and comb his hair. Boyo went to the darkroom at the newspaper to develop film, then to the Riverdale Zoo to clear his head. Clouds like white lambs covered the sun. Knowles rode the elevator up to the fifth-floor city room. His editor said the story earned him a byline.

Knowles began typing: *Frederick L. Davis, 46, wanted on the charge of murdering Philip Goldberg, a nine-year-old boy, was arrested last night at Auburn prison, Auburn N.Y., by D/Sgt Geo. Porter . . .*

Porter reached home before Knowles filed his story. When he arrived, he crossed the road to pick up Badge from the neighbour. He paid a boy to watch the dog in his absence. Attaching the leash to the collar, he walked Badge to the corner and home.

"Today was my last day, boy," he told the black-and-tan retriever. "I quit."

HEART'S CONTENT

Having given no thought to how he would occupy his time in retirement, George read a great deal. Thanks to a book provided to him by the Chief Constable, his initial interest lay in popular biographies.

After George tendered his resignation, Chief Constable Dickson, recently promoted to the rank, summoned him to his office at police headquarters. Dickson, seven years younger and two inches taller, had an impressive chevron moustache and grey-green Irish eyes that changed colour according to what was passing through his mind. He spoke with the clipped cadence of someone who liked to keep things going.

George followed the duty desk man into the Chief's office. "Sir, Detective Sergeant George Porter to see you."

Dickson stood behind a black walnut standing desk. A red leather desk pad with brass corners sat in the middle, flanked by a radio set for receiving and broadcasting police bulletins, bulky headphones, and a telephone fitted with a new Hush-A-Phone to reduce noise and to better relay confidential messages. Rereading George's resignation letter, he looked up and said, "Close the door."

George closed the door and looked for a chair, but there wasn't one.

The Chief gestured at the communication equipment. "They tell me that, in the future, every police car will be equipped with apparatus for receiving and transmitting dispatches. Difficult to imagine, though."

"That will be something to behold," George remarked.

"Chitchat aside, you're leaving?"

"Yes, sir."

"When did you come on, Detective?"

"'77."

"Me, I came on in '90."

George nodded.

"Hmm. Could you remain for an additional year or two? Force is short. Can't lose another one."

"With all due respect, sir, I'm through."

"Hold-ups are increasing. Housebreaking is up—"

"Sir. It's final."

Dickson tried in vain to talk the detective into remaining and suggested he revisit his plans in six months. Finally, he recognized George's resolve. "A luncheon, then. Speeches. A send-off."

"No, sir."

Dickson nodded. "You really are a lone hand, aren't you?"

"I've been told."

"Retirees receive a silver tea set."

"Unnecessary."

"Gold cuff links?"

"No, thank you."

"Nothing?"

"Nothing, sir."

"Thrifty, too."

Dickson walked around the desk to shake George's hand, and as he did, he picked a book up off a side table. "Here. At least accept this. A biography of Florence Nightingale. Signed, too. Written a few years ago by a member of the ambulance department on the centenary of her birth. Take it. You'll like it."

"Did you—"

"Like it?"

"No. Read it."

"No time." Dickson clicked his heels, straightened, and saluted. "Thank you for your devotion to duty, Detective Sergeant Porter. Good day."

George mirrored the Chief Constable's salute but with considerably less vigour.

"Good day."

After completing outstanding investigations, the detective had to fill out forms to initiate his pension. He turned in his Colt revolver, cleaned his locker, and packed the contents of his desk.

A few weeks later, a letter from the Police Commissioner expressing appreciation for his years in uniform as a member of the Toronto Police Force arrived in the mail. The letter also contained an enamelled gold lapel pin with the force's logo.

George had trouble sleeping after Susan's death. In retirement, his insomnia worsened. Beatrice suggested a visit to the doctor for a prescription. Instead, he read voraciously through the night. Other times, he leashed Badge and went on night-time strolls through the neighbourhood.

Beatrice recommended he get a library card. Visiting an area branch, he filled out the application form, presented evidence he was a taxpayer, and was granted borrowing privileges.

He spent a lot of time in the stacks. On Mondays after school, staff facilitated free art classes, mainly charcoal and pastels, for boys and girls in the Teachers' and Children's Room to the left of the main entrance. The same free course occurred on Wednesdays for mothers.

George approached the dour-looking librarian behind the circulation desk, inquiring if the library offered the same for men. As he suspected, they didn't, but he was welcome to join the mothers.

Tired of checking out biographies, he returned to the books of his boyhood: penny dreadfuls, westerns, and dime novels about desperate hand-to-hand battles, mortally wounded gunmen getting a last shot off on the narrow running board of a careening taxi roaring down an empty street after midnight, sawed-off shotgun-wielding detectives, police gun battles, a revolver to the head, and a bullet through the skull.

When he told Beatrice he would sell the house and move, she said that would be rash. He would regret it, she told him, suggesting he put the decision off for a year or two. When he informed her that he and

Badge had found a spacious first-floor flat in a three-storey walk-up on Davenport Road, she came to help him start packing.

Recently retired from her position as chief of the stenographer staff at Osgoode Hall, she was enjoying moderate success with her series of mystery novels starring Miss Brown, a private tutor-turned-detective, and her Japanese sidekick, Yuka-chan.

The basement, George's sovereign territory, was stuffed with debris from decades of investigations: piles of sketching pads, court transcripts, crime scene photographs that didn't belong to him, and files that should have been returned ages ago. There were also glimpses of another side of detective work: brass knuckles, false ID, a pistol with a filed-off serial number, bump keys, a lock-picking kit, burglary tools, and a balaclava.

George intended to dispose of everything.

Beatrice stood in the basement, surveying the accumulated paraphernalia, and said, "You can't throw all of this away."

"Why not? Who wants it?"

"Someone in the future might be interested in what we looked at down here," she said, opening the small blue satin gift box containing the lapel pin. "You can't get rid of this, too. You just received it."

"Then you keep it."

Later, Beatrice collected some sketches and photos and placed them in a shoebox with the lapel pin and a few other items, along with a hastily jotted note.

The day of the move arrived, and when the last piece of furniture was carried out and the house was finally empty, the siblings walked through each echoey room.

"This place always felt too big," George confessed.

"Who bought it?" Beatrice asked.

"A family."

"Do they have children?"

"Believe so."

"Hope they enjoy it as you and Susan did."

Back downstairs, he put on his hat, walked Badge outside, and locked the door behind them.

Beatrice paused on the porch. "That Borsalino I bought you ages ago is looking shabby. You need a new one."

"No. It's fine."

No.12 police station was in a handsome Beaux-Arts-style New Street building within walking distance of George's apartment, where he'd now resided for a number of years.

Around 9:30 on a moonless early autumn evening, George took Badge for a stroll around the block. The streets were still. In the city tonight, people gathered outside drugstores and theatres, in athletic clubs, in their homes, and on front porches glued to a live radio broadcast from Philadelphia's Sesquicentennial Stadium of the much-anticipated Jack Dempsey–Gene Tunney world heavyweight title bout.

It was balmy, and windows everywhere were wide open. From house after house, George heard the shrill voice of the announcer calling the fight as Badge, advanced in age, trudged along the sidewalk.

Up ahead, on the other side of the street, a man and a woman engaged in a drunken row behind an automobile at the curb. Stopping to observe, George remained out of sight. Their cursing interrupted the steady chirp of a field cricket. Someone leaned through a window from the dark and shouted, "Shut up. We're trying to listen to the fight."

The inebriates shouted back almost in unison, slurring, "Shut up *yourshelf*," and eventually staggered away.

On the way back, plodding Badge stopped to relieve himself near where the row had occurred. George spotted a white, expensive-looking purse discarded under an automobile. It contained keys, a fountain pen, a gray ribbon, two one-dollar bills, and an engagement ring.

Before returning home, he took the purse to the police station.

The lights in the lobby were blazing. George encountered the pungent stench of disinfectant and sweat combined with the scent of lemon shaving soap. Badge's paws clicked on the black-and-white checkerboard patterned linoleum floor.

The night station duty man, appearing unswervingly grim and even harsh, sat on a stool behind a high wooden counter almost the width of the lobby, listening intently to the Dempsey–Tunney bout on a radio with other constables.

On the side where George remained, a gaggle of drunks and vagrants leaned in to listen, too.

From behind a Florentine glass-panelled door marked SERGEANT in gold leaf lettering came the sound of someone methodically pecking the keys of a typewriter.

"Dempsey will put him to sleep any second now," a shabbily attired old man predicted.

A constable countered, "Cinch for Tunney to win in a knockout."

A coarse-looking woman with a bruised eye, spindly legs, and a missing front tooth, wearing an outfit resembling a gunny sack, sat on the long wooden bench by the door. She leaned against the wall and mumbled, "If you ask me, left hook's Dempsey's best punch, like someone else I know."

A young boy, about eight years old, white-faced from worry and fear, was sitting quietly on the same bench in what appeared to be pyjamas.

George set the purse on the counter. He beckoned the duty man. "Hey. You," he pointed. "Come here. You're responsible here?"

The duty man gazed confoundedly at George. Turning their attention away from the radio, the other constables stared at George in disbelief.

"That tone in here, old man. You think you can take it with me?"

George ignored him and continued, "Found this. On the sidewalk under an automobile walking my dog. Left behind by a drunk couple going at it."

The duty man gritted his teeth and said, "Fellas, won't you listen to this one?"

The glass-panelled door opened, and the Sergeant emerged. "What round are we up to?" Spotting George, he put his hands on his hips and said cheerily, with a pronounced English accent, "Well, well, well. Look what the dog coughed up."

The duty man, who'd been about to come from behind the counter, stopped midstride.

George didn't recognize the Sergeant until he said, "It's me, Detective. McPherson. Remember? M-c capital P-h-e-r-s-o-n?"

George thought momentarily, then said, "House on Defoe Street. Right. The cadet." He grinned in recognition and nodded.

"I'd remember you anywhere, Detective, even that long ago. Always ask. You taught me that that day, and I always do."

One of the vagrants hanging off the counter interrupted, "We're listening here. Pipe it down, will ya?"

"Get a load of that one," McPherson laughed, pointing at the vagrant. "Man thinks we're at the front desk of the King Eddy Hotel." He asked George, "What's the mutt's name?" and then introduced the former detective to the night duty desk man. "Detective, meet Constable Dave Floody."

George extended a hand to Floody. "George is fine. I'm retired."

McPherson ordered the constable back to his stool and winked at George. "Mate's all shot, no powder. And Floody," he said, "learn a thing or two from Detective Porter. He's counted among the greats. Ask the Chief. Before you do, though, man, process the lost purse the detective returned. Got it?"

McPherson invited George back to his office to catch up. George looked down at Badge and then at the little boy. "You're here a while longer?"

"They're taking me to the children's shelter when the fight's through 'cause my parents left me behind."

"Too bad. Keep an eye on Badge for me?"

The boy perked up. "Does he bite?"

"Course not. Hardly has any teeth."

In the ninth round, the crowd roared when Dempsey's knees appeared to buckle. The announcer described a cloudburst followed by a deluge of rain. The fight continued. The fans got soaked.

George followed McPherson behind the counter and down the hallway.

McPherson said over his shoulder, "What a bout, eh? Too bad for Dempsey. He's pretty well used up."

"I used to follow the fights but haven't for ages," said George, glancing into the cells. "You know, Sergeant, I didn't treat you very well that day—"

"Nay, you didn't. But that's the past and the past is dead. And by the way, call me Norman."

In the last cell sat a despicable-looking man. Porter stopped, studied the pathetic figure, and asked, "What's he here for?"

"Caught robbing a charity box."

Porter pulled a small sketching pad and a stick of charcoal from his pocket, and asked McPherson, "May I?"

"Aye. To your heart's content."

I SLEEP

E. Steward,
1930

I sleep when a white-capped doctor hoists me up by the ankles slippery as an eel and slaps my bottom I sleep bawling I sleep as a nurse cuts the pulsing umbilical cord connecting me to my mother I sleep at her breast I sleep christened Edwin Allan Steward I sleep swaddled in a bassinette in the nursery I sleep doted on by my parents I sleep in a brass crib I sleep in a house with good furniture on a leafy street in Winnipeg I sleep happily through infanthood I sleep when my brother John is born three years after me I sleep wearing Sunday clothes attending church weekly with the family I sleep through elementary school I sleep daydreaming I sleep when Sadie Hodder coaxes me under the bleachers at Red River Speedway and kisses me I sleep when my cheeks blaze red and I run away I sleep horseplaying with my brother I sleep struggling to make friends with anyone except John I sleep when I am nine and our father dies unexpectedly after a cataleptic fit I sleep when his body is taken to the city dead house laid out in a casket and respectfully buried I sleep when mom tells me I am the man of the house now I sleep preparing her a ginger tea I sleep while John coils in her lap

THE WAY OF TRANSGRESSORS • Edward Brown

howling like a sore cat I sleep when I pat her shoulder telling both it will be okay because we'll see Dad again in heaven I sleep when banks take back our home and possessions I sleep when I leave school to work as a farm as a hand I sleep when John has to perform scrubbing work at a tannery I sleep when at fourteen on a whim I flee for Edmonton on the 6:19 freight train I sleep with feelings of guilt I sleep when I promise myself I will send money home I sleep when I never do I sleep when I get a job as a fireman with Swift Canadian Company I sleep when I quit I sleep tramping east a thousand miles to Moose Jaw and then Rat Portage I sleep feeling so hungry I sleep drifting further east for a decade I sleep in boarding houses I sleep missing John and Mom terribly I sleep on benches I sleep thieving three brown eggs from a henhouse I sleep when the farmer catches me red-handed I sleep when his hired man sits on my chest pins my arm to the earth as the farmer raises a dull hatchet to cut my hand off I sleep as I wriggle free and escape I sleep in hobo camps I sleep not speaking to another person for months on end I sleep performing itinerant work I sleep at times startled by the sound of my own voice I sleep when war starts in Europe I sleep under bridges I sleep with a prostitute in a Halifax brothel forking over all my money in the world totaling $8.78 I sleep propped against the headboard after I'm done and she listens while I confess the depth of my loneliness I sleep when she replies poor thing and returns my money I sleep watching divine sunrises and sacred sunsets I sleep when I am jumped by men in a Johnstown trainyard I sleep unconscious and bloodied in a culvert I sleep at a charity hospital in a ward with an ocean view I sleep recovering at a Salvation Army shelter I sleep as I heal I sleep when an auxiliary captain aids a failed attempt to locate family back west I sleep when provided three dollars plus cigarettes and directed to the recruitment office in Woodstock New Brunswick to enlist I sleep when I proceed overseas with the 65th Battery I sleep at Camp Witley I sleep through training I sleep watching soldiers play poker and smoke in the Y.M.C.A. hut and attend dances in Surrey England I sleep when I am transferred to 19th Battery and go into action in France I sleep behind the trenches I sleep with a team of six manning an eighteen pounder I sleep pressing

I SLEEP

my eye to the telescope following shells to burst I sleep killing enemies at 6,500 yards I sleep at Vimy Ridge I sleep at the Battle of Mons I sleep at a place called Nine Elms I sleep receiving a chest wound I sleep convalescing at the 12th Field Ambulance hospital I sleep with the scent of iodine and iron in my nostrils I sleep when a chaplain delivers a telegram reading JUST INFORMING YOU YOUR MOTHER IS DEAD IN WINNIPEG I sleep when he kneels and asks to pray with me I sleep when I tell him leave me alone I sleep rereading the telegram I sleep crumpling it in my palm and discarding it on the dull plank floor I sleep beside a fellow in the cot next to me whistling Hanging on the Old Barb Wire I sleep when a grim-faced officer wakes me to pin a Victory medal to my pillow I sleep as he salutes I sleep when discharged in April I sleep returning to Canada on a grey steamer I sleep when I arrive in Montreal I sleep when I disembark and assume the name Edward Stewart I sleep when I can't find work anywhere I sleep when I give up and leave for Chicago on a whim I sleep in that city working various jobs for God knows how long I sleep when I meet a store clerk named Mable Anderson I sleep when she teaches me the Lindy Hop at the Municipal Ballroom I sleep when we eventually live together in an inexpensive flat I sleep when she tells me she wants to get married I sleep when I reply gosh I'm not sure besides I don't own a suit I sleep as she throws her arms around my neck and says it doesn't matter what we wear when we get married so long as we get married I sleep thinking how I've never met anyone like Mable I sleep giving the idea of marriage lots of thought I sleep when Mable blushes and says she has something important to tell me I sleep when she makes reservations at a restaurant we can't afford called Berghoff's I sleep when she blurts out halfway through dinner I'm pregnant I sleep pretending to be happy I sleep bolting Chicago for Winnipeg I sleep seeing John for the first time in fourteen years I sleep when he breaks down and cries burying Mom alone was hard I sleep when he begs me to stick around because I am all he has I sleep repeating I can't stay I can't stay I sleep bound for Toronto I sleep in a rented room on River Street in the east end I sleep when butcher John Freeman hires me to work in his Gerrard Street shop I

THE WAY OF TRANSGRESSORS • Edward Brown

sleep when he fires me months later suspected of stealing from the till I sleep visiting the zoo where I concoct a rash plan to rob Freeman in his shop I sleep when I break in early one morning prior to Christmas I sleep when he arrives to open I sleep hiding under the staircase in the darkened basement with a lead pipe resting on my shoulder I sleep when he clomps downstairs I sleep when he never sees me I sleep striking the back of his skull I sleep rifling his pockets I sleep concealing the body in the corner behind barrels I sleep covering it with sawdust I sleep when a messenger boy witnesses me leaving the shop I sleep the morning spending the one hundred and some dollars I stole on a suit shoes and cigarettes I sleep the afternoon at the movies I sleep the evening looking for a girl named Liz I owe $25 I sleep when I find her outside Eaton's I sleep when we argue on the street corner I sleep when I go home because it is too cold outside I sleep at two in the morning when plainclothes policemen and uniformed policemen burst into my River Street room rouse me from my cot and arrest me I sleep at No. 12 police station charged roughed up fingerprinted photographed questioned sign a full confession and locked in a cell I sleep in the middle of the night when the station is quiet except for the noise from the night station duty man shuffling papers and listening to the radio I sleep when a retired detective named George Porter unexpectedly appears and drags a heavy stool over and sits on the other side of the bars outside the cell I sleep when he crosses his legs and props a bulky pad of paper on his knee and rolls up his sleeves I sleep when I ask What are you doing here I sleep when he directs me to sit on the edge of the cot and face him I sleep when he makes small talk asking if I'm comfortable I sleep when he tells me to lean a little to the left to get better light I sleep when he tells me to stay perfectly still and stares at me a long time I sleep when he stops talking altogether and begins to sketch I sleep when I ask him what he is doing I sleep when he replies I told you already I'm making a sketch I sleep when I ask him why I sleep when he replies It's what I like to do when I can't sleep at night I sleep when I ask Why he can't sleep I sleep when he admits he doesn't know I sleep when it is quiet enough that I can hear the charcoal strokes lightly

I SLEEP

grazing the page I sleep when I break the silence and ask him if I can ask him a question I sleep when he answers No not now I sleep when I say any way Do you want to know the real reason why I really did it I sleep when Porter replies No I sleep when I move suddenly because I am pissed off by his response I sleep when he says Stay still I sleep when I tell him I want to tell him why I killed the Freeman man I sleep when he replies All that matters now is you killed him and I'm here and you are in there so sit still I sleep when I think about what he said about being in here I sleep when I get pissed off again I sleep when I throw myself down on the hard cot and tell him Fuck off Just fuck off I sleep when he mutters I will when I'm done I'm almost done Sit up for another few minutes Don't act like a child Act like a man I sleep when I obey I sleep when the silence returns and I wonder if Porter is married if he has children of his own I sleep when Porter seems to read my mind and breaks the silence admitting I'll confess something to you I'm a widower We had no children I would have liked to have at least one Recently it occurred to me if I hadn't joined the force when I did or hadn't married Susan when I did That was her name I would have liked to have become an artist Or a farmer I sleep when I ask Why I sleep when he answers Is why all you ever ask I sleep when he finishes the sketch and says Do you want to see it I sleep when I hesitantly stand up and say Sure I sleep when he holds up the sketch I sleep when I cross the cell and take a good look at it and think it looks exactly like me I sleep when I have to admit It's good It's me I sleep when Porter's face softens for an instant and he says Thank you We've all done things we shouldn't have done some are just more serious I sleep when he abruptly replaces the stool and rolls down his sleeves and says Did I mention I had a dog that died and then leaves without saying another word not even goodbye I sleep when I shout after him Go home asshole Leave me alone asshole Go home asshole I'm glad your dog died asshole I sleep when he shouts back I'm not I miss him I sleep during my trial in January I sleep when the Crown subpoenas 28 witnesses to testify against me I sleep when my war record is put into question I sleep when I take the stand in my own defence I sleep when the jury deliberates

THE WAY OF TRANSGRESSORS • Edward Brown

seventeen minutes before returning a guilty verdict I sleep when Justice Garrow orders me to rise before sentencing and asks Do you wish to address the court I sleep when I answer No I sleep when he sentences me to be held in custody until the 24th of March and hanged by the neck until I am dead I sleep in the death cell for two months I sleep writing John a letter asking him to visit one time I sleep when I play cards with guards who remain in the cell to prevent me from ending my life before they can I sleep when a letter arrives from Mable beginning Dear Ed I hope you get this letter all right I have a baby boy he's three already I sleep when a square-jawed guard asked if I'm scared I sleep when I tell him I'm terrified I sleep when he asks Then why do you act like you don't care I sleep when I tell him I've always been like this I sleep when John writes back he's too sick to travel but volunteers to pay for a nice coffin I sleep the night before my execution when a priest requests to pray with me I sleep when I say If it's all the same to you no thanks I sleep composing an abecedarian poem for no one in particular I sleep when shortly before 8 o'clock the next morning the sheriff, officers and guards enter the cell and walk me to the death chamber I sleep thanking the guards for being nice to me I sleep with hands and feet restrained and a black hood placed over my head I sleep when a noose around my neck is tightened I sleep when the muffled voice of the jailer asks Any final words I sleep when I reply No Maybe I sleep when the bolt is sprung and the floor beneath my feet vanishes I sleep freefalling I sleep while the oddest thoughts collide in my brain like I guess this means I'm not going to heaven Mable's green eyes why we never had a dog when I was a little boy I wish I stayed in Winnipeg with John why did those fellows in Johnstown beat me so savagely I stole more from that farmer than three eggs I sleep in the time it takes the cord around my neck connecting me to the world to become taut I sleep while my lifetime blurs past like a fast train before a tremendous jerk and stop I sleep hearing rope creak swinging silence I sleep involuntarily writhing I sleep seven agonizing minutes as life drains from me I sleep cut down examined put in a coffin painted white with silver hardware featuring a crucifix at the midline I sleep lowered into burial shaft number nine I sleep buried seventy-seven years in the exercise yard until an excavator operator named Glen splits my coffin open and golden dawn sunlight kisses my skeletal remains I sleep when my bones are exhumed examined put in an ossuary and reinterred in St. James Cemetery in 2008 with fourteen other transgressors I sleep with the realization I sleepwalked through life and death.

A POLICEMAN'S FUNERAL

Beatrice discovered George in his apartment after dinner. He hadn't been gone long.

He'd given her a key ages ago, and she periodically popped in on a whim, believing her brother spent too much time alone. When she suggested George replace Badge, he replied that he was too old for a dog.

Ted accompanied her this evening. George was in his recliner, eyes closed beside the radio, tuned to his favourite show, *Crime File*. A tepid cup of tea and a half-eaten sandwich on a plate sat on the small side table at his elbow. A novel was open on his lap, and his drawing pad had fallen to the floor. Dozens of sketches covered the dining room table.

Beatrice assumed he was sleeping.

"No, dear," Ted comforted her. "He's gone."

Beatrice lowered herself to the ottoman and sobbed.

Through the open window, a robin's trill welcomed twilight.

George's plain wooden casket rested on the metal lowering device over the open grave beside a mound of earth concealed under canvas. He had selected the spot under a chestnut tree by the broken fence at the back of Mount Pleasant Cemetery to be interred beside Susan.

A satin sheet of asparagus fern and white roses from the few remaining family in East Gwillimbury, too old to make the trip, was placed upon the casket. Beatrice tucked a sketchbook, charcoal pencil, and many of his completed sketches inside.

The retired detective had requested a simple graveside funeral ceremony, declining the honours entitled to him. Mourners were few except Beatrice, Ted, grandchildren, and a lady from George's building. Hatsu, who had remarried, was there with her husband.

George had requested no words of eulogy be spoken.

The minister cleared his throat and prepared to commence the service as a man approached with a friendly expression, winding his way around tombstones. Lowering his head, he laid his palm on George's smooth wooden casket, closed his eyes, and moved his lips in prayer.

The stranger introduced himself to Beatrice and Ted. "I was fond of George. A friend, I'd say," he said, shaking Ted's hand. "I'm Norman. From the twelve." He embraced Beatrice, whispering, "Our brother is protected in heaven."

Beatrice said, "George mentioned you."

"He should've. Trotted into the station practically every other evening with that sketch pad tucked under his arm."

Beatrice smiled.

"Others from the station weren't sure if they should attend but wanted to."

"Give them our thanks. You know how George was."

In the distance came the whir of a push lawnmower.

Norman turned toward the noise, aggravated. He shook his head. "Don't they know it's a policeman's funeral?"

"How would they?" Beatrice countered. "No tributes, no piper."

"If that's what he wanted, then—"

The minister opened his Bible. "Let us begin."

THE GRAVE (An Epilogue)

Luigi owned one suit, a loose, ill-fitting number with pinstripes and a wide collar, which he wore with a matching wide tie.

When he showed up at the venue for the premiere of the documentary, Glen asked him, "How long have you owned that suit?"

"Since my nephew Stefano's wedding."

"When did Stefano get married? 1990?"

Luigi gave it some thought. "*Si*. Around then. My brother-in-law, Frank, Stefano's late father, God rest his soul, knew a guy with a shop. That's where I get it. You like?"

As the credits rolled, Luigi crept down the carpeted aisle, tapped Glen's shoulder, and crouched. "Eh. Let's talk. We go outside," he whispered.

Glen slipped out of his seat and trailed Luigi up the dark aisle to the lobby, down the block, and across the street. "Where are we going?"

"I show you something."

When they stopped at Luigi's van, he fished keys from his pocket and slid open the side panel door. The interior dome light came on. "Look inside."

Glen climbed into the van to examine a cast bronze grave marker on a granite base. "What's this for?"

"Those men they reburied. The grave is unmarked."

"So?"

"We dig up bones. We disturb the dead. They sleep for so long then we wake them up. Now I can't sleep. All the time, I think. It is in my mind. So, we honour them. We put marker on grave." Luigi lit a cigarillo. "We finish the job."

Glen looked at the marker. "How much does this thing weigh?"

"Less than one hundred pounds. Easy for us."

"Are you nuts? You think we can just do this?"

"We're excavators. Twenty-minute job. No more."

"When?"

Luigi opened the passenger side door and tossed a pair of coveralls at Glen. "Now."

"What?"

"We go now. We go *right* now."

It was after dark when they arrived at the cemetery. The grounds were closed, but Luigi had arranged for the security guard to open the wrought iron gates. He remembered them.

The last time Glen and Luigi were here was when the documentary crew filmed the final burial scene. Tonight, they followed the same narrow winding road into a ravine, cutting out noise from the city before stopping beside an unmarked single plot where fifteen ossuaries were buried, stacked in three rows of five.

It was considerably darker down in the ravine. Luigi disturbed the quiet by turning on a portable generator to power a set of trouble lights. They changed into coveralls, and then the old Italian removed a shovel from the van and gave it to Glen to dig a small patch of earth. Luigi used a pry bar to uncrate the plaque. Together, they strained to lift the marker from the van and lower it flat on the ground.

"This weighs way, way more than a hundred pounds," Glen huffed.

Glen and Luigi stepped back to admire their work.

"Luigi? Umm, a question: who paid for this thing?"

"No worry. I know a guy."

"You seem to know a lot of guys."

They stared at their handiwork in silence. Luigi crossed himself before switching off the generator. Now, in darkness, he said, "Maybe we say a few words?"

"Like what?"

"You know, when Cristo was on cross, he forgave the criminal on cross beside him," Luigi said.

"True." Working with the director and producers of the documentary, Glen had discovered the stories of the criminals hanged in the exercise yard of the Don Jail. Glen poked the earth with the tip of his shoe. "These guys did pretty awful stuff, but then again, they paid the ultimate price for it."

Luigi looked at him. "Good understanding giveth favour: but the way of transgressors is hard."

ACKNOWLEDGMENTS

Thank you, Lynn Duncan and Kilmeny Denny at Tidewater Press. Kilmeny's advice and keen eye significantly improved the story, and I am indebted. Thank you, Lynn, for accepting the original submission.

Thank you City of Toronto Archives, Imām Yūsuf Badāt, Anastasia Borisova, Carol Brown, Eddy Ryley Brown, Ken Leyton-Brown, Nick Burton, Barry Callaghan, Michael Callaghan, David Chilton, Library and Archives Canada, Exile Editions, Keith Greenbury, Jeff Gray, Holmes, Hennick Bridgepoint Hospital, Cherri Hurst, Archeological Services Inc., Shannon Leigh, Toronto Public Library, *Spacing Magazine*, *The Globe and Mail*, Lidia Monaco, Marianne Mullen, Lynn Peach, Randall Perry, Rev. Louise Peters, ProQuest, Julia Noble, my first readers, Sarah Reynolds, Wendy Shaw, Weston Historical Society, *Toronto Star*, Sally Szuster, Susie Toney, Paul Traviss, Linda Traviss, Alanna Waugh, Heather Wood.

I found many books helpful, but most especially: Ken Leyton-Brown's, *The Practice of Execution*, UBC Press, 2010; Jeffrey Pfeifer's, *Death by Rope: An Anthology of Canadian Executions*, Vanity Press, 2007; Terry Boyle's, *Fit to Be Tied, Ontario's Murderous Past,* North 49 Books, 2001; Mark Johnson, *No Tears to the Gallows*, McClelland & Stewart, 2000. I borrowed the title of this last book for "The Treatment."

Also helpful was the report titled, *The Exhumations of the Burial Area of The Old Don Jail*, prepared by Archeological Services Inc. and published in 2010.

I am especially grateful to you, the reader.

ABOUT THE AUTHOR

Award-winning writer Edward Brown lives in Toronto. He is the author of *Playing Basra, On Toronto Train Bridges,* and *I Am a Pedestrian.* His writing appears in the *Toronto Star, The Globe and Mail* and *Spacing Magazine.*